THE WITCHES OF WYLDEDEN
CHRONICLES

THE MARK OF THINGS UNWANTED

ALEX CLIFFORD

THE MARK OF THINGS UNWANTED

BOOK ONE OF THE WITCHES OF WYLDEDEN CHRONICLES

ALEX CLIFFORD

ISBN: 978-0-6450201-0-6

Alex Clifford

www.alexclifford.com.au

spcafcs@gmail.com

Nir
Ahrenhale
QIRI
North Mountains
Northern Spine
The Vein
Pirevia
VERTLYN
TERVEDA
Dusarn
Womb
Heart Lake
Soul Lake
Orhn
Teppa
ANFAR
Southern Spine
Wyldeden
Dividing River
BERNT
Hyrsch
Belden
OFORD

PART I

A MATTER OF LIFE AND DEATH

CHAPTER 1

THE KINNER

He didn't let himself hope that this wasn't a dream until he smelled the fresh air. From inside the moldy laundry bag, through his own reek, the cold night air whipped life into his senses. Outside—he was *outside*. The smallest kernel of hope was blooming, drawing him from the deep recesses within where he had long since retreated.

"Halt!"

The laundry cart came to a stop. As the sound of boots crunching over gravel grew closer, he refused to move or make a sound. Refused to tremble. To breathe.

"Where are you going? The laundry room is that way," demanded a tired, gruff voice.

"We were told to take these to the orphanage," one of the women who had coaxed him out of his cell explained.

"In the middle of the night?"

"Has the time of day ever dictated when we work?"

A moment passed. Two. His lungs burned with the need to

pull in air, but he would hold his breath forever if it meant getting out of the palace.

"Would you ladies like an escort?" asked the guard, softening.

"Thank you, but we'll be fine. It's not the first time we've had to brave the streets of Hyrsch at night."

The cart started rolling again, but he still didn't dare breathe. Not until the cobblestones turned to gravel, then to dirt beneath the wheels; although, even then his breaths were shallow and silent so as not to wake the sleeping city.

The women didn't speak as they pushed the cart through Hyrsch, much farther than the orphanage ought to be.

Distantly, rushing water pushed out the silence, gradually becoming louder until it overwhelmed the clattering of the wheels. Gravity shifted as the cart tipped over, spilling its contents onto the ground. A gentle hand pressed his side.

"There are spies along the river, but if you can stay in the bag until sunrise you should be out of the city. Get as far from this place as you can."

"And if you're ever in need"—the other woman huffed as she grabbed the end of the sack—"look for the seven-pointed star."

As they dragged the sack across the dirt, he braced himself for the cold, breathing deeply in preparation for the lack of air.

He wished he could thank them.

Wished he knew their names.

A final heave sent him plunging off the edge of the bank and into the freezing water of the Dividing River.

Staying conscious was a greater challenge than staying submerged as the night passed by slowly. The lack of air and the water that he hadn't been able to keep from his lungs made his brain foggy and limbs leaden. It seemed impossible, but he'd done the impossible before. Had thrived on impossible.

The current dragged the sack, bumping him against rocks and debris that tore tiny holes in the canvas. Battling through the stiffness, he forced his fingers through one of these holes, tearing apart the cloth, pulling and stretching until he managed to slip out.

He didn't have the strength to swim against the current that continued to push him along. Slamming against another sharp rock, vision spotting, he began to panic; if he passed out now he could be washed all the way out to the ocean. Clumsily, he grabbed a hold of the next rock sticking out from the muddy riverbed, set his bare feet against it and propelled himself weakly up the steep slope.

One more push.

A second one, and his head broke the surface.

Blinding sunlight glistened on the water, the heat of it scalding as he choked the water out from his lungs. Frozen fingers reached for something to pull himself to shore by, finding only clumps of clay and reeds that were too easily ripped from their roots.

Gasping down painful breaths gave him back some control over his body until he was finally able to catch on to a gnarled root. Shivering fiercely, he scrambled out of the river and crawled up the bank to collapse.

The songs of birds in the trees and the rustling leaves tumbling beyond the muddied riverbank competed with the burbling of the water behind him. A light breeze brushed over his skin, making him wince. It was one thing to smell the fresh air, but to feel it . . .

Free.

Joy pulled a sob from his parched throat, but it was quickly swallowed by a familiar panic. He needed to get up. To run. If he were found and made to go back . . .

Cracking his eyelids, blinded by the day, he forced his aching body to rise. Mud hardened to soil once he passed the tree line into the forest, harsh light filtering through the oppressive canopy. Sensible thoughts eluded him, but he knew he needed clean water, food and rest. Not necessarily in that order.

The forest blurred, his knees buckled and the world went dark.

When he woke, he was not alone.

Perhaps the fact that he was not alone had been what had roused him. The sun was low in the sky, bathing the autumnal forest in gray light. Cicadas were screaming, and yet he barely heard them as he stared at the face peering down at him. Deeply tanned skin spattered with freckles and framed by a long curtain of brownish-red curls. Symbols had been drawn with mud on her forehead and cheeks, framing the black beady eyes locked on his prone frame. Her feet were bare and she wore layers of fur that shifted as she crouched over him, sniffing deeply.

A forest witch. He'd never seen one, either wild or clan-bound, but there was no denying what she was.

Hissing quietly, the sounds almost word-like, she nudged him with her dirty foot. When he didn't respond to her, continuing to lie as still and unthreatening as possible, her brow furrowed and she struck forward. Fast as a whip, grabbing a handful of his matted hair in one hand and the collar of his ragged shirt in the other, the witch ripped them in opposite directions to expose the back of his neck. Hissing again, she got off him and stalked to a sack by a nearby tree. He didn't dare move as she rifled through it, pulling out a waterskin and a ball of cloth. Tossing them at him, she snatched up her sack and darted into the forest.

For a moment, he still didn't move. Only when the sound of the cicadas began to register again did he force himself to get up, drink a little and unwrap the cloth to find a handful of black berries. Not even caring what they were, he ate a few.

There was no sign of the witch; no footprints in the earth beside him, nor leading into the forest where she had disappeared. Reaching up, he brushed his fingers against the birthmark on the back of his neck that had caused so much grief—two mirrored S's that overlapped, their tails turned out like the caps of an hourglass. If the witch recognized it, would she approach Hyrsch to report him?

Unlikely, but it wasn't worth the risk to linger.

Grunting, he got to his feet. The river still roared away to the left, the darkness of the forest to the right. The sun—that blessed sun—was on its way beyond the horizon meaning the forest would only get darker. There were worse things living in that endless expanse of trees than witches and he had no desire to run into any of them. Keeping to the tree line and following the river downstream, his emaciated body barely capable of a dozen steps at a time before he needed to rest again, he walked.

For three days, he picked his way through the forest. When the sun was high he traveled beneath the canopy of firs and pines, eyes struggling with the brightness and skin red from exposure. The browning leaves littered the ground in a crunchy layer of needles and twigs that scratched raw the soles of his bare feet. It was easier during the twilight hours when he could walk in the mud by the river. The farther he got from the city, the clearer the water ran and drinking it didn't send him into fits of cramps anymore.

Rest was scarcely come by. Anytime he was still for more than a moment his body began to tremble, the shadows closing in. Nights were the worst. Walking too close to the river's edge was a risk because with clearer water came the beasts that lurked within it; things with iridescent eyes that watched him for miles. Beyond the tree line wasn't safe either, especially when the cicadas went quiet. He'd seen the remains of midnight snacks the creatures that lurked in the wild would leave. Though he couldn't be killed, he would still rather not experience being eaten.

Cold and damp from the night's mist, he wrapped his bony arms around himself, eyes scanning the darkness ahead. There wasn't a plan beyond getting away from Hyrsch, finding food and keeping safe. He couldn't think that far ahead.

To the right, among the trees, a shadow moved.

Stilling, fists clenching, he focused on the space with the alertness of a wild hare. Heartbeats passed, but nothing stirred. It would be terribly ironic for him to have somehow kept it together through everything he'd come from just to go insane in the forest after escaping.

A low chuckle echoed through the darkness.

Every hair on his body stood to attention, his breath catching. Wild beasts didn't laugh.

"Found you," a rasping voice called, drawing out the two words into a songlike taunt.

The voice was unfamiliar, but his heart beat fitfully anyway as he stepped back toward the river, more willing to take his chances with the shiny-eyed monster than risk being dragged back to Hyrsch.

"No, no, don't run," the voice called, somehow closer. "I haven't smelled your kind in an age. Such sweetness. Such an eternal feast."

Another step toward the river.

The air to his left rippled, a mild suction pinching his skin. He flinched away just as hot teeth raked his neck. Whoever it was had blocked off the river; feet slipping in the mud, he fled to the forest instead.

There was no way to be stealthy as leaves crunched beneath his feet, branches scraping his hands and face as he pushed through close-knit shrubbery. Shins close to snapping, knees grating with every step, weak lungs burning in protest . . .

Your mind will quit before your body does.

A hazy memory, but the words had never left him. The tip of a finger gently pressing against his forehead.

Conquer this and you will be unstoppable.

Needle-sharp claws sunk into his back, tearing loose a strained scream as the beast hauled him to the ground. A vacuous weight descended, sapping at the air around them until his scream became silent. Dirt filled his nails as he clawed at the ground, but when razor-sharp teeth punctured his throat, filling his veins with acid, there was nothing he could do but surrender.

A keening howl bellowed nearby.

The darkness stilled and shifted. Another howl, and the

shadow lifted away entirely. The air rippled. His ears popped with the sudden absence of the vacuum above.

Meeting the beast that could scare off whatever that thing had been was not on the agenda, but he needed a moment. Pressing a hand to his neck, the hot pulse of boiling blood already slowing as the healing itch pulled his skin together, he counted to ten. The blood loss and the poison in his veins would take longer to recover from but he couldn't afford to wait.

Panting hard, he rose to his feet.

When dawn came and there was still no sign of the river, he knew he was lost. The wounds on his neck and back had healed and, after finding a patch of wild turnips to feast on, his body felt better than it had in a long while. At some point during the night the waterskin had been lost, so finding a fresh source of water became a priority.

Moving quietly through the brush, he spotted a doe and her foal. They sensed him, but didn't run, so he stalked them for most of the day until they came to a small pond. Crouching by the edge, he cupped his trembling hands and brought the water to his chapped lips. The pool mirrored back his reflection.

Flinching, he scrambled away.

He didn't know that gaunt face; the skin that had once been richly tanned but now hung sallow. Or it would have, if there wasn't a layer of grime in his pores. The dark hair might have been his but it was long and matted, thick with sweat.

Rattled, he slapped the water until the ripples took the reflection away.

The ground around the pond was damp and when he pressed

the soil with his toes, it made puddles. Exploring a nearby incline revealed a trail that might lead him to a larger source of water, or even back to the river. If he could find it, figure out a way to cross it, he would be out of Oford. Once in Anfar, the Royal Guard wouldn't be able to follow. Maybe he could find a witch clan and trade labor for protection.

It was as good a plan as any.

~

He didn't find the river. Or at least not the one he was looking for.

Trying to picture a map of Oford, to remember where the Narrow River was in relation to the Dividing River, was hopeless; his mind was barren. All he knew was that the sun was setting and for the past few hours there had been eyes on his back. When night came, he didn't want to be in the forest and before him there were options.

The trail from the pond had led to the Narrow River and across it was a small estate. Sitting on roughly an acre, encased in a barbed-wire fence, were three small stone houses and a large wooden barn. An array of livestock wandered freely among raised garden beds laden with vegetables and herbs. Along the northern edge was an orchard, the smell of rotting fruit pungent in the air.

On the one hand, the forest wasn't safe. But neither were people. He needed rest and food, but to trespass and risk theft seemed like tempting fate. There didn't seem to be anybody around, but that didn't mean the place was abandoned.

Just as he turned to leave, an odd gleam caught his eye. The top wire of the fence was barbed steel, but the second shone like silver. Beneath the wires, a shallow trench had been dug and filled with salt. Looking closer at the farm, he noticed the wooden edges of the garden beds had been painted with the sloppy skill of a child in an array of yellow suns, moons and stars.

Dozens of seven-pointed stars.

Hanging from the awning of one of the houses was an old wind chime, its sail carved into another septagram.

Chewing his filthy fingernails, stomach growling furiously, he took another step forward. Then another.

He didn't have to let them know he was there. He could take a little food, just enough to satiate his hunger, find shelter in the barn and wait out the night.

Just one.

The eyes on his back only urged him forward faster.

CHAPTER 2

EAVHA

DEEP IN THE FREE FOREST OF ANFAR STOOD A BOAB, LARGER than any other tree in Nir. It hummed with unnatural energy from a witchmark carved over a deep crease in the trunk. With a single step, the spell transported witches to Wyldeden—a pocket of spirit realm the Anfar Forest Clan called home. It was a gift from the nature spirit Terra; a place of eternal springtime, a sanctuary of cool sunlight and rolling fields. A mirror copy of the Great Boab stood upon an island in the middle of a lake from which rivers and streams threaded through a city of towering marble and quartz, reaching for the insipid sky like enormous stalagmites. Paths of moss curled between them, leading to the valleys where dwellings had been carved from stone, the narrowing streams plummeting off the edges of steep cliffs, its spray leaving the wilderness below in perpetual mist.

In a dandelion clearing by a trickling stream stood a sprawling, lichen-encrusted manor. Eavha Nemuse sang quietly to herself as she strained a lavender infusion through a mesh bag, measuring a careful quantity to add to her brew. At only twenty, she hadn't yet graduated from her tertiary studies and thus wasn't meant to be brewing outside the healer's clinic, but she saw no reason to let her mother's tools gather dust in the infirmary while her brother was in need.

As soon as the tonic was ready, she followed the smell of breakfast to the kitchenette in the wing of the house reserved for Eavha's immediate family. It was the only wing in the entire manor still in use. Once, the Nemuses had been hundreds strong, residing together in one of the largest properties in all of Wyldeden, but now their ghosts left dust on every surface that none who were left bothered to wash away.

Kailevi was at the hot plate, cooking Eavha's favorite scrambled eggs. At the small table, Eaon sat holding his head up with his fists.

"Drink up, buttercup," Eavha teased as she placed the vial of tonic beside him. Skipping across the colorful rugs Kailevi had collected during his travels, she peeked around his shoulder to see how close to ready the food was. "Have I ever mentioned how wonderful your eggs are, Da?"

"Why do you think I keep making them, petal?" Kailevi smiled and turned to kiss Eavha's forehead.

It was a smile that didn't meet his eyes anymore. None had in the three months since their ma had passed to the Lover, leaving the three of them to carry the Nemuse legacy alone.

All Wyldeden witches were blessed by Terra to some degree, but only a handful received a second blessing. Sanni, the Spirit of Healing, had blessed the Nemuse bloodline for centuries but, of the three of them, Eavha was the only one dual-blessed. Kailevi had married into the family, and Eaon had been the first Nemuse ever born without a Sanni-blessing. Without much of a Terra-blessing, either. As if the Spirits had looked over him and given them all to Eavha four years later instead.

The most promising young witch in an era, they called her. The next heir apparent to the high priestess, when she finished her training under Elder Esther.

"It's lovely to have you home again," Eavha told her da, then went to sit across from Eaon. "Both of you. Even if you do smell like stale hay."

Eaon rolled his eyes and gestured rudely, downing the tonic she'd brewed him in one gulp.

Kailevi worked as a traveler for the clan, taking messages and trade deals to the other clans in Nir, and was often gone for months at a time. For the last six years, Eaon had been going with him. That had changed after their ma passed and Kailevi was needed to stay home as Head of House, trapping Eaon as well. At least for a while. On his quarter-century birthday, Eaon would be given a clan role and Eavha knew he hoped for traveler. His only other option was to labor, and nobody wanted that.

"At least you're dressed today!" Eavha grinned, trying to rile some life back into him. "The just-rolled-out-of-bed look really suits you."

His dark, knee-length pants and beige cotton shirt were rumpled, and the dark circles under his eyes didn't help. Eaon and Eavha had a lot in common—mousy hair, golden-brown skin, honey eyes—but their commitment to self-care was not one of them.

"Go rogue," Eaon groused, laying his head down on the table. Eavha clenched her teeth at the insult.

"Eaon, sit up. Eavha's right, you look a mess. Laboring for High Teacher Teagan is an incredible opportunity and you're jeopardizing it by walking around looking like you don't care."

Kailevi brought three bowls of scrambled eggs to the table and handed them out as he joined his children. Eaon sat up reluctantly and picked at his breakfast. High Teacher Teagan ran the elementary school and had taken Eaon on as a laborer-in-training until his birthday as a favor to Kailevi. Rather than have him serve her, she gave him research to do and even let him teach a few classes. Other laborers would have given a limb for that kind of opportunity.

"Teagan doesn't care."

"Maybe not, but she reports directly to Elder Bodhi and he will definitely care," Kailevi warned him.

Eaon grimaced. "Don't you think it's a little optimistic to think Elder Bodhi even knows I exist?"

"You are a smart, talented witch, Eaon. You have a lot to offer this clan, with or without magic. *Make* him notice."

"Mother spare me, alright already, I'll fix my shirt." Eaon finished his breakfast before stalking down the hall.

Eavha waited until the door closed before whispering, "Is he going to be able to keep it together?"

"Don't worry, petal. Eaon knows how to do what's needed." Kailevi's gaze followed his son down the hall, laden with a sadness Eavha couldn't begin to understand.

For three months the three of them had grieved privately, silently, so as not to offend the Spirits. It was the natural order of things; Mother formed them, nurtured them, until her Lover decided they were perfect and took them to the after-realm. Gifts, passed from one to the other. Most witches lived for centuries before being taken, their physical aging slowing once they reached their prime. Some witches lived far longer and spent their days at the temples, atoning for whatever wrongdoing they had committed to still be deemed unworthy.

To die young was an honor, they said.

All Eavha knew was that she missed her ma.

Eavha smiled at all the witches who waved and pointed as she walked the winding paths toward the city center. She didn't know most of them, only stopping outside one house on the way to wait for Apaete. The two of them worked closely at the clinic and Apaete was one of the only witches who didn't seem intimidated by Eavha.

"I heard Neanna was being reassigned as a brewer," Apaete whispered as they continued their journey to the healer's clinic.

"Serves her right for cheating on the exams."

Eavha flicked back her long curls and waved to a male who had stopped to gawk at her. The healer's uniform drew a lot of attention: the beige, gauzy skirt that brushed her ankles was slit down the front, while a binding across her chest left her heart and solar plexus open for spellmarking if a patient required it. Around her neck dangled her Blessing Charm—a daisy she'd plucked twelve years ago, tied to a piece of twine. Every morning and every night she said a prayer to Sanni and Terra as she wound a piece of hair around the stem, as thick as her thumb now. A simple spell she'd seen her ma perform over and over to strengthen the blessings she'd been given.

Eavha knew how she looked as she breezed by the gardeners and scouts, the makers and the guardians as they all made their way to classes or work.

Theirs wasn't the attention she wanted.

"There's Dearmead," Apaete pointed out, blushing and

hiding her face behind the curtain of ashy hair falling over her shoulder.

Jogging towards them down a steep hill, Dearmead Bayfield was a vision in leather. The supple brown of his guardian uniform stretched snuggly across his broad frame, his long black braid swinging from side to side as he moved. "Eavha!"

"Good morning." Eavha raised her chin and smiled.

Dearmead returned it, nodding towards Apaete as well. "Good to see you, Appy. I'm glad I caught you both. Do you know if Eaon's back at work today?"

"He was dressed this morning, so I assume so." Eavha shrugged, twirling a curl around her finger.

Dearmead was Eaon's only friend and he'd been around as long as Eavha could remember. For a while, Eavha had worried Dearmead saw her as more of a sister than a romantic option but this last year he often brought freshly picked flowers and gourmet pastries to the house. These last three months since her ma's passing he'd also spent more of his free time at the Nemuse house, helping them maintain their gardens and crops.

"Great, thanks." Dearmead smiled widely, making his cheeks dimple. "Well, have a good day."

Eavha returned his smile as she waved goodbye, then watched him jog back up the hill.

"You two would have beautiful babies," Apaete sighed, fanning her face.

Eavha's ma had been talking to her about babies for almost a year before she had passed. Their bloodline was dying out, and breeding with another affluent family was their best bet at growing again.

Like Dearmead's family.

The Bayfields were three-hundred strong and had produced

powerful guardians for generations. Rumor had it the Bayfields even guarded the high priestess herself, though nobody knew for sure. The high guardians kept their identities secret behind wooden masks; a tradition lingering from a time of discord among the clan. Nobody would ever try to usurp the high priestess now, but many initiatives from that terrible time remained.

"If only he'd actually ask me out. At this rate I might have to make a move myself." She sighed and rubbed her cheeks; the day had barely started and her face already ached from all the faux smiling.

Apaete took Eavha's arm and gave it a gentle pat. They'd never spoken about the blight that had decimated her family these past fifty years, but of all the witches Eavha had ever met, Apaete was one of the few who didn't scold her for her grief.

The healer's clinic was one of the largest structures in the city center, made of polished quartz that glittered dazzlingly under the high sun. The ground floor was for the hospital, glistening ivy-covered pillars between beds of the sick and injured, both Sanni-blessed and medicalist healers tending to them as they recovered. The second floor was reserved for practical work and storage for supplies where the best brewers worked tirelessly to prepare ointments, salves and tonics. The third floor was mostly classrooms but also contained the extensive library dedicated to medical knowledges. Above that, the highest level was reserved for Elder Esther and her high healers.

On this morning, Elder Esther was in the hospital, carrying her satchel.

"Are you leaving?" Eavha asked.

"There's been an accident in the barley fields that requires my attention," Esther explained.

"Let me get my—"

"Both of you can go and assist Yvette until I return," Esther interrupted, giving Eavha a pointed look before hurrying out the door.

Eavha sucked her teeth, her narrowed eyes following the raven haired elder as she hurried from the room.

"Do you think she's punishing us for what happened with Kaela yesterday?" Apaete said quietly, glancing along the rows of beds for the witch they had treated the day before.

Eavha had been in a foul mood, gotten impatient, and accidently flooded the nerves of a poor witch with magic. Not a dangerous mistake, but a painful one. Apaete had tried to cover for her, but Kaela's screams had echoed all the way up to the top floor.

"Probably," Eavha scoffed, ignoring the stares of the other healers as she stalked to a large archway that divided the ground floor into two sections.

On the other side, the hospital beds were replaced by pens where the sick and injured animals of Wyldeden could recover. An older witch was sitting at a bench, inspecting a squirming hummingbird, but as she noticed Eavha coming down the hall her face crumpled into a scowl.

"Guess who's back," Eavha sung, forcing herself to grin as she turned in a graceful pirouette.

"Lover take me; I'd hoped Esther was joking when she said she was sending you here."

Eavha ignored Yvette and crouched to look at the emerald-and-turquoise colored bird in her hands. "Oh, she is beautiful."

"Good morning, High Healer," Apaete said softly from behind her.

"A pleasure, Apaete. Would you mind blessing the bandages for me?"

"Of course."

Eavha wasn't listening as the kernel of magic inside her unfurled. Burrowing into it, she let it wash over the bird in a quick assessment that told her its wing had fractured.

"May I?" Eavha asked, reaching for the hummingbird without waiting for an answer.

From the mass of her power, she whittled down a tiny thread and fed it into the bird, testing each nerve and ligament. The critter twitched in her sun-kissed palms but didn't fret.

Yvette's stare was cold as river pebbles as she watched Eavha begin the healing. Wordless spells, commanded by sheer will alone. A rare talent.

A high priestess's talent.

However, even Eavha had to obey the law. High Priestess Lorelei had declared to the Anfar Forest Clan at the beginning of her reign some many centuries ago that magic was not to be something a witch *did*, per se, but rather something a witch offered. To force her will was an act of abuse, so Eavha offered up her intentions to Sanni and waited for the Spirit of Healing to accept, just as she had while brewing Eaon's tonic that morning. A spell, like a potion, was only as strong as the witch who cast it.

As soon as Sanni accepted the offering, Eavha's magic surged forward. Gasping, she quickly reigned it in.

Slow.

Gentle.

As the magic spilled into the bird's injuries, Eavha conjured everything she remembered about the anatomy of a hummingbird. The way their bones, muscles and nerves were built and connected, reimagining the damaged ones she sensed into something whole.

She'd barely broken a sweat before the bird gave a chirp and began fluttering its wings in her hands. Eavha smiled as she watched it zip into the air, laughing airily as it sped around in circles. Inside her, the magic fluttered, waiting for more direction.

"I'll find a scout to take it back," Yvette sulked, rising from the bench. "You might as well take a look at the goats in bay five."

For a moment, Eavha forgot about her grief. Forgot about the insult of being made to work in the veterinary clinic when her talents were better appreciated on the other side of the arch. She stood and watched the bird fly, admiring her little miracle.

Once she was alone, she quietly wandered by Yvette's desk and slipped a key out of her chest binding, tucking it back into a cluttered drawer.

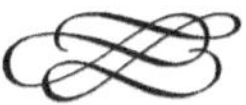

EAON

HIGH TEACHER TEAGAN TOOK ONE LOOK AT EAON AND TOLD him to go back home; that he couldn't and shouldn't be teaching if he was still unwell. Eaon didn't argue. He didn't want to teach anyway.

Rather than return home and face Kailevi's questions, Eaon wandered the sprawling grounds of the elementary school until he reached the educators' offices. He didn't have one of his own considering he was technically only a laborer, but a history instructor named Selina had made room in hers for an extra desk where he could work.

The school was set out in adjacent circles, each building domed and constructed from braided willow. It gave the rooms a more natural feel than the formal buildings of the secondary schools or the ostentatious construction of the tertiary establishments. Eaon found the pale coloring of the willow rooms soothing, and the rug on the floor made of rich red and gray wools that Selina had acquired during the biannual trading festival was soft underfoot. Judging from the pattern woven into it, Eaon guessed it had been made by a mountain witch dual-blessed by Terra and Ignatius, the Spirit of Flame. The way the red and browns blended together was reminiscent of glowing embers; beautiful, had he not known that Ignatius-blessed witches were secretly heathens.

Crammed against the wall, Eaon's desk was piled high with books and scrolls from all over Wyldeden. Most were written in Terranian but a number of them were in Nirnish, the common tongue shared by humans, witches and the rest of the speaking kind living in Nir. One of the projects Teagan had given him was to write Terranian translations of those books for the Wyldeden libraries, but he hadn't been able to focus on that for weeks.

Sitting at his desk, Eaon pulled two books from his satchel. One was a history tome he'd gotten during his last expedition with Kailevi to the Southern Mountain Clan, written in an old stone dialect that was unique enough that Eaon had needed to make an effort to study it. The book was an account of Mountain Clan families and covens who'd gone extinct over the last ten centuries. It was a loan, but now that he was Boab-bound he honestly wasn't sure when he would be able to return it. Selina had procured a similar record from her own collection detailing the history of the Anfar Forest Clan bloodlines, but there were fewer instances of an extinction ever occurring, let alone one that decimated a family in the span of five decades.

An honor, everybody kept saying. The Nemuse family was so blessed to have reached perfection in such numbers and embraced so enthusiastically by the Lover.

Except, the thing that irked Eaon was that the healers could not determine a cause of death. One by one, the members of his family had just dropped dead. The priestesses had not detected a curse, putting it down to the Lover's will, but Eaon needed to know why. To find out if there was a way to stop it before it took the rest of them, no matter how blasphemous it made him.

Swallowing the lump in his throat, he opened the second book. The one Eavha had stolen for him from the healers' restricted resources. He needed it to decipher the coded anagrams in the records as he searched for instances of similar plagues in the past.

The office door creaked open and Eaon suppressed a smile. There were only two witches who would come in unannounced, and he knew Selina had classes until after noon.

"There you are." Dearmead snuck inside and closed the door. He was carrying his staff—the weapon given to junior guardians until they graduated and received their spears. "I haven't got much time before Teagan realizes I'm not at my post."

"And why, exactly, are you not at your post?" Eaon raised an eyebrow and smirked.

Leaving his staff against the wall, Dearmead held the back of Eaon's chair and leered over his shoulder at the open books. "I saw Eavha. She said you might be back today. How is your fatigue?"

"Better. Benefits of having a healer for a sister."

It wasn't a lie; the fatigue that had left him bedridden for almost two weeks was mostly better, even if he was still tired. This latest bout was a delayed reaction to their ma's passing. When it had happened, Eaon had picked up a lot of the extra work that needed to be done so Eavha and Kailevi could grieve. It wasn't until recently that he'd stopped busying himself long enough to feel the loss. Perhaps he and his ma hadn't been as close as he was to his da, but she had loved him. Had defended him against their relatives who'd sneered at his lack of blessings.

"Still, you should spend some time outside. The sun will help." Dearmead frowned at the small window over Eaon's desk before reaching to angle one of the books. "What are you reading?"

Eaon pushed it away.

"Nothing that will interest you. But I have something at home you'd like," he said, turning in his chair. "It's a history book but it details a minor war between the ancestors of the Swamp and North Mountain Clans. The Swamp Clan used to believe that healers, anyone blessed by Sanni, was blasphemous to the Lover because it contradicted the Lover's right to take her gifts. It took the North Mountain Clan twenty years to convince them that to reject any of the Spirits, including Sanni, was blasphemous to the Mother. The whole dispute was transcribed and—"

Eaon stopped talking and bit his lip.

"And?" Dearmead prompted.

"And you'd like it, but I talk too much. You don't care about the language."

"So?" Dearmead smiled warmly, bumping Eaon with his elbow.

After a moment of trying to control himself, he gave in. "And, it was all written in one of the ancient dialects. One I haven't had a chance to study as much as I'd like to. I'm thinking about petitioning the elder traveler to return to the Swamp Clan and see if they have anything else written in the language so I can better my fluency."

"You'd travel on your own?" Dearmead tensed.

"If I wait for Da I might never get to leave the Boab again. But, if you're worried, I could always use a guardian to accompany me." Eaon looked up and winked.

"Good luck finding one willing to venture that far."

"Coward."

Dearmead flicked Eaon's ear, chuckling deeply. "I suppose it would be marginally less boring than standing around here all day."

"We could go during the winter. You could see snow," Eaon suggested, enjoying the way Dearmead's eyes lit up.

"Snow. I heard it's just slush."

Eaon laughed quietly. "Come with me. Find out for yourself."

Dearmead grinned widely, leaned down and kissed his cheek. Eaon closed his eyes, holding his breath. Holding on to the giddiness bursting in his chest, even as guilt descended on him. His bloodline was dying. It wasn't fair to leave the responsibility of breeding up to Eavha; his sister, who had set her sights on Dearmead, completely oblivious that Dearmead only had eyes for him.

Dearmead's breath warmed Eaon's cheek as he chuckled, then stepped back to retrieve his staff. "If you get approval for travel, I'll come."

Eaon bit his lip and turned to his desk. "I should get back to work."

"Okay. Have fun with all your books."

"Have fun standing around guarding a musty old office." Eaon smirked once more, watching Dearmead poke out his tongue before rushing back to his post.

When his head began to ache and his stomach growled viciously at him, Eaon decided to track down some food. There were provisions in the staff room that Teagan told him he could have, but the other witches always stared at him when he went in there. Besides, it had been a while since he'd foraged for his own meal. During his travels he'd learned things not many other young witches got to learn, like how to find your own food. Not grow it, not coax it from the ground, but to find what has grown naturally. With very little of Terra's blessing in his blood and considering the politics of his family back then, Kailevi had thought it pertinent to teach Eaon to fend for himself.

Leaving the school grounds, Eaon made his way to the forest that bordered the eastern edge of Wyldeden. Scouts often ventured into the forests of the spirit realm, but no matter which direction they went or how deep they traveled, they always wound up back at the settlement. There was no fear of getting lost; not that any forest witch had ever experienced such a thing.

Out in the woods, Eaon roamed beneath the green canopy— the ground warm beneath his feet, the air sweet and clean. Unnatural, in every sense of the word. Nothing about Wyldeden resembled the real wilderness, and the invisible wards that kept the clan close to the Boab were like a cage. Some days, it was suffocating. Eaon longed for the brutal cold and sweltering heat of the different territories in Nir, the mud between his toes or the sand in his hair. The ocean, the mountains, the desert.

As he picked some low-hanging fruit, he watched a ruddy fox slink out of a warren carrying a baby rabbit in its maw. The fox froze at the sight of him, and it took Eaon too long to realize why his heart was racing. There weren't supposed to be foxes in Wyldeden. There had never been a predator within the confines of the Boab.

With the fluidity of a loosed arrow, the fox darted into the brush. Without thinking about it, Eaon gave chase. He was fast, but the crafty fox still managed to disappear into a cluster of shrubs. For the better part of an hour, curiosity drove Eaon to search the woods, but there was no trace of the critter. He'd have to tell Dearmead about it, and maybe they could hunt it down later that night.

Just another mystery for Eaon to solve.

CHAPTER 4

EAVHA

After a long day at the clinic Eavha just wanted to be alone, but she didn't protest as Apaete asked to walk with her.

"I have to make a stop at the lavender fields," Eavha explained.

"Oh, my cousin would love a fresh bunch. I'll come with you."

As soon as they were alone, Eavha's whole face dropped. Her cheeks ached from smiling and laughing all day, the pressure behind her eyes almost overwhelming. Again, Apaete took Eavha's arm as they walked.

The lavender fields were a communal supply maintained by the clan's gardeners, mostly used by healers and the occasional artisan at the markets for dyes and baking. Eavha was well-known enough that the guardians patrolling the supply didn't question her, letting the two witches roam deep into the fields.

"Do you ever wonder why the fields need guardians if it's supposed to be a communal supply?" Eavha asked.

"My family's laborer said she is always stopped from accessing the communal supply of anything until she can provide proof one of us sent her. Didn't Eaon ever tell you that laborers are barred from the supply?"

"What? Since when?" Eavha asked, a deep frown creasing her brow. Eaon didn't talk about the time he'd spent laboring for their family before Kailevi took him traveling. Then again, she had never asked.

Apaete shrugged. "At least a few decades, I think. Then you get the magic-poor families trying to steal things."

"I thought that was what the communal supply was for?"

"No, it's for community members who are actually useful. How do you not know this stuff?" Apaete shook her head, bewildered as she snapped the long stems, the scent of the flower so heady Eavha found it difficult to muster any outrage.

Perhaps she hadn't been paying attention in some of her community classes at school, but there had been other things on her mind. She was tired. Tired of worrying and grieving and pretending she wasn't. This blight had been ravaging her family her whole life, but no matter how much death she saw, no matter what her teachers had preached, the idea of the Lover's greedy fingers snatching even one more Nemuse soul was enough to buckle her knees.

"Oh, Eavha." Apaete crouched beside her and shielded Eavha's shaking form as she grit her teeth against the tears threatening to break her. If the guardians saw. . .

"I'm okay. I'm alright," she said, taking a steadying breath and pushing down the crushing weight in her chest. Apaete rubbed her back as she wiped her face. "Thank you."

"Of course. I understand. You know I do."

Eavha nodded and let Apaete help her to her feet, letting her long, mousy hair veil her face. The two of them gathered what they needed and waved to the guardians as they left. Outside Apaete's house, the two witches hugged briefly before Eavha continued the journey back along the stream alone.

Her house came into view, the sun hanging low on the horizon. Eaon sat on the porch steps, holding his head in his hands.

"You alright?" she called out, quickening her steps.

"He's gone," Eaon croaked.

"What?" she asked, heart already seizing. "Who? Gone where?"

Stupid questions.

Leaving Eaon on the steps, she hurried into the house, dropping the armful of lavender as she saw Kailevi collapsed on the floor, lips and eyelids blue. The washing trough was still full of their breakfast dishes.

An honor. She shook her head.

What was the last thing she had said to her da this morning? Had she hugged him? Kailevi had been seventy-two years old. Dearmead's da was two hundred and seventy-two and had never been in better health. It wasn't fair.

Eaon's hand settled on her shoulder and she turned into him, letting out the sobs she'd held back in the lavender field. They only had a few moments before they ought to report the passing. A few more minutes before they had to pretend to be proud their da had been selected.

Eavha hid in the house for three days while Eaon made the arrangements for the funeral. He told people she was working on her ceremonial dress, which was true, but she'd also been burning smudge sticks and casting protection spells on them both, as well as on the house. If the clan found out what she was doing they'd have charged her with conspiracy against the Lover, but Eavha was beyond caring. She would pray for the Lover's forgiveness and atone for her sins after she and Eaon had both lived long, healthy lives.

On the third night, Eavha had no choice but to emerge. To smile at the neighbors and accept their offerings and congratulations as the siblings made their way to the Lover's temple. She was grateful to see Apaete, the faintest sign of pity pulling at her features.

"He was a good man. Reached perfection much sooner than most," she said, wary of the listening ears all around them.

Reached perfection. As if Kailevi had been a barrel of whiskey and not her father.

"Thank you." Eavha hugged her friend.

Eaon was a better actor than she was, his face beaming with pride. Even knowing it was fake, she couldn't help but clench her fists in the folds of her white gossamer dress as she listened to him sing of the honor their family had received.

Drums marked the beginning of the ceremony with the slow steady rhythm of a beating heart. The witches who'd gathered to celebrate Kailevi's passing fell back, leaving Eavha and Eaon alone at the front of the temple. It was a grand structure by the edge of the lake, polished into a mirror except for the black, white and gray mosaic depicting the story of the Lover and Mother: the purest truth, a beautiful purpose, the embodiment of Balance.

The witches knelt as the doors to the temple opened once more, the procession of representatives moving slowly to the dais. Eavha already knew how the evening would go. An acolyte representing each of the twenty elders would meet Eaon and Eavha, clasp their hands and mutter praise for Kailevi. The drums would quicken and one of the clan's priests or priestesses would come billowing in like doily-lace curtains during a storm. They'd bow at the altar and speak the passing prayers while the crowd bruised their knees waiting.

Eavha recognized the priestess who stood by the altar, dressed in a shimmering gray robe, a hood lowered over the top half of her face, golden curls unbound and spilling down to her hips. She'd procided over the funerals for all the Nemuse passings, full of sanctimonious nonsense.

Gathering her skirts, Eavha tried not to sigh too loudly as they were finally allowed to stand. She *had* actually worked on the gown these last three days as well, adding Kailevi's initials to the long list down the length of the fabric. A new line for every family member she had worn the dress for. Eaon's white tunic was similarly stitched, though his needlework was much more elegant than hers.

As they listened to more of Aadya's antics, Eavha worked hard to control the snarl curling her upper lip. Given the opportunity, she would have spat in the Lover's face.

When the prayers were finally finished, Aadya led the procession out of the temple and across the single bridge between the shore of the city and the island. Eaon reached for Eavha's hand as they approached the fold in the Boab that would take them to Anfar, and despite her bitterness at his display of sycophantism, she took it.

One step, and they were through.

Reeling back from the shock of the cold, the earth mud beneath her feet, trees heavy with decay, Eavha was grateful they only had to walk a few minutes before reaching what was meant to be a clover field but looked to her like nothing more than a patch of weeds. In the center was a hastily built altar upon which lay Kailevi's cloth-wrapped corpse.

"I've never had to do this part before," she whispered to Eaon, trying to swallow the thickness in her throat.

"It'll be okay," he whispered back.

They stopped and waited for the crowd to gather. Aadya stepped forward, holding two jaw bones of some large animal into the air, lowering her head as she declared: "Behold! The digging bones."

In one shaking hand, Eavha took the bone that was offered to her. Eaon took the other, and together they dropped to their knees to prepare the grave. The clan stood watch, the drums continued to beat, and Aadya would sing for as long as it took them to gift their da's body to Terra.

More than once, Eavha had to stop and repress her gagging. Eyes burning, she was unable to feel the holiness of the moment beyond the stiff chill in her fingers and the sickening humiliation clawing at her throat. The process took longer than it should have because Eaon had to do most of the work, and by the time they were done, her whole body aching and trembling, Eaon had to lift her out of the grave.

Drenched in sweat, they approached the altar. Eaon was older, so he stood by Kailevi's head while Eavha took her position by his feet. She didn't want to touch him. The wrappings were meant to mask how stiff and cold the body was, but she felt it all the same.

At Eaon's nod, they lifted. Bare feet slipping in the mud, knees buckling under the dead weight, Eavha stumbled. Kailevi's legs banged back down on the altar, and she nearly fell face first onto them.

Pressing her lips together against a sob, she looked up to Eaon in apology.

"It's okay. I can do it," he said quietly, walking around the altar to center himself.

Eaon wasn't going to be strong enough. There was no way he could get their father's body in the ground with any amount of grace.

A hand fell on Eavha's shoulder.

Murmurs of surprise and outraged overshadowed Eavha's shock as she turned to see who had interrupted the ceremony. With a solemn look on his face, Dearmead silently handed Eavha his staff and took position at Kailevi's feet. She couldn't keep in the gasp as her heart squeezed painfully.

Aadya's raised hand silenced the gathering. Once the drums regained their rhythm, she nodded for the Nemuses to continue.

Eaon stared at Dearmead for a long minute before moving back to the other end of the table. The males lifted Kailevi's body from the altar, breathing hard as they carried him to the grave and carefully lowered him down.

After the two of them climbed back out of the grave again, Eavha joined them to scoop dirt back into the hole, one hand still clutching Dearmead's staff. The guardian was using his bare hands to shovel mud back into the grave, jaw set in a hard line as they worked.

It was done.

The three of them stayed on their knees as Aadya sung the final prayer, then Dearmead stepped back to let Eavha and Eaon give their thanks. Eaon spoke so softly Eavha could hardly hear him, the words clearly not Terranian. Whatever he said was between him and their da.

A final beat of the drums. Time stilled in the moment of silence that followed.

With a grand bow, Aadya led the procession back to the Boab. Gossip about Dearmead's intervention during the ceremony swelled, but the three of them ignored it as they meandered their way back to Wyldeden.

Eavha stepped back into the velvet grass of the island, but the spring air brought no relief to her chilled bones. A bonfire had been lit in the Lover's Meadow where the music had already begun, tables of food and wine prepared for feasting.

"Thank you," Eavha croaked as she handed Dearmead back his fighting staff and pulled him into a fierce hug. "Thank you."

His large, warm hand held her head against his chest.

Eaon turned away, a vacant expression flattening his face. "I need to give thanks so they can start the wine ritual."

"We should talk later," Dearmead said to him, letting Eavha go.

Nodding once, Eaon left for the bonfire. Eavha glared at her brother's back, but it lacked sincerity.

"Our da is dead and he's worried about the wine."

"You know it's more complicated than that," Dearmead sighed, worrying as he watched after Eaon.

Eavha sniffed and wiped her filthy hands on her white dress, grimacing at the mud all over Dearmead's gray tunic and pants. Her body bubbled like champaign as the reality of Dearmead's declaration tonight, the commitment to her family, set in.

"Will you dance with me during the odes tonight?" she asked.

Dearmead smiled and nodded. "Of course."

She took his arm and the two of them walked to where Eaon was kneeling again in the Lover's Meadow.

"As eldest, do you swear to protect and care for every Nemuse under your roof? To nurture them until the Lover deems them worthy of embrace?" Aadya asked him with exaggerated stoicism.

"Let the Spirits see that I do," Eaon answered.

He lifted up the first goblet of wine and Aadya prayed over it for an exorbitant length of time before finally sipping from it. Lowering the cup, Eaon closed his eyes and turned up his face, letting Aadya spit the wine into his waiting mouth.

"Then I name you Head of House."

The clan roared and the lutes began a merry melody. The acolytes tapped into the barrels of wine as the revelry began. Apaete brought Eavha a goblet—the first of many she would drink tonight.

Eaon stayed on his knees, shoulders bowing as he lowered his head to the ground.

CHAPTER 5

EAON

STUMBLING, EAON AND DEARMEAD HELPED AN INCOHERENT Eavha back to the house and into bed, leaving her in her mud- and wine-stained dress. The removal and cleaning of the burial clothes was a significant rite, and Eaon wouldn't take that from her.

Closing her bedroom door, Eaon rubbed the heel of his palm into his dry and itchy eyes. Smoke from the bonfire saturated his skin, filling his lungs with the thick scent of patchouli.

"Are you alright?" Dearmead asked once they were back in the dark kitchenette, lighting a single candle in the center of the round table.

"No."

"Are you angry with me?"

"No." Eaon sat down and put his swaying head in his hands. "Can we talk about this tomorrow?"

"Except tomorrow you'll want to talk about it the next day, and the next after that." Dearmead sat across from him, running

39

his hands through the stray hair that had fallen from his braid during the dancing. "I'm sorry, but I couldn't just stand there."

"Eavha will think you did it for her."

"We should have told her ages ago."

"I know." Eaon sighed deeply.

The two of them sat in silence, watching the small flame dance in the slight breeze blowing through the open window, until Dearmead slid his hands onto the table, palms up and wide open. "What else can I do?"

Eaon shook his head. There was nothing left to do.

With a sigh, Dearmead pulled his hands back and stood, the chair scraping as he did.

"You know where to find me if you need anything."

There was a pressure growing under Eaon's skin. He was twenty-four years old, Head of House, and trapped inside the Boab for the rest of his life. Decades, maybe centuries, of living his worst nightmare. Breath hitching, he raised his head.

"Stay."

Dearmead stilled, looking back in shock.

"Please. I don't think I can be alone right now."

Gently, Dearmead walked back around the table and placed a palm on Eaon's cheek. Leaning into the touch, Eaon turned to press his lips to Dearmead's wrist.

"Stay," Eaon repeated.

Smoothing back Eaon's hair, Dearmead leaned down and answered with a soft kiss. First his forehead, then his cheek. His lips. With a hand on Eaon's elbow, Dearmead helped him stand, then guided him to bed. There wasn't room for shame as Eaon pressed himself into Dearmead's side, letting the warmth of him lull him to sleep. There was a storm brewing in his head; all he could do was cling to his anchor.

Duty called Dearmead away before sunrise and Eaon couldn't sleep after he left, so he took his burial clothes to the stream and began cleaning them. The water ran brown with the remnants of Kailevi's grave that Eaon had taken home with him. Seeing it hollowed out his chest.

Let Terra guide you. His da had taught him how to walk in the forest without leaving footprints. Had taught him how to listen to the trees, how to read the earth. *Magic doesn't make a witch, no matter what anyone else says. It's your heart, your devotion to the Spirits. Let them guide you and you'll never need magic a day in your life.*

Kailevi had been the only one who'd understood what Eaon was going through, and he felt strangely untethered now that he was gone.

Once the clothes were clean and flung over a branch to dry, Eaon sunk into the stream to bathe. Like everything else in Wyldeden, the water was perfectly tepid. It did nothing to ease the tension in his shoulders.

He'd have to double down on his hunt for answers and a way to stop this blight from taking the last of them. If he was going to somehow keep the Nemuse home functioning, he would have to fill his days with work and his nights with Dearmead.

For a year, the two of them had been sneaking around in empty rooms, the guardians' barracks, and in the forest. Eaon wasn't sure when it had changed from being the culmination of years of flirting and carnal attraction, but he knew that he was going to need Dearmead if he was going to keep from falling into another episode.

Once clean and dressed in his regular clothes, Eaon collected the eggs. The crops that had once been bountiful were barely producing now that there wasn't anybody with the right kind of magic for gardening to care for them. Wandering into the forest that bordered their property, he found some scallions that would have to stand in as a substitute for chives.

It didn't take him long to familiarize himself with the kitchen, and as he'd expected, the smell of breakfast roused Eavha from her room.

"Ugh. I hate wine," she moaned, collapsing into a chair at the table, still wearing her burial clothes.

Eaon didn't have the energy to tease her, so he just passed her a bowl of eggs and took a pot of water to the hot plate to make tea. Plucking a peppermint leaf from the few remaining herbs in their window, he began to grind it down.

"I see you didn't waste any time shedding your funeral whites," Eavha scolded. Then gagged and shoved the bowl away. "Lover spare me; didn't anybody ever teach you how to cook?"

Eaon flinched.

Throwing the pot of water into the trough with enough force to crack the ceramic, he stormed out of the kitchen. Eavha could fend for herself.

"Very mature, Eaon!" Eavha shouted after him.

"Go rogue!" he spat back before shutting himself in his room.

Crawling under the blankets, he took deep breaths that smelled of Dearmead. Fists clenching in the sheets, he bit the pillow to keep from screaming as something feral clawed beneath his skin. He ought to go back out there and throw his relationship with Dearmead in her face, but he wouldn't sully what was between them like that.

He's as useless as they come.

Eaon buried his head under the pillow, his heart galloping painfully in his chest.

I've petitioned the Head of House to disown him.

He's a stain on this family and we want him gone.

Send him to the labor camps. Or better yet, have Kailevi trade him to another clan for a sheep. Or a hen.

There was a knock on his door.

"Eaon, I'm sorry," Eavha whined. "Come out. How about I cook the eggs from now on?"

It was his job to take care of them and he was already screwing it up.

Useless.

Useless, useless, useless.

Eavha began a steady rhythm of knocking until Eaon, ready to lose his mind, rolled out of bed and threw open the door. His rage dissipated in the space of a breath. She was so much smaller than him, and such a mess. Her hair was oily, her hands and feet stained with mud, face darkened with soot.

"I'm sorry," she said again.

His shoulders sagged. "Me too."

It was unclear which of them leaned in for the hug first, but for a while, the two of them just stood there and held each other. Eavha clung to his shirt, shuddering through deep, soothing breaths.

"We'll figure this out together," she said. "I'm going to keep us safe."

Eaon nodded, exhaustion sapping the strength from his voice.

"Me too."

CHAPTER 6

WILLIAM

FOR ALMOST A MONTH, WILLIAM HAD NOTICED VEGETABLES going missing from the garden, but now the chicken eggs were being stolen and he'd had enough. A hazard of living close to the forest was that the occasional beast or faerie would try its luck, and while the silver and salt at the fence line deterred most of them, it wasn't always enough.

"What are you doing?" Sarah asked at the sight of her husband carrying his silver hunting knife, his iron one tucked into his belt.

"Taking care of whatever's thieving from us."

"Don't you dare!" Sarah darted through the living room to block to door. "Do not mess with the faeries, William. You'll bring a world of pain down on this house."

"I'm not going to kill it. Just give it a good scare."

"Report it to Lord Dustin. Let him deal with it," Sarah argued.

William gave her a pointed look. The Lord of Belden was as

useful in dealing with the wildlife as a mouse was at dealing with a fox.

"Shut the doors and windows, and don't open them unless I give you the knock," he told her.

They'd been fooled before by a faerie that could mimic voices, and it had taken two days to get the fist-sized pest out of the house. Most of their curtains had been destroyed in the process.

Sarah grimaced, but moved aside. "If the land wasn't so good for business, I swear, I'd make you sell this place."

"You wouldn't have to twist my arm, love," he answered.

William waited to hear the door snip before wandering out into the evening light. The air was bitterly cold with winter on their doorstep, a layer of frost greeting them with every sunrise. That morning, he'd seen footprints breaking the ice; a trail of bare feet leading from the chicken coop to the barn. It couldn't be a rogue witch because he'd never seen a witch leave tracks, so he assumed it was some large faerie type or beast hybrid.

Sliding the large barn door open, there was a scurry of movement on the mezzanine. The horses were docile, grazing quietly, and the fat tabby was asleep on a bale of hay with a dead mouse under its paw. A fox slipped through a crack in the wall and William made a mental note to check the fox-proofing in the chicken coop later.

As he climbed the ladder to the mezzanine, William had to swallow the lump of nerves knotting in his throat. He'd dealt with large fae before, but it had never been a pleasant experience. The one time he'd faced a beast—a shtryg—it had almost cost him his life.

The mezzanine had become a storage place for things he'd been meaning to fix. He'd tried to keep it tidy, but he still had to step carefully over discarded tools and broken furniture. In the darkest corner near the back of the barn, an old door had been moved. Instead of lying flat against the wall it was shielding the corner, making a little den for something to crawl up and hide behind.

"Alright. Come on out. Just want to have a chat."

There was no movement, no sound, so he approached the door with his knife raised. Taking a steadying breath, he pulled the door away and flung it aside. Already half lunging, he choked when he realized what he had found.

A boy. Maybe human, but probably demi-kin judging by the state of him. Too skinny. And filthy. Couldn't be older than a teenager.

"Whoa, hey," William softened his voice, putting the knife away.

The kid bolted.

Cussing, William chased him.

The boy leaped from the mezzanine, forgoing the ladder, unafraid of the fall. William swore again, trying to hurry down as the kid tore out of the barn, making a beeline for the forest.

"Wait!" William shouted after him.

It was like a bear chasing a rabbit as William lumbered after the boy, who vaulted the wire fence and fled into the forest without hesitation. William had to stop. He couldn't risk going any farther. What would happen to Sarah if he never came out again?

"Kid!" He cupped his hands around his mouth as he bellowed into the dark. "It's dangerous in there! I'm not going to hurt you!"

Nothing.

He stayed a while, listening for trouble, but the sun was

getting low and he couldn't wait forever. Swearing viciously, William returned to the house and knocked.

"It was a demi-kin," he said as Sarah let him back inside. "In bad shape and scared out of his mind. He ran into the damned forest."

"Alone? No smuggler?" Sarah paled.

"No, and I'd bet my thumbs he's come down from Vertlyn, judging by the state of him. I'll be a donkey's ass if I can figure out how he did it alone though."

"I'll fetch some supplies. Put together a bowl for him. We'll leave it by the fence and hope he understands," Sarah suggested, heading for their linen closet.

William prepared some porridge and took what Sarah gave him, leaving them just within the salt line where he'd seen the boy disappear. He also left his silver knife.

Neither of the Copelands slept well that night, but when William went to check the fence the next morning, the pile was gone.

CHAPTER 7

THE KINNER

For a week, he lingered in the forest. Every morning and every night, the farmer left things for him: food and water, clean clothes, socks and shoes. He ate and drank greedily, hoarding the rest, never putting the blanket or knife down for more than a second.

A blanket. Gods, how long had it been since he'd held a blanket?

The knife had kept at bay the hissing things that watched him from deeper in the forest. He sat awake at night facing the darkness, waiting. He still dreamed of the beast that had attacked him and he had no desire to face it again.

On the seventh day, the farmer brought out more food and water, leaving them by the fence before taking a step back and sitting down.

"I know you're there," the farmer called out. "I'd hoped you might believe me when I said we're not trying to hurt you. We want to help."

He clenched his teeth and crouched lower, watching the farmer from behind a tree and hoping he would go away.

Hours passed, but the farmer stayed.

The sun was setting, the temperature dropping so quickly both he and the farmer started rubbing their arms against the chill. There was a part of him that still couldn't believe how crisp clean air was, or how bright colors seemed. He couldn't risk losing this freedom.

The farmer swore, his face falling.

The hatch to his cell opened, torchlight blinding. A guard looked down at him, mouth popping open, eyes widening. "Oh Gods. Oh Gods." A loud clunk somewhere far away. "I'll be back. I'll bring help."

He blinked rapidly, watching the farmer rub at the salt-and-pepper stubble on his face.

"C'mon kid," he muttered.

This sanctuary didn't feel real, but he'd been sure he'd hallucinated that guard, too. Yet help had come, and now here he was.

Holding his blanket tight to his chest, keeping the knife on display, he took a deep breath and stepped out from behind the tree. The farmer didn't see him until he was mere meters away from the fence line. As he spotted him, they both froze. The farmer raised his hands, scooting away from the food.

Unblinking, each step forward brought the kinner closer to the ground. His stomach clawed furiously as he reached for the bowl.

"Would have been better this morning."

He flinched back, snatching the bowl as he did. The farmer hadn't moved, but he kept his wary gaze on the man anyway as he picked at the rice and cheese. Four weeks ago he wouldn't have been able to stomach the grain or dairy, but he'd gotten stronger since then; more than capable of wielding the knife in his hand.

"My name is William. My wife is Sarah."

Human names. He hadn't seen any slaves when he'd hidden in the barn.

"You don't have to tell me your name if you don't want to. Are you hurt?"

He snorted lightly and shook his head, ripping into the chunk of cheese. The creaminess of it melting on his tongue elicited an intoxicated whine.

William glanced over him, unconvinced, but he wouldn't see any marks. Not so much as a bruise. "Okay, well, you're welcome inside. If you'd prefer the barn, you're welcome there too, but there's a bath and a bed in the house when you're ready."

He froze, mid-bite. A bed. A bath.

Too much.

Turning away, he tried to hide the tears blurring his vision.

A dirty fireplace. Three small bodies curled up together in front of it. Crumbs on their lips and fingers—cinnamon and sugar.

Clenching his eyes closed, he willed the images away.

"It's okay," William said gently.

Wiping the dampness from his cheeks, he made quick work of what was left in the bowl before pushing it back toward the farmer. Then he turned and ran back into the forest, ignoring the farmer's disappointed cussing.

Later that night, once the lights in the farmer's house went out, he gathered his supplies and crept back over the fence.

It took the farmers a few days to realize he was back in the barn, but once they had they started bringing supplies to him there rather than leave them by the fence.

A torrential downpour had begun outside, heavy rain cascading through a hole in the roof and pooling in the fresh hay in an empty stall. He stripped off, stood under the shower and scrubbed at himself as best he could.

The barn door rolled open and William quickly entered, soaked through his coat. The boy watched him warily as he replaced the morning's empty bowl with something steaming.

"We can run you a hot bath inside," William reminded him.

As the rainfall became needle-like and his teeth chattered, the temptation to follow the farmer inside grew sharper.

"You're looking better," William continued, running a hand over his jaw. "You don't need to shave. How old are you, exactly?"

Blinking, the boy turned away and picked at the dirt caked under his nails. It was a question that plagued him. How old was he? How long had he been imprisoned for?

When he realized he wasn't going to get an answer, William sighed. "Well, do you need anything else? Are you warm enough out here?"

Stepping out from under the stream, he pulled on one of the fresh shirts William had given him, ignoring the way it wafted around his thin frame. The blanket draped over the stall door was a decent woolen thing, but even that wasn't enough anymore to keep out the cold that was too cold, and the dark that was too dark. Too often, he woke up back in his cell.

Eventually, William gave up and left.

Wrapping himself in the blanket, he went and sat by the barrel William had left the bowl on top of. Soup and fresh bread.

The animals paid him no attention as he ate. The

chickens had been moved inside since the winter weather had settled in, huddling together in their pen. The two cloaked horses in their stall nibbled at their hay, uninterested in him or the critters that had started swarming in, looking for shelter. He'd witnessed a few amusing exchanges between the farm cat and a fox as they fought over mice. The fox also had a habit of sneaking up to the mezzanine and trying to steal his blanket. He'd tried to catch it, to share, but the stupid thing kept barking at him and slinking away again.

The fox watched him now, eyeing his hot meal. Carefully, he singled out a chunk of meat and offered it to the animal. It hopped around and darted to the barn door.

He shook his head at it, then froze. How was he any better than the fox, running away from a helping hand?

As he ate, he mulled it over. He could always run if things went wrong. He had more strength now and could probably make it through the forest on his own if he really needed to.

Gathering his things, he went to the barn door and looked out into the rain. He could barely see the house, but there was light shining through the window and smoke rising from the chimney in a soft haze that filled his lungs with nostalgic comfort.

Before he could talk himself out of it, he ran for the house.

Through the kitchen window, he saw William and Sarah sitting at a small table. Both of them had gray hair running through the black, their backs bowed with age, bellies soft. He wasn't sure he'd ever seen a human less threatening.

Raising a hand, blinking back the rain on his eyelashes, he tapped the glass.

William and Sarah sat up straight, staring at him with

matching shocked expressions. Then Sarah was out of her chair, running to the door and flinging it open.

"Come in, quickly, before you catch your death."

He edged through the door, reeling from the heat inside and the smell of cooked meats and sourdough. The sound of the fire popping and crackling in the next room could only barely be heard over the rapid dripping of his wet clothes on the tiles.

"Get him a dry blanket," Sarah said to William as she herded the kinner to the table. "We'll get you warm in no time, sweetheart. Are you still hungry? I'll get you more soup."

Sitting at a table was foreign, and he couldn't help his squirming as Sarah fussed about him. Rich paneling lined the walls, and through the door to the living room he could see thick rugs on the tiles. There were paintings hung on the wall, so unlike the masterpieces that had lined the palace corridors; colorful finger paintings clearly drawn by children, stuck on with pins rather than kept in frames.

He couldn't stay seated, his body magnetized to the fireplace. The heat was nothing like the sun, or a warm blanket. It was the heat of home. Family. Their faces clouded his vision as he sat down, eyes stinging. Were they safe? Did they miss him? Had they even noticed when he'd disappeared?

A fresh blanket was placed over his shoulders, but he was too lost to feel it.

He slept the night on the floor in front of the fire. The storm got worse, thunder rolling over the hills in waves of violence, making the flames stutter. The rain was still belting the house in the morning, but William left to tend to the animals anyway.

Sarah brought him porridge and hot tea, sitting beside him by the hearth.

"We're going to have to do something about that hair," she sighed. "Would you let me cut the matts out?"

He reached back to feel the knots stuck to his scalp. It would be nice to be free of them, so he nodded.

Sarah went to the kitchen and returned with a pair of scissors that made him nauseous.

"It's okay," she assured him.

At the feel of her fingers on him, he flinched back.

"It's alright."

She reached for him again, and he focused on staying still. On breathing. His heart was beating so hard he was sure she could hear it.

"You know, when I was a little girl I would play in my family's barn, and I came home one night with my hair so tangled my mother had to shear my head."

As she talked, she snipped. Within five minutes his head was lighter, his scalp tingling from the sudden looseness. Layers of dirt and oil caked under his nails as he ran his hands over his head.

"Well, look at that." Sarah smiled at him. "There's a handsome young man under all that mess after all. How about I run you a bath and you can wash properly? Then we'll do something about those nails of yours."

His breath caught in his throat and he turned back to the fire, pulling his knees up under his chin.

"I know. It's alright," Sarah soothed. "It's safe here. You're safe."

He glanced back at her. How did she know?

"This is what we do, sweetheart," she explained, reading the question in his eyes. "We house refugees until they're ready to move on. Nobody should go through what your people have gone through."

She assumed he was demi-kin. It was what everybody assumed, and he let them.

Forcing a smile, he let go of his knees.

"Bath?" she asked.

He nodded, body stiff as he rose to his feet.

As Sarah led him through the house, she pointed out the different rooms, eventually bringing him to the bathroom. It had a simple tub, a toilet and a basin with a small mirror over it.

"Would you like some privacy?" she offered.

He nodded, so she left.

Leaning against the wall, holding a hand to his throat, he took a moment to gather himself. Clean. He was going to be truly clean. The civility of it, the dignity she was offering him . . .

A few wobbly steps took him to the faucet. The tap screeched as he turned it and water began to dribble into the tub. There was a small boiler hidden in the corner he could use to make hot water if he wanted, but the idea of such a luxury made him nauseous. So he undressed and slipped his aching body into the cool tub and began scrubbing.

After lunch, he sat in a chair and let Sarah fix his hair some more while William stood at the sink, washing dishes. The distant braying outside, the gentle clinking of crockery, and Sarah's quiet humming had lulled him into a state of peacefulness he hadn't known was possible.

"We should talk about your next move," William said, shattering the peace.

"Later," Sarah dismissed.

"I'm not saying we need to make any decisions right now, but if he wants to move before the snow falls we need to know."

The kinner glanced between the two farmers warily.

"Do you have anybody down here that could help you?" Sarah asked, putting the scissors down and taking the seat beside him.

He shook his head.

William sighed deeply. "Figured as much. Look, kid, it's up to you but your best chance at a fresh start is in the city of Hyrsch. Have you heard of it?"

His chest dropped into his gut, eyes snapping to the door. The window. The scissors by Sarah's hand. There wasn't enough air. The fire was sweltering.

"It's okay," Sarah reached for his hand, but he pulled away. "It's a safe city. The princess liberated it years ago. The demi-kin are free inside the walls. You could go to school, or get a job—"

Lurching from his seat, he dashed for the door. Heavy footsteps came after him, William's hairy hand slamming on the handle.

"Wait."

Skidding on his heels, he turned for the other door in the living room. Nobody stopped him this time as he flung it open.

"You don't have to go! Please!" Sarah called after him, twisting her fists in her stained apron. "You can stay! You can stay as long as you like!"

He was halfway out the door, but paused. Back warm from the fire, face tingling with the unrelenting rain outside, he dared to glance back.

"Please don't run," Sarah begged.

"If you don't want to go to Hyrsch, you don't have to. It was just a suggestion. Sarah's right, you can stay here as long as you want."

He'd gotten too comfortable too quickly, but no temporary comfort was worth the risk of being sent back.

"At least wait until morning." Sarah's voice cracked.

"It's not safe out there at night. But if you really want to go we'll pack you some things to take with you," William added.

A valid point. Much of the forest was obscured from where he stood, but he knew what was out there waiting for him. He wouldn't make it to Anfar by nightfall.

One more night, he promised himself. Just one.

Stepping back inside, he closed the door and put his back to it. The Copelands wore matching expressions of relief and sadness. Or they did, until William's eyes narrowed.

"When you ran from the barn, you went north."

He said nothing. Did nothing.

"Where are you from?"

If they thought Hyrsch was a safe city, what would they think of someone who ran from it?

His grip tightened on the door handle.

"William, you're spooking him again," Sarah hissed.

"We haven't been to the city ourselves in years. Has something changed? Is it no longer free?" William pressed. "We can't be sending refugees there if it's no longer a haven."

Sarah froze, looking back to the kinner with wide eyes.

"I know you don't want to talk—" William started, but Sarah held up a hand, placing it on her husband's chest.

"*Can* you talk?"

Heat flushed his face. It was too hard to explain, even if he could, so he shook his head. The Copelands both stiffened. Sarah took her seat again and grabbed William's arm.

"Did you come from Hyrsch?" There was such a hot rage in William's voice that the boy shrunk in on himself. Nodded.

William swore and kicked the table. Sarah kept her hold on her husband's wrist, unphased by the outburst.

"Stay," she demanded.

It was dawning on him that their rage was not directed at him. Swallowing the bile that had risen in his throat, he nodded again.

CHAPTER 8

EAVHA

Eavha stood at her bedroom window and wound another strand of hair around her Blessing Charm. Before Eaon woke up, she walked through the house burning sage again, then tended to the gardens, bringing some tomatoes and mushrooms inside for breakfast. As much as she detested Eaon's cooking, she would let him do it. He needed to do it.

The kitchen door creaked and Dearmead stepped inside, smiling tightly.

"Hi," she said quietly, breaking the lull over the dim morning light. "Eaon's still sleeping but he'll get up soon if you want breakfast."

Dearmead grimaced. "No, thank you. How are you doing?"

Eavha shrugged. Keeping a smile on her face was easier if she didn't acknowledge how much she wanted to scream.

"I brought something for you." Dearmead came to stand beside her, the air between them growing warm. He pulled a slip of paper out of his pocket. "I got this from my senior guardian. It's a protection ward. You'll want them on every window, every door."

Blinking in surprise, she took the paper to inspect the ward. Her eyes widened as she realized what it was and quickly shoved it back into his pocket.

"What are you doing with a spellmark like that?" she hissed.

"What's wrong with it?" Dearmead frowned, fondling the paper.

"It's archaic, for starters, and only a grade below a witchmark. You have no business carrying a spell like that around in your pocket." She paused. "Why do you have it?"

"I thought it might help with the blight, and . . . I worry about you two here alone. Are you saying you can't cast it?"

Eavha flicked her hair as she straightened her shoulders. "Of course I can cast it."

"Great."

"You know, if you're that worried about us you could always move in. We have plenty of spare rooms and it would be good to have another magic user around."

Eavha's pulse was racing as she watched Dearmead shift his weight and scratch at his chin. Had she been too bold?

"Maybe. I'll talk to Eaon about it. What do you need to cast this?" he changed the subject and took out the spellmark again.

Eavha took another look at it.

The Barring Mark of Things Unwanted. Even on paper, it radiated power. She'd been in the presence of witchmarks before, and this wasn't that bad, but still, casting this mark would be taxing. Not to mention it wasn't intended for the kind of problem the Nemuses were having, but for keeping out intruders and curses.

"Salt, blood and earth," she told him, eyes narrowing.

"That's it?"

"Older spells tend to be simpler in design. You said your senior gave you this? To give to us?" she queried, even as she and Dearmead began scooping soil out of the herb pots and searching the pantry for salt.

"Not . . . specifically." Dearmead shuffled his feet, unable to meet her stare as he passed her a jar. "We should get this done before Eaon gets up. You know what he's like with this kind of thing."

Eavha nodded. She would find out what he was hiding later.

Grinding the salt and soil together, Eavha whispered a binding enchantment while Dearmead took a stone dagger from his belt.

"Not your hand," she scolded him as she saw him place the blade against a faded scar on his palm. "I don't fancy patching up nerves this morning."

Dearmead blushed and began to unlace his leather cuff.

Eavha's heart stuttered at the color in his cheeks, biting her lip at the blemished skin of his forearm. She almost didn't care why Dearmead had brought the spell anymore, grateful to just be spending time with him.

"A little higher," she told him as Dearmead put his knife to his skin. He looked to her for approval once more before making a cut. Blood like mulberry wine trickled into the jar.

When the incantation over the paste was finished, she brushed her fingers over Dearmead's arm to seal the wound. He watched in fascination as she used more soil to mark her face with Marks of Concentration before dipping her fingers into the blood. Letting the kernel of Terra magic inside her unfurl, she began to trace the spellmark onto the windowsill. Her muscles contracted as she dragged her fingers over the wood, every movement leeching at her strength. Sweat rolled down her spine but she completed the mark, its intensity humming against her skin.

"That will have to do," she panted, passing the jar to Dearmead who promptly sealed it and hid it in their chiller. "I'll do another tonight after I finish at the clinic."

Dearmead began to speak, but the creak of a door down the hall stilled them both.

Eavha quickly washed the stain from her hands and face as Eaon shuffled in from the hall, hair tousled as if he'd just rolled out of bed. The shadows under his eyes were worse.

"What's going on?" Eaon's voice cracked with sleep as he looked between them.

"Nothing," Dearmead said quickly, leaning awkwardly against the counter. "Just came by to help with the gardening. And to invite you both to dinner tomorrow night. Sorry. Ma insisted."

Eaon groaned loudly. "It's too early for this level of torment."

Eavha leveled a glare at her brother and straightened her shoulders, forgetting the heaviness in her bones.

"That's very generous of her. Thank you."

The smile Dearmead gave her was strained. "Anyway. I have a meeting to get to. I'll be by again later."

Eaon grunted as he shuffled to the counter and began slicing vegetables.

"Thanks for your help this morning," Eavha said, but suspicion was gnawing at her again. In all the years she had known Dearmead, she had never seen him lie to Eaon.

Dearmead nodded at her before rushing from the house. Eavha waited a moment before tying back her hair with a piece of twine she kept wrapped around her wrist.

"I just have a few more things to do. I'll be back in a minute," she said to Eaon, who just grunted at her again.

Silent as a shadow, Eavha followed Dearmead. Not toward the city, like she expected, but to the forest. Once he was under the canopy, she nimbly scaled the nearest tree and tracked him from above, leaping effortlessly between the overlapping branches. Her hard feet found purchase on the bark time and time again, never faltering, and so delicate that not a single leaf shook free.

Dearmead jogged through the wilderness until he caught up with a small group congregated at the invisible boundary of Wyldeden. Eavha halted some distance away, recognizing the witches who'd gathered. Herbe, the elder guardian, and Milnova, the elder keeper, stood stoically by the priestess Aadya, clad in her standard oversized robe, and three masked high guardians. Behind them was High Priestess Lorelei, the clan's spearhead and one of the most powerful witches in all of Nir. Terra incarnate, or so the rumors said. Eavha had turned into a jittering mess both times she'd met Lorelei. Dressed in a stately gown of cotton, the threads as thin as spider-silk and embellished with golden moss, the high priestess glittered under the diluted light filtering through the canopy. Her skin was dark like Dearmead's, and her long black hair was pinned up beneath a diadem of polished quartz.

What in the Mother's realm was Dearmead, a junior guardian, doing with them?

All questions emptied out of her head when she noticed what had drawn the high priestess out of her sanctuary. There was a rip in the fabric of the realm separating Wyldeden from Anfar; a shimmering tear through which all sorts of creatures might have come through.

Covering her mouth, Eavha had to remind herself to breathe. Every twisted bedtime story she'd been told as a witchling came rushing back. Her older relatives—who'd worked as battlefield medics during the rogue's attempted coup on Wyldeden—used to tell her horror stories of what rogue witches would do to the guardians, priests and priestesses fighting to protect the rest of them. She'd had nightmares about it for weeks.

Lorelei raised a hand and the elders stepped back. From within her robe, Aadya pulled out the ceremonial bone knife, its blade carved from a femur and etched with powerful spellmarks. The swell of magic quieted the air as Lorelei took the blade and sliced her fingertip. Slowly, she drew a witchmark over the rip.

Eavha's head began to pound, her bowels weakening as the aura of the spell rippled through the forest. Below, Dearmead vomited.

The wound in the realm sealed, and Eavha nearly fell out of the tree from relief as the magic ebbed. She'd barely steadied herself before the gathering of witches were heading back toward her, their voices finally within eavesdropping range.

"It's an old tear reopened," Milnova said. "But even then, the strength that would have required . . ."

Herbe quickened his steps to catch up to Lorelei. "My heir apparent is already hunting for what may have crossed the border, but with your permission, High Priestess, I would like to organize—"

"No." Lorelei held out a hand as Aadya wrapped a binding around it. "We keep this contained. Nobody else is to know."

"If the public is attacked—"

"Let me worry about the public," Lorelei interrupted him again. "Just find her. Or him. Any sign of them and I want to know. Immediately."

Numb, Eavha followed them back out of the forest. Dearmead was still pale as he trailed after the group.

The Boab had been violated. It was all she could think about as she stumbled home. Nothing unwanted had ever gotten inside the Boab before, or so she'd been led to believe; Milnova had called it an old tear.

Eaon had left a bowl of burnt tomatoes and mushrooms on the table and left. If he had gone looking for her, he would probably think she'd fled from his cooking. Maybe he was better off believing that.

She ate, not tasting. Slowly, the numbness waned and her breaths began to hitch. Despite what her teachers had told her, there must have been a breach in the Boab at some point. Perhaps during the rogue attack. Maybe they were coming back to try again.

Lurching from her seat, she vomited into the sink.

Rogues, prowling the forest. Stalking her through the garden. Breaking into the house and killing her in her sleep.

There was no way she could work today. Elder Esther would have to manage without her.

Still trembling, Eavha wandered back into the garden and plucked a leaf from a nearby shrub. She let her magic touch it before whispering her message. Terra accepted her offering, the leaf spiraling up into the sky to be delivered to Esther.

Eavha didn't care if she passed out from the effort, she would ward the rest of the house immediately.

～

"Eavha!"

Eaon's shout woke her from where she'd fallen asleep in a wicker armchair. Six cups of chamomile tea hadn't eased her nerves, but expending the depths of her Terra-blessing warding the house had put her out for hours.

Straightening, she quickly ran her fingers through her curls. "What?"

"What in the Lover's embrace have you done to the house?" he snapped, stalking into the living room with a heavy satchel over his shoulder.

"I..."

"You know, I can ignore all the constant sage and muttering but this . . . ugh, I'm getting a headache. I've been here thirty seconds and I have a headache."

"There are rogues inside the Boab," she squeaked, clasping her hands in her lap.

Eaon blinked. "That's impossible."

"I saw the high priestess in the forest today. She was drawing a witchmark over a tear in the realm. They said it was an old wound . . ." Her throat tightened and she had to focus on keeping her tears from betraying her panic.

Eaon put down his bag and sat at her feet, taking her clenched fists.

"Tell me everything."

The hallway Eaon led her down was covered in dust that their steps didn't disturb. Behind every closed door, Eavha could almost hear the ghosts; the cousin who'd taught her to braid hair and the one who'd taught her how to sew, sharing gossip about how Unk Beesa had been caught with their neighbor Freeda.

Eaon opened one of the doors. The living quarters of Unk Reevon's wing had been cleaned, the furniture pushed aside bar a large table laden with moldy books and yellowed scrolls. Behind it, the wall had swathes of parchment pinned to it with Eaon's tidy scrawl listing names and dates, sweeping lines connecting groups of them in a pattern Eavha didn't understand.

"What is this?" she asked.

"I've been thinking." Eaon left her to stare, traipsing to the desk and splaying his hands over the open pages of a book.

"I can see that. Where did you even get these?" she asked, following him to inspect the tomes. She didn't recognize any of them. The books in the clinic were in much better condition.

"We really ought to have one central library."

Eavha looked closer at Eaon; at the way his eyes darted too quickly over his work.

"I think we've been lied to," he continued. "This is a timeline of families and covens from different clans that went extinct in the last millennium from a nameless plague. One or two families are affected, but not at the same time. Then it jumps to a different clan, but never in two clans at once."

Eavha followed Eaon's hand as he showed her the path between groups of names. A path of plague. A pressure released in her chest as she realized they weren't alone. There were dozens of family names, thousands of witches, taken en masse.

"The thing is, in every single clan, the extinctions begin almost right after an attack by rogues. Every time. History books claim none of the attacks were successful, but this blight always follows. It can't be a coincidence."

Eavha hummed, sucking in her bottom lip. Fifty-two years ago, Wyldeden had been attacked. Fifty years ago, the Nemuses started passing without cause.

"Aadya says it is."

"Aadya is a liar."

Eavha flinched and stared at Eaon. She'd never heard him openly blaspheme before. Their priestesses were the holiest of them—witches touched in the womb by the Spirits. Eavha aimed to ascend to their ranks one day.

"What if the attacks are a distraction?" Eaon asked, so much fire burning in his gaze that Eavha had to step back. "Keep our priestesses and priests busy so they don't sense the breach. Keep the guardians occupied, so something else can sneak in from behind."

"It sounds paranoid, Eaon." Eavha kept her voice soft and soothing.

She should have seen this coming. Should have seen the signs he was on the brink of another frenzy. How many times had she seen him cycle through these moods? Fatigue and frenzy, fatigue and frenzy . . . Ma would have been disappointed in her.

"Besides, let's say you're right; why us? Why these families? These clans?"

"I don't know. Yet." Eaon dragged his hands down his face, paused, then snapped his attention to a random book across the room.

"How long have you been working in here at night?" she asked, watching him stalk to a pile of tomes discarded on a footstool.

"I'm fine, Eavha. Don't start fussing. How long were you passed out in the living room before I got home?"

A fair point. Eavha looked over the wall again. She had seen the rip in the realm with her own eyes, and the pattern was too pronounced to be marked down as a coincidence.

"I just don't believe that Lorelei wouldn't know about this. She'd have to know. If this is all true, she would have done something."

Eaon glanced at her, grimaced, then went back to searching for whatever book he was looking for. He plucked one out and brought it back to the desk. "Do you think you could get the medical records for our family?"

"Yes." Eavha stepped around the desk and put a hand on Eaon's shoulder. "But you should leave it for tonight. Get some sleep."

"You shouldn't tell anyone about this," Eaon muttered, ignoring her. His finger moved down the page as he scanned it. "We don't know who might be involved. Who . . . who appeared in the clan after . . . census. Where's the census."

"Eaon." Eavha grabbed his wrist as he made to dart off again. "You need to sleep."

"I'll sleep when we're safe," he snapped, pulling away.

Sighing, Eavha pinched the bridge of her nose. Eaon crouched by a stack of scrolls on the floor and began sifting through them.

"Alright then. I'm going to make some dinner and I'm going to brew you something, okay?"

Eaon froze.

"It's *my* job—"

"You're busy. I can do it."

"I don't need a tonic."

"I know." She raised her hands, stepping back toward the door. "It's just something to help clear your head."

He went back to the pile of scrolls and Eavha left.

Eaon was the Head of House, and she knew he was doing his best, but the harsh reality was that Eaon wasn't cut out for leadership. So Eavha went to the kitchen, lit the oven and pulled out her recipe for a tonic that would make her brother sleep.

CHAPTER 9

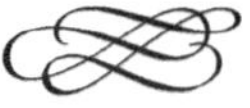

EAON

Eaon couldn't decide if he was furious or grateful for Eavha's deceit. She had lied to his face, but he'd slept for the first time in days and felt much better for it. Teagan even let him teach a class—six young witches had been identified as being low-magic and needed to begin learning Nirnish in case they became travelers.

They sat on the floor of a hut in varying states of misery and resentment. Eaon knew how they felt. The promise of *beyond*, of getting out, had been his only comfort, so Eaon broke up his lessons with stories of Nir. Like the time he and Kailevi had chanced upon a sacred faerie site and seen the whimsical creatures dancing through the night. Or a type of human shoe with a blade on the sole, designed especially for skating over frozen lakes.

By the end of the day, Eaon was ready to sing Eavha's praises. His head felt clearer than it had in a long time, meaning dinner at the Bayfield residence would be significantly easier.

Dearmead's parents barely tolerated him as it was; he didn't need to show up out of his mind with exhaustion.

Still, it took all his restraint not to go directly to his unk's quarters and continue his research. He was close to something. Every time he closed his eyes he could see the lines on the parchment leading him to the truth, the way he sometimes saw the lines of the universe connecting the world around him. Dearmead and Eavha had both told him time and time again that the lines weren't real, but every time he saw them it was harder to deny it.

Eavha was bathing in the stream when he got home, so he set about completing the endless list of chores he had to keep up with. He couldn't do much to help with the gardens, but he could manage the cleaning and what little livestock they had left. Aside from a few hens and a goat for their eggs and dairy, he'd traded the rest of the animals to larger clans for sacks of grain and small repairs. So he cleaned the chicken and goat pens, then cleaned the few rooms in the house they still used.

The old Heads of House never had to do all of this. They could delegate, or take on laborers to do the work for them. The fewer witches in the family the less prestige came with the title, apparently.

When Eavha returned, Eaon went to the stream. The sun was close to setting so he didn't waste time. From his closet, he found one of Kailevi's nice linen shirts to wear. After making sure the pearl buttons were aligned, he rolled the sleeves up to his elbows and tried to tuck the hem so it wasn't so obvious the shirt wasn't his. Kailevi had been built like a barrel and, while Eaon might have filled out these last few years, he wasn't his da.

Eavha was waiting on the porch. When Eaon came out she immediately went about trying to flatten his hair.

"You look nice," he admitted.

"I was going for 'radiant' but I suppose 'nice' will do. Do you think Dearmead will like this skirt?" she asked, stepping back and running her hands down the layered emerald folds of her dress, the fabric cut in the shape of butterfly wings. Around her neck hung a large moonstone pendant that had been their ma's.

Eaon had trouble swallowing the thick lump in his throat.

"I'm not sure Dearmead notices female fashion, to be honest."

Eavha laughed. "Well, I'll have to see if I can change that." She paused suddenly, biting her lip as she glanced up at him a little ruefully. "I mean, you're okay with it, right? What's going on between Dearmead and I?"

Eaon's chest was getting too tight, his hands shaking.

"I'm worried you might be reading too much into things," he said quietly.

"What do you mean?" Eavha frowned.

"Oh, you're both ready."

Eaon turned to see Dearmead striding down the path to their house wearing a dark shirt and matching knee-length pants.

"Is that a new shirt?" Eaon asked.

"You came to escort us?" Eavha said at the same time.

"Uh, yes." Dearmead looked between them. "Was I interrupting?"

"We can talk about it later." Eavha skipped down the steps and looped her arm through Dearmead's. "Besides, Eaon and I have something to discuss with you."

Eaon crossed his arms as he followed, trying not to grind his teeth. His mood had soured and his question came out sharper than he'd intended.

"Why are you involved with the high priestess and the rip in the border?"

Dearmead choked, looking back over his shoulder with wide eyes.

"Eaon, shh," Eavha hissed, glancing at the long shadows stretching across the grass.

"I was the one who found it while I was out tracking that fox you saw," Dearmead explained.

"We were supposed to do that together," Eaon groused.

"Wait, how did you . . ." Dearmead looked to Eavha, frowning deeply. "You followed me."

"You're a terrible liar and I'm not stupid," Eavha scolded.

Dearmead sighed and pulled his braid over his shoulder, twisting it in his fist. "My family don't know. Nobody does, okay? If they find out you two . . . just, stop talking about it. It is what it is. I don't know anything more and I don't know what it means."

"It means there are rogues inside the Boab." Eavha's tone was scathing. "That's why you came to tell me to ward the house. Don't lie."

"Don't ask me to talk about things I'm not allowed to talk about. Don't put me in that position."

Eaon clenched his fists and huffed loudly, but the conversation came to a stop as the Bayfield residence came into view.

Dearmead's family estate was larger than the Nemuse home, his family twice the size theirs had been at its peak. Eaon had been there plenty of times, often visiting immediately after returning from travel. Sprawling clay buildings peppered the crest of the hill, the family separated into clusters based on clan roles, each compound connected by stone paths to give them the illusion of being a cohesive unit.

The garden leading up to the complex was lush and laden with fruits, vegetables, herbs and flowers, while the back half of their land was dedicated to larger crops of wheat, barley and maize, as well as a large collection of livestock. Food enough for all, as well as enough to trade for other supplies. Maintenance would be a nightmare, but a large portion of the family was generously blessed by Terra and were not only capable of tending to their gardens, but to the communal fields of medicinal herbs the clinic relied on.

Torches led the way up the hill, conversation and laughter filling the sweet night air. Young guardians were outside playing with worn-out staffs, their clacking reminding Eaon exactly who he was about to have dinner with. A pity dinner, he knew, but possibly an interrogative one too. No doubt Dearmead's intervention during the burial was still a point of contention.

A laborer opened the door as they approached, and just inside it stood Calla Bayfield—Head of House, and Dearmead's ma. She was tall and muscular, and had been that way for over three hundred years. With her dark hair chopped short and a pale scar running from her lip to septum, Calla looked the warrior she'd proven to be.

Eavha curtsied and clasped the hand offered to her, bowing her head.

"Eavha Nemuse. Welcome." Calla smiled warmly.

"Thank you for inviting us," Eavha answered, straightening.

Calla didn't offer her hand or greet Eaon before leading them down a long hall that ended in double doors. There was another laborer waiting to open them for her, bowing low as they passed into the cavernous space the Bayfields used for dining. The walls and ceiling were made of loosely woven willow, allowing a stunning view of the impossibly bright stars speckling the evening sky. The walls were laced with phosphorescent flowers Eaon knew were native to the northern mountains. They would have required an exorbitant offering at the trading festivals to have procured so many.

The guardian section of the estate needed four long tables to seat everyone. More laborers milled around carrying plates of roasted vegetables, chickpea and lentil salads, freshly baked breads and platters of exotic cheeses. It was a feast suitable for one of the largest and most powerful families in Wyldeden; a feast that had once adorned the tables of the Nemuse home as well.

Eavha's mouth had fallen open, and as they followed Calla toward the head of a table she whispered to Eaon, "We live in a hovel."

Eaon rolled his eyes.

Calla took the plush seat at the head of the table and rolled up the sleeves of her tunic. Dearmead took the chair to her right and nodded for Eaon to sit beside him. Patting the chair on her other side, Calla smiled for Eavha, who beamed and flattened her skirts again.

"Your home is so beautiful," Eavha said, awed by the cascading hydrangeas arranged like chandeliers from the ceiling.

"As are you. It's been a long time since we've had someone so civilized sitting at this table, let alone someone with such prestige. How are things at the clinic?" Calla asked.

Eavha's cheeks pinked as she shot a glance across the table at Dearmead, practically batting her eyelashes. Grabbing the glass of red wine beside his place setting, Eaon took a long drink.

Dearmead's hand found his knee beneath the table, giving it a tight squeeze.

"Wonderful, thank you," Eavha answered. "Of course, we're always so grateful for the supplies the Bayfields grow for us."

"It's an honor to be useful." Calla nodded, then turned and looked down her nose at Eaon. "Speaking of such things, I heard you're laboring again. At the elementary school this time."

"Ma." Dearmead gave Calla a dark look. Eaon took another drink and looked for something to put on his plate. Something to do with his hands.

"Did I say something untrue?" she asked, blinking in faux innocence.

"Why don't we talk about something other than clan roles? Eaon's been working on some really interesting projects lately."

"Oh?" Calla asked, reaching for a salad. "Is that why my sister saw you loitering around the guardians' training grounds a couple of weeks ago?"

Eaon focused on spreading cheese on a slice of sourdough.

"I just had to ask Dearmead something."

"Do you not have anything useful to do with your time that you can make social visits during working hours?"

"Ma!" Dearmead snapped.

The other witches at the table were keeping their heads down, trying to contain their smirks. Eaon felt twelve years old again.

"It's fine, Dea," he muttered.

"It's not fine," Dearmead hissed, glaring at his ma. "You said you wanted to get to know them. If I'd known you were going to—"

"I do want to get to know them," Calla smiled crookedly. "I want to understand why my youngest son made such a public declaration of commitment to the Nemuse family. I'm hoping it was for more than a friendship based on pity for a floor-scrubber."

"I'm so sorry." Dearmead turned to Eaon beseechingly. Eaon just put his hand over Dearmead's under the table and squeezed.

"Actually," Eaon kept his eyes on his plate as he took a bite of his bread. "Mm. Delicious. Dea and I's friendship is based on our mutual disdain for bigotry and self-righteousness."

He heard Eavha's sharp intake of breath but ignored it. Dearmead closed his eyes and pulled his own wine glass closer. The cacophony of conversation throughout the room became a backdrop for the rapid staccato of Eaon's racing heart.

"Fascinating." Calla's crooked smile disappeared as she turned to Eavha. "Anyway, tell me dear, how long has my son been courting you?"

Dearmead choked on his drink, eyes widening at he stared at his ma in horror. Eavha had gone completely red, face twisted as if she might be violently ill right there at the table.

"May the Mother help me, Ma, I'm not . . . you know that . . . Eavha is just my friend." Dearmead shot Eavha an apologetic look. Eaon cussed under his breath. He should have told her. The moment he realized she had a crush on Dearmead, he should have told her.

"I swear, boy, if you have embarrassed this family by declaring mere *friendship* at that burial I will throw you out as a rogue myself," Calla spat as she whipped her head around to glare at him, eyes burning with a blistering rage.

"You're the one embarrassing this family," Dearmead hissed back, but Eaon could feel Dearmead's knees shaking against his own.

"Really," Eavha's trembling voice sliced through the tension.

"Dearmead has been so close to our family for so long, he's like . . . like a brother to us. It's not just . . . friendship."

Eaon's heart was getting heavy. Mother of all, Eavha was trying so hard.

Calla wrinkled her nose. "Dearmead has plenty of family already."

"Enough." Dearmead narrowed his eyes, his shaking coming to an abrupt stop. Eaon had seen that expression on his face too many times; he needed to put an end to this. Now. Before Dearmead got into a much more dangerous fight.

"You know, as much as we appreciate the fine hospitality, Cal, I think I'm feeling a little unwell. Perhaps we can reschedule this delightful conversation for another time."

He didn't wait for a response before rising from the table. Eavha didn't hesitate to follow suit. Silence fell over the hall. They were being rude. Kailevi would have smacked him senseless for this display of disrespect. But Eaon had heard enough; Eavha was mortified and Dearmead was moments away from bursting a vein in his forehead.

"I'll walk you home," Dearmead said coldly.

"Sit down," Calla hissed, but all three of them ignored her.

Eaon didn't realize how hot his skin had become until they were walking down the hill and sweat rolled down the back of his neck. Eavha's constant sniffing made him clench his fists. If he didn't know for a fact that Calla could break every bone in his body without even picking up her spear, he'd be tempted to turn around and show her those fists.

"I'm so sorry," Dearmead repeated once they were beyond the property line. "I had no idea she was going to be like that."

"It's not your fault, Dea."

Eavha said nothing as she strode ahead. Her tears were likely as much about Dearmead's rejection as anything else. Dearmead's shoulders fell as he watched her, his face pinching as he took in Eaon's angry gait.

"I should have known. She always does this, and I know what she thinks about—"

"Dearmead," Eaon slowed his stomping, taking Dearmead's hand. "It's not your fault."

Dearmead hung his head but didn't apologize again. Wrapping her arms around herself, shoulders stiffening, Eavha picked up the pace as they continued home in silence. As they passed the song and laughter pouring out of the houses between the Bayfield and Nemuse residences, stones filled Eaon's chest as the familiar sensation of feeling like a foreigner washed over him. Their world was one he would never belong to.

Eavha didn't stop as she approached their house.

"Can we talk?" Dearmead asked her, but Eavha refused to face them. She grabbed a candle by the porch and flipped her hair over her shoulder.

"For what it's worth, your home really was beautiful and the food looked delicious."

Eaon watched her stalk into the house. Her light disappeared down the hall.

"I'm sorry," Dearmead repeated.

Eaon loosed a deep sigh, turned, and cupped Dearmead's face in his hands. "Eavha will be fine."

"I'm sorry about Ma."

"Dea. She is just one nasty old crone. As soon as you're ready, we can go. I'll show you the city, the beaches, the snow. We'll be free."

Dearmead closed his eyes and pulled Eaon closer, resting his chin on his shoulder. "I just . . ."

Eaon waited. Sometimes Dearmead needed time to get the words out when he was upset. They stood on the porch for a few minutes before Dearmead stepped back, took Eaon's face in his calloused hands and kissed him.

"Thank you."

"Stay tonight. I don't want to think about you going home to her."

"I know. But if I don't it just gives her more time to get riled up. Besides, you should talk to Eavha. She walked into a minefield tonight."

Eaon sighed and closed his eyes. Dearmead was right.

"Let me know you're okay."

"Of course I'll be okay." He kissed Eaon again, lingering. There was such longing on his face. "Tomorrow. I promise."

Eaon nodded once before letting Dearmead go. Then he took a candle of his own and went to find Eavha.

He didn't have to look far. She was standing in the hall with her candle blown out, murder on her face.

She'd seen everything.

"You filthy, rogue-rutting . . ." she stuttered over an insult foul enough.

"I—"

"No, you don't get to speak! You're a liar!" she spat. "You could have told me! But you let me pine after him for . . . it . . . it's humiliating! I'm humiliated, Eaon! How could you!"

Eaon grabbed his candle with both hands to steady it.

"And, ugh," she continued, wrinkling her nose as she stepped back from him. "I suppose you two will just disappear and go live happily ever after in some cottage somewhere. I suppose I'll have to save our bloodline by myself."

"I'll do what I have to, Eavha. I won't leave you."

She scoffed. "Don't ever speak to me again."

"Eavha . . ."

"You really are the most useless Nemuse ever born."

It would have hurt less if she'd hit him.

"I'm sorry."

"Go rogue, Eaon."

She'd said it a hundred times, but this time she truly meant it.

CHAPTER 10

EAON

TRUE TO HER WORD, EAVHA HADN'T SPOKEN TO EAON FOR two weeks after discovering the depth of his relationship with Dearmead. Every day he felt heavier. Sometimes when he was teaching class his vision would go blurry, his body numb. He'd forget what he was saying and have to sit down.

All the teachers had been gathered in the staff room for a meeting, but Eaon couldn't remember a single thing Elder Bodhi had said in the last hour. He didn't care. Teagan or Selina could fill him in later.

There was a tap on his shoulder. Eaon glanced back to where Dearmead stood, staff in hand. It wasn't unusual for a teacher's guardian to be present at staff meetings, but it wasn't often Eaon missed Dearmead's arrival.

"How is Eavha?" he whispered.

Eaon shrugged.

"How are you?" Dearmead tried, but Eaon didn't know how to answer him.

The meeting dragged on, but Dearmead's fingers on his elbow kept him grounded. He needed to be kinder to him. Dearmead was working so hard for his family, for him, and he deserved better than Eaon's emptiness.

When the meeting finally ended, Eaon reached back and gave Dearmead's hand a squeeze.

"I'll come and find you later," Dearmead promised, worry creasing his brow as he left to follow Teagan to her office.

Eaon didn't have class that morning, so he was free to sink himself into his research. Having compared the census from the year of and the year after the rogue attack, Eaon had a surprisingly long list of discrepancies to investigate.

"Eaon!" Elder Bodhi grabbed his arm as he stepped out of the staff room. "Didn't you hear me call for you?"

"What?" Eaon blinked.

Elder Bodhi. Elder Bodhi was talking to him. He gave his head a little shake and bowed deeply.

"My deepest apologies, Elder."

"Are you ill again?" Bodhi asked, pulling on Eaon's arm to make him straighten.

Eaon paled. Bodhi knew about his fatigue?

"No. No, I'm fine. I'm sorry." Eaon forced himself to take a breath and make his mouth smile, bowing again. "What can I do for you?"

"I need your assistance with a particular apprentice of mine. Olevia Morse is engaged to a witch from the Southern Mountain Clan and, as you know, they speak a different dialect down there. She needs to be fluent by the end of the month and you happen to be the most qualified witch for the job."

Eaon's head was full of cotton wool; he wasn't sure he was hearing correctly.

"Of course. I'd be honored to help with anything you need. I can get started right away."

Eaon would agonize about the fool he'd made of himself later. This was the kind of opportunity Kailevi had hoped Eaon would get, and he'd almost squandered it. The urge to drop to his knees and repent almost overwhelmed him.

"I appreciate it," Elder Bodhi smiled. "I'll clear your schedule with Teagan and let Olevia know you can start with her tomorrow."

"Of course." Eaon bowed again, clasping the hand Bodhi offered him in farewell.

As soon as Bodhi was out of sight, Eaon practically ran to Selina's office and shut himself inside. Selina glanced up from her desk to where Eaon was leaning against the wall, a hand at his throat.

"Do I dare ask?"

"I just made a complete idiot of myself in front of Elder Bodhi."

"Oh, Eaon," she said, putting down her quill. "I've got a minute if you want to talk about it."

"No. No, I've got a lot of work to do. He asked me to train one of his apprentices," Eaon explained.

Selina gasped. "That's fantastic!"

"Thank you," he rasped as he sat at his desk, clearing his throat.

"Let me know if you need anything. Did you find what you needed in that history book I loaned you?" she asked, tucking her auburn hair behind her ears.

"Yes. Thank you. I'll bring it back soon." He smiled, then coughed. The whole encounter had put his body into shock. He coughed again and rubbed his chest. "I might just get some water before I start. Need anything?"

"I'm alright. If you're sick . . ."

"I'm not. I just . . ." He shook his head, unsure how to explain it. His lungs couldn't find their rhythm.

The door creaked open and both Eaon and Selina looked up to see Dearmead poke his head in. When he saw Selina sitting at her desk, he grimaced.

"Ah, sorry."

"I thought you were coming later," Eaon frowned.

"I saw Elder Bodhi talking to you," he explained, coming inside and closing the door. "Didn't realize you weren't alone."

Eaon coughed again, rubbing at his tightening chest.

"Go and get some water," Selina reminded him.

"You alright?" Dearmead reached over to keep Eaon steady as he rose from his desk.

"Yeah," he wheezed, his chest getting tighter and tighter. "Just . . . fresh air."

Selina stood, running to get the door as Dearmead helped Eaon stumble outside. He couldn't seem to pull in a deep enough breath, and his growing panic wasn't helping. The air outside was cool but he couldn't get it inside his body. His legs failed, and only Dearmead and Selina holding him up stopped him from collapsing.

"What's wrong? What's happening?" Dearmead asked, but Eaon couldn't answer. He couldn't *breathe*.

Dearmead swore, hoisting Eaon up into both arms and broke into a run, leaving Selina behind. Eaon closed his eyes, commanding himself to breathe. But he couldn't.

He just couldn't.

CHAPTER 11

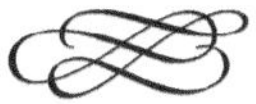

EAVHA

Eavha was in the middle of inspecting an infection when she heard her name being shouted. She'd barely had time to turn around before Dearmead was running through the clinic door carrying an unconscious Eaon.

For one second, she froze. Her brother's lips were turning blue.

"What happened?" she snapped as she left her patient, rushing to the bed Dearmead was laying Eaon down on.

"Nothing. He just . . . stopped breathing." Dearmead patted Eaon's face, trying to rouse him.

Eavha laid her hands over Eaon's chest, trying not to compare the way Kailevi's face had looked in death to the way Eaon was starting to look. She felt a pulse but it was weak.

Apaete arrived beside her and pinched Eaon's nose, turning his head up to inspect for an obstruction. Closing her eyes, Eavha rallied her magic and sent it through his body, looking for the problem.

But there was no problem. No disease or illness or injury.

"No, no, no," she muttered, searching desperately. "Damn it, where's Esther?"

"Not back yet," Apaete said before closing her mouth over Eaon's and blowing air directly into his lungs. Eavha waited to feel Eaon's chest rise, but it didn't.

"What's wrong?" Dearmead asked, looking between the two healers.

"I don't know."

Reaching for a bowl of burnt herbs, she hastily drew spellmarks over her face to amplify her power. With her hands over Eaon's slowing heart, she dove deep into her magic and offered it all to Sanni.

Nothing happened.

"Come on." Eavha grit her teeth. "Take it."

Her magic pushed against her skin, waiting for the connection. For permission.

Eaon's heart faltered, then stopped.

"No. Not him too," she hissed, climbing onto the bed to start compressions.

"Eavha," Dearmead begged.

"Eavha, he's gone," Apaete said quietly.

"I said, no!"

A pulse of magic beat through the clinic, silencing the chatter around them. She could feel her power writhing inside her, boiling her blood.

"Take it!" she screamed, not even sure who she was asking anymore: Sanni, or the Lover.

Not that it mattered; there was no answer from either of them.

All she could feel was the gaping absence inside him where

his essence, his soul, should be. Something dark and foreign lurked there.

Damn the Spirits. Damn permission. Damn everything.

"Take it, you wretched beast," she hissed, then shoved her magic into the abyss.

Apaete gasped. "What are you doing?"

It was so dark in the void. So cold and so vast, as if there were an empty galaxy inside him. She kept tunneling, forcing her magic farther and farther. Body cramping, head pounding, she knew she shouldn't be there. She didn't care.

She couldn't let the last words she'd said to Eaon be ones of anger.

"He's gone, Eavha. Stop." Apaete's voice echoed somewhere far away.

Then she felt him.

Just a spark, slowly sputtering out in the abyss. She grabbed a hold of it and gasped at the pain that tore through her. Something inside her began to fray, but she wrapped herself around that spark and started to pull.

Mother help her, it was like trying to drag a rooted tree through the ground, but she was doing it. Inch by inch, she dragged his soul back to his body.

Bones on fire now, skull splitting, she shoved Eaon's essence back through the void and welded it there, emptying every drop of magic she had left into starting his heart again.

A deep nausea rolled through her, red bursting behind her eyes.

Strong hands hauled her off Eaon, but she didn't care about that. All she cared about before she passed out was that Eaon was gasping for breath.

CHAPTER 12

EAON

EAON WOKE UP ON A DIRT FLOOR, BODY STIFF WITH COLD. HE didn't recognize the room he was in; windowless, the tall walls made of stone, no ceiling or furniture, and one door that had two masked guardians standing in front of it—the high priestess's personal guard. Their masks were shaped like helmets and carved with animal faces. A wolf and a leopard were with him now.

"What's going on?" he asked, wincing as he pushed his aching body off the ground.

The leopard stepped forward. In one swift movement, the guardian whipped his staff, striking Eaon's back.

"Ow!" He crumpled back into the dirt.

Clearly he was in trouble, though he didn't know what for. The last thing he remembered was the conversation with Elder Bodhi and his coughing fit.

"Am I sick?" he asked.

The guardian hit him again.

Eaon hissed through gritted teeth, backing away from the leopard-masked witch. He didn't try asking anything else.

During the hours he was left waiting, the coldness ebbed from his skin and the room became stifling. Overhead, he watched the sun inch across the open ceiling, eagerly awaiting shadow. Nobody offered him water and the guardians didn't relax their stance by the door for a second. He didn't know what they thought he was going to do. If he had done something wrong, he would face the consequences without argument.

Without a cue, the guardians stepped forward and aimed their spearheads at Eaon. The door behind them opened and Eaon lost his breath as the high priestess glided in.

He was in serious trouble.

"Eaon Nemuse."

Bile rose up his throat at the surrealistic sound of his name coming from her lips. Swallowing it back down, he bowed his head and kept it down.

"Tell me what you remember."

"I . . . I was sick. It came on suddenly," he admitted.

"And after that?"

"Nothing."

"Nothing from the Lover's realm? From beyond?"

Frowning, Eaon dared to raise his head high enough to see the way her eyes glittered in eager curiosity. For a moment, he forgot how to breathe again. The Lovers realm? Had he died? How was he—

Another brutal blow from one of the guardians knocked him down to his side, scattering the spiraling thoughts.

"Cold," he remembered, rubbing his shoulder but staying where he'd fallen. "It was cold."

Lorelei waited, but Eaon had nothing else to add.

"This is your only chance to give me something to take to the council. Give us a reason to spare you."

Tendrils of magic pressed against his mind, colors bursting behind his eyes.

In the clinic, Dearmead pulled Eavha off the bed. Guardians came rushing in, taking her from him. Apaete placed two fingers on Eaon's throat to check his pulse, but immediately recoiled. Her hand began to rot.

Nobody moved to help her as Apaete started screaming. They all stared in shock as the witch's meat slid off her bones, the decay spreading until all that was left of Apaete was a pile of putrid entrails.

Lorelei released Eaon, who promptly lurched forward and vomited. The cold beneath his skin was creeping back as he began to shake.

"If you can tell me anything about how that was possible, you need to tell me now. There's a reason necromancy is forbidden. The Lover's blessing does not belong in this world."

Eaon heaved and vomited again.

"Get him some water," Lorelei told one of her guardians, taking a step back from where Eaon was going into shock. "In the morning, the council and I will announce a course of action. You understand what has to be done, don't you?"

He could barely hear her over the screaming still ringing in his ears, but the consequences of what Eavha had done were slowly dawning on him.

Whatever Lorelei thought was best . . . he would not resist.

Apaete's screaming haunted Eaon all night. He doubted he could have stomached anything even if someone had offered him food. The dawn didn't bring a new day, but it did bring a third guardian who commanded him to stand. One in front and two behind, they kept their spears pointed at his chest as they led the way from the prison.

He didn't blame them. If he could, he'd have ripped his skin off with his bare hands. A part of him hoped the council sentenced him to death so he didn't have to live with what he'd done. They couldn't do it outright, but there were ways around the law.

As they walked along the lake, his chest tightened painfully. A death sentence meant he'd never stand on the line between sand and sea again; never see the way an ocean mirrored the explosion of color from a setting sun. He would never feel the press of bodies in the human cities, or the first snowfall on his cheeks.

At the Elder Circle, a large crowd had gathered. Witches fell silent, scampering out of the way as the guardians led him toward the stone platform in the center of the amphitheater. The braziers at each corner had been lit and Wyldeden's elders stood in a ring around the dais. In the center of the stone, Lorelei was waiting. Eavha knelt at her feet.

They had beaten her.

Even from the base of the dais, he could see the bruising on her skin, the dried blood on her neck. A chill spread through him again, his lip pulling back in a snarl as a guardian prodded him forward. As he reached the first step leading up the platform, the wolf-masked guardian jerked his staff. The impact bit the back of Eaon's knees.

"Wait," the wolf-masked guardian hissed, ignoring Eaon's glare.

Eavha had not seen him, her head bowed low as Lorelei raised her arms, the long sleeves of her black ceremonial robe draping on the floor.

"Witches of Wyldeden," she called for attention. "The council has ordered this gathering to sentence Eavha Nemuse for the crime of necromancy."

A murmur went through the crowd and Eaon's stomach twisted again. Some Head of House he'd turned out to be. This stain on their family name would never wash away, and it was his fault. He had failed Eavha miserably, and whatever happened to her today was his fault, too.

"You abused Sanni's blessing, and for that you have already atoned. However, for thieving from the Lover, the council hereby excommunicates you from this clan."

Eavha gave a short sob. Lorelei looked down at her almost gleefully.

"And lastly, for upsetting the Balance, to protect this clan from the Mother's wrath, and to warn all other clans of your blasphemy, we sentence you to bear the mark of a rogue."

"No!" Eavha screamed. Jumping to her feet, she ran for the stairs.

Two guardians near the platform grabbed her by the arms and dragged her back to the high priestess, bored with her pathetic attempt to escape. They held her, even as she struggled against them, screaming, as Elder Milnova approached a brazier and withdrew the branding iron.

Eaon tried to stand. Three simultaneous blows to the side of his neck, his ribs and the back of his legs left him gasping facedown in the grass. He didn't rise in time to see them brand

Eavha's hands, but he heard it. Every witch in Wyldeden heard it.

He wished himself dead rather than know what his sister's burning flesh smelled like.

It was over by the time he got back to his knees. The guardians were dragging her, still weeping, from the platform.

As she raised her head, Eaon caught her eye. All the color left her face as she reached for him with her burnt hands, his name on her split lips. The guardians hit him preemptively, sending him back down to the grass.

He didn't see them throw her out of Wyldeden, either. Couldn't remember what might be out there waiting. When she landed in the Anfar forest alone and afraid, would winter greet her?

"Get up," the wolf commanded.

Eaon glared at him as he rose once more to his feet. Glared at the elders, at the crowd who'd just stood there and watched . . .

Dearmead.

Dearmead was there, face ashen, eyes red.

Climbing the stairs, he held Dearmead's eye until he knew he had to kneel before Lorelei, but she held out a hand.

"Stand, Eaon."

Again, the high guardians crossed their spears between him and Lorelei.

"This clan has never had a witch brought back from the Lover's realm before and the council has deliberated on what is to be done with you. Elder Bodhi and Elder Milnova have made the argument that to reproach the Lover's blessing would be blasphemous, despite the danger you now pose. I agree with them and will not declare your power an abomination."

Eaon didn't know how he felt about that.

"Furthermore," Lorelei continued. "As all witchlings are given grace when learning to control their magic, you have been pardoned for the accidental passing of Apaete Laeser."

He definitely didn't agree with that.

"Also, considering you played no willing part in the crime that has been committed against the Balance, the council has decided you are not to be punished."

He should feel relieved. He did not.

"However." Lorelei's voice lowered, and the gleeful sparkle in her eye returned. "The Balance has still been disturbed and the council is of the unanimous agreement that the Mother's wrath will descend upon this clan if it is not restored. You were denied the honor of your rightful passing—"

The honor. The honor of cold and dark and nothing.

"—and so I will not deny you a choice now."

Aadya stepped forward and presented the bone knife.

"Nobody can force you, but for the sake of the Balance you are permitted to return to the Lover of your own volition. Or, alternatively, to appease the Mother, the clan must denounce you. You will be excommunicated and marked as a rogue for failing to restore the Balance."

Eaon looked to the blade. He knew what the right thing to do was.

Or he thought he had. Doing the right thing by the Balance was not the right thing to do as Head of House. He had a responsibility to Eavha, and right now she was alone in a strange place she didn't like, didn't understand, and wouldn't know how to navigate.

She would die.

Eaon turned to look over the crowd. Many of them were

already nodding, assuming he would choose the blade. Assuming he owed them that decency. Assuming he would put his own salvation before Eavha's life.

Dearmead was visibly shaking. Eaon swallowed the bile in his throat.

"Burn me."

Complete silence fell over the gathering, but Eaon didn't look away from Dearmead.

This was it. The moment had come for them to finally leave.

Dearmead averted his gaze and turned away.

Another sharp blow to the back of Eaon's knees made him cry out. The bone knife was gone. Furious magic swirled around him and the two spears beside him softened, wrapping themselves around his wrists like snakes. The wood yanked his hands up, palms exposed. Eaon clenched his teeth as Milnova brought the branding iron over once more.

He tried not to scream, but one tore its way out of him anyway.

Too dizzy to stand when ordered, the high guardians dragged him down from the platform, toward the Boab. Something cold churned inside him again. He couldn't find any strength to rally. To leave Wyldeden with some shred of dignity.

The air was freezing as the guardians tossed him into the gray morning light of Anfar, their spears retracting and solidifying once more. Mud splattered in his eyes as he landed. The portal sealed with a zap.

For a moment, he couldn't move. Couldn't see or think or hear. Pain wracked every inch of his body, the cold consuming him.

"Eaon," Eavha sobbed.

He gasped, wiping the mud from his eyes in time to see her crawling toward him. Reaching for him.

"Don't touch me!"

She froze, face crumpling.

"I'm sorry," she wept, lowering her forehead to the ground. "I'm sorry. I'm sorry."

"No," he wheezed. Forcing himself to rise, he sighed at the relief of the mud on his burning palms. "No, it's . . . my skin. My skin will hurt you."

Eavha raised her head, mud caking the ends of her hair. "It's true?"

"Yes. Can you heal the brands? Your face?" he asked.

She shook her head, voice cracking. "Sanni is furious with me. I have nothing. We have nothing. I'm sorry."

"Eavha," he sighed, reaching for her before remembering that he couldn't comfort her. Would never be able to touch another living thing ever again. He dropped his hand. "They gave me a choice. I chose this."

Eavha's eyes widened. Eaon closed his own as they started to burn.

CHAPTER 13

THE KINNER

Sleeping in front of the fire was still his preferred place of rest but his clothes were constantly sooty and Sarah insisted on cleaning them for him every time she noticed, so he'd started sleeping on the couch. His resolve to stay only one more night had deteriorated when he'd seen the letters the Copelands had been preparing to send out.

Letters to the other smugglers, they'd explained, to let them know that Hyrsch might be compromised.

Guilt gnawed at him. For most people, Hyrsch was a perfectly good city. The demi-kin truly did live free there. The problem was that he wasn't demi-kin.

But there was something about seeing how dedicated the Copelands were to helping the demi-kin that had settled his anxiety, so he'd stayed, spending his time helping William prepare the crops and land for the coming snow. The work and a steady diet of meat and vegetables had put some padding back on his bones, his joints no longer aching through the night.

The farmer had also shown him their other means of making coin; a pottery shed attached to one of the guest cottages on the estate.

"Try," William had said, getting off the stool and making room for the kinner.

He shook his head, but William smiled and tapped the stool insistently. Warily, he'd sat down and watched William prepare some clay for him. His hands shook as he peddled the wheel, the clay wobbling around messily. William made to guide him, but he flinched at the feel of the farmer's calloused hands, crushing the clay.

William made him try again, over and over, until he managed to make something. It wasn't sellable, but he'd smiled as William moved the pot into the oven.

Whenever William wasn't working, he'd let the kinner play with some clay. With the oven burning and the mindless whirring of the wheel, the rhythmic movement of his foot on the peddle and the silky earthen feel of wet clay on his hands, everything else faded away. For just a few hours, he got to be nothing more interesting than a simple farm boy.

Sarah kept every one of his misshapen creations.

The kinner had also taken to helping the farmer's wife in the kitchen, learning how to make soups and stews, and how to bake bread and biscuits. It was during the latter that he'd discovered a jar of cinnamon sticks, and literally collapsed to the floor at the sight of it. He couldn't stop himself as he'd torn the lid off, breathing in the rich smell.

Home. His eyes had burned behind closed lids. The mix of worry for his family's wellbeing and the painful longing to go back made it hard to think. There was nothing he could do for them now except stay away.

Sarah had lowered herself to the floor beside him.

"Do you like cinnamon biscuits?" she'd asked softly.

He hadn't even cared that his breath was hitching as he smiled. When he'd opened his eyes, the kitchen was blurry. He'd had a life, once. He'd let himself forget it during the time he'd spent in the dungeons of Hyrsch, but he'd had one.

Sarah sat patiently with him as he'd struggled to get himself under control. Things he hadn't thought about in years came barreling back; like playing games with rocks and sticks in the alley behind his master's house instead of cleaning the bedpans like he was supposed to, his new brother and sister with him. Running barefoot through the streets when they were caught rummaging through a bakery's trash can for scraps, the three of them howling as the fat baker chased after them. All three of them had been walloped viciously when they'd been caught, but they'd had full bellies that night.

Wiping his face, cheeks flushed, he'd managed another smile to tell her he was okay. Sarah chuckled lightly and helped him up off the floor.

"You know, if you're going to be here for a while, we're going to need something to call you. Would you mind terribly if I gave you a name? Since you can't tell us what yours is?"

The smile lingered as he nodded, passing her back the jar so she could take some out for grinding. He'd had a name. Then he had been given a new name when he'd arrived in Hyrsch. When he'd been freed and stupidly joined the Royal Cadets, he'd used another new name. All things considered, he wasn't too upset about leaving them all behind. The versions of him that had existed in Hyrsch could stay in Hyrsch. He didn't need to be that person anymore. He could have a new name, for a new life.

Sarah smiled too.

"My mother named me after her favorite character in a novel, because she loved it so much. So, I thought, we should call you Cinnamon." Her face had twisted in suppressed amusement as she said it.

Wrinkling his nose, he'd given her a dubious look. His disdain for the name had only made Sarah burst into raucous laughter. Reaching over, she'd pinched his cheek.

"That face. That right there has settled it. Cinnamon it is. Cinn."

He hated it. It was a terrible name. The kind of name you gave to a pet, not a person. But Sarah was so joyous . . . what did it matter what she called him? So Cinn had just sighed, shaking his head in defeat as he watched her blend the ingredients for the biscuits together.

That night, he startled awake, his hand already beneath the pillow he slept on, clutching his hunting knife. The wailing wind outside shook the windows, the curtains fluttering as a wisp of it snuck through a gap in the framework, but that wasn't what had woken him. Carefully, he inched back the blankets and exposed himself to the chill night air, planting his bare feet on the hard slate tiles. There was a chance it had just been a dream, or some benign sound triggering his vigilance, but there was also a chance that it wasn't. Pushing up his sleeves, ignoring the bite of cold on his flesh, he took his knife and stood.

His eyes had not stopped being adept at peering through darkness, so he scoured every corner, every shadow as he first checked on the Copelands, both sleeping heavily, before wandering through the rest of the house. He found nothing, but when he returned to the living room one of the windows was open a crack, the curtains billowing inside the house like a loose sail.

Clenching his teeth to stop them from chattering, he made his way to the window and slid it closed. Flicked the latch. From there, he surveyed the room again, his eyes almost passing over the deep shadow in the fireplace that had burned out hours ago. A normal shadow, except something about it wouldn't let him look away.

"Found you . . ." A low, smooth chuckle followed the taunt.

Cinn froze, grip tightening on the knife. He would never forget the sound of that silken voice—the way it moved as impossibly as the creature that spoke with it. He was not defenseless this time, but he couldn't help glancing back to the hall. He needed to shout a warning. Wake the Copelands so they could run, or arm themselves.

The air to his left rippled and Cinn didn't hesitate to slash out where he expected the creature to appear. A shrieking hiss made the hair on his arms rise and he quickly darted away from the shadowy claws lunging for him. He'd trained only six months with the Royal Cadets before being found out, and it had been a long time since then, but it was coming back to him quickly.

Slash, dodge, slash, dodge; his breaths rasped painfully, his footfalls slapping loudly through the house. He didn't manage to strike the shadow creature again as it came after him, but the injury he'd caused with that first blow was dripping some kind of pale ichor onto the floor.

Heavy footsteps sounded from the hall and candlelight warmed the room. The shadow creature hissed again and flitted back to the corner, slithering up the wall to get as far from the light as possible.

"Fuck," William cussed.

"I'll get the—" Sarah started, but the creature flitted across the ceiling, dropped down behind William and blew out the candle.

Cinn made a panicked sound, gritting his teeth as he ran for them. Sarah screamed and crashed to the floor, but another swipe from Cinn's knife forced the creature to refocus on him. William dragged Sarah away.

Cinn couldn't move quick enough as the shadow pounced at him. That impossible weight dragged him down to the ground and he felt the sharp sting of teeth in his neck. The burning of acid filled his veins and his throat cracked with a scream.

William barreled down the hall with a long serrated blade, roaring furiously. The beast was too busy feasting on Cinn to even notice until the blade sunk into whatever was solid within the shadow. Shrieking, it arched back. Something cold and sticky dripped onto Cinn's face. Retracting its claws, the shadow slithered away along the darkest corners of the room before shooting up the chimney.

"Gods, oh gods," Sarah was crying. A candle was relit. William stood over him, panting, turning paler by the second as he stared down at Cinn.

Forcing himself to sit up, Cinn bit his lip to contain a whine as he clamped a hand over the pulsing wound in his neck.

"We need to get the healer. I . . . I'll go, I'll take the horse . . ." Sarah climbed shakily to her feet, uninjured.

Cinn shook his head, wincing as the itching begun deep beneath his skin.

"That was a shtryg," William said, crouching down to help

put pressure on the wound. "Even for your kind, if we don't get a healer, the toxin—"

Cinn shook his head again, grabbing William's wrist with a trembling hand. He didn't need a healer. That thing, the shtryg, was still out there. It was the middle of the night and a winter storm was setting in. Yet, after exchanging glances with William, Sarah stepped back toward the door.

Groaning, Cinn pulled his hand away. William tried to cover it again.

"No, keep—" he started, but stopped when he felt Cinn's neck. The lack of blood still pulsing from his torn artery, the shifting of muscle and skin as it worked to pull itself closed.

Even Sarah stopped to stare.

It only took a few minutes now that he was healthier; the wound healed and Cinn lowered his hand completely to show them that he really was okay.

His heart hammered as he watched the shock on their faces, waiting for the moment they realized what he truly was. For any indication that this had suddenly become a much less safe place to be.

Would they turn on him? Report him to their lord? Sell him back to Hyrsch?

"You're a . . . a kinner. A full-blooded kinner," Sarah breathed.

Cinn nodded, the toxin making his head heavy.

"But . . ." William shook his head, at a loss for words.

His people were gone. Had been gone for a very, very long time. Long before he was even born, most of his people had vanished. His parents never told him what happened to them, just that the two of them and three others had escaped and stayed hidden for centuries. The Kinner had become a myth, a legend, and they'd let themselves be nothing more than a bedtime story for children.

His parents . . . he didn't want to think about them. Slammed what little memories he had of them behind thick mental doors, and went back to watching the Copelands for signs of betrayal.

"It's okay," Sarah said, whimpering slightly as she lowered herself to the floor beside him, rubbing her elbow. He wanted to believe her, but . . .

"Does anybody else know what you are?" William asked.

Cinn swallowed, shutting out the faces that came to mind. William understood that for the answer it was.

"It's okay," Sarah said with more force. "Nobody will find you here."

"Nobody," William promised.

Cinn looked to the chimney.

He was a danger to them. Not just because there was a shtryg who'd caught his scent, but because the royal guards and soldiers would be hunting him, too. Not to mention the rogue witch who had fed him when he'd first crawled out of the Dividing River. Who knew what had become of her.

"Don't even think about it," Sarah snapped. "You are staying right here."

"It's safe. For all of us. You see this?" William picked up the serrated knife he'd used to stab the shtryg. It was coated in a congealed substance the color of curdled milk. "It's made with silver. Deadly to beasts. That leech-turd isn't going to make it to morning. Living as close to the forest as we do, you learn a few things. And as for the palace soldiers? We've been hiding people from them for years. They won't find you here."

"I can look after myself, too," Sarah promised with a wink as

Cinn looked to her reddened elbow. "I don't normally go down quite so easy."

It wasn't enough to put him at ease, but he also didn't want to leave. Selfish. Foolish. But staying was a better option than trying to get into Anfar. He believed the Copelands really did want to help him, and he was starting to think maybe they actually could. Maybe this could be his new home.

CHAPTER 14

EAON

THEY STUCK TO THE PATHS EAON KNEW THE CANOPY WAS thickest, protecting them from the worst of the wind and rain. Eavha struggled with the sharpness of a real forest floor, but bit her tongue and followed him without complaint.

A pack of timber wolves stalked them for a few days, sending them sprinting over splintering roots and logs until they couldn't run anymore. Desperate, they climbed a tree, the bark tearing at their raw, blistering hands. But the wolves must have been as hungry as the witches were because they waited.

Rescue came in the form of an arrow-shooting witch who took down the alpha with a single shot. The relief didn't last long as the rogue caught their gaze and aimed her next shot right at Eaon.

The two of them fled through the canopies, leaping from branch to branch like a couple of spider monkeys. They hadn't had time to eat in days and Eaon stumbled on a landing. An arrow split the hairs on his arm.

He knew from previous travels that there was a coven of cannibals who'd marked out a territory nearby. Taking a gamble, he led Eavha and the hunter across that invisible line. The rogue slowed as she realized where she was. When the cannibals appeared, she turned and fled.

Putting himself between Eavha and the coven leader, Eaon let the cannibal scent him. For a long moment, he and the cannibal stared at each other, but the threat of necrotic flesh was enough for the coven to back off. Still, Eaon didn't want to linger.

Staying in Anfar was a death wish. The weather was freezing overnight and it would only be worse if they went south to Oford, but going north to Vertlyn meant traversing the thickest parts of the forest and Eaon wasn't sure they'd make it.

Sometimes, when the nights were really bad, he wished he'd made a different choice back in Wyldeden.

The morning after leaving the cannibal's territory, the ground was covered in frost. Eavha squealed as they leaped from a tall oak, their bare feet burning on the ice. The ache in Eaon's belly wouldn't let him offer her any sympathy. Every time his sister started to get upset about something, all he could think was: *you should have just let me die.*

They hadn't discussed it. He wasn't sure he wanted to.

His head spun as he dragged himself to a narrow creek to drink. They had to find food soon, or the next predator who caught their scent would get an easy meal.

Color flashed beneath the surface of the water.

Eaon lunged for it, not even sure what he was doing until he plucked the fish from the stream and watched it give a pitiful flop. He dropped it quickly before it could rot further.

"What did you do?" Eavha gasped.

Eaon stood slowly. "We need to eat."

"No. No, absolutely not," she hissed.

"Would you rather die?" he snapped. A deep shame was hollowing his chest.

"You can't just start murdering animals now that we're rogues!" she shouted back at him.

Poisonous words sat on his lips. He didn't need to say them. Eavha scrunched up her face and took a deep, shuddering breath.

They ate the fish. Eavha gagged on every bite, but she ate. Then they both sat and prayed to the Mother for forgiveness.

Eaon led them south. It would still take them a few days to reach the border at the pace they were moving, but once they crossed the Dividing River and reached a village, they should be able to find somewhere to rest. Hopefully by then Eavha would have recovered enough of her magic to offer potion brewing services in exchange for supplies.

If they even survived that long.

"What are the ch-chances one of the r-rogues might help us?" Eavha asked, her rain-soaked hair sending rivulets down her shivering body. "I mean, we're r-rogues and w-we wouldn't k-kill someone who n-needed help."

Eaon rolled his eyes. "Next one who f-finds us, w-why don't you ask?"

"Don't be an ass."

"Sorry," he said, though it still sounded snappish. "Just . . . keep an eye out f-for anything tradable. Or edible."

Hands tucked under his arms, he stepped onto a large

boulder. Black ice had crusted over it and he slipped. The snap of his teeth as he landed burst black spots behind his eyes.

Eaon and Kailevi stood, shivering on the Southern Mountains as a blizzard descended on them.

"Are we going to die?" he'd asked his da. For a moment, Kailevi didn't answer.

Eavha nearly grabbed Eaon to help him stand, but flinched away at the last minute.

"Are you okay?" she asked as he got to his feet, brushing the frozen dirt off his healing brands.

"Yeah," he panted, blinking his vision clear. That day on the mountains . . . "Do you trust me?"

"Of course."

Eaon was unsure if he liked that answer. "When I traveled to the Southern Mountains, Da and I got caught in a blizzard. I think . . . we need to get downhill. We'll build a shelter and wait out the winter."

Eavha didn't answer. When he turned to face her, she was crying.

"I know it's not ideal, but—"

"I'm just . . . sorry."

"Not now." He couldn't do this now.

Eavha took a deep breath and wiped her face, cradling herself. "What about rogues?"

"I'll handle it," he told her with more confidence than he felt.

He'd killed a fish that morning. It was different, but in many ways the thought of killing a rogue was easier. A fish was innocent, but the Spirits already despised rogues. Besides, Eavha had sacrificed everything to save his life. Even if he hated her for it, even if he wished she hadn't done it, he could do nothing less for her now.

At the bottom of a basin they found a small lake. The ancient trees that surrounded them in every direction created a dome that kept the worst of the weather at bay. The magnificence of the towering oaks was overwhelming, and Eaon could understand why the dryads protected them so fiercely. Not even the most savage of rogues would dare offend an Anfar tree.

While Eavha drank from the lake, Eaon surveyed the area carefully. They weren't encroaching on any more coven territory, from what he remembered, and while a number of trees gave off enough energy to know there were dryads living within them, he did find a sturdy willow that seemed empty.

"If you're going to start messing with the trees, I'm ditching you." Eavha cracked a small smile as she joined him at the willow.

"Sure, okay," he snorted, laying his hands against the tree. "Can you feel if it's safe?"

Eavha pressed her finger tips and forehead against the bark and took a long breath. "No dryads. Strong roots. Old, but not old enough to be offended if we make a nest. If we're careful, I think it will let us stay."

Eaon climbed onto a sturdy branch and inspected the reeds dangling around them. His body scolded him, but he couldn't afford to rest yet. It would take time to weave the reeds into a shelter, but right then it felt more achievable than making it to Oford.

By the time the sun set, they'd woven a couple of hammocks and a net above them to keep off the frost. Tomorrow, they would make walls. Eavha had found some dandelions to chew on as they both settled down for the night.

"You should get some sleep. I'll keep watch," Eavha offered.

"I don't know if I can."

"I don't know if I can be around you much longer of you don't."

Eaon's nostrils flared as he considered his next words.

"I'm not just snapping at you because I'm tired."

Eavha averted her eyes. "I know. I'm sorry."

"Why?" He turned to face her. "I mean . . . how?"

"I don't know," she said softly. "I don't know how I did it. I panicked and I got mad and I . . . I forced my will. I didn't think, I just did it. And as for why, do you really need to ask?"

"It was arrogant, Eavha. Selfish."

"Would you have done it differently?" she snapped. "If you had my power, would you have let me die?"

"It's not a matter of letting me die; I was dead! What you did—"

"I know what I did!"

Eaon grit his teeth and huffed, glaring at her as he ripped the stem of his dandelion and chewed the end of it.

"Don't look at me like that," she hissed. "You didn't exactly do the right thing either. You could have gone back to the Lover, but you didn't."

"I did it for you!"

"So did I!"

"No, you did it for yourself. You didn't want to be alone."

"Oh, go rogue!" Eavha's voice cracked, eyes gleaming in the

moonlight. "You want to be all self-righteous about it, go jump in the lake. I won't stop you."

Eaon snarled. "I can't keep up with you. This morning you were crying and now you're trying to justify yourself."

"I am sorry. I'm sorry for what it cost us. But if given the chance, I'd do it over again."

What it had cost them.

He knew the grief that pulled at Eavha's tired eyes was for her friend. Apaete had been a sweet girl, and her death made him feel stupid for mourning his own loss. But thinking of Dearmead turning away from him again made him curl up on himself. Eavha straightened, watching him.

"You alright?"

"I asked Dearmead to come with me." They hadn't talked about this either. Eavha sat silently while Eaon tried to catch his hitching breath. "It wasn't fair. I shouldn't have asked that of him."

"I'm surprised he didn't," Eavha spoke gently. "He loves you."

Eaon closed his eyes, the words worse than branding irons.

"You love him too, don't you?"

He couldn't answer. Couldn't unclench his jaw.

"I'm sorry, Eaon."

"I'm sorry about Apaete."

Eavha didn't say anything, and the two of them sat in silence as night fell around them.

CHAPTER 15

EAVHA

EAON HAD STAYED AWAKE MOST OF THE NIGHT BUT WAS ASLEEP when Eavha woke up the next morning. The cold burned her limbs, but she forced herself to her feet despite it, stretching and moving her body to create warmth. It hadn't been an easy night's sleep, Apaete's name like a foot on her neck. It hadn't been her fault, she told herself. It wasn't Eaon's fault, either.

Her conviction didn't release the pressure in her throat.

As she had every day since the sentencing, she knelt and prayed, then tried to conjure something from the ground. But like every other day, Terra wasn't listening. Food had never been her strength, anyway. Flowers were more receptive to her, so she started doing laps of the lake, coaxing out a few more dandelions and some chamomile flowers, but nothing substantial.

Once Eaon woke up and they ate their meager findings, the two of them worked tirelessly on their shelter until they'd boxed themselves in.

The forest went still, and both Eaon and Eavha froze.

From where they stood, they watched a green-and-black leopard slink from the tree toward the lake. Eaon raised a hand but stilled again when a rogue stepped from the shadows, spear raised and aimed for the wildcat.

Eaon pointed up, and Eavha slipped from the nest and sprung silently onto a higher branch. Crouching by the small opening they'd left, Eaon focused on the witch creeping along the tree line.

A breeze blew through the clearing, and both the rogue and the wildcat snapped their heads in willow's direction. The leopard ran, but the rogue crouched even lower.

Magic tingled against her skin, in the air, and it took Eavha a minute to realize it wasn't coming from the rogue. Nausea churned her empty stomach. The rogue stepped back, aiming his spear. A pulse of power swept through the clearing and Eavha gasped, a coldness so pure she found herself slipping from the branch. The rogue staggered back, doubling over, before stumbling away into the woods.

Eaon didn't move, wave after wave of magic rolling off him.

"Eaon," Eavha wheezed, losing her grip and tumbling through the branches.

He whipped his head around, made a move to catch her, but remembered at the last minute he couldn't. Eavha dropped through the branches and landed on the ground, the impact winding her. Like a wildcat himself, Eaon leapt down after her.

"Damn it, are you alright?" he asked.

"Reel it in," she gasped, recoiling from the cold still pouring off him.

"What?"

"Reel . . ." she choked on her breath, her skin itching painfully.

Eaon's eyes widened. He stared at his hands, then at her, before running. The farther away he was the better she felt until, finally, she could breathe properly again. Pins and needles rushed through her limbs as the pain receded.

Across the clearing, Eaon sank to his knees, hands clasped over his mouth as he stared at her in horror.

"It's okay. I'm okay," she called out, but Eaon was shaking his head, wild with fear. "I can teach you to control it. You need to calm down."

She tried to recall her earliest lessons, but it was useless. Magic had been such an integral part of who she was that the lessons had been redundant. Getting to her feet, she took a few shaky steps toward him. Panic flitted across his face.

"I can't . . ."

"You have to, or you're going to kill everything in this clearing."

She stepped closer and Eaon put his fists in the soil, lowered his head and steadied his breathing. As she walked, she could feel the point in the air where Eaon's magic was waiting to bring her to her knees again, but it was retreating.

When she was a few meters away, he looked up.

"Get back," he hissed.

"You're doing it. You're not going to hurt me, Eaon," she soothed.

"I can't . . ."

"You can."

He lowered his head again and took deeper breaths, knuckles turning white as he pushed them harder against the ground. The air tingled a moment longer, then the energy dropped away. Eaon sagged, collapsing to his side in the mud.

"You're okay." Eavha knelt beside him, not knowing what to do. "We're okay. You're okay."

His eyes were open, staring at the empty space above her head.

"How do I make it stop?" he wheezed.

"What does it feel like?"

Eaon shook his head, lip trembling. All those books he read, and he didn't have the words to describe how it felt to keep a raging death inside his body.

Eavha picked up a stick close by and used it to push Eaon's hair out of his face. Rubbed his back with it. Eaon blinked, focusing on her properly.

"Are you petting me with a stick?" he asked breathlessly.

"Maybe."

He snorted, closing his eyes. Slowly, his body began to relax.

"You got it?"

"I hate it."

"I'm sorry." Another thing that was her fault.

"If it ever happens again, promise me you'll run. Just run and don't stop."

Eavha winced. Hopefully it wouldn't come to that, but she nodded anyway. "I promise."

CHAPTER 16

AISLING

Princess Aisling Aurnia sat in a plush velvet chair and considered the glass chessboard set before her. She played the frosted pieces and, although no companion sat across from her, the clear bishops had her in quite the predicament.

Eventually, she reached forward to move her queen three places. "Checkmate in four."

There was nobody to hear her stern voice break the frigid morning air. The winter was going to be brutal but, this far south, such things were expected and prepared for. The ability to keep her people warm and fed through the worst of the storms was essential if she wished to maintain their favor. Loyalty. Things she desperately needed.

Things that were already fracturing.

The small rebel forces that had been nothing more annoying than a couple of flies buzzing on a summer day had quite suddenly grown some spine. The prison break from her dungeon some months ago proved as much. She'd done her best to keep word of both the existence and the escape of her prisoner from her advisors, lest the king and queen hear about it. The pool of people she trusted with the information was small, which was making the search problematic. She couldn't send out a large force without raising suspicions.

Rising from her chair, she walked to her dressing room to prepare for the meeting that was about to take place. With a steady hand, Aisling dipped her brush in the pot of fresh bird's blood on the vanity and painted her lips. She wore her most courtly gown; dark burgundy swathes of silk, embroidered with golden sparrows down the skirt, and a black bear-fur cape over her shoulders. Dark silk gloves adorned her hands, concealing the last of the tattoos marking every part of her body from the neck down. Her pale skin was a stark contrast to her attire, exacerbated by the river of liquid steel hair flowing down her back. It made her look older than her years, but she didn't mind. Age was a welcome illusion that helped her establish authority over the city below. Finally, atop her head, she wore a crown of bird skulls and bone roses.

Edwina knocked on the door before peeking through.

"Princess?" the demi-kin woman's soft voice was barely a whisper. "He has arrived."

Pressing her lips with translucent powder that set the blood, she practiced her grin to make sure the color didn't crack. As usual, it was perfect.

"Good." She kept her voice hard and low, straightening her shoulders as she strode from the dressing room into the foyer of her suite.

Her Second, Nora Turlough, and her guard, Captain Clayton Grint, were waiting for her with hands on their hilts. Silently, her entourage followed Aisling from the room where two more guards joined them, keeping close as she powered along the hall, down the spiraling stairwell of her tower, and through the palace until she reached the throne room. Usually she would take meetings in the parlor, or the council room, but not this one. She would need every weapon in her arsenal for this one.

The guards in front of her pushed open the large ornate doors. Aisling didn't pause as she stormed past the foreign guardsmen standing in formation around her guest. She might as well have been carved from bone herself for all the life she showed walking to the dais, taking a seat on the black velvet cushion atop the marble throne.

From behind his guards, her brother smiled wickedly.

"Aisling," he cooed, curtseying mockingly.

"Nevan."

The wall behind her was made entirely of stained glass, the light dousing the scene in red and purple. The braziers and chandeliers had been lit, their fire flickering over the polished black floor.

"Thank you for gracing us with your presence."

Aisling narrowed her eyes, folding her hands in her lap. "I have other things to attend to today, so I suggest you get to the point."

The prince smirked before nodding to his guards. As one, they turned and marched through a door to the left where a waiting chamber was prepared for them. Aisling's guards followed, Nora and Edwina leaving with them.

Even though they were alone, they spoke in Kurv, too wary of prying ears.

"I do believe I've never been to your palace before. You never invited me." Nevan rested one hand on the rapier at his waist, glancing around the room sourly.

"That was intentional."

"Interesting company you keep." Nevan ignored the jab and wrinkled his nose. "Employing demi-kin. Appointing one as your Second. How you can stand to debase yourself with such filth is beyond me. They're vermin, Aisling. Sport, at best. You'd be better off washing your streets with their blood."

Like him.

Such a waste. Both her parents and her brother were so consumed by the old feud with the Kinner they were blind to what an asset their half-breed offspring were. Her coven's stupidity would be the ace in her sleeve.

"Say, I wonder what mother and father would think of your soft-hearted approach to the infestation." Nevan tapped his chin, eyes sparkling gleefully. "Then again, I did notice your rather stunning decorations outside the gates. So maybe you haven't forgotten your loyalties entirely."

The bodies of the guards on duty the night of the prisoner's escape, as well as one of the two rebel laundresses who had done the deed, were currently staked on the gates as a warning to those in Hyrsch who still thought to oppose her. None of the citizens in the city knew what had happened, of course; rumor had spread that Aisling had uncovered a group conspiring to enslave the humans dwelling in Hyrsch as revenge for the years the demi-kin had suffered that fate. Both the loyal demi-kin and the humans had rallied support for her. A silver lining.

"Is this really why you sullied yourself traveling this far south on the cusp of winter, Nevan? To amuse yourself by insulting me?"

Nevan chuckled darkly and pinched the bridge of his nose as he began to pace.

"I wish it were. There is news I didn't trust the messengers with. My spies have reported that the queen is with child. A third heir is to be born."

Nevan and Aisling had been given their own cities to run, both to keep them from getting too bored in Dusarn and as a test for their suitability to leadership. Everything outside the city walls was still under the control of the king and queen, but Aisling had always made sure to include the Oford lords in her winter plans anyway.

"The child will be too young to contend for the Sparrow Throne when mother and father pass." Aisling waved a hand dismissively.

"You can't know that. The Lover has not claimed them in six hundred years," Nevan argued. "Unless you plan to take matters into your own hands."

"No, I'm counting on you being stupid enough to make a move."

Nevan chuffed. "You think I'd make a grab for kingship without taking care of you first?"

Aisling tilted her head, eyes glittering.

The death threats had been going on as long as they both could talk. Only the promise of disgrace in the eyes of their parents had stopped them from trying openly. It had barely been a month since Nevan had last sent an assassin to poison her. Not a very good one, as he now decorated her prayer room with his bones.

"Help me get rid of the infant," Nevan finally asked. "Let this remain between you and me, as it should be."

"I'm surprised you even need to ask for my help. You've single-handedly murdered a quarter of your city, but can't manage a babe?" she teased.

Nevan sucked his teeth, fists clenching at his sides.

"Father will suspect my motives if I return to Dusarn unsummoned. But you? You've had our parents wrapped up under your skirts since the day you were born."

Aisling bristled, digging her black nails into the arms of her throne.

"Well, Nevan, as much as I've enjoyed your visit I have no desire to murder a baby. I am confident I will ascend whether I am the only Aurnia left or if the king sires a hundred other brutes like yourself."

"You *will* help me," Nevan snarled, stepping onto the dais with his hand on the hilt of his blade.

In a liquid motion, Aisling stood and pulled a dagger from the secret pocket in her skirt.

Nevan only grinned. "There's the sister I know and love."

Aisling stared coldly, daring him to put his other foot on the dais.

He didn't.

"One way or another, Aisling, you will help me," he told her smugly. Whistling loudly, Nevan's guards came marching back through the door with Aisling's own close behind them. "Are there rooms prepared for us?"

"No." She slid her weapon back into its pocket and resumed her seat. "I'm sure you'll find a tavern or something in town with a room available."

The insult struck a chord as Nevan's upper lip curled, but he didn't argue. The Pirevian guards stayed in tight formation around their prince as they stalked from the room.

"Nora," Aisling called for her Second as soon as they were alone.

The demi-kin female stepped forward and knelt. "Yes, princess?"

"Assign someone to keep an eye on my brother."

"Of course."

"Any news on our missing friend?" She needed him back. Now. Though maybe a taste of freedom would convince him to cooperate. Nothing else in the last two years had managed to.

"Towns closest to the Dividing River are still being investigated."

There was a tightness in Nora's tone that made Aisling purse her lips.

"You're still mad that I sent Owen."

The rest of the guards were silent as Nora composed her features. Large, flat features marred viciously by her years of slavery. Aisling supposed the demi-kin was beautiful, but it had still taken her by surprise when Officer Owen Turlough from her Royal Army had asked to marry her. But perhaps that had been unfair; Nora was clever and ruthless and indomitable. In the past five years since Aisling had taken over the city from Lord Hawthorne, freeing the demi-kin and donating heavily to their equity in her city, Nora had proven herself to be loyal and dedicated beyond measure. It made sense for a male to notice these things too.

"No. Owen is reliable. He was the right choice," Nora said, though her shoulders had tensed. Later. Aisling would talk to her later.

"Any news on the missing laundress, then?"

The one laundress the guards had been able to identify had refused to name her co-conspirator, taking her identity with her to the Lover's realm. Aisling had forgotten how much weaker human bodies were.

"We're still investigating."

Aisling sighed deeply and waved her hand, letting Nora rise.

"I have meetings scheduled with the mountain clans from the Southern Spine this afternoon to discuss our coal and lumber collection for winter. Then I'm meeting with the lords of Oford to discuss provisions. You will not be needed."

Nora nodded. It was more than a dismissal—a silent command to *find* something. Time was running out for her to get her pieces in position.

She needed the kinner back.

PART II

CITY OF BLOOD AND ASH

Three months later

CHAPTER 17

NORA

Nora Turlough sighed deeply as she stepped beyond the palace wall, turning her face up to the dull sun. These had been the hardest months of her entire career; from the moment the report of an escaped prisoner came across her desk, through the organizing of a secret manhunt, sending Owen away, the interrogations, finding the laundress who'd been minutes away from escaping the city, the executions . . . Then winter had broken, during which everything had come to a halt. Only the letters that arrived from all over Oford reassured her that Owen was still alive out there. Still searching.

The weight of it all had only grown heavier, as if the knowledge that there had been a young kinner imprisoned beneath the palace hadn't been heavy enough. In the years Nora had known Princess Aisling, she had never thought her capable of such atrocities.

Savior, they called her. The Great Equalizer.

When Aisling had arrived in Hyrsch and abolished slavery,

the world had held its breath as they waited for the Sparrow Coven to punish her. They hadn't, and demi-kin had begun to flee to her from all over Nir. She'd given them opportunities to go to school, to start businesses and families. Nora's people had hope for the first time in centuries, their longer life spans and superior healing no longer a burden.

She owed it all to Aisling.

Yet, being asked to stomach the torture of children was beginning to feel like too much. Especially considering who was living in her house.

As she walked home, Nora stopped by the bakery in her old neighborhood. Before moving in with Owen, she had lived in a small apartment in Hyrsch's market district, Westgate. The bakery was one of the first demi-kin owned businesses that had emerged and she liked to continue supporting them.

A little bell rung as she opened the door, drawing the attention of the middle-aged man behind the counter, who beamed widely at her.

"Good to see you, Nora!"

"Buka," she returned his smile. "The new sign looks amazing."

"Dellis's handiwork. Let's just hope the Guard caught those damned traditionalist vandals. I don't want to have to hire security."

"I know. Just have patience. It's going to take a little longer than five years to clean up the city," Nora sighed, leaning on the counter. "Do you have any honey cakes? And can I grab a rye loaf?"

"Yes, and yes." Buka nodded, continuing to talk as he grabbed a paper bag for the bread. "And also, yes. It helps that so much of the Guard is demi now. Gods, or Spirits, if you're that way inclined, bless Aisling."

Nora smiled tightly. Gods bless Aisling, indeed.

The bell rang again and Nora glanced over her shoulder as two more customers entered the store. Humans. She could tell from the nervous way they clutched at each other's arms in barely concealed trepidation.

"Good evening, ladies." Buka smiled at them, putting Nora's bags on the counter and ringing up the till.

"Is it okay for us to shop here?" one of the women asked.

"Of course. All are welcome." Buka waved a hand around the cabinets. "Everything is made here from local ingredients."

"Is it your recipes or did you steal them from your master?" the other asked. Her friend slapped her arm, blushing madly and muttering under her breath as she pulled her friend toward a display cabinet.

Buka didn't acknowledge the accusation, but Nora saw the way the muscles in his jaw twitched.

"Patience," Nora said quietly, handing over a few silver coins.

"This is too much."

"Hire some security." She pushed the coins into the baker's hands and took her bags, eyeing the two women warily as she left. Standing at the crossroads, she spotted a tall demi-kin guard in his dark red-and-gold uniform. He caught her eye and she nodded, raising her chin toward the bakery. The guard dipped his head and began a slow stroll in that direction.

It was a risk, because not all the Guard could manage their tempers. More than a few humans had lost hands or tongues for expressing traditionalist views. She just hoped that her position in the court meant this particular guard would keep a low profile.

There was no doubt that he knew who she was. The scars on her face and scalp were distinctive, as was her closely shorn haircut. Her tunic was embroidered with the Sparrow crest, two hands cradling a bird, while the addition of a crown above the crest identified her as Aisling's Second. Pride and anxiety rode her equally as she strode the city streets, meeting the curious eyes of strangers unafraid to stare. The tunic marked her as a target, but she knew how to use the sword at her hip. Had made sure traditionalists knew she knew how, too.

The streets she took on her way home had morphed over the last five years. There was still filth, but people had been hired to clean the gutters daily. Housing still needed development, but there were enough tradespeople and coin to do the work since Aisling had decreed slave owners to pay restitution taxes. As she moved into Northgate where the wealthier humans resided, the consequences of that decree became more apparent. Hostile glares from people out watering their gardens or walking their dogs; not from everyone, but from enough to make her walk a little faster.

On a corner block stood a double-story bluestone house with high wrought-iron gates, a thorny hedge growing just inside the grounds. Home.

Nora unlocked the gate and waved to the gardener as she walked up the footpath, still reeling from the fact she and Owen could afford staff at all. Inside, the smell of roasting pork warmed the air. Following the smell to the kitchen, Nora found Paulette preparing carrots and potatoes to accompany dinner. On the counter, Siobhan sat in one of her pretty pastel gowns, swinging her legs and laughing at some gossip Paulette must have shared.

"Mrs. Turlough!" Siobhan gasped as Nora came into the room, slipping off the counter. "We weren't expecting you."

The girl was in her mid-twenties, with thick black hair and soft olive skin, plump lips and large green eyes. She reminded Nora of herself before she'd been disfigured, which was entirely the point. If they were going to hire a surrogate to help grow their family, she wanted the child to at least look like her.

"I wasn't needed at the palace, so I thought I'd come by to check on things," Nora explained, putting the paper bags on the counter. "And I brought treats."

"Honey cakes?" Siobhan asked, clasping her hands in excitement.

"Of course."

Siobhan squealed and grabbed the bag, rummaging through it for one of the sticky golden cakes. Paulette smiled fondly at her, then at Nora.

"Nothing's out of order, miss. Though the pantry is getting a little bare."

The winter had been brutal, so Nora had told the staff they were welcome to wait out the freezing months at the Turlough home if their own wasn't suitable. Many had, bringing their children with them. It had made her weekends a delight, even with Owen gone.

"I'll give Aria extra coin to stock it tomorrow."

"Thank you, miss."

"I'll leave you to it. If you need anything, I'll be in my office," Nora told them, heading back into the hall with her satchel full of paperwork.

"Wait." Siobhan hurried after her, wringing her skirt and biting her lip. "I feel terrible. With Owen away . . . is there something else I can do to earn my keep?"

Nora bit her tongue at the way Siobhan said her husband's name. She'd known what was involved in this process before agreeing to hire a surrogate and it wasn't fair to lash out at either Owen or the girl just because it was uncomfortable.

"You do plenty," she said, turning away.

Then stopped.

Looking Siobhan over, an idea began to form.

"Actually." Taking the girl's arm, Nora led her farther into the hall where Paulette's curious ears couldn't hear them. "There is something you could do. Not for me, but for the crown."

Siobhan gaped, head bobbing. "Of course. Anything."

"I will give you money, but I need you to go to the East Markets and do some shopping. A new dress, or some shoes. Whatever."

Siobhan blinked, confused.

"You don't need to do anything; just . . . listen. There's a woman, either hiding or missing. She's not in trouble, but I need to find her. The people there won't talk to me, but they won't look twice at a girl like you."

"Does this have anything to do with the rebels on the gate?" Siobhan asked, a hand at her throat.

The bodies of the guards and the laundress had frozen solid over winter, only recently thawing and resuming their decomposition. The smell was putrid and wafted through the city for blocks.

"No. This woman is sympathetic to the demi-kin, and is being hunted by traditionalists," Nora lied. "Do not risk yourself. Do not go around asking suspicious questions. Just listen for news of any missing laundresses or disappearing seamstresses. She may have had access to palace uniforms and think she's in trouble, so if she knows she's being looked for she might run. So please, be discreet. This woman's life depends on it."

"Of course. I . . . thank you for trusting me with this."

She *did* trust Siobhan with this. The girl had come from a poor farming family that had never owned a slave and had a reputation for being kind to the demi-kin before they were liberated. She'd lived with her for six months now, sharing meals and sometimes even a bed. Trusting her was not an issue, but dealing with Owen's disapproval when he found out Nora was roping their surrogate into this mess with the kinner was not something she was looking forward to. But until the girl successfully conceived, she didn't see the harm.

Besides, it's not like she had many other options. Aisling was growing more impatient by the day and Nora was afraid of what the princess would resort to if she didn't get what she wanted soon.

CHAPTER 18

CINN

Even with an extra mouth to feed, the Copelands hadn't struggled to keep themselves warm and fed through the long winter. Cinn had spent the months eating, learning to cook and turn pottery, trying to learn to read and write, and helping work the little farm with William and Sarah.

The physical work meant that the weight he'd put on had turned into lean muscle, his body becoming something he didn't entirely mind being trapped in. A lot had changed; he barely recognized himself in the little mirror in the bathroom. He'd grown at least a foot taller, facial hair making a sudden albeit patchy appearance. William had taught him how to shave, while the hair on his head had grown back out, smooth and shiny. The eyes he'd been so afraid to look at had a little spark back in them.

He sat on the couch beside Sarah, listening to the crackle of the fire as the sun sank below the horizon. Vision blurring from trying to concentrate on the book in his hands, the first inklings of a headache creeping in, he handed it to Sarah.

"My turn?" she asked, watching as he pointed to where he was up to. He still hadn't spoken. Doubted he ever would. "You got through a whole paragraph. That's so much better."

He yawned and lay his head down on the back of the couch as she began to read to him.

William finished cleaning the dishes and came to stoke the fire. "Spring starts tomorrow. Thought it'd be nice to take Cinn to the festival."

The blood rushed from his face as he sat up, shaking his head. Leaving the farm . . . it was too much of a risk. He was still in Oford, and he doubted the princess would ever stop looking for him.

William raised his hands. "No problem, it was just a thought."

Sarah put the book down, smiling sadly at him. Cinn managed to return the smile before yawning deeply, gazing longingly down the hall.

He'd started sleeping in the spare bedroom and had cursed himself for waiting so long to try it. Laying in a bed was almost as wonderful as soaking in the tub, though he had to leave the door open at night. It helped keep the nightmares at bay.

It was a simple space, but it was more than he'd had in his entire life; a narrow bed with thick blankets and soft pillows, a set of drawers to keep clothes, and a number of candles in case he needed them. On top of the dresser he kept a small wooden box that William had bought from a local turner, which is where he kept his collectables: the iridescent feather that none of them could identify, a button with only one hole, a startlingly blue snail's shell, and a single green leaf that had clung to a tree long after the others had all browned and blown away during the winter storms.

"Get an early night, sweetheart," Sarah told him, giving his hand a squeeze.

"Sleep well, bud."

Cinn smiled at them both, eternally grateful that he had found them.

The following day was gray but warm as he helped Sarah remove the protective sails over the vegetable garden. William had left early with the horses and a cart full of pottery to take to Belden for the Spring Festival, promising to bring back new books and fresh meat. Although they hadn't had any trouble all winter aside from a stray nymph taking shelter in their well, Cinn kept his hunting knife in the leather scabbard at his waist. William had fashioned it for him when he realized the kinner had trouble relaxing without the weapon close by.

When he heard horses galloping toward them, his hand went right to the hilt.

Sarah hissed at him and he quickly ducked behind the nearest planter box. His mouth had gone dry, but knowing he could get away if discovered kept the true panic at bay. He had the strength to run, or to fight if he had to.

"Oh, blessings of barley. William, you gave me a heart attack!" Sarah shouted across the farm.

Cinn rose, heart still hammering as the horses came to a still. William's face was hard-set as he leaped from the cart.

"Soldiers," he called back. "In Belden. They're coming."

Resignation dulled the sharp edge of grief that made Cinn's

breath catch in his throat as he eyed the forest. He couldn't put the Copelands in danger.

Sarah grabbed his arm tightly.

"Do we have time?" she asked William.

"A little." He nodded, glancing back to the dirt path he rode in on. "There were four of them splitting up to see the other farms. They'll come here next."

Cinn tugged his arm away from Sarah, but William blocked him from making a dash to the tree line and grabbed his jaw.

"We have a hidden room. Nothing is going to happen to you. Go inside with Sarah while I tie up the horses."

Cinn swallowed hard but nodded. William let him go, and he quickly followed Sarah inside.

In his room, he spread a blanket over his bed and took all his clothes, his spare boots and his box of collectables over to it, tying them up into a sack. Sarah was in the living room, carefully pulling nails out of the wall beside the hearth. Within minutes, she was pulling back a false wall to expose a cramped space big enough for him to hide.

"I know its small," she said, cupping his face. "It's only for a little while. You're not locked in, okay?"

If it meant never having to go back to Hyrsch, he'd stay in the wall as long as he had to. Stepping into the space, his sack barely fitting beside him, Cinn focused on keeping calm. Distancing himself from his body.

"It's going to be alright," William reassured him as he came inside, knocking the mud from his boots as he did.

The two of them apologized as they closed the door on him, pressing the nails loosely back into the paneling. It was so dark. So small. He couldn't breathe. He didn't want to be alone; to be trapped again.

"You're alright. You're okay," Sarah said through the wall. "It's not long. Just stay quiet, okay?"

If he could be still and stay quiet, he would be fine. This wasn't Hyrsch. William and Sarah would let him out when it was safe. So even though every fiber of his being screamed to pound against the wall until he broke through, he kept still.

Quiet.

CHAPTER 19

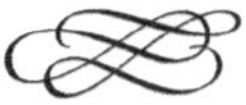

OWEN

THE SOLDIERS RODE UP THE LONG DIRT ROAD, TENSION THICK as cream between them. Owen didn't approve of Ralph's antics in Belden but he was outranked, so he kept his mouth shut and did what little he could to compensate for the damages.

Something gnawed at him as they approached this next farm though. There was something familiar about the odd cottages across from the main household and the organized chaos of the raised vegetable gardens. The forest came right up to the fence line and the Narrow River's gurgling could be heard from the road.

"You know, this might be it," Ralph said, raising his eyebrows.

Owen grunted.

As they dismounted, he noticed the yellow paint on the wooden boxes of the vegetable gardens, and it suddenly hit him where he was. The sloppy swirls and flowers had faded over the years, but he remembered painting them. Remembered the man who'd guided his hand as he'd drawn the seven-pointed stars hidden among the other shapes. Even before Aisling had come, Hyrsch had been a better city than Pirevia. A life of slavery was better than being bred for the arena. So he'd gotten out. The smuggler had left him here, and when he was strong enough the Copelands had gotten him to Hyrsch.

Seeing his childhood paintings, Owen very nearly vomited right there on his boots. The boy was here; he knew it in his bones. Knew it the way he knew he couldn't take him back to Aisling.

The couple who came out of the house looking at the soldiers with feigned confusion were older and grayer than Owen remembered, but there was no forgetting who they were. But it had been too long, and they must have seen so many faces in the past twenty years, he doubted they would know him.

"Officers," William nodded. "To what do we owe your company?"

"We're looking for a fugitive," Ralph declared, swaggering toward them.

"Oh, my." Sarah put a hand to her chest, looking around as if expecting to see a criminal lurking behind the tomato vines. "Well, by all means, please."

"It's been a number of months since he escaped. Either of you seen anything suspicious?" Owen asked, playing his part.

"No, sir. We pay attention to the forest, you know, because of the fae and the beasts. Haven't seen anything out of the usual," William denied.

The couple followed the soldiers as they searched the property. In a desperate attempt to keep Ralph from finding the boy, Owen made a big show of raiding the place as fast as he could so Ralph would have less to search. He had to find him first so he could look him over and pretend there was nobody there.

They went through the grounds, the barn and the cottages before venturing into the house.

"I assure you, if there was a criminal in our house we would know," Sarah said, staying behind her husband as the two officers ransacked the house.

"I would hope so." Ralph grinned wickedly.

William's fists clenched as he pressed himself closer to his wife.

They searched the place from the rafters to the rugs, finding nothing unusual. William and Sarah stood by the fireplace, trying to stay out of the way. Maybe he was wrong. Maybe the farmers weren't harboring anyone at the moment.

"Nothing," Owen declared, trying to hide his relief.

"Huh." Ralph looked around at the mess. "I suppose we should move on then. Except, I don't know about you, Turlough, but all that work has tired me out. Got some ale, lovey?" he asked Sarah.

"No ale, but there's some wine." She slid out from behind her husband, stepping over broken crockery as she picked her way into the kitchen.

Ralph watched her, eyes glittering.

William glanced between the two demi-kin, furious but confused. The latter expression was for Owen. He'd recognized the last name, no doubt.

"Wine before a long ride might not be the best idea," Owen tried. "Let's just water the horses and be off."

"What's the rush?" Ralph grinned wider. "I'm a little bored, too. This town's festival was rather pathetic. How about some entertainment? I saw a lute before and I don't think I broke it.

Which one of you knows how to play? Maybe we can have a little dance."

The soldier made a move to grab Sarah. Owen didn't try to stop William as he lunged. Ralph spun, pulling his sword. Sarah screamed and picked up a saucepan from the floor, flinging it at Ralph's head, but he raised his arm to block it without even glancing in her direction. His blade was pointed at William, who skidded to a stop mere inches from death.

"Damn it," Owen cussed, drawing his own weapon. "We weren't given orders to kill civilians, Lieutenant."

"This human peasant challenged me," Ralph sneered. "Once upon a time, a man like you could have made me do anything you wanted because of this mark on my neck. Should we find out what I can make you do, now?"

"Lieutenant . . ."

"Turlough. Unless your blade is out to skewer this pig, I suggest you put it away."

Obviously he could not kill William, but he couldn't keep arguing with Ralph, either.

Owen hesitated, hand tightening on the hilt as indecision dampened his brow.

Crack!

The wall to his left exploded and the kinner emerged, snarling like a wild beast and brandishing a long silver hunting knife.

Owen's jaw dropped.

Ralph started laughing. "Look what we have here."

"Cinn." William held a hand out toward the kinner, sweat beading on his forehead.

The kinner ignored the warning and made a move for Ralph, his knife pitiful beside the steel blade swinging for his head.

"No!" Sarah screamed.

William made a grab for the boy, but he was too slow. Cinn took the sword deep into his shoulder.

The impact sent him to his knees with a short, guttural cry. Only down for a second, Cinn wrenched himself off the blade and lunged again, swiping for Ralph's throat.

The lieutenant dodged, eyes widening at the wound already closing in Cinn's shoulder. He should have known that fighting a man who cannot die wouldn't be so simple.

Knocking the boy's arm aside and pushing him off balance, too close for the sword, Ralph slipped his own dagger from his belt and rammed it into Cinn's throat.

Without hesitating, the kinner grabbed Ralph's wrist and slashed out again. A gash opened the soldier's neck and Cinn shoved him back.

Dropping his weapons, choking on a gasp, Ralph stumbled back and grabbed at his throat to stem the blood spurting from the cut.

Without hesitating, Cinn pulled the knife out of his neck and turned to face Owen, growling deeply, face twisted with rage. The wound gave a single spray of red before slowing to a trickle.

Owen dropped his sword and held up his hands.

"My name is Owen Turlough."

The words meant nothing to Cinn, but William put a hand out to stop him from attacking.

"Damien Turlough brought me here twenty years ago, and I still honor him," Owen continued.

The panic in the room was waning. Looking down at his superior officer who was still choking on his lethal wound, Owen raised his chin.

"He deserved it. And I can make it go away, but it's going to take some time. There are other soldiers here. You . . ." He looked to Cinn. "You can't be here."

Cinn snarled again, but Sarah stepped forward to place a gentle, shaking hand on his shoulder. Despite his ferocity, the kinner was swaying a little, eyes darting around the room too quickly, his breaths too sharp.

The door to the kitchen opened.

A wild looking witch stepped inside.

Not a single person in the room looked like they had any idea who she was or what she was doing there. Owen didn't understand a word she said, either; the witch languages were a mess of vowels sliding like sand over stone. But when she stomped her foot and pointed to the forest, eyes locked on Cinn, the message was clear enough.

"Do you know this witch?" William asked Cinn warily.

The kinner nodded slowly, a deep frown on his face.

"Go," Owen suggested. "Give me a few days to get things sorted. When it's safe to come back, we'll leave a sign. I promise, I'll take care of them."

He wasn't entirely sure how he was going to fix this, but he would. He owed the Copelands everything. Cinn leveled an icy glare at him that suggested there would be bloodshed if Owen gave anything less.

"It's okay." Sarah stroked back Cinn's hair as she pulled him in for a hug.

"Come back," William said, pointing a stern finger at him. "I mean it. Come back."

Cinn gave them both a long, pained look, but nodded. Holding the two knives in one hand, hiking his sack over his shoulder with the other, he chased after the witch who was already making a beeline for the forest.

Sarah covered her mouth as she watched him go.

William turned to the corpse releasing its fluids on the floor.

"I'm sorry about your house," Owen started, but Sarah held up a hand.

"Damien Turlough."

Owen nodded, bowing his head. The smuggler who'd gotten him from Pirevia to Belden had recently been caught. News had spread quickly through the rebel forces.

"I took his last name when I was allowed to have one," he explained.

"Owen . . . Owen . . ." Sarah looked over the framed finger paintings on the wall, stopping when she reached his. She smiled sadly. "I remember you."

William stepped forward and clapped a hand on his shoulder, looking back out the kitchen door. The witch and the kinner were gone.

Nora would never forgive him if she found out.

CHAPTER 20

CINN

CHASING THE WITCH WAS A STUPID IDEA, BUT HE DID IT anyway. Twice now she had appeared in a moment of crisis. He didn't understand where she'd come from or what she wanted, but she was leading him north, so he didn't resist.

He was still shaking, blood slick on his hands, dampening his shirt. In those early days, or weeks or months, he didn't know, but for a while he'd tried to fight his way out of the dungeon. Every time somebody came to take him from his cell, he would fight. But back then, the feel of a blade against his skin had been foreign and frightening and he hadn't fought as hard as he should have. By the time the bite of steel was as familiar to him as the smell of his new namesake, he'd lost the will to fight entirely.

That feeling of helplessness had risen up in the darkness of that cramped room beside the hearth as he'd listened to the soldiers on the other side. He hadn't thought about what he was doing, but he didn't regret it. That red-and-gold uniform had stained his vision, and he'd darken it with blood over and over again if given the chance.

His make-shift sack bounced on his back as he ran through the orchard, leaping over the fence at the northern boundary. The forest was different this time. He had boots on his feet and a body that could move, though he was aware of the tracks he was leaving. He tried to keep to the drier areas but the witch was not waiting for him, a streak of orange and gray through the trees.

After half an hour, she finally slowed down. Panting heavily, Cinn took the opportunity to put his sack down and clean the blades on the grass before slipping his silver one into its scabbard. His head was spinning, the blood loss not agreeing with him.

Finally stilling, the witch watched him closely. He returned her stare. The soldier's dagger was still in his hand, shining strangely off the two different metals of the double-edged blade. Cinn would be willing to bet one side was silver, for the beasts, while the other was laced with iron, for the fae.

The witch began to circle him, tying her long brownish-red hair into a knot. Her black eyes were just as shrewd as he remembered. When she stepped forward, he raised the blade. Head tilted as she inspected his stance, the witch crept forward. Closer. So close he could have cut her.

He didn't get the chance.

In the space of a breath, she knocked his arm away, hooked her foot around his knee and toppled him over. He slashed upwards, but her foot slammed down onto his wrist, pinning him. So he swung his other fist, but she caught it and pinned that arm too. Huffing, he brought his legs up, trying to get them around her, to knock her off balance, but she hissed viciously. It sounded a lot like a command to stop.

He wasn't sure why he listened.

With her free hand, she reached over and tapped the back of his neck where his birthmark glimmered just below his hairline. The only difference between his mark and the demi-kin's was the color; his opalescent while theirs was freckle brown.

The witch got off him, staying in a crouch as he rose, rubbing the back of his neck with a frown. Cleary she knew what he was, but it didn't explain anything.

She ran a finger through the mud and began drawing lines on her face; a curve like a bowl between her brows with an upside down triangle over it, and a sharp horizontal line under each eye, dragged down her cheeks to a fade. Cinn stood transfixed as he watched the witch take a deep breath and raise her face to the sky, the air crackling with energy.

With a sound like wet clay squashed between his fingers, the witch's body turned to mud. Cinn took a step back, nauseous as he watched her shrink and shift until she finally reformed as a ruddy-brown fox.

A fox.

He knew that fox.

Before he could catch his breath, she was shifting again. Growing larger, longer, into something Cinn had never seen before. A creature the shape of a wolf, except instead of fur it had olive-green reptilian scales and a fleshy frill around its neck. She stood on all fours, longer than he was tall, her face level with his own. As she exposed her long yellow canines, dripping with saliva, the stench of rotting meat wafted up his nose. Only her eyes stayed the same, beady and intelligent, like a rat.

She turned her maw up and let loose a deafening howl that

sent him scrambling away. But not far, because the sound pulled at a recent memory. A night, many months ago, when he hadn't wanted to know what kind of creature could scare away a shtryg.

As the witch shifted back into her normal body, a warmth spread through him as if he'd just had a sip of hot tea. She'd been following him this whole time, keeping him safe. He couldn't ask her why, but . . .

He showed her his second dagger, then made a point of putting it in his boot. It was the only way he knew how to show her that he was willing to trust her. At least a little.

When she started moving north again, he followed.

It was getting dark by the time they reached the Dividing River. Cinn repressed a shudder as he looked across the rushing water. Putting his sack down, he took the opportunity to wash his hands and face, figuring they'd settle here for the night.

The witch drank, then fixed the markings on her face. When she noticed Cinn watching her, she pointed across the river.

Raising his eyebrows, he shook his head. It was dark, and there was no point. In a few days he'd go back to the farm anyway.

The witch stomped her foot and pointed again. Then pointed back the way they'd come and ran a finger across her throat.

Cinn spread his arms, looking around the riverbank. It was a perfectly good place to wait.

She began muttering and stomping, gnashing her teeth at him, but it was clear he didn't understand. With a last huff, she began to shift again and the reptilian lupine creature replaced her once more. As she stalked toward him, his hand instinctively settled on his knife. She stopped in front of him and lowered her forelegs, bowing her head as if expecting him to climb atop her.

Cinn shook his head. The witch bared her fangs, then snatched his sack and strode for the river. Hissing at her, he followed and made a grab for his blanket but she pulled it away, circling around him and even gave a little mocking prance.

Throwing his hands up, he pointed across the river in defeat. *Fine.*

Crouching again, the beast practically smirked as he climbed on. Her skin was cool and smooth, loose enough that he could grab fistfuls of it to keep steady.

As soon as he settled, they were running. Cinn forgot to breathe as the wind whipped at his face, making his eyes water.

The river's edge came up too quickly.

The witch leaped in a high arc over the water with such velocity Cinn's stomach curled up behind his spine. He clung to her wildly, bladder weakening as the surface of the river came hurtling toward them.

The impact bruised every bone in his body and the cold stole the air from his lungs. His throat burned as water rushed up his nose, gushed between them, the pressure of it pushing his body away from hers. For one fleeting moment, he was lost.

Arms and legs kicking out for something, anything, unable to tell which way was up . . . he was nowhere.

Then something cold and hard pushed against him. Witch or beast, he didn't care; he clung to it and let it drag him through the current. Just as his lungs were about to fail, his mouth opening to pull in air that wasn't there, his head broke the surface.

Gasping loudly, he clung to the creature's back as the witch paddled quickly, giving her a sharp whack on the back of the head.

It didn't take long before the things that lived beneath the surface came to investigate. Cinn kept a wary eye on the shadows that neared, but as soon as they scented the witch they promptly sped away.

Except one.

Iridescent eyes stared at him from murky waters, growing closer much too fast. Its head breached the surface and Cinn whined, tugging the witch's frill. Covered in seal skin, teeth black and pointed, a horses head rippled the surface as it moved toward them with liquid grace. There was an intelligence behind its shining eyes—a hunger. Like the shtryg, it knew if it captured him it would earn itself a sempiternal feast.

The witch let loose a blood-curdling growl. Unperturbed, the kelpie gnashed its teeth and echoed back a violent huff.

This was not going to be fun. Scary wolf-lizard versus scary horse-monster in the middle of a faerie-infested river? No, Cinn was not going to fare well in this at all.

The witch drew a breath, so Cinn did too, holding on tight as they submerged again. The kelpie's maw reached for him, but the witch maneuvered around and slashed out with her thick, curved claws. Screeching, the kelpie swum beneath and around them to come at a different angle, moving with a fluidity that wasn't natural. It had the body of a horse but the flippers of a seal, spinning effortlessly in a dodging maneuver as the witch made another swipe at it. Cinn kept his arms locked around the lizard-wolf's neck as he drew back his knees, kicking out as the kelpie grew close again. It didn't avoid him, thrusting into the attack and locking its jaws around his ankle.

Cinn opened his mouth to scream, water gushing down his

throat. The kelpie tugged at him sharply—if he didn't let go of the witch, it was going to rip his leg off.

His hip dislocated as the kelpie tugged again.

Cinn let go.

The witch swum for the surface and Cinn cursed her silently, pulling the silver knife from its scabbard. Thrashing against the kelpie who dragged him deeper into the river, slashing out uselessly, unable to reach it, his lungs burned from the lack of air. He could already imagine what it would be like, pinned to the bottom of the river forever, burning as he was eaten alive, over and over. Not for the first time, his heart ached with hatred for having ever been born.

Through the murk, another large shape sped toward them.

Great. The kelpie had a friend.

As the shape grew larger, Cinn shook his head; the oxygen-deprivation to his brain must be kicking in. The lupine beast plunged towards them, overshooting Cinn and aiming its sharp teeth for the kelpie's neck. The monster panicked, releasing Cinn's ankle. Without hesitating, he forced his arms and one good leg to move, propelling himself slowly towards where he thought the surface was. Coordinating was getting harder. This wasn't like crawling out of the river the first time; there was nothing to hold on to, nothing to drag himself by.

Dark, ink-like blood bloomed around him.

From beneath, something was rising. Cinn stopped swimming and tried to focus on his knife hand. On keeping his fingers around the handle.

The witch snagged the back of his pants and dragged him toward the surface.

As the water broke around his head, Cinn immediately began choking the water from his lungs. Maneuvering herself beneath him so he was laying across her back, the witch continued paddling across the river. After vomiting into the water, Cinn finally took a fresh breath, shaking as the riverbank came into view.

He never would have made it across on his own, and he would never be able to go back without her help. The weight of his predicament distracted him from the pain in his hip as the witch climbed awkwardly up the muddy slope and dumped him gracelessly on the ground.

Grimacing, he braced himself against a twisted tree root sticking out of the ground, grabbed his leg and wrestled it back into his hip socket. His jaw ached from clenching his teeth through the pain, but after a moment it all ebbed away leaving nothing but a dull throb.

The witch didn't transform back right away, picking up his soaked and filthy sack between her teeth and stalking into the forest without waiting to see if he would follow.

As if he had much of a choice anymore.

CHAPTER 21

EAVHA

Eavha would not have survived the winter on her own. She'd never seen a storm, or snow; had never truly been cold or hungry. Every morning and every evening, Eaon had made her climb one of the taller trees and shown her the sky. He'd point out the way the clouds moved, their color and shape, and taught her to notice the direction of the wind so they could predict bad weather and prepare for it.

She hated it. She hated looking across the endless canopy of the Anfar forest, knowing the world had no end. Knowing there was nothing there to turn her back home if she strayed too far.

"I'm not a damned sky witch," she'd hissed the first time he dragged her up there.

"No, you're a spoiled little Wyldeden bird. Learn or die," Eaon had snapped back at her.

Unlike her, Eaon looked completely at ease standing at the top of a redwood, the world laid out at his feet.

But the winter had passed. Flowers poked their heads out of

156

the ground, the lake thawed and fish glittered as they swum beneath the surface. The nights were still brisk, but the sun had begun to thaw Eavha too. Berries and wild onions started growing, and she and Eaon quickly began to regain their strength as they gorged themselves.

As the direness of their situation waned, Eavha noticed Eaon changing. He'd begun to sleep longer, his energy draining quicker each day. That afternoon when she returned from gathering something for them to eat, she found him sitting by the lake, just staring.

Putting the greens by their willow, she sat beside him and washed the dirt from her feet. Cold seeped from him. Not enough to worry her, but his magic was clearly roiling. Whatever he was feeling, it was feeding off it.

"I don't think I thanked you," she said softly.

"You don't need to." His voice was flat. Apathetic.

If they were home, she'd have already started brewing him a tonic. She'd found some chamomile flowers and sage leaves, but it wasn't enough.

"Thank you, Eaon." He needed to hear it. "You saved my life."

"Makes us even."

"No, it doesn't."

He didn't answer her, tucking his hands under his arms.

"So, now that we can move again, where do you want to go?" she asked.

Eaon shrugged. "Doesn't matter."

"Come on," she teased, picking up a stick so she could poke his shoulder. "The whole world is yours for the taking. There wasn't a favorite place when you used to travel?"

She should know these things, she realized. Her brother's

favorite place. What he wanted in life.

Eaon didn't respond. She didn't know what else to say. So she didn't say anything and just sat with him for the rest of the afternoon.

The next morning, Eaon wouldn't get up. She wished she could do something as small as make him some tea, but they had nothing to keep water in and she didn't even know how to start a fire.

Spoiled, Eaon had called her. It was true, and she resented it.

She coaxed him to sit up and eat, then she went out in search of something that might help. What, exactly, she didn't know, but she couldn't just sit there and watch Eaon spiral into the dark place where she couldn't reach him.

For an hour, she walked laps of the lake. It was too early in the season to find much. Gritting her teeth, she cussed under her breath until she realized there was nobody around to reprimand her.

"Wretched, shitty forest with your stupid seasons and your miserable, ugly weeds. Selfish, fickle Spirits. Give me back my magic!" she spat.

A rabbit that had been nibbling on a thistle darted back inside its warren. Eavha dropped her shoulders and crouched by the entrance.

"Sorry. I didn't mean to startle you," she cooed.

After a moment, a pink nose appeared, twitching as it scented the witch. Eavha smiled as the long-haired critter hopped out, letting her pet its floppy ears.

At least some things hadn't changed.

"No!"

Birds flocked to the skies as Eaon's scream reverberated through the clearing. Eavha was running before she remembered standing.

As she neared the willow, Eaon came tumbling out of their shelter and hit the ground hard. The pulse of power that burst from him made her skid to a halt, nausea rolling in her stomach.

"Eaon!" she called.

Curled onto his side, clawing at his chest, Eavha didn't know if he was in pain, if he was dreaming, or if the blight had returned. She had to step back, vision blurring.

"Run," Eaon groaned.

"Breathe. Just breathe."

"Run!"

A second pulse surged through the clearing. Animals fled to the forest in every direction as red burst behind her eyes, skin crawling with a thousand fire ants.

There was nothing she could do for him if she died.

Choking back a sob, Eavha turned around and ran.

CHAPTER 22

CINN

THAT MORNING, THE TWO OF THEM CROSSED INTO ANFAR. Cinn had gotten used to the pine and firs of Oford, its canopy filtering light softly, the shadows hiding beasts that were always waiting for them to stop paying attention.

One step changed everything.

The air cracked with energy as they crossed the invisible boundary into Anfar, where the trees seemed to whisper, judging if the trespassers were worthy of every step. The witch had moved through Oford like a wraith, but in Anfar the shrubbery moved aside for her, branches swaying in the breeze to allow her passage. It wasn't as generous for Cinn, but it didn't outright stop him as he trailed after her. The trees began to change, trunks thickening, the canopy closing over until so little light came through the scenery was washed in gray.

Yet, he had never seen anything so beautiful.

The moss beneath his boots was softer, the clovers that came up to his knees greener than any plant he'd ever seen. He tried his best not to trample them, awed by the way the witch glided through the field without leaving a trace.

She belonged here. She was as much a part of the forest as the clovers, the bark, the air. The trees he didn't have names for. The wildlife that watched them without fear.

They stopped by a stream to drink. Cinn rolled his shoulders, tired of carrying his sack. He'd changed out of his wet and bloody clothes, but the night still left him shivering. He missed the fire at the farm and hot meals. When the witch nodded her head for them to keep walking, he shook his head and pointed back.

The witch's nostrils flared as she hissed and stomped her feet. She was mid-gesture when a windless breeze blew by, raising the hair on both of their necks. The witch sniffed, the tip of her tongue sticking out between her lips as if tasting the air as well.

From the left, a rabbit darted through a bush, leaped over the stream and disappeared into the forest behind them. A moment later, a couple of elk hurtled madly by, followed by a second wave of that strange breeze, leaving an aftertaste of rot on the back of his throat.

The witch frowned, tilting her head. Listening.

Heavy panting, broken by short sobs.

Cinn watched a gap between two thick trees, flinching when four wolves came barreling through, blowing right past them. He turned back in time to see another witch come flying through the shrubbery, dirty feet barely touching the ground, face streaked with tears.

She shouted something at them as another breeze pulsed through the clearing, stronger than before. The witch he'd been traveling with doubled over and gagged. Staggering back, she turned around and ran.

Cinn began to follow, but something made him pause. A part of him knew he ought to be afraid, but he wasn't. There was a sadness in the breeze, calling so desperately he couldn't help but step toward it.

Panicked animals lumbered past him as he pushed deeper into the forest, following the tug in his gut. The farther he went, the more urgency consumed him until he broke into a sprint.

The forest grew impossibly silent, all living things having vacated, and ahead he could see a line in the grass slowly creeping toward him. Across that line, everything was dead. The grass, the trees, everything had wilted. The remains of animals that hadn't moved fast enough lay rotting in heaps.

It made him pause. Anything with that much deadly power wasn't something he wanted to mess with, but it also occurred to him that he might be the only one who could.

Rallying, he stepped over the line.

His skin crawled, guts cramping, as whatever it was destroying the forest tried to destroy him too. As fast as his cells were dying, they were replenishing. With little more than discomfort to stop him, Cinn pushed on.

Breaking through the tree line, he found a clearing around a small lake. There was a pitiful shelter in a bare willow, and beneath it lay a man. Or a male, he supposed, taking in the bare feet and strange clothes. The energy was coming from him, the ground around him so rotted that the grass had turned to dust. Dead fish floated on the lake's surface, the stench so vile Cinn resisted taking another breath.

The witch was curled up on himself, shaking on the ground, eyes, teeth and fists clenched. Whatever was happening clearly wasn't intentional.

Cinn didn't know what to do, but he knew what it was like to be alone and in pain. So he knelt by the witch and put his hand on his shoulder. The witch jerked away from him, so Cinn shuffled closer and took his hand.

The witch gasped and opened his eyes, staring up at Cinn in disbelief. Where their skin touched, the pins and needles intensified to the point of pain, but he could tolerate it. There was nothing he could say, so he just wiped the sweat off the witch's forehead.

He gasped again, whimpering quietly at the touch. Tension eased off the witch's shoulders and the tingling sensation lessened, so Cinn sat there, holding him tightly as the witch took deeper and deeper breaths, slowly getting himself under control.

By the time the air cleared, the witch was only half conscious. His hand still tingled, but it was almost pleasant now, like a humming. Cinn lifted the witch's limp hands to his cheeks, letting the sensation shiver into his jaw, down his neck. The witch sighed, sagging heavily, fingers digging in.

He said something, voice cracking, but Cinn didn't understand. He didn't need to. The desperation in those hands, clutching him as if his life depended on it, was clear enough. So Cinn stayed as the witch slipped completely into sleep.

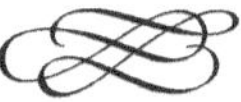

CHAPTER 23

EAVHA

WHEN THE WILDLIFE STOPPED RUNNING, SO DID EAVHA. THE rogue she'd passed had kept up with her, sniffing the air for signs that the danger had not yet passed. If the surging had stopped, either Eaon had it under control or something had happened to him. If he had died again, Eavha wasn't sure what she was going to do.

The thought made her double over, winded.

"By the Mother, what was that?" the rogue asked, spitting on the ground.

Eavha gave the rogue a once over. She was older, though how much older was impossible to tell. She could have been in her thirties or three hundreds. The eyes were startling, feral and animalistic in a way Eavha had never seen before. When she sniffed at her, Eavha bared her teeth.

"What kind of magic is that?" the rogue asked, sniffing again, unintimidated.

"Who are you?" Eavha snapped. Without Eaon with her, if the rogue wanted to kill her she would die. No question.

"Kaelean. You?" She held up her hands, exposing branded palms. Not quite Wyldeden's mark, but similar. Old.

"Eavha." She bared her own palms.

"A baby," Kaelean cooed, cracking an amused grin. "What did you do?"

"What did *you* do?" Eavha countered, shooting a glance to the forest.

"Dabbled in forbidden magic." Kaelean grinned wider, sniffing at Eavha once more. "As have you. What is that? I've never smelled it before."

Eavha stuttered over a lie, but ran out of time to think of one. With a gasp, Kaelean looked between Eavha and the forest, beady eyes sparkling as she loosed a barking laugh.

"Necromancer. Incredible! That magic . . . a Lover's blessing? From the Returned?"

Eavha shifted her weight. She needed to get back to Eaon.

Kaelean made the first move, darting back into the forest in the direction they'd come from.

"Shit," Eavha hissed, chasing after her all the way to where the greenery ceased.

Lover be damned, Eaon had killed the plantation, too.

Skidding to a stop, Kaelean crouched over the line between life and death and sniffed at the necrosis with that nose so much keener than Eavha's own.

"It's passive now," she said, but tossed a blade of grass over the edge anyway, to make sure. When it didn't wilt, the rogue stood and ran. Again, Eavha followed.

At the lake, she nearly fainted at the sight of Eaon skin to skin with a young male. Her brother was drowsily regaining consciousness, the other male holding his hands to his face.

Kaelean stopped, eyes flashing.

"How?" Eavha dropped to her knees. "Has he cured him?"

"He is a kinner."

"What is that?" she asked.

Kaelean tilted her head as she looked down at Eavha. "You truly are a babe, then."

Eavha bristled, but Kaelean just laughed.

"It means he cannot die. Ever. Immortal, invincible, invulnerable. Neither disease nor injury will ever claim him, and he heals faster than anything else ever made. A species trait, though nobody has seen or heard from the Kinner since the Second War."

Eavha stared at the male in awe as he helped Eaon sit up. Her brother was staring at their hands, pale and in shock.

"It's miraculous."

"It's certainly something," Kaelean chuckled.

They watched for a moment, then Kaelean looked down at Eavha again with a wry expression. A moment of silent debate before explaining: "I've been keeping an eye on him since I found him in Oford. I have a territory up north, and I figured having a kinner as an ally wasn't a bad idea. A necromancer and her Returned wouldn't make terrible company, either."

Eavha narrowed her eyes as she climbed to her feet. This rogue was nothing like the ones she'd met during the winter, and she didn't know if it was safe to trust her.

"You certainly can't stay here any longer," Kaelean went on. "Others will come to investigate. Balance fanatics and witch-killers who believe the Lover enjoys the odd sacrifice."

Her stomach turned. Eaon was in no condition to defend

them and Eavha's own ability to do so was abysmal. The idea of actually following this rogue was insane, but she didn't know what other choices they had. And if this kinner was with her, if he could help Eaon . . .

"Give us a moment," Eavha told her, keeping a wary eye as she approached her brother. "Eaon . . ."

The kinner flinched and backed off, but when he saw Kaelean in the clearing he relaxed a little. Rising to his feet, he gave Eaon's hands a pat before leaving the two of them alone.

"Are you alright?" Eaon breathed, holding his head.

"I'm fine," she promised, crouching down so she could explain about Kaelean and the kinner. The promise of safe territory up north.

Eaon winced as he struggled to stay upright. Eavha remembered the exhaustion after bringing him back from the dead and wished she could help, but his skin still hummed with power.

So much power. So much destruction.

Eaon grayed as he noticed what had become of the clearing. To see so much of Terra's dominion wilted and rotting was a sacrilege only they could understand.

"Maybe I should be killed."

"Don't you even think about it," Eavha scolded. "I need you."

Eaon hung his head and took a steadying breath, then looked to the rogue hovering nearby. The kinner was just returning from the forest beyond with a feeble sack.

"I don't know if I have it in me to keep doing what we've been doing," Eaon admitted, rubbing his temples. "And she has valid points. My head is killing me though. I can't think about this."

"I think we should go. Be ready to run if things go sideways, but at least let her help us get north," Eavha suggested.

Eaon nodded and tried to stand. When he couldn't, the kinner dropped his sack and came to help. Fascinated, Eavha watched as the kinner grabbed Eaon under the arms and hauled him to his feet, slipping an arm around his waist and pulling his arm over his shoulder.

"Listen," Eavha said, turning back to Kaelean, who was picking up the kinner's sack for him. "We've had some rough dealings with rogues over the winter. Your offer is generous, but you can't blame us for being suspicious."

Kaelean stared, jaw tensing as Eavha spoke. "Of course. Though mind who you call a rogue now that you're one of us."

Eavha bit her lip. "Sorry."

"Your suspicion is testament to your wisdom," Kaelean said in acknowledgment of Eavha's apology. "The unbound witches in Anfar are vermin and exactly the reason I established a territory in Vertlyn instead. I've grown bored of my usual company and only offered you to come with me because you seem interesting. I won't bite if you don't want to follow us."

Warily, Eavha gave the rogue another once over. The furs she wore were filthy but, after spending the winter in only her gauzy healer's clothes, she could understand why the rogues she'd seen had all slaughtered animals for their skins. She'd be lying if she said she hadn't been tempted. Hadn't looked for something to kill when she and Eaon had been on the brink of starvation.

"Well, we wouldn't mind joining you for a while, if that's okay with . . ." Eavha indicated toward the kinner.

"He doesn't talk, so he doesn't get an opinion." Kaelean shrugged.

"He doesn't speak Terranian?" Eavha asked, noticing the way Eaon's ears perked up at the talk of language.

"Doesn't speak at all, as far as I can tell. Doesn't understand a word I say. We mostly just point and glare at each other, but he's being hunted, so he doesn't have a lot of options besides doing what I want." Kaelean fixed her hair, pulling the tangled reddish curls into a knot.

"Hunted by who?" Eaon asked as the four of them began to walk.

"Sparrows," Kaelean spat. "I'm out of touch with the human world, but I recognized Hyrsch's colors."

Eavha saw Eaon grimace, but she had no idea what they were talking about. There was so much she didn't know. The world outside the Boab was complicated and confusing and dangerous, and she absolutely hated it.

"This territory of yours . . . is it safe?" Eavha interrupted.

"Not a lot of things in this forest, or anywhere, dare to bother me." Kaelean grinned wickedly. "Once we're out of range of the locals, you'll have to tell me how all this came about. I love a good story, and the kinner hasn't exactly been titillating company."

Eaon was focusing on his feet, trying not to drag them as they reached the edge of the clearing, but Eavha took one last look at the willow tree that had been their sanctuary, now dried out and buckling to one side. They definitely had to leave. If the rogues didn't come to kill them, the dryads just might.

Thank you. I'm sorry. She pressed her lips to her fingers and brushed them against a decaying shrub as they passed, vowing to pray properly later.

Eaon spoke, looking at the kinner, in a dialect Eavha wasn't familiar with. He didn't get a response, so he tried another. And another. Kaelean and Eavha watched closely as Eaon tried language after language until, finally, the kinner's head snapped up.

"He knows Nirnish," Eaon told them. "But not the demi-kin's native language. He must have been born after it was outlawed."

Eavha didn't particularly care. She didn't know what he was talking about and she didn't speak any Nirnish anyway. But seeing Eaon engaged again was worth listening to his jabbering. The kinner had given him a new puzzle to solve, and if that's what he needed to get through this fatigue then she would happily listen to it all day long.

CHAPTER 24

EAON

Eaon's body was a sack of dead meat being dragged through the forest, but he didn't focus on that. The destruction he'd caused went farther than expected, and he tried not to think about that either. Something inside him was still raging, clawing to get out, but the feel of hands on his skin was like a salve. He hadn't realized how much the lack of touch had been bothering him until he'd felt warm hands on his freezing skin. Until a complete stranger was holding him.

"Does it hurt you?" Eaon asked, looking at where his arm was slung over the kinner's slender shoulders, pale hand holding his wrist.

The male shook his head, dark hair tousling as he did.

"What about the rogue. Is she safe?"

The kinner frowned and glanced behind him to where Kaelean and Eavha were making careful conversation about the territory up north. His narrowed eyes and twisted mouth, along with a slow nod suggested it was a tenuous truce, then.

"My name is Eaon. My sister is Eavha, and the other witch is Kaelean," he told him, watching as the kinner mouthed the words to himself. "Thank you for what you did back there. I'm . . . it was an accident."

He'd tried to breathe through the ache in his chest, but it had gotten worse and worse until it felt like his skin was ripping apart and the only way to make it stop was to let it out.

The kinner nodded, as if he understood.

"I know you don't speak, but can you write? Could you write your name?" Eaon asked.

They stopped walking and Eaon held on to a tree as the kinner let him go. There was a pained expression on his face as he found a stick to write in the dirt with. The letters were barely legible, but Eaon was used to it.

"Cinn? Am I saying that right?"

Cinn nodded and scrubbed the word out with his foot, tossing the stick and retrieving Eaon.

"Are you very old?"

A shake of the head was his answer.

"Are you from around here."

Another no.

"Have you known Kaelean long?"

Another no.

"She said you were being hunted. Are you hiding from the princess?"

Stiffened shoulders and a small nod.

"I thought she was kind to the demi-kin."

A nod.

"But you're not demi-kin." Eaon frowned, trying to figure it out.

He didn't know a lot about the Sparrow Coven that ruled the

human territories except that most of them were a disgrace to the Mother. Princess Aisling had seemed different, but Cinn's reaction suggested otherwise. Kinners were practically mythical, so he supposed Cinn's presence would be a novelty. Plus, there was the old feud between his kind and hers. The Second War.

"Were you a prisoner?" he asked softly.

Cinn didn't respond.

"I'm sorry."

The kinner just tightened his grip on Eaon's wrist and waist as they finally crossed the line where the flora of the forest had stopped wilting.

"My sister and I were"—Eaon struggled for the right word —"rejected, from our clan just before winter. I had a . . . friend, there. I miss him a lot. I think I will miss him forever now that I have this magic that kills people who touch me. I don't know how to live with it. I don't know if I want to."

Eaon wasn't entirely sure why he was telling him this. Maybe because he could; Cinn could never tell anyone. It was a relief to say it aloud, knowing the females behind him couldn't understand. Maybe getting it out of his head would stop it from hurting so much.

Cinn stopped walking, turning to face Eaon with such a deep sadness it stole his breath. The kinner nodded slowly.

"I'm sorry. You don't know me. I shouldn't be . . . I just . . . I don't . . ."

They started walking again, but Cinn raised his eyebrows and nodded in encouragement. That concession, the permission, broke a damn in Eaon's head. Everything that had happened, every thought he'd had, the pressure he'd felt since the day his da had died came spilling out of him in an unstoppable torrent. He sounded like a lunatic, but . . . Cinn could touch him. Cinn had brought him back from the brink of insanity, sat with him through the waves of necrotic poison wafting from him. He didn't even know him, but he had not abandoned him.

The whole time, Cinn listened. He had no choice, but he didn't seem to mind.

When Kaelean announced they were stopping for the night, Eaon translated and the kinner helped him sit. He crouched beside him and, with two fingers, Cinn lifted Eaon's chin. He tapped it twice, raising his own in defiance, and refused to look away until Eaon nodded.

CHAPTER 25

CINN

Dinner was simple: onions, radishes, pine nuts and spring berries. Eaon passed out before he'd even finished eating, while Eavha and Kaelean talked among themselves until the sun went down.

Cinn doubted he would sleep. Listening to Eaon unravel had been overwhelming, but he knew how it felt to reach a breaking point. There had been days upon days of sitting in front of the fire at the Copelands farm, lost in his head, unable to stop crying no matter how much he hated himself for it. In all honesty though, Cinn didn't mind the sleepless nights. He didn't want to know what he'd find in his dreams when he eventually closed his eyes.

The night was cold and Eavha was shivering so hard Cinn could hear her teeth clacking. Opening his sack, he pulled out his last clean shirt and passed it to her.

Her mouth popped open as she took the shirt with trembling hands. Cinn didn't need to understand the words she spoke to know she was thanking him. There were tears in her eyes as she pulled it over the chest binding she wore, tucking the hem into her skirt. Cinn took out his clean socks too, giving one pair to Eavha and putting the other pair over Eaon's bare feet while he slept.

It didn't take long after that for the other witches to fall asleep, soothed by the petrichor lacing the frigid night air. Cinn took up a vigil perched on a nearby boulder, every sound and movement stiffening his shoulders. Tightened his grip on the blade resting across his knees.

He could remember too clearly the softness of the soldier's throat as he'd cut it open. The coppery tang of blood on his tongue.

The adrenaline had worn off, and the blood-stained shirt in his sack was a dirty reminder of what he had become. William and Sarah had been in danger, but . . . Who had that soldier been? Did he have family? Children? Would he be missed? Nobody would ever mourn for Cinn the way that demi-kin would be mourned, because nobody could ever take from him what he had taken.

This was why his kind were hated.

Just before dawn, someone got up behind him, shuffling and grunting as they wandered into the trees. Cinn stiffened his jaw and tried not to smirk at the sloshing of an emptying bladder, keeping his attention on a dark shadow he didn't entirely trust.

Eaon came and sat beside him, massaging his feet through the socks.

"Thank you."

Cinn nodded.

"Were you awake all night?"

He nodded again, glancing over quickly when he sensed Eaon watching him, a puzzled expression pulling at his brow.

"Does your kind not sleep, or is it just you?"

Cinn smirked and tilted a hand from side to side. He'd always needed less sleep than the demi-kin he'd lived with, but he did need to.

"In my clan, I sometimes was a teacher. A language teacher. In the Southern Mountains there's a clan who, during the frozen seasons, can only communicate in hands. Um, in gesture. Or they get the... um, the frost. Frostbite. I could teach you, if you want."

Cinn blinked. A teacher. A language of gestures. What would be the point if only one clan of witches in the Wastes could understand him? And there was no guarantee that he'd be any better at learning it than he had been at reading and writing.

"You could try. You could teach others."

Cinn narrowed his eyes and glanced sideways at the witch. Was his face really that expressive?

Eaon smirked. "Unless, of course, you have something better to do. Like glare at shadows and trample clovers."

Lifting his boots, Cinn grimaced at the flattened weeds. He was a cow among a herd of gazelles. Eaon chuckled, raising his face as the first rays of sunlight grayed the canopy above them. Cinn watched as Eaon held out one arm, then moved his other in a slow arc.

"Sunrise."

Putting his knife down on the boulder, Cinn copied the movement. Eaon smiled and nodded, then made another gesture that was a little more complicated.

"Forest."

Cinn tried it, but it wasn't right.

"Slower. Don't think of it like words. It's more like a dance. Smooth and jerky movements can mean different things. Watch." Eaon repeated the movement. "Forest."

{Forest.} Cinn copied.

Eaon's grin rivalled the dawn.

After foraging for breakfast, which was surprisingly satisfying, the four of them continued north. Eavha and Kaelean were talking again, and Eaon occasionally translated for him, both in Nirnish and in sign. He couldn't keep up with all the gestures, but the ones Eaon kept repeating were becoming familiar.

He stopped walking.

Eaon noticed first, calling for the others. "What's wrong?"

Cinn frowned, looking between the witches and the direction they'd just come from. For a moment, he'd been so caught up in his new company that he'd forgotten what he was meant to be doing.

Kaelean said something, glaring at Cinn and throwing her hands up until Eaon raised a hand to quieten her down. Looking at his hands, Cinn took a deep breath.

{Shelter.}

"Did you forget something back there?" Eaon asked.

Cinn shook his head and huffed. Tried again.

{Sunrise.} Three fingers. {Shelter.} Pointed south. {Shelter.} South.

Eaon frowned, turning to Kaelean to ask her something, but she shrugged and the two of them had a snappish conversation. Eavha just looked between them, chewing her lip.

"The farmhouse?" Eaon turned back and asked.

Yes! He sagged with relief, nodding eagerly.

"Your home?" he asked, making a new sign that Cinn copied immediately.

{Home.} {Sunrise.} {Three sunrise.} {Home.}

"Kaelean said she found you at a farmhouse, and that there were soldiers there. That it was dangerous, and so you came with her."

{Three sunrise.} {Home.}

"You want to go home? You didn't want to come this far?"

Cinn nodded so fast he made himself dizzy.

Eaon sighed and pinched the bridge of his nose, translating for the other witches. Kaelean hissed viciously, flinging her arms and stomping the ground. The three of them began arguing loudly until Kaelean stormed off and Eavha turned away, busying herself with the plant life nearby. Eaon grimaced, giving Cinn an apologetic look.

"Sit down for a moment."

Cinn crossed his arms.

"Or not. Listen, it's not surprising that there's been a mistake. Kaelean didn't know you intended to go home. She was taking you to her territory in Vertlyn."

Vertlyn. It was as far from home as he could possibly go.

"She said those soldiers . . . the farmers have most likely passed."

He shook his head. {Home.}

"We're not going that way."

{Home.} His hand's started shaking, eyes burning as he made the sign more aggressively.

"Cinn, it's not safe. Not for us and not for you. If the farmers are still alive, it's not safe for them either. Not with the princess hunting you. Kaelean says she just wanted to keep you safe."

The forest had gone blurry, but Cinn had to admit that Eaon made a good point. It was what he'd been afraid of all along, wasn't it? Bringing danger to the Copelands? If Owen hadn't known them, what would have happened?

"I know." Eaon stepped closer, but hesitated to comfort him. At least until Cinn raised his chin, dropping his hands as he tried to blink back the tears. Stepping forward again, Eaon pulled him into a tentative hug, skin tingling pleasantly where it touched the magic coursing through Eaon's.

When he stepped back, Eaon smiled sadly and gave Cinn a gentle tap under the chin. Closing his eyes, Cinn nodded.

CHAPTER 26

NORA

FISTS CLENCHED, IT TOOK EVERY OUNCE OF NORA'S SELF-control not to run through the halls of the palace. Servants and courtiers alike hurried out of the way as she navigated the passages to her office.

The door was ajar when she got there. Slipping inside, she locked it behind her and threw her arms around Owen.

"Thank the gods," she muttered into his neck, the tension in her back melting away as she felt his arms tighten around her. It didn't look or smell like he'd taken the time to wash before coming to her office, but she didn't care. "Are you alright?"

"Of course. Are you?"

"Yes." She let go and held him at arm's length.

He was just as broad and warm as she remembered, if not a little scruffier and a lot more drawn. There were deep shadows under his light brown eyes, so bright they were almost yellow. There were also deep lines on his heavy brow that never used to be there. Taking his face in her hands, she tried to smooth them away. Both of them were paler than they should be after the Oford winter, but there was a gauntness about his usually lively face that worried her.

"What happened?" she asked.

His rough hands settled gently over hers. There was visible pain on his face as Owen closed his eyes.

"We found him. Hiding at a farm near Belden."

"Your farm?" she asked, biting her lip.

Owen nodded, stepping back to fall into one of the high-backed wooden chairs Nora kept by her tidy desk. Aisling had offered her anything and everything for her office but she liked to keep it simple. A plain rug over the marble floor, a plant in the corner, and draws upon draws along the wall to keep her filing in. The only concession she had allowed Aisling to install was the long, cushioned chaise for nights she stayed in to work. Nora hadn't minded sleeping on the floor, but the princess had taken one look at her Second curled up beneath the desk and thrown a fit.

You may insist on working like a dog, but Lover be damned if I let you sleep like one.

The chaise had come in handy more times than Nora would ever admit. She took a seat on it, leaning forward to take Owen's hand as he continued.

"They had no idea he was even there. The kinner killed Ralph before running. The others went after him while I tried to . . . I thought I might be able to save him. I couldn't. The others never returned, so I went looking for them. Followed their tracks all the way to the Dividing River."

"Shit." Nora turned to look out the window, worrying her top lip.

"I know you needed to get him back . . ."

"No, I'm glad you didn't follow them. If they made it through the river, two demi-kin crossing into Anfar will be enough of a headache if the witches decide to confront Aisling about it." She turned back to him as he brought her hand to his lips.

"I'm sorry, love."

Nora narrowed her eyes at the endearment and let go of his hands.

"What else?"

"That's all. I sent a message for the coroner to collect Ralph and paid some townsfolk to return the palace horses. The signed statements from the farmers are in my satchel. They were innocent."

She waited for whatever it was he was holding back but Owen just sighed, running his hands through his curly black hair.

"Will you be in trouble if the boy is lost?"

Nora grimaced and looked away. "I'll think of something."

If the princess deigned to share her plans with her, perhaps Nora could convince Aisling of a different path. Letting the boy stay lost would certainly help her sleep better at night.

"What should I tell Commander Gogh?" Owen asked.

"Tell him you were attacked by fae, and that it was Ralph's final command that you fall back rather than engage."

Commander Gogh was decent for a human, entrusted to lead Hyrsch's armed forces, but he did not make Aisling's inner circle. There were things the princess had to do that a human just wouldn't understand, and the last thing they needed was a revolt.

Owen nodded, struggling up from the chair with a grunt.

"When will you be home?"

"In the morning," she sighed. Whatever he was hiding, maybe she could convince him to tell her then. "Siobhan will be there waiting for you."

Again, he ran his hands through his hair, then leaned down to cup the nape of her neck and kiss her. The scars across her face, her scalp, and her prerogative to have them on show, had never bothered him. There were parts of him that were just as badly marred.

"It will happen for us," he whispered.

"I know. I just hate this." She closed her eyes.

"Do you want to stop? We could adopt."

"No, just . . . try not to enjoy it too much," she grumbled.

Owen chuckled. "Nora, Nora, Nora. Haven't I already told you? You're all I think about. Every day, and every night. You."

Nora's face cracked in a wide smile, her eyes lighting up. "Even so, maybe I'll join you both later."

Owen's throat bobbed as he swallowed loudly. Nora covered her mouth to dull her laughter.

"Go. See Gogh, then get home. Clean up. Rest. I'll be there in the morning."

"Yes, ma'am," he saluted, giving her a wicked grin.

Nora watched her husband leave, feeling the laughter die in her chest as he went.

She spent the evening preparing the report for Aisling, eating a quick dinner at her desk before sending it off with a trusted messenger. The princess would be annoyed that Nora hadn't come to her with the news directly, but she didn't want to deal with her anger.

The messenger returned in the early hours of the morning, rousing Nora from a nap. Aisling was summoning her.

Checking her uniform was orderly, Nora made her way

through the halls to the council room where Aisling was waiting. Another room with a stained-glass wall, but at this hour only the torches faint firelight illuminated the space. The walls and floor were stone, and a long mahogany table had been carved into the shape of a wing. At the head of the table, Aisling sat in a soft black gown with a large glass of red wine in her hand.

Nora took a seat beside her, glancing at the papers on the table between them. One was her report, the other a list of names.

"Owen is on this list."

"Yes, he is," Aisling said flatly, sipping her wine. "I trust him."

Nora shuddered as she realized what Aisling was planning. "You're sending him into Anfar?"

Staring out the window, Aisling nodded as she took a longer drink.

Nora pressed her fingers to her lips. "It isn't wise."

"Excuse me?"

"If you violate the treaty, it will be more than just the Anfar Forest Clan and the wild witches who live there who will be angered. Negate that deal and who's to say you won't negate the deals you made with the Southern Mountain Clan? Or the Sea Witches by the port cities? Or the Old One by the Wastes? They will unite against you."

Aisling pursed her lips. "I know."

"Is this one boy really worth the risk?" Nora pleaded.

"Yes."

The lack of hesitation made Nora sit back. "Why? You executed the demi-kin guards after only three weeks. The human rebel lasted only two. What could a teenage boy possibly have done to warrant two years in that box you call a cell—"

Nora stopped as Aisling aimed an icy glare in her direction.

Rolling her suddenly dry lips, she continued cautiously. "I will always respect your decisions. I just wanted to make sure you'd thought it through. If you would just tell me . . . I want to understand. To help."

Aisling turned back to the window and drained her glass. From the corner, Edwina stepped forward with the decanter to refill it. Nora hadn't even noticed the girl there, but she supposed that was entirely the point. She gave Edwina a small nod; the girl may be a servant, but she was Aisling's servant and a part of the inner circle.

"I didn't enjoy it, if it eases your conscience," Aisling said softly as she nodded at Edwina, taking another drink. "It is necessary, and that is all I will say on the matter. Go home, Nora. Spend a few hours with your husband, then send him to Gogh. He will have fake orders. Make sure Owen knows what to do."

Aisling slid a third piece of paper toward Nora with her instructions for the deployment. There was pressure behind her eyes, but she wouldn't let them water in front of the princess.

"Thank you, Your Highness."

Nora stood and bowed. If Aisling sensed Nora's upset, she didn't acknowledge it. Edwina gave her a pitying look as she tucked the instructions into her pocket and strode from the room.

The rooster crowing woke her. Rolling to her side, Nora snuggled in against Owen's firm shoulder, sliding her arm over the barrel of his chest. His breath warmed her face, chin dipping to nuzzle the top of her head. The peace was ruined by Siobhan's light snore.

"Let's hope that's not genetic." Owen chuckled lightly.

Nora grinned, but it felt hollow in light of the news she had to give him. The tears she'd held back a few hours ago obscured her vision.

"Are you absolutely sure nothing else happened at the farm?" she asked quietly.

Owen groaned. "It's a bit early for this, isn't it?"

"Owen."

"Nothing else happened, love. Okay?"

Nora closed her eyes. After listening to a few more of Siobhan's snores, she carefully sat up, unable to meet his eye. Owen sat up too.

"You don't believe me?"

"Aisling is sending you out again today."

Getting out of bed, she went to retrieve the letter from her discarded uniform, unable to enjoy the way Owen's gaze lowered to watch her walk. As he read, she slipped on a nightgown and robe, the morning chill raising goosebumps across her skin. Owen sighed deeply, the corners of his mouth pulling down as he dropped the letter and hung his head.

"Why can't she just drop it?"

"I tried, but she must have her reasons. You know she would never insist on this if it wasn't important."

Owen blew out a harsh breath, rubbing his hands over his weary face. "Here I was hoping to catch up on some sleep. Does she realize that by having us cross into Anfar, we're declaring war?"

"She does."

"Fuck."

"So I'm going to ask you again, Owen. Are you sure he

crossed the river?" She sat on the edge of the bed, wiping her eyelids to stop the tears from falling.

Owen shifted so he was beside her, taking her scarred head in his large hands and pressing his brow to hers.

"We will get through this. Like with everything else, we will survive this and we will see the true dawn. It will take us a few days to get to the bridge, and I can delay the crossing by insisting we do it secretly. Try to get her to change her mind. I'll wait as long as I can."

Nora nodded. It was the best they could do.

Siobhan yawned loudly and rolled onto her back, her flawless skin making both Owen and Nora blink twice. Jealousy was hard to justify when, if she was being honest with herself, she enjoyed these moments as much as Owen did.

"Oh, it's cold," Siobhan croaked, pulling the covers up over her head.

"I'll get Liz to light the fires," said Nora, giving Owen's hand a pat before getting to her feet.

"We'll get dressed and meet you for breakfast. I'll just explain to Siobhan . . ." Owen grimaced.

Nora nodded, slipping from the room and leaving the door ajar.

Three days. Maybe four, depending on how long Owen could delay the deployment. That was how long she had to convince Aisling to change her mind.

It would be easier changing the path of the sun.

CHAPTER 27

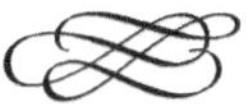

CINN

"Make it stop! Make it stop, make it stop."

Eaon's screaming startled Cinn out of his sleep. Kaelean and Eavha were scrambling away, a hint of rot in the air panicking the nearby wildlife.

Cinn rolled to his feet and dove for Eaon, grabbing the witch's hands. It didn't work. The starlight above illuminated the twisted expression on his face as he fought whatever pain was causing his back to arch like that. The pins and needles in his hands were like a thousand fire ants trying to eat him alive.

Eavha shouted something at them, even as she backed away.

Through clenched teeth, Eaon drew a breath and forced himself to look at Cinn.

"I'm sorry," he rasped. "I don't know where else to send it."

Cinn frowned, but as he felt the tingling intensify, becoming painful, he gave a sharp nod. He could take it.

As the full force of Eaon's magic hit, Cinn doubled over and gagged. In the moments between his cells' death and rebirth, he could taste the decay. Red burst behind his eyes as every inch of his body was razed. This was worse than he'd thought it would be. How could it be worse than it had been in the clearing?

A thousand years of agony condensed into a minute. Slowly, the pain receded and Cinn collapsed to the ground, panting hard. Eaon passed out.

Dropping to her knees beside them, Eavha's hands fluttered over Eaon, then Cinn. She started to speak, then bit her lip.

{Hurt?} she asked him.

In the past three weeks of traveling together, Eavha had picked up a few words during Eaon's lessons.

{No,} he signed. Not permanently.

{Thank you.}

Cinn nodded. {Eaon?}

{Alive.}

He nodded again, then closed his eyes against the spinning canopy.

Neither Cinn nor Eaon could move the next day. Kaelean lit a fire, unconcerned about the attention it might attract, and started roasting some nuts over hot stones. Eavha had to drop them into Eaon's mouth to get him to eat, and while Cinn acknowledged the sweetness of them he couldn't find the energy to enjoy them.

"I'm sorry," Eaon said quietly.

Cinn frowned and shook his head.

"Was it awful?"

He shook his head again. Eaon seemed too fragile, like he had during his meltdown after the outburst in the clearing. He didn't think the witch needed to know right then what his magic had really done to him.

{Nothing was hurt. Nothing died,} he signed instead.

Eaon nodded, but didn't seem relieved. "I'm going to ask Kaelean to put out the fire. I don't want rogues to find us while we're like this."

Cinn snorted. {Kaelean can handle. Change into wolf.}

Eaon frowned. "Change into wolf?"

He was too tired to explain. Didn't care enough to make the effort. He wrapped his arms around himself and curled into his chest. What was the point in having left Hyrsch and endangering the Copelands if pain was just going to follow him anyway?

Eaon started talking to the other witches, and before long they were all arguing. He didn't care. If he didn't already know it wouldn't work, he was tempted to take his knife and cut the mark off the back of his neck just so he could have peace. But the mark only identified him for what he was. The curse was in his blood.

"Cinn." Eaon called for his attention. He glanced over to where Eaon was forcing himself to sit up. "Kaelean is explaining."

As Kaelean spoke, Eaon translated using the sign language that Cinn had found easier to learn than written Nirnish.

"I was bored with clan life, so I dabbled in some forbidden magic," Kaelean was saying. "Nobody had ever had a blessing from the Mother, and I wanted to know why. So I did some research and found a way to get one."

"You . . . you *took* magic from the Mother?" Eavha gaped.

"Yes. It cost . . . a lot. And it's harder to do than I thought it would be, but I don't regret it." Kaelean shrugged.

"Can you change into anything?" Eavha asked, resting her chin on her fists as she leaned closer.

"No," Kaelean chuckled. "To change into an animal, I have to eat the heart of one during a new moon."

The three of them stared at her in horrified silence. Cinn thought of the giant reptilian wolf thing she'd become and paled. No wonder nothing in the forest bothered her if she'd been able to kill one of those monsters.

With a smug grin on her face, Kaelean took another handful of nuts from the fire and cracked open their shells, passing the treats around.

Another week of traveling north without incident passed before Cinn felt a familiar shift in the air. The trees became simple trees again with their ghostly bark and bitter leaves, the animals growing fearful again, darting under shrubs or into burrows as the witches neared. The Vertlyn forest was strangely colorful, speckled with vibrant red nettle flowers and hakia buds, a soft feathery grass tickling their knees as they strode through it.

Within a few hours, the four of them stepped out of the tree line. Cinn's eyes went wide as he took in the expanse of grassland before him. The feathery grass was waist high, stretching uninterrupted in every direction for as far as he could see. The wind sent the stalks rippling, glistening under the spring sun in rays of gold, lavender and jade.

In all his life, he'd never seen such wide, open space. At the brink of freedom, Cinn could breathe again for the first time since Eaon's surge.

Eavha had stopped, turning a ghastly shade of gray. Her

words were breathy as she wrapped her arms around herself, stepping back beneath the canopy. Eaon went to talk to her, but Kaelean stepped up beside Cinn and turned her face to the sun. In this light, her eyes were almost brown and there was such relief on her face that Cinn smiled. Anfar might have been where she belonged, but this was her home. She grinned giddily, and he understood it. Standing in this field, he could see how big the world really was. How it might be possible to get far enough away from where he'd been that he could truly start to live.

"Eavha needs a moment," Eaon explained as he came up beside him. "It's a lot to take in when you've lived your whole life in the Boab. The world is so big. Makes you feel small."

Cinn nodded, though feeling small didn't bother him. He wanted to be as insignificant as possible. To disappear in the enormity of the world.

Kaelean said something and Eaon translated in sign. Always signing, even when he spoke Nirnish. Cinn couldn't follow all of it, but he was getting better.

"She said her territory is two more days through the grassland. We'll be safe there. I thanked her for letting us come along. She said she'd always wanted a little coven of her own." He chuckled as he shook his head.

{Coven?} Cinn made the sign uncertainly, adding the marker that made it a question.

"Covens are different from families. Family is blood or marriage. A coven is chosen. They're rare amongst rogue . . . unbound witches. Wild witches do it more often."

Cinn bit his lip and looked over the plain. A chosen family. Sarah's smiling face came to mind, as did William's calloused hands. And before . . .

He loosed a breath and shook the images away.

{What is different between unbound and wild witch?}

"Hey, that was good." Eaon smiled as he watched Cinn's hands. "Some witches leave a clan by choice. Some are born by wild or unbound witches. They have committed no crime, so they are not rogues. Not unbound."

Cinn couldn't help but glance at Eaon's hands. The scars he shared with Eavha, similar to the ones Kaelean had.

It didn't sit right with him that the Nemuses had been punished for what happened. Eavha had performed a miracle, and they had cast her out. And Eaon . . . all Eaon had done was not kill himself. It wasn't fair.

Eavha was finally stepping out of the tree line with Kaelean at her side, holding her arm gently. The young witch looked to her brother, to Cinn, still pale as a banshee.

{Safe,} he signed to her.

She managed a whisper of a smile.

They didn't light a fire that night; the grass that swayed in the gentle breeze would have burned too quickly if an ember flickered away. Instead, Kaelean shed one of the outer layers of her fur coverings to drape over Eavha's shoulders. The young witch looked ill, but she smiled anyway. Cinn gave Eaon his spare socks and boots again.

{I have a shirt but it is blood.}

"Bloody," Eaon signed, reminding him to use the adjective signifier. "Thank you anyway. I'll be fine."

Cinn nodded, but twisted his mouth at Eaon's gruff tone. Any trace of the wanderlust that had been written all over the witch's face earlier in the day had vanished, replaced with a melancholy that made Cinn nervous. The last thing he wanted was for Eaon to have another surge.

The spot they had chosen to settle for the night was beside a slow-trickling stream. Kaelean pulled a couple of fish from the water and ripped out the bones, turning both Eaon and Eavha green. Cinn wasn't as fussy, happily taking what Kaelean gave him and filling his belly on the pink inner flesh.

"How long have you been . . . unbound?" Eavha asked, picking at a handful of roots and berries she'd saved from Anfar. When she offered some to her brother, Eaon shook his head, signing as he explained he didn't have much of an appetite.

Kaelean smiled mischievously. "Trying to work out how old I am, little witchling?"

"You keep calling us witchlings, children, babies; for all we know, you're not any older," Eavha grumbled, jutting out her chin.

"Alright, how about... if you can guess, I'll tell you," Kaelean challenged, tilting her head.

"Have you celebrated your half century?" Eavha asked, earning a snort of derision.

"Don't insult me."

"At least a century," Eaon chimed in with feigned enthusiasm, pushing at the dirt with his toes.

Kaelean shook her head, licking the fish bones clean before threading them into her furs. "Not even close."

"Two centuries," Eavha guessed.

"Were you around for the Sparrow insurgence?" Eaon asked at the same time.

"Ah." Kaelean leaned back and stretched out her legs. "Now you're asking better questions."

"How long ago was that?" Eavha asked.

Cinn had trouble keeping up with Eaon's hands after the mention of the Sparrows. The delicate bones between his fingers made his skin clammy. Dropping them, he rubbed his fingers through the sand-like soil, digging up loose pebbles. He pulled one out to see if it was interesting.

"Eaon!" Eavha's sudden shout made Cinn flinch.

Eaon had stopped signing, so he didn't know what was happening as Eavha continued talking, a pained look on her face. The air wasn't tingling, so it wasn't another surge. Eventually, Eaon managed to sooth whatever had upset her but a sad smile lingered.

Cinn tugged Eaon's sleeve. {What?}

"It's my quarter-century birthday tomorrow," Eaon explained. "We only celebrate the first year after a witch is born, because it's often a harrowing year, then their quarter and half centuries. After that the celebrating is limited to each passing century. If we were home . . ." He bit his lip and stared at his hands, eyes distant. "Not that my family would have celebrated mine anyway. If they were still alive."

Cinn bit his lip, glancing at Eavha who still looked like she might start crying. Taking a deep breath, hands trembling slightly, he asked Eaon: {What is that in witch years?}

Eaon frowned, translating his question to the others. All three of them looked at him in confusion.

{Is quarter century grown? Or are you really just a baby?}

Eaon blinked. Raised his eyebrows. "Are you . . . making a *joke*?"

Cinn grimaced, but Eaon was suppressing a smile as he translated for the others, who burst into hysterics.

"I'll have you know that the quarter century is our marker for full maturation. I can't believe you called me a baby."

{You sulk like one.}

Eaon gaped and gave Cinn a playful shove, a little light back in his eyes.

"Alright, smart ass, how old are you then?"

The laughter died in Cinn's chest.

Eaon's face dropped. "Did I say something . . ."

{I don't know how old I am.}

"You don't know? I thought you said you weren't that old."

Cinn smirked, but it hurt to do so.

{I don't know how long I was . . .} He looked at his hands, not knowing the word he needed.

"Imprisoned?" Eaon asked quietly.

Cinn nodded, hands shaking as he copied the sign.

"How old were you when you were imprisoned?"

{Seventeen.}

Eaon flinched.

Cinn's heart was working too hard as the memories of that day in the training field clawed its way out of the hole he'd buried them in. The arrogant cadet who'd been careless with his crossbow, accidently loosing a bolt that had found its way into Cinn's throat. The panic of the lieutenant in charge who'd tried to stop the bleeding, carrying him to the infirmary. Demi-kin healed better than humans but a fatal wound was a fatal wound.

When the injury healed right in front of the medic, no amount of dye over his mark could disguise who he really was.

"How long had the princess been in Hyrsch?" Eaon asked.

{Close to three years.}

Eaon jerked again, looking away guiltily to field the questions coming from Eavha and Kaelean. After explaining, Kaelean said something Cinn didn't need translated.

"You're nineteen, maybe twenty depending on your birthday and when you were . . ."

He couldn't breathe. Eaon warily touched the back of his hand, but Cinn flinched away from him. Nineteen. He felt older and younger at the same time. His body felt wrong. Too big and too small; too heavy and too light.

"I'm so sorry."

It took Cinn a long time to find the strength to move his hands.

{It doesn't matter.}

It couldn't. He had to leave it behind if he was going to live. He wasn't *there* anymore; he was in the most beautiful meadow he'd ever seen, with people he almost trusted.

A sledgehammer of a thought broke through his dissonance: what if he wasn't? What if this was some elaborate hallucination and his nightmares were actually real? What if this meadow, these witches, this body . . . didn't exist?

"Cinn. It's okay," Eaon said, reaching for his hand once again.

Rolling his tongue across his dry lips, Cinn nodded and forced himself to sit still as Eaon touched him. The sensation was grounding. He couldn't make up a feeling like that.

Eavha said something, but Eaon hissed at her.

Cinn glanced between them until Eaon sighed.

"It's okay if you don't want to talk about it anymore."

{What?}

"She wants to know if you're okay. She can try to find some herbs . . ."

{I am okay.}

"Cinn . . ."

{I am. I must be. I was made to be.} He frowned at his hands again, knowing they weren't the words he wanted.

Eaon translated for the others, who had huddled in as the night descended, bringing the worst of the chill with it. When they all looked to him, questioning, he took a deep breath and tried to explain.

{There are monsters who imprison our kind and eat us forever. There are people who keep us for work. My family are gone. Alive, but that is not a comfort. I didn't know before why they made me ready, but I do now.}

It was the most he had ever managed to communicate. Eaon sucked in his lips, fists clenching. Eavha asked another question.

"When did you last see your family?" Eaon translated.

{Seven years old. A monster came. They told me to run. I was found and taken to Hyrsch.}

Cinn didn't remember much of it, or have any recollection of where it had happened. He just remembered the screaming, running, and then a cold that he wished had killed him.

"You were enslaved?" Eaon asked, voice cracking.

Cinn nodded, copying the new signs, trying to commit them to memory. He didn't want to think about that either, his neck itching with the weight of a collar that was no longer there.

"And nobody ever figured out what you were?"

{No. Many humans don't believe I exist. The demi-kin helped keep my healing hidden until we were all . . . unbound.}

"Free." Eaon showed him the sign.

{Free.} For three blissful years, he had been free.

"They didn't notice your mark was different?"

Cinn shook his head. {They see what they want to see. And we used . . . color to cover it}

"I've never actually seen one of the marks up close. Are they that similar?" Eaon frowned.

Cinn nodded, turning his head to let him see it. Eaon leaned close, then flinched back with a gasp. Looking to him, to Eavha, to Kaelean, he started signing to ask what was wrong, but Kaelean was nodding at Eaon with a knowing look on her face.

{What?}

"It's . . . a spellmark." Eaon shook his head in disbelief. "Maybe even a witchmark."

{What is that?}

"Um, it's . . . spellmarks are used when the magic a witch wants to perform is more complicated than what occurs naturally. It's a language to itself, really. A witchmark . . . it is the highest order of spellmark. Many are believed to still be undiscovered. To make one without sufficient magic . . . it will kill you. Only the high priest or priestess usually has the power. That mark . . ." Eaon put his fingers to his lips.

Cinn lost his breath again. {It's a spell?}

Eaon nodded.

{Could it be broken?}

Eaon raised his eyebrows. "I . . . I'd never thought of it. I suppose so. Is that something you'd want?"

{Maybe.} Cinn looked away. {I want the choice. There are some things I'd rather die than feel again.}

He'd had enough. He didn't want to talk anymore.

Eavha said something, but Eaon snapped at her. Instead, she came to hug him, then cupped his face and smiled sadly. She smelled like sweat and earth and smoke, and, on her, he didn't terribly mind it. Almost missed it when she went back to her spot, huddling under the fur Kaelean had given her.

Kaelean, who gave Cinn another knowing nod before getting to her feet and making some kind of declaration. Eavha and Eaon both went slack-jawed, and it took Cinn tugging on Eaon's sleeve again to get him to translate.

"She . . . she's nine hundred and fifty years old," Eaon breathed.

Cinn raised his brows and looked up to where Kaelean stood, proudly basking in the shocked expressions on all their faces. Eavha was full of questions, and once Kaelean had settled down to answer them, Eaon turned to Cinn and signed:

{When I can, I'll look into breaking the spell for you.}

{Thank you.}

Eaon reached over and tapped him under the chin.

CHAPTER 28

EAVHA

Eavha took the first watch that night, unable to sleep with the weight in her heart anyway. It was Eaon's quarter century birthday and she had nearly forgotten. No matter where they were, it was always going to be a difficult day for him, but thanks to her he would be spending it as a rogue.

Better than spending it dead.

Still, under the cover of the wind whispering through the grass, she threaded her fingers through the soil beneath her knees and prayed.

"Mother, forgive him. Love drives him, and you of all should know what we do for the sake of love. Lover, forgive him. Your power punishes him for a crime he did not commit. Of all the Spirits, it is you who should know we don't get to choose our fates. Terra, forgive him. He grieves deeply for the damage he has caused. Spirits, bless him. Give him the strength he needs, and the courage to use it. Give him a purpose to fill his days until the Lover deems him worthy of her embrace."

She paused. In her years at the clinic, she had felt the Lover's presence when a witch's time was near. The day Eaon died, she hadn't felt it. Had felt nothing but fear and pain and rage. Yet another thing that didn't add up.

"And may every day until then shine upon him."

Eavha whipped her head around to stare at Kaelean.

"Did I wake you?"

"I make a point to sleep lightly," Kaelean answered. "Rest. I will take watch from here."

"It's still early . . ."

"Then you will be well rested for your brother's celebration in the morning." Kaelean smiled softly.

Her breath hitched as she returned it. "Thank you."

She had nothing to give Eaon to mark the day of his maturity, but among these people who seemed to actually like him, maybe it would still be okay.

"Oh, wow, thank you."

Eavha dragged her gritty eyelids open. The others were awake already, Kaelean with a small pile of fruits the bright orange color of tulips. Too small to be an orange, she sat up and sniffed at the citrus tang in the air.

"What are those?" she croaked.

Kaelean smiled and tossed her one. The skin was looser than an orange's, too.

"A type of tangerine native to Vertlyn. They're very sweet," she explained.

Eaon had already peeled back the skin, taking a large bite, unphased by the juices dripping down his chin.

"Merry day, Eaon." Eavha smiled, picking at the peel of her fruit. He returned it with a sparkle in his eye as he savored the fruit.

Cinn lifted his fruit like a glass of wine, nodding at them both as he ate.

"Wait," Eavha frowned. "When did you get these? Did you leave us unguarded? I would have stayed up—"

"Oh, unclench, Eavha. Cinn was up." Kaelean rolled her eyes and gestured for Eavha to eat. "I have this little stove at my place. I like to cook these—"

Cinn gagged, lurching forward to smack the fruit out of Eavha's hands. Eaon dropped his, blinking frantically as his body sagged.

"What . . ." Eavha stood up.

"Run," Eaon rasped, a hand at his throat.

Kaelean's beady eyes glittered as she rose into a crouch, tilting her head, a smirk pulling at her upper lip. All around them, the grass rustled.

Before Eavha could move, a ring of humans rose from the field. The black-and-cobalt-blue uniforms with golden sparrows embroidered on the breast were stark against the crisp greens and yellows of the meadow; they shouldn't have been able to sneak up on them so easily.

Cinn had gone bone white.

From where he sat, Eaon lunged for Kaelean and tried to grab her bare ankle, coldness radiating from him in a dark aura. The rogue danced out of the way, scowling as the closest human hurried forward with a metal staff. It had hinged crescents on the end, and Eavha noticed the spellmarks etched on the steel a moment before they clamped around Eaon's neck. He snarled, clawing at the collar with one hand while still trying to reach for someone to grab—to kill.

Cinn reached for his dagger, but it was gone.

"You filthy, maggot-eating rogue," Eavha spat, finally climbing to her feet.

"Run!" Eaon shouted at her again, but she wouldn't leave him.

Kaelean's head whipped around. The rogue snarled and tackled Eavha to the ground, her head bouncing off the hard-packed earth with teeth-shattering force. A pained whine cracked her throat as she lashed out, scratching at Kaelean's face and grabbing a fistful of her tangled hair. Yanking hard, Kaelean's head snapped back, but it wasn't enough to stop her from pulling away Eavha's arms, pinning her wrists with a crushing grip. Bucking wildly, Eavha clamped her teeth on Kaelean's forearm.

"Ah! Don't make me hurt you!" Kaelean growled as she tried to shake her off.

Eavha bit down harder, sharp metallic blood staining her teeth and coating her tongue. She would not lay docile this time. If they were going to beat her, she would fight.

Kaelean arched back, then slammed her head down onto Eavha's brow. Spots burst behind her eyes in an agonizing display, but her jaw only clenched tighter. Kaelean hissed between her teeth as she wrestled around, pushing a knee into Eavha's abdomen until bile scorched her throat.

It was too much. Eavha let go of Kaelean's wrist as she choked on a scream, shoving at Kaelean to get off her.

Close by, Cinn had staggered to his feet. Eyes wild, he bared his teeth at the soldiers surrounding him before lunging, throwing a handful of dirt at the nearest human and making a grab for the sword in his hand. The soldier swung blindly and managed to knock

Cinn in the head with the hilt. Staggering, the kinner ducked under the soldier's arm and got his hands on a dagger at the soldier's waist. In a single swipe, he slashed the soldier's throat open, blood spraying over Eavha's face as she squirmed under Kaelean.

"Get. Off!" she panted, running out of breath as Kaelean pushed down with more weight.

"Stop. Fighting. Me," Kaelean hissed back, but glanced up as a guttural scream tore through the clearing.

Cinn had rammed the knife into another soldier's gut and torn his belly open, innards spilling in a foul cascade. A distant ringing filled Eavha's head as the smell assaulted her, body slackening, the bile already in her throat filling her mouth.

Without looking back, Cinn sprinted into the fields.

Kaelean swore and got off Eavha, chasing after him.

"No!" Eavha cried, jerking away and spitting at the two men who came to haul her to her feet and clamp her wrists and ankles in shackles.

Kaelean caught up to Cinn, nimbly dodging his blade. In the same movement, she caught his wrist and pulled him forward, ramming a fist into his throat. Cinn gagged and stumbled, dropping the dagger. Caught it in his other hand.

Swiping out at Kaelean again, she wrenched the arm she was still holding and spun him away before the blade could touch her, then bent back and kicked up into his face with such brutality Eavha heard his nose break from where the soldiers were holding her. More uniformed men descended on Cinn as he struggled to get off the ground, clamping shackles on his wrists and ankles too.

"No," Eavha sobbed, looking from the rabid kinner thrashing against his restraints to her brother, still pinned to the ground by his neck and clawing to get free. One of the soldiers was yelling something, but she didn't understand. Eaon hissed in Nirnish back at him, turning his panicked gaze to her, then to Cinn, who looked like he was trying to break his own arms to get free.

Kaelean wiped her bloodied arm on her furs as she swaggered back to the center of the clearing, breathing heavily. It didn't stop her from smirking at them all.

"Welcome to Pirevia."

Then, for Cinn, she gloated in perfect Nirnish.

For an hour, Eavha, Cinn and Eaon were dragged through the grasslands until they finally crested a hill and saw how close to the city of Pirevia they actually were. A steep cliff lay before them with a narrow dirt path curving tightly down it. Some many meters below them stretched out a muddy bog, cut through with a wide stone bridge that went on for miles until it reached the city gates.

The city was unlike anything Eavha had seen before; a mass of ugly, pointed buildings crammed together behind a tall wall, the sprawl of it so large she knew it would take days to cross to the north-eastern side where the sky wedged against a mass of sapphire blue. The sea. Eaon had told her about the sea, once.

The poison from the fruits had spread through Eaon's veins; he could hardly walk as the soldiers dragged them to a horse and cart at the edge of the dirt path. The cart was barred like a cage, and they shoved Eaon inside with no regard for the way the collar choked him. One of the soldiers picked Eavha up and tossed her in after her brother, while four more struggled with a frenzied Cinn. The sounds he was making weren't human as the soldiers tried to wrangle him into the cage, battering his legs when he braced them on the bars.

"Eaon, what's going on? Who are they?" she begged, but Eaon was using all of his strength to stay upright as the soldiers lashed the pole attached to his collar to the bars.

Cinn came sprawling into the cart, promptly flinging himself back at the door as they slammed it shut and locked them in. A desperate moan grated his throat as the cart lurched, the horses breaking into a canter that sent Eavha sprawling far too close to Eaon's bare feet. Her short scream pulled Cinn out of his rage long enough to help her away from her brother's deadly skin. She grabbed hold of the bars across the cage from him, huddling against it as violent shivering wracked her limbs.

They hit a hole in the road, bumping the cart sharply. Eaon gagged on the collar, head beginning to loll.

"He's going to choke," she cried, looking to Cinn who'd already gone back to wrestling with the cage door. Nobody around them seemed to care. Kaelean was nowhere to be seen. "Cinn. Cinn."

They couldn't understand each other, but he recognized his own name. She pointed at Eaon, and the kinner's eyes widened as he realized how sick Eaon really was. The fruit didn't seem to be having the same effect on him.

Swaying unsteadily, Cinn made his way to sit beside Eaon, holding his head up with his cuffed hands to ease the pressure on Eaon's throat.

"Is he dying?" she asked, earning a confused and panicked glance from Cinn.

Taking a deep breath to steady herself, she reached in for her healing magic. A tiny kernel of what used to be there sputtered awake. Focusing on Eaon, she sent a tendril over him for a rudimentary check of his most vital signs. She almost choked on her relief, both at having used magic again and at what it was telling her. Eaon was hurt, but he would be okay.

By the time the soldiers decided to set up camp for the night, they'd managed to get down the precarious cliff face and halfway across the seemingly endless bridge. Eavha ran her dry tongue over her drier lips and pulled her knees up to her chest. She hadn't been able to hold her bladder, but neither had either of the others.

At least we're together.

Or so she'd thought. Cinn wasn't quite with them anymore. He'd become very still and very quiet with a vacancy to his eyes she'd only ever seen before on corpses.

Eaon had recovered enough to hold his own head up, to speak, to try to comfort Cinn, but nothing seemed to be getting through to him.

"Who are they?" Eavha whispered, watching where the soldiers had settled down to feast.

"Pirevian soldiers."

"What do they want with us?"

"I'm not sure they want anything to do with us at all," Eaon said, grimacing as he glanced back to Cinn. When he didn't respond to Eaon's hand squeeze, his expression withered into cold rage. "If I ever get my hands on Kaelean . . ."

"Rotten old hag." Eavha wiped her cheek on her shoulder, wriggling her fingers and toes to encourage circulation.

"I'm sorry—"

"Don't even start with that self-blaming shit, Eaon. We all trusted her."

They were all stupid.

Someone banged their fist on the cage, shouting aggressively. Both Eaon and Eavha flinched. Cinn did not. Holding a finger up to his lips, Eaon lowered his chin and waited for the soldiers to pass by.

"If there was ever a time for you to figure out how to use that power of yours, now would be it," Eavha muttered.

"Even if I could summon it on purpose, this stupid collar is doing something. It's still there, but it's like . . . I don't know. It feels caged, too." He craned his neck as if trying to loosen the steel.

Another soldier was heading toward them, so they fell silent. The smell of food wafted over from the encampment and Eavha bit her lip to suppress a groan. She'd hoped her days of being hungry were over.

"Listen," Eaon hissed as soon as it was safe. "We're going into Pirevia tomorrow, and it's not going to be pleasant. It's not like where Cinn is from; it's a lot worse for the demi-kin. You're going to see some horrible things, but I need you to stay focused."

Eavha closed her eyes. For the first time, she regretted everything she'd done that had led her to this moment. She wanted to go home. She hated Nir, and everyone in it.

"Act weak," Eaon continued.

"I am weak," she hissed.

She couldn't fight, had hardly any power . . .

"You are not," Eaon hissed back. "But pretend to be. Be a scared little witch and let them underestimate you. As soon as an opportunity arises, run. If I can't go, leave without me. Run for the Northern Mountains. There are covens there who might not turn you away. But don't hesitate, Eavha. Run."

She licked at her lips again and looked away, blinking back tears.

"Eavha," Eaon growled. "I know that look."

"Shut up."

"I am still the Head of House, and I am telling you—"

His tone made her whip her head back around. "You can shove your head right up your house, Eaon. Don't tell me what to do."

The two of them glared at each other.

One minute.

Two.

Eaon's face cracked with the smallest smile she had ever seen, the weight of the world in his eyes. "Glad to see you can still bite."

"We will all get out of this, Eaon." She sniffed. "Somehow."

He nodded, then looked to Cinn. Gave him a gentle nudge.

Nothing.

CHAPTER 29

EAON

THE PEOPLE OF PIREVIA STARED IN CURIOSITY AS THE procession of guards led the prisoner cart slowly through the city streets. In broad daylight, right down the main road. A cacophony of gossip swelled as they passed, and Eaon singled out a few blood-chilling words: *the arena . . . a hunt . . . demi-kin . . . wager . . .*

Cinn had completely shut down. Eaon couldn't blame him. Couldn't blame the way Eavha started whimpering as she looked around the city streets either. He'd tried to warn her, but there was no way to truly prepare someone for the things that happened in Pirevia.

The red stain of the cobblestones beneath the horse's hooves gave Blood Boulevard its name, taking visitors from the city gates to the palace. On either side of the road, corpses hung from street lights in varying states of decay, the white pile of scavenger filth beneath them making an unpleasant break from all the crimson. Many of the citizens wore strips of cloth over their face in an attempt to filter out the smell, but Eaon knew it didn't help. He'd tried it when he'd come here with Kailevi, but the reek of Pirevia was the kind of horror that could only be scoured away by death. And maybe not even then.

Eventually the spectators fell away and their cage was hauled through the palace gates. Immediately to the right was a courtyard where the soldiers all came to a halt.

The stopping of the cart roused Cinn. His nostrils flared, pupils dilating as he climbed to his feet and began to pace the length of the cage.

"Settle down, kinner," one of the soldiers growled as he banged on the cage.

Both Cinn and Eaon flinched at the word. They had not mistaken him for what he was, then.

In the middle of the courtyard was a small square structure, and from within it came five royal guards, one of whom was brandishing a crossbow. As soon as they were within range, the bolt was aimed at Eaon's head.

"Behave," the first soldier spat, pointing for Cinn to sit down.

There was such feral rage in Cinn's eyes as he paused his pacing that Eaon doubted he had the capacity to comply. The likelihood of Eaon dying in the next ten seconds was high, and the only reason his stomach churned at the thought was because of Eavha.

Eaon opened his mouth, unsure exactly what he could say to calm the situation.

He didn't have to figure it out.

Cinn crouched down, levelling a glare so hateful that the man holding the crossbow shuffled his feet.

The long metal prong attached to the collar around Eaon's neck was untethered and the door to the cage opened.

"Out," the soldier in charge demanded.

Slowly, Cinn crept forward. He didn't fight as guards grabbed hold of his arms, yanking him from the cage.

"Now the girl."

"Your turn," Eaon said to her.

Every soldier in the courtyard drew their weapon.

"What did you say!" the guard with the crossbow pressed forward. Eavha sobbed as she clung to the bars.

"She doesn't understand you!" Eaon explained, raising his hands. "I just translated."

The clamor of the city beyond the wall couldn't penetrate the bubble of tension in the courtyard. After a moment, the guard in charge dipped his chin. Eaon cleared his throat and tried again.

"Eavha, you need to get out."

Releasing a shaking breath, she nodded and began to scoot herself closer to the door. Soldiers grabbed her ankles and pulled. Eavha screamed and began to thrash. A soldier drew a baton.

"Don't! Don't!" Eaon begged them. Then, to Eavha, "Calm down! Just get out! Please, Eavha, just get out."

They weren't gentle with her as they hauled her from the cage and got her upright, but nobody hit her. Eaon wasn't sure what he was going to do if they did.

Nobody asked Eaon to do anything; the soldiers holding the pole dragged him out and flung him away from the cart. He couldn't keep his feet, hooking an elbow over the pole to keep from choking.

Cinn moved, just a step, and the crossbow fired.

The scream that rang through the courtyard as the bolt pierced and stuck in Cinn's knee sucked the air from Eaon's lungs.

"No!" Eavha gasped, her knees buckling.

"Do you think we're stupid?" the soldier in charge snapped. "The fox-witch made sure we knew how to handle the three of you. Now, move!"

With a smirk, the man holding Eaon yanked sharply and led the trio to the small room that housed a descending stairwell.

Cinn had to be dragged. Rasping cries echoed as they let his injured leg thump on every step.

Eaon had never been to a human prison before, so he didn't know if they were supposed to smell like that. Like rotting and feces and death, so potent it made the streets above seem like potpourri. The taste of it stuck to the roof of his mouth, making him gag the whole way down.

At the bottom of the stairwell, the hall branched off in two directions. The torches lit intermittently weren't enough to break the crushing darkness, but the smell was worse to the left. To his relief, the guards took them right.

Through a heavy door was a large room lined with small stone-walled cells, empty of even somewhere to put their bodily fluids. A bench with leather restraints was bolted to the middle of the floor, the wood spattered with dark stains and scratch marks.

Eavha and Cinn were taken to adjacent cells, the barred doors letting in the merest fraction of light from the torches in the chamber. Eavha put on a convincing show of crying and pleading as they shoved her in, while Cinn had become pliant again. After dropping him on the ground, one of the guards pulled the bolt from his knee. The scream barely drowned out the wet sound of flesh being torn apart.

Eaon was not put in a cell.

The soldier manning the pole pushed him toward a gibbet,

tall enough for him to stand in but so narrow that once inside he wouldn't be able to move. The bars on the cage had more spellmarks etched into the iron, both outside and in. Eaon got an up close look at them as he was pushed inside and the chafing collar around his neck was finally released, the cage locked behind him.

"Wait here," the soldier in charge sneered before the entire squadron turned around and left.

Once they were gone, Eaon gave the gibbet door a useless shove. The cage was quickly becoming stifling. Pressing his fingers through the narrow gaps in the bars, he focused on taking deep breaths, even though the reek of the chamber made him nauseous.

"Eavha, are you alright?" he asked.

"Yes," she spat. "Though I'm starting to wish I'd just let you die in Wyldeden so I didn't have to be here."

A hiccup of laughter broke the tension riding Eaon's spine.

"How dare you joke at a time like this," he said, grateful she was trying.

"How dare you assume I'm joking."

He smiled shakily, but the jesting died when he looked to Cinn's cell. The kinner had dragged himself to the back corner and curled into himself.

"Cinn, we're going to get out, okay? Keep your chin up."

No response. Not even an acknowledgment he had heard him.

"Cinn," Eavha said softly, crouching by the corner closest to Cinn's cell, twisting her arms to get her chained hands through the gap. If Cinn looked up, he'd be able to see her fingers. "I'm here."

"Eavha's right there," Eaon translated. "You can hold her hand if you want to. You're not alone."

Nothing.

～

Time passed painfully slow; Eaon didn't know how long it had been since they arrived, but it was long enough for the hunger clawing at his insides to become all he could think about. Long enough that he had no choice but to relieve himself standing up in the gibbet again. His body cramped as the hours passed by, unable to stretch or sit. His magic wanted to lash out, but the spellmarks on the hatching around him were an unrelenting pressure on his skin.

The only distraction was Eavha as she sang folk songs from home; a soft, calm melody like a still pond. He clung to the sound of her voice echoing through the chamber like the lifeline it was, trying to measure his breaths to the swell of sound.

When they were kids he had hated listening to her sing. She was going to be a healer and sometimes, when the medicine and the spells didn't work, that meant sitting with someone and trying to ease their suffering while they passed. The songs had been another reminder that she was special and he was useless. But now, he hoped the sound of her voice followed him to the after-realm.

The latch on the door scraped against stone and Eavha fell silent.

Four human guards wearing polished golden chest armor marched in, the same cobalt blue tunics as before underneath. Behind them, a male witch glided in. Even without knowing that Prince Nevan didn't keep other witches in his court, the heavy gold crown molded into interwoven feathers atop his head gave his status away. He stood tall and broad, silver hair curling beneath his pointy chin and watery gray eyes surveying his prisoners with a satisfied smirk.

"A rogue necromancer, a kinner, and a Lover-blessed Anfar witch." Nevan smiled coyly, pacing along the length of the cells. "Sounds like the beginning of a bad joke, but my oh my, the Spirits have truly blessed me today. I will have to reward my little fox handsomely for collecting you all for me."

Eaon bristled, but kept silent.

"As I understand it, the necromancer doesn't know Nirnish and the kinner doesn't speak at all. So, tell me . . ." Nevan stopped in front of Eaon's gibbet. "From one Returned to another, can you see well enough from in there to translate for me?"

"Let me out and I could see better," Eaon answered, ice sliding down his spine. Knowing the Sparrow Royals were Lover-blessed and being face to face with one were very different things.

"Funny," Nevan deadpanned, tilting his head. "I've heard your blessing manifested quite spectacularly. A necrotic touch. Surges that result in mass destruction. Play your cards right and there might be room for you in my court once this is all over."

With perfect aim, Eaon spat between the bars with enough force to land it on Nevan's neck. He was slightly disappointed his spit wasn't necrotic, too.

Nevan grinned, wiping his neck with his sleeve.

"Yes, I would very much like to have you. Until then . . ." Nevan turned away to stand outside Cinn's cell. "Kinner. Stop your pathetic cowering and come here."

Cinn didn't move.

"You want another bolt to the knee?" Nevan cooed.

"Leave him alone," Eaon hissed.

Pick on me. Leave them alone and pick on me.

"Or should I put one in the necromancer and see if she can bring herself back to life?" Nevan's eyes glittered at the idea.

Eaon stiffened, then flinched as Cinn sprang from the corner like a death adder, clawing between the bars an inch from the prince's throat. Nevan howled with laughter, mocking him as Cinn twisted around, trying to give himself that extra inch.

"Oh, dear, my sister really did a number on you, didn't she?"

Cinn dropped his hands, panting hard.

"Yes, I know all about that, too. You can imagine my surprise when my little fox reported that Aisling was keeping a genuine kinner in her dungeon. My ancestors rid the world of your kind a millennium ago, but Aisling... oh, that sly little minx. She should have reported you right away, but she didn't, did she?"

Cinn stood utterly still, eyeing the prince with deadly calm.

"Did you really think it was a coincidence that, after two years, a rebel guard just happened to find you down there? Was it pure luck that Kaelean was wandering exactly where you happened to wash ashore? Just chance that the rogue who found you was a lonely, bored old hag who felt compelled from the goodness of her heart to protect you?"

Nevan's glee was palpable as he watched Cinn's face fall. Stepping back from the cells, Nevan came to gloat to Eaon.

"Was it also a coincidence that she just happened to be in the area where a necromancer and her Returned had set up for the winter?"

Eaon bared his teeth.

"I knew you were coming," Nevan continued. "I wanted you.

I wanted your sister. It took a lot longer for my little fox to get you here than I wanted, but she did it."

"You love listening to yourself talk, don't you?" Eaon snarled.

How did he know? Every molecule of Eaon's brain came alive with the question, running through every possibility at once.

Nevan narrowed his eyes and walked away. For some reason, Eaon's remark had irked the witch.

"Now, kinner, if I know my sister, and I think I do, I'd be willing to bet she spent the first few months trying to court you. Am I correct? She wined and dined you, offering you the world in exchange for your cooperation. But when you turned her down, things got nasty, didn't they?" Nevan's grin returned as Cinn flinched. "Tell me, did she lock you away in solitary confinement before bringing out the toys? I taught her that, you know."

"In my experience," Eaon interrupted, "males who brag about how tough they are tend to be compensating for other . . . shortcomings."

Leave them alone. Pick on me.

Nevan flashed his teeth at Eaon but turned back to Cinn.

"My point is, kinner, that I am much older and much more creative than my sister and I will not waste time trying to court you. You are an abomination to the Balance and you will get what you deserve, rest assured. What you do have control over is how much your friends here suffer for your silence."

Cinn stared at the prince, eyes hard as glaciers.

If anyone moved toward Eavha's cell . . .

The pressure of Eaon's magic beneath his skin was cyclonic, his body nothing but a glass jar trying to contain it. He would beg, if he had to. He would beg Cinn to talk.

"What did Aisling want from you?"

For a heartbeat, the world went black. Cold consumed his body and Eaon had to grit his teeth against the formless claws shredding his chest from the inside out. All around him, the sparks of life his magic craved lit up like stars in the night, but whatever spell the Sparrow witch had used on the gibbet kept it from reaching out. A sharp jab through the bars made him blink back the pain. A soldier had approached, prodding Eaon's chest with a long baton.

Cinn was watching him. There was an eerie vacancy in his eyes.

Unable to unclench his teeth, all Eaon could do was plead silently. Talk. For Eavha, please talk.

Cinn raised his hands and began to sign.

{Know where Kinners are.}

The shock emptied him, the magic easing enough to let him unclench his teeth and suck down a shallow breath.

"She wanted to know where the rest of the Kinners are," Eaon wheezed.

"And do you know where the rest of your kind are?" Nevan asked.

Cinn shook his head, breath hitching. Nevan watched him for a moment before rocking back on his heels, running a thoughtful hand over his jaw.

"You know what? I believe you. Aisling didn't though, did she?"

Cinn shook his head.

"Why does she want to know about the Kinner?"

Cinn shrugged. Again, Nevan waited and Eaon began to sweat, the air in his gibbet too thin.

"A matter for another time, then." Nevan let his hand fall onto the rapier at his waist. "What else?"

Cinn's hands trembled. {Know how the healing works. To study the mark.}

Eaon explained again, even as dizziness made it hard to focus. If he wasn't so constricted he would have collapsed.

Later, he promised his magic, trying to calm it down. To his surprise, it listened and Eaon drew a more satisfying breath as the pressure eased.

"You're being terribly helpful." Nevan narrowed his eyes again.

{No need to keep . . . stories.}

"He has no reason to keep her secrets after what she did," Eaon elaborated.

"True. Why don't you speak? Did she find a way to permanently injure you?"

Cinn shook his head.

Nevan bit his lip as a smile spread across his face.

"Are you afraid, little kinner? Are you afraid that if you let yourself speak, you might give something away?"

Cinn shook his head, but Nevan's grin turned maniacal.

"Liar."

Cinn flinched, signing adamantly.

"He has no reason to lie," Eaon grabbed the bars. "He stopped talking while in confinement and hasn't figured out how to start again since then."

Nevan laughed.

"We'll see. Tormund, have one of the slaves feed the witches. Let the kinner starve. And keep an eye on that one." He pointed at Eaon, then sauntered over to the bench in the middle of the chamber and stroked the wood with grotesque affection. "And kinner? I'm looking forward to our conversation later."

Cinn stood there with his head against the bars, disappearing inside himself again.

Once the guards left and the three of them were alone again, Eavha appeared at her cell door and reached through it for Cinn's hand. Her cheeks were damp, but she smiled as Cinn looked at her.

This time, he took her hand.

CHAPTER 30

AISLING

Aisling had been drinking since noon and had no intention of stopping. The full moon bathed her suite in silver light, glistening off the crystal decanter on the tray beside her as she lounged on a chaise. Her dress and shoes had been discarded as soon as she was behind closed doors, the soft silk of her robe a relief from the heavy layers she wore as a part of her costume.

It was the part of the primping princess, turning her back on her cruel family, that had gotten her more leeway with the mountain clans than she had ever hoped for. Likewise, the ditsy, curious female was the role that had won over the traveler who had come to teach Hyrsch about mining oil to fuel their fires.

The city would thrive for another season. Her people rejoiced.

The victory did nothing to ease the tension in her neck.

"Your Highness?" Edwina said softly as she replaced the empty decanter and brought two fresh goblets. "Nora is here."

"Send her in."

Aisling drained what was left in her glass and handed it to Edwina, immediately pouring the new wine into fresh glasses. Nora's heavy footsteps clacked on the marble as she made her way to the chaise.

"I'm sorry to disturb you at this hour, but you said you wanted to know immediately if there was any news about Nevan." Nora stood stiffly, surveying Aisling's barely concealed nakedness. "Are you drunk?"

"Nora, please. I'm in no mood for your chastising," Aisling sighed, rolling her wrist. "What's my brother up to now?"

Frowning, Nora pulled a slip of parchment from her pocket.

"A spy reported that a squad of his troops escorted three prisoners into the palace dungeons this afternoon, making a big show of it."

"More of his demi-kin murdering antics, I presume." Aisling pursed her lips, but the news was hardly worth disturbing her brooding.

"Shortly after, a letter arrived by crow. It has his seal on it."

Nora passed her the parchment. Sure enough, it had Nevan's blue wax and sparrow seal on top.

Sitting up, Aisling didn't need a letter opener; she slipped one of her sharp nails beneath the wax and sliced it off. The moonlight was enough to read her brother's scratch by, but the words made her eyes blur with rage.

"He has the kinner."

Nora froze.

"Stop our troops from crossing into Anfar immediately."

"Edwina, fetch me some ink," Nora demanded.

Aisling crushed the letter in her fist, head pounding as she tried to figure out how this had happened. Nevan couldn't possibly have chanced upon them. No, there was a tone of intent in his words:

I have your pet. You know what I want.

"Fuck," she spat, hurling the paper across the room.

Nora finished writing a message on a scrap piece of parchment. "Please, get this to Walter as fast as you can and tell him to send it to the bridge."

Edwina nodded, taking the note and darting for the door.

Warily, Nora perched on the edge of the chaise. The wine was heavy in Aisling's head and she had to lean back before she fell from the couch.

"Are you alright?" Nora asked quietly.

"What a ridiculous question."

After giving the princess a moment to collect herself, Nora placed a gentle hand on her shoulder.

"What can I do?"

"Nothing."

"Then, what are *you* going to do?"

Aisling sighed, running her hands down her face. There was too much riding on the information the kinner was hiding to let her brother's pettiness get in the way. To let her own weaknesses be an obstacle.

Levelling a weary look at her Second, Aisling decided on the only course of action she could take.

"I'm going to poison my mother."

CHAPTER 31

CINN

HE KEPT FORGETTING WHERE HE WAS. HIS OLD CELL HAD BEEN different, little more than a hole in the ground with a solid metal hatch door above him. Every now and then he'd blink and realize he hadn't moved in hours, and either Eaon or Eavha were trying to talk to him.

Orchestrated. The whole thing had been orchestrated. He'd been too desperate to see it. Pulled from one nightmare just to be dumped into another.

He couldn't feel his body. Flashes of Hyrsch, of looking down at himself and seeing it dissected, pinned open on the table, feeling Aisling's fingers digging through his organs, his head so full of stimulants he couldn't pass out . . .

Breathe. He couldn't breathe.

The door to the chamber opened and a mental shroud enveloped him.

Distantly, he recognized that it wasn't the prince, or even a guard, who came shuffling into the room. A large witch wearing a raggedy dress and a worn-out cloak, wrists and ankles loosely shackled, carried in a bowl of something steaming. She came to a stop in front of their cells, sad and tired eyes taking in the three of them.

"I'm sorry," she said from beneath the hood of her cloak. "I'm sorry I had to bring you here, but as you can see I could not come to you."

Cinn twitched his fingers, blinking back the shroud. This witch was no threat, though her words confused him.

"My name is Yomra," she continued. "I am from Qiri, above the Northern Mountains."

Eaon gasped, speaking Terranian for Eavha. The old witch waited patiently, nodding as Eavha too gasped, asking a question Cinn couldn't understand.

"Yes, Morvia blessed me many, many centuries ago. Here. Eat, then we can talk."

Yomra came to Cinn first, holding a bowl of steamed dumplings toward him. He looked from the bowl to Yomra, brow heavy with suspicion.

"The others need to see it isn't poisoned," Yomra explained.

She knew what he was, then.

Reaching through the bars, he took one of the dumplings and sniffed at it. Nibbled at the edge. It didn't make his gut churn the way the tangerine had, so he took a second one and nodded.

Eaon told Eavha it was safe, so she took some and broke a few down so Yomra would be able to pass them through the space between the bars around Eaon.

"Listen carefully," Yomra said, her voice low. "I have been cursed so that if I speak prophecy to anyone besides Prince Nevan, I will die. Again, I'm sorry. Giving him the information he needed to bring you all here was the hardest decision of my life, but I had to speak with each of you. There will not be much time once I begin."

"Wait, what?" Eaon asked. "No, you—"

"It is why I am here. It is why I asked Kaelean to play spy for the prince when she failed to rescue me. The fox and I have known each other for centuries; the royal prick is an imbecile for thinking someone so powerful bows to him."

Cinn put his head against the bars and closed his eyes. He didn't know what to think anymore.

"It won't be long after I'm gone that she will arrive. She brings the key."

Yomra put the bowl down on the stained table and looked around at the three of them. Cinn was sure his face was as painfully perplexed as Eaon's was.

"Look at the three of you," the witch said with a sad affection, putting a hand to her chest. "I will pass with honor knowing I got the chance to meet you.

"Yomra, please, what—" Eaon began to ask, but fell silent as the witch pushed back her hood, revealing the stark white constellation tattooed on her forehead. As she began to speak, the stars glittered like diamond.

"Eaon Nemuse." Her voice took on a hollow quality, eyes clouding over. "Soon, you will have all the pieces you need to save them all. You are exactly who you need to be. Stop fighting it."

Immediately, Yomra began to age. Her bright hair turned ashen, back bowing under a crippling weight.

"Eavha Nemuse. You have forgotten where your strength truly comes from. Start again, but be aware. Power corrupts. Trust yourself."

Yomra's skin began to flake off her body, which was withering down to bone.

"Ryson Tacenda."

Cinn flinched at the sound of his true name.

"Go to Ahrenhale. Find Moyra Thorne. She has the answers."

As if struck by a strong wind, Yomra disintegrated into dust and blew across the stone floor.

"Did that just happen?" Eaon whispered.

Cinn nodded, then shook his head. If he was being honest, he wasn't convinced he hadn't hallucinated the entire thing.

The door slammed open.

A male witch came barreling in, throwing the door shut behind him just as a terrible growl reverberated into the room. He was tall with a dark braid down his back, barefoot and dressed in simple brown leather that couldn't hide the definition in his body. A long wooden staff tipped with a stone spearhead was in one hand, a chain with a key on the end in the other.

"Dearmead?!" Eavha screeched.

She and the new witch exchanged rapid, panicked conversation as he fit the key into her cell door. The key unlocked the shackles on her ankles and wrists, too. As soon as she was free, Eavha flung herself at him and began sobbing.

The new witch soothed her, glancing to the gibbet. Eaon told them something, and Eavha promptly took the key and came to release Cinn.

"Cinn, I'm going to need your help for a minute," Eaon explained, something wild and slightly panicked in his voice.

Dearmead watched Cinn stoically as Eavha released him and gave him the key. When the door to the gibbet swung open, Eaon sagged and Cinn had to grab a hold of him to stop him from collapsing on the floor. His skin burned like acid, tendrils of magic brushing over Cinn, looking for weakness.

"Give me a second," Eaon wheezed, face slicked with sweat.

Cinn glanced to the door, listening to the sounds seeping into the room. He knew that growl. Knew what was waiting for them in the hall. Pulling Eaon's arm over his shoulder, Cinn raised his chin at the door.

Dearmead argued, pointing at Eaon, then at the door. Eavha put her hands on his chest, trying to calm him even as she argued over the top of him.

"Give me another second," Eaon grunted, forcing his legs to support him.

Bouncing on the balls of his feet, Cinn had to resist the urge to run. He made another sweep of the room, but whatever weapons the prince used to torture his prisoners weren't kept in the chamber. Cinn would have to earn one again.

Once Eaon was ready, the four of them headed for the door. Dearmead took the lead, spear poised, red glistening on the stone. The hall was just as dark as before, but now growling, ripping and screaming echoed so loudly the walls shook. Eavha froze and Cinn signed quickly: {Kaelean's wolf.}

His knee still ached as they climbed the steps to the courtyard above. When they pushed open that final door, they were greeted with a slaughter field.

Half a dozen mangled bodies lay in pieces across the span of the paved courtyard, those still with faces frozen in desperate denial. Kaelean's lupine form was tearing out the throat of another guard, deep gauges in her scaly hide. The moonless night made it hard to see if she had any other injuries.

"That is not a wolf," Eaon breathed.

More guards were racing towards them, swords already drawn

as they crossed under the stone archway, fanning out to block the exits. One noticed the witches and Cinn standing stupidly by the stairwell.

"Stop them!"

{Stay with Eavha,} Cinn signed before running for the nearest attacker.

The man swung his sword for Cinn's legs, clearly not knowing who he faced. Cinn dived over the arc of the blade and tackled the guard. Stupid, but not slow, the guard drew a dagger and stuck it in Cinn's side. Gritting his teeth, he ignored the bite and punched the guard in the throat. It stunned him long enough for Cinn to pull out the dagger from his side and plunge it into the Pirevian's neck, taking his sword as he stood.

Behind him, Dearmead was a weapon unto himself. He swung the staff so quickly most of the humans didn't have a chance to consider dodging, only using the spear tip as a last resort. The cracking of ribs and legs filled the courtyard. It would be more efficient if Dearmead aimed for their heads—the force of the blow would cave in their skulls, killing them—but the witch only left a trail of broken bodies in his wake. For the most part, anyway.

Cinn ran to where Eaon had put Eavha against the wall, shielding her with his own deadly skin. The kinner gave her the dagger, quickly corrected her grip, took three seconds to show her how to get the best use out of it, before turning to parry the sword of a guard who'd been trying to sneak up on them.

The courtyard was filling with more and more soldiers. Every time Cinn thought he saw a way out, a fresh batch of guards came running in. He remembered the road of blood and the hours it had taken to get through the city streets. It should be deserted at this dark hour, but it would still take them too long to fight their way to the city gate.

"Cinn!" Eaon shouted. "Take Eavha and run!"

Frowning, he barely blocked a sword swinging for his head.

Then he felt it.

The air crackled with power and Eavha screamed, clambering away from her brother. Cinn raced to cut down a guard who'd moved to grab her, spraying blood over her face, but she didn't seem to care. Her shouting at Eaon drew the attention of the others. There wasn't time to hesitate. Kaelean bit Dearmead's braid and pulled the witch away as he turned toward Eaon, eyes widening. Cinn grabbed Eavha's arm and roughly dragged her, grunting as a throwing knife imbedded itself in his shoulder.

When the first wave of magic pulsed through the courtyard, the guards stopped. A few of them groaned, grabbing their heads as they stumbled back.

Another bitter, magical pulse. The entire courtyard took a step back.

"RETREAT!"

The clipped screams of people who couldn't move fast enough weren't only from guards and soldiers; Cinn passed a number of courtiers and servants on the way to the palace gates, their wide eyes following the fleeing witches in startled confusion. Their agonized screams chased after him, cut short by a chilling silence.

The sky was graying as they reached the gates. Kaelean bounded over it in a single leap, and neither Dearmead or Eavha hesitated before scaling the wrought-iron bars.

Cinn skidded to a stop. Eaon's surges could be huge, and beyond the gates lay a city of sleeping civilians. For a split second, he thought of his siblings. They still lived in a city just like this, back in Oford.

Turning around, he tried not to look at the piles of dust that he knew just moments ago had been people. The clouds were turning purple as the sun rose higher. If all the screaming hadn't woken people living nearby, the morning soon would.

As he reached the courtyard, Cinn expected to find Eaon curled up on the ground, writhing in pain.

He wasn't.

Eaon stood, staring vacantly across the yard, lips parted. The witch blinked when he noticed Cinn, pupils dilated.

"I stopped fighting it." His eyelids fluttered as he turned his face up to the sky. "I can feel them. It's so . . . pure."

{Stop,} Cinn signed, his skin crawling, organs twisting. The desire to sleep descended heavily.

Eaon shuddered in ecstasy, a fresh pulse of magic sweeping through the courtyard. Gritting his teeth, Cinn lunged forward and grabbed Eaon's face.

Something cold and vicious tunneled inside him and Eaon dropped, as if every bone in his body had liquefied. Cinn went down with him.

For a moment, he couldn't see. Couldn't breathe, or feel, or hear. Then the pain crashed into him, washing out the darkness. He couldn't bear it. His body lay on the cusp of decomposing as the two powers inside him warred.

Eaon's magic depleted slowly, retreating bitterly from the battle it couldn't win. Even once the enormous outpouring was over, the point of contact between him and Eaon still tingled.

Weakly, Cinn reached over and checked Eaon's pulse. It was slow but it was there.

Rolling away, Cinn closed his eyes. Was this ever going to stop?

Conquer this, and you will be unstoppable.

A fingertip pressed against his forehead.

Five seconds. He gave himself five seconds to wallow in self-pity.

Then he got up.

Eaon's dead weight was too much for Cinn; the best he could do was grab him under the arms and drag him through the courtyard. They had to get out of there before the sun could get much higher and people began to wake.

Eavha, Dearmead and Kaelean were rushing back through the gates just as Cinn reached them.

"Eaon," Eavha cried, twisting her skirt in her fists.

Kaelean had shifted back. Cinn bared his teeth and snarled.

"I'm not the enemy right now," she said clearly.

Cinn put Eaon down and picked up another sword laying near a pile of dust. Dearmead's staff whistled through the air, slapping Cinn's wrist hard enough to make him drop the weapon.

"Can we do this once we're out of the city?" Kaelean snapped.

A bell started ringing.

Cinn snarled once more, but moved to pick up Eaon again. After letting Kaelean wrap Eaon's bare feet in one of her furs as protection, Dearmead looped his staff under Eaon's knees, using his body to counterweight Eaon's core so they could carry the unconscious witch properly.

Outside the palace gates, the bloody road was coated in ash.

CHAPTER 32

EAVHA

IT WENT AGAINST EVERY INSTINCT TO FOLLOW KAELEAN DOWN a set of stone stairs and into what she called a "basement apartment," but Eavha didn't see that they had much of a choice. The cobblestones had bruised her feet, Eaon was unconscious, both Dearmead and Kaelean were bleeding, and Cinn looked on the verge of a mental breakdown. So, once again, they followed the rogue.

Small, frosted-glass windows lined the very top of the walls, letting soft filtered light into the apartment. The floor was covered in rugs of varying tones of greens and browns, as if trying to replicate the forest floor, and instead of furniture there were piles of furs, blankets and pillows to nest in. The only remotely civilized aspects of the open room were the hot plate and wash trough in the corner that Eavha presumed was supposed to be a kitchen, and the large tub and latrine in the opposite corner.

Cinn and Dearmead set Eaon down, both of them sinking to the ground and panting heavily. Shaking from the effort, Cinn dragged Eaon onto a pile of cushions and propped up his head before laying down on the rugs and closing his eyes.

Kaelean ignored all of them, stripping out of her furs as she limped to the tub. Grabbing a cloth from the floor to stem the bleeding from her thigh, she turned a metal knob and water started pouring from a spout over the bath.

The silence felt fragile. Shock was setting in, so Eavha did what she did best. She went to the pile of clean cloths on the floor, ignoring Kaelean, and took two. One she dampened under the tap, then took both over to Dearmead.

"Where are you hurt?" she asked quietly.

Dearmead forced his gaze away from Eaon and blinked. Dropping the spear, he started unlacing his leather sleeves, then his shirt, peeling them away to expose the myriad of cuts still oozing blood. Crouching beside him, she did her best not to stare at the physique she had once so openly admired, focusing on cleaning the wounds.

"The leather's not enough against royal weapons," she commented, just for a respite from the smothering silence.

"No." Dearmead's voice cracked and he winced as she pressed on a particularly deep cut. At least the wounds were starting to clot.

"Did I thank you?"

"Yes, you did," he said, a small smile pulling at his lips as he watched her work. "I've missed your gentle hands."

Eavha's face burned and she scowled furiously at him. "Don't flirt with me."

He flinched. "I wasn't . . ."

"What are you even doing here, Dearmead?" she asked, unable to keep the awe and accusation from her tone. "How did you . . ."

Dearmead sighed deeply, hanging his head. "It's a long story, and I'd rather not tell it twice. If he'll even listen to me." His gaze swept back to where Eaon lay, Cinn pale and blank faced beside him. "Is he alright? Are you?"

"No."

Kaelean hissed loudly from the tub as she sunk her body into the water.

"That's not a good idea," Eavha called out.

"Do you know much about shape-shifting, child?"

"No, but—"

"Then be quiet."

Eavha jutted out her chin. The rogue could bleed to death; she'd deserve it.

But her voice had pulled Cinn out of his trance. Springing to his feet, fists clenched, he took a few steps toward the witch. The way he held himself . . . Eavha couldn't help but think of how he'd looked wielding that horrible sword. The way he'd braced his lithe body to compensate for the weapon's obvious weight, and the cold fury in his eyes as he'd cut men open like sacks of grain. Her heart stuck in her throat as she tried to blink the image away.

Kaelean snapped at Cinn, making him stop. Dearmead had tensed, slowly reaching for his staff, but Eavha took his wrist.

"Let them sort it out," she told him.

"She saved your lives."

"She's also the one who put them in danger in the first place." Eavha scowled, but softened as Dearmead mimicked her. "You didn't know. How do you even know Kaelean? How—"

"I'd done a perfectly good job of sneaking through the city, all the way inside the palace walls, just to find this rogue strangling the guards at the prison entrance. She sniffed at me, then called me by my name." Dearmead shook his head in bewilderment. "We were spotted and she just grinned, threw the keys at me and told me to get you out. She would hold them back. It seemed insane, but . . . she was there to help you too, and I didn't think an ally would be a bad thing."

Eavha sighed. "Kaelean appears to be a very complicated witch."

Most of the cuts on Dearmead weren't too bad; the kind of thing she should have been able to heal with the brush of a hand. If she had to resort to a needle and thread, she was going to lose it. Nudging the kernel of magic inside her to see if it would respond again, she nearly cried when she felt it stir. Rousing it a little more urgently, she laid a hand over one of the deeper wounds and offered her intentions to Sanni.

Please, let me heal him.

The Spirit took her offering without hesitation. She had to focus more than she was used to and the process was much slower, but as she rested her hand over each wound the clean edges stitched back together, leaving a pink scar behind.

Shaking and exhausted, she sat back to admire her handiwork. Sloppy, but better than nothing.

Cinn made a snort of disgust, snagging her attention in time to see him make a gesture at the witch that didn't need interpreting. Kaelean sunk deeper into the water, glaring across the room.

"He really is a kinner?" Dearmead frowned.

"You've heard of them?"

"Eaon used to tell me stories. Myths."

"Apparently not." She looked to Cinn, who was giving Dearmead a stern appraisal. She made herself smile, making one of the few signs she knew. {Safe.}

Cinn crossed his arms and came to take back the knife he'd given her, then stood by the door in another of his silent vigils. He was doing what he knew how to do, just like her.

"I didn't want to believe he could really do that," Dearmead said softly, looking at Eaon again. "I saw the meadow, but—"

"He can't control it," Eavha snapped. "He didn't grow up learning how to live with power like we did, let alone a foreign magic he has no business having. When he realizes people have died . . . wait, you saw the meadow?"

Dearmead nodded. "Later, I promise. There's a lot I have to tell you both."

He reached for his leathers, but Eavha stopped him. "Lie down. Get some rest. You look like you could use it."

Dearmead nodded, keeping his eyes down as he found a pile of blankets across the room to ease into. Eavha went to Kaelean next, who was still soaking in the pinkish water of the tub.

"Would you like some help?"

"Will you give it to me?" Kaelean asked, the words laced with hostility.

"Not if you keep talking to me like I'm the one who did something wrong." Eavha crossed her arms and raised an eyebrow.

The old witch sat stoically, refusing to meet Eavha's stare.

"Your friend told us you weren't really working with that prince."

Kaelean's lip curled. "Despite what you think of me, until today I had never killed a person. Animals and fae and beasts, yes, but not a person. Eaon is not the only one who will mourn what they have done today. And yet, if his power has reached Nevan I will not pray for the prince's safe arrival in the Lover's realm. Let him rot in the in-between for what he did to Yomra."

The pain in Kaelean's trembling voice had nothing to do with her wounds. Eavha perched on the edge of the tub and grabbed a clean cloth.

"Show me your leg."

Kaelean's brow creased, but she turned to her side and raised her hip out of the water enough for Eavha to inspect it.

"I won't thank you for betraying us, but I will thank you for coming back," she said, letting a tendril of magic check the cuts for anything insidious.

"Was it worth it?" Kaelean asked, closing her eyes.

Eaon had explained what the prince had told them—about how everything from Cinn's escape to finding them in Anfar had been orchestrated by Kaelean so she could bring them to Nevan. Bring them to Yomra, so they could receive their prophecies. She had lied, betrayed them, fought and killed, and now the witch wanted to know if it had been worth it.

"I don't know," Eavha answered honestly. "I don't understand Nirnish and Eaon didn't have time to translate what she told us before we were escaping. But, honestly? You wouldn't have done all this if you doubted her. Clearly Yomra thought it was worth her life, so we have to trust that it was."

"I'm sorry," Dearmead interrupted, sitting up from the pile of blankets. "I can't keep pretending I can't hear you. Who is Yomra? What happened?"

Kaelean's skin had pulled back together and Eavha slid from the tub to the floor, resting her sweaty forehead against the cool porcelain. Between breaths, she begun to explain what had happened in the dungeon.

"Wait," Dearmead held up a hand. "So, you knew you needed to get Eavha and Eaon here, but how did you even know when and where they would be? Nobody could have . . . Wait. Wait, you were the rogue, weren't you? The one who tore a hole in Wyldeden."

Eavha stilled, and Kaelean's eyes narrowed to black slits.

"Call me that again, boy, and you'll lose your tongue."

"They're called unbound witches," Eavha explained.

"I'm sorry. I didn't know."

Kaelean hummed, then rose from the tub and pulled the plug from the drain. Eavha watched in fascination as the water was sucked into a hole.

"But you are the witch who came through, aren't you?" Dearmead pushed.

"Yes," Kaelean admitted, drying herself off. "I used a witchmark to cut into Wyldeden. I watched the Nemuses for a while, trying to discern how I might get them out. Seems I didn't need to do anything at all. They were quite capable of getting themselves thrown out. Then it was just the timing of things. The kinner wasn't strong enough to move through winter, and too broken to cope with coming here, so I let him recoup."

"Did you bring the blight to our people?" Dearmead asked, tone heavy with accusation.

"What blight?" Kaelean frowned.

Eavha had stopped listening. "You can use witchmarks?"

One of Kaelean's wicked, cocky grins spread across her face. She opened her mouth to speak, but a groan from across the room drew everybody's attention.

Eaon held his ribs as he rolled onto his back. "Ow."

"Eaon." Eavha jumped to her feet and rushed to his side. "Are you alright?"

He grunted, opened his eyes to look around, then closed them again.

"You're going to feel terrible for a while. Rest." She almost reached out to touch him. Even after all this time, it was still an effort to remember.

"I . . . what did I . . ." He blinked his eyes open again, the edge of panic creeping in.

"Shh, it's okay."

Kaelean came and crouched beside Eaon, pity marking her face as she dripped water all over the floor. "When you are ready, we will pray. But rest knowing you saved our lives."

He closed his eyes again, chin wobbling as he turned back onto his side and pressed himself into the pillows. Eavha left him to do what he needed to do; there weren't words to comfort him.

"I need to sleep," Kaelean announced. "Use the bath if you wish."

She sauntered off to a pile of well-worn furs and nestled into them, covering herself until she was nearly invisible.

Eavha and Dearmead both went to the tub. Too tired to worry about modesty, realising Dearmead probably didn't care anyway, she stripped down and ran the water to clean the filth off her.

"Let me help." Dearmead dampened a cloth.

Eavha set her jaw. "I can manage."

"Please, Eavha. I owe you."

Eavha wasn't sure how to answer that without starting a fight, and she didn't have the energy to get into one. Dearmead stepped behind her and gently coiled up her hair, cleaning the skin on the back of her neck and shoulders while she wiped down her legs.

"Is it alright to leave the kinner on watch?"

"He's inclined to do it whether anybody wants him to or not. But if you mean whether we can trust him while we sleep, then yes. I would and have trusted Cinn with my life for more than a month now. He's a friend."

She could feel the tension between them thickening as he cleaned her back. Whatever Dearmead's problem was, Eavha wasn't having any of it.

"He was there for us when no one else was," she added.

Dearmead's hand stilled. Glancing over her shoulder, there was shame lining his eyes.

"Tell me," she continued as she recalled Eaon's grief these past months. "Do you not trust Cinn because you don't know him, or because he's close with Eaon?"

Dearmead's eye twitched, looking over to where Eaon had passed out again. "How close?"

Eavha shrugged. Partly to annoy him, but partly because she truly didn't know.

"He told you about . . ."

"Yes," she said sharply. "And he vacillates between feeling guilty for having asked such a thing of you, and feeling guilty for how devastated and angry he is. I've told him to stop, repeatedly. After everything that happened, he had every reason to believe in you."

"I had—"

"I don't care, so don't waste your speeches on me." She sniffed and rose from the tub.

Dearmead leaned back, gaping at her; she had never been like this with him before. Her days of seeking his affection were over.

Leaving her soiled rags on the floor, she made her way to a pile of blankets and curled up underneath them. For the first time since before winter, she was inside, safe and warm. As the blankets soothed her aching muscles, she covered her mouth to bury the sound of her sudden crying.

More than ever, she just wanted to go home.

CHAPTER 33

EAON

EAON WAS VAGUELY AWARE OF BEING MADE TO SIT UP. OF A quiet voice telling him to open his mouth, and of being fed. Given water. He didn't have the energy to open his eyes.

He felt the cool change against his skin as his clothes were removed and something soft and warm was placed over him. Forcing his eyelids to crack, he took note of Cinn and Eavha around him. He went back to sleep.

Running water.

Opening his eyes this time was easier, though his body still felt leaden. Dearmead was crouched by the hot plate in the corner, working on something with Eavha. His sister looked clean—damp hair twisted up into a knot and wearing a fresh dress. The skirt was thick and went all the way to the ground, the bodice covering from her neck to her wrists. It was a simple dress, but the deep emerald color suited her.

Cinn crouched down into Eaon's line of sight, also wearing fresh clothes in the city fashion. Brown leather pants and an ill-fitting dark-blue shirt with a deep V down the front, tied closed with leather laces.

{You need to clean,} Cinn signed slowly.

Eaon nodded, letting Cinn help him sit up. He couldn't be bothered wondering too hard about where they were as he staggered on shaky legs to the bath. Cinn kept him steady as he climbed into the water.

Warm water. Eaon closed his eyes and sighed as it pulled the ache from his body. Relief, almost a bliss, washed through him . . .

"No," he croaked, sitting up sharply and scrambling for the edge of the tub. He knew that bliss. The overwhelming sensation as pure energy passed through him. He was killing them again.

Cinn put a gentle hand on Eaon's chest and pressed him back into the water. Eavha and Dearmead had stopped, watching Eaon warily.

They were fine.

So many other people were not.

{I killed them,} he signed, eyes burning.

Cinn bit his lip. {I killed too. Kaelean killed. Dearmead killed.}

Eaon had enough room in his head to flinch at that, but it wasn't the same. He had killed hundreds of innocent people. Had felt their lives winking out as his power touched them.

{It felt good,} he admitted. {I lost my mind to it. I liked it.}

Cinn grimaced, leaning his elbows on the side of the tub as he met Eaon's miserable gaze. Even with his limited vocabulary, he was trying. {I don't know about magic, but I know you. You are not bad.}

Stop fighting it.

He'd heard Yomra's words echo in that moment in the courtyard and he would never forgive himself for listening to them. The pain had gone, but he'd rather fight it for the rest of his life than kill anybody ever again.

Perhaps that was exactly Cinn's point.

{Thank you.} Eaon gave a small nod before resting his head against the lip of the tub and closing his eyes.

Kaelean had been venturing out into the city, first as a fox to find out the state of things, then as herself, albeit in a human disguise. Eaon hadn't been able to stop staring when she'd come back to her den with her hair untangled and braided into a coronet, wearing a dress like Eavha's. Kaelean's was a gaudy orange color designed to distract the humans from her aura and empty black eyes.

She'd brought back food and some more clothes for Eaon; pants like the other males, a long-sleeved charcoal shirt as well as a heavy cloak, socks and boots. At the bottom of the bag, he found a pair of snug-fitting supple leather gloves. Eyes wide, he looked up at her in gratitude. She nodded solemnly, lacking her usual cockiness.

"How long have I been sleeping?" Eaon asked as he pulled the socks onto his feet.

"It's been three days. We need to leave before the inquisition party arrives from Dusarn. Do you feel ready?" Kaelean asked.

He didn't, but he nodded.

Aside from food, clothes and information, Kaelean had also gotten supplies that Eavha had requested. She and Dearmead had been brewing a tonic to combat his fatigue, feeding it to him while he slept.

Dearmead.

He could barely look at Dearmead.

"Once we are out of the city we need to get back to Anfar," Kaelean continued. "The Sparrows won't risk following us in there. Before we cross the border though, we need to find time to talk. There's no time now, but I don't trust the trees in Anfar not to listen."

The witches all nodded, and after Eaon translated in sign for Cinn, he nodded too. It was still deeply unsettling to know that Kaelean knew Nirnish and had been eavesdropping on them the whole time. Listening in on conversations Eaon had thought were private.

They feasted on the bread and cheese, fruits and vegetables that Kaelean had brought. No meats. As if even Kaelean was making an effort to appease the Mother.

Remembering why she might feel the need to atone made it difficult to swallow the soft bread in his throat. His struggle didn't go unnoticed. Kaelean waited for him to get himself together, then shifted around until she was on her knees, bowing her head low and offering up her palms.

"Mother forgive me," she started.

Eaon knelt down as well. Dearmead and Eavha followed suit, joining in the Prayer of Forfeiture. The origin of the prayer was unknown, but most clans he'd met used it as punishment for serious crimes that didn't quite deserve excommunication. During his travels, he'd seen witches make the offering and be struck down on the spot.

"I offer my life and soul forfeit, if it be your will," he said, holding his breath as he waited for the cold. All four witches looked around to see if any of them would pass.

Nothing happened.

That afternoon, they packed for the journey. Kaelean had kept the bags she'd brought their food and clothes in, and they repacked them with canteens of water, dried fruits, and small weapons she had hidden around the den. Cinn had slipped the soldier's dagger into his boot. The idea was that they would look like a group of shoppers preparing for the public memorial dedicated to the victims of the "mysterious blight" that had struck the palace and surrounding streets.

"You'll have to leave the spear," Kaelean told Dearmead.

"No."

"We can't be seen lugging a weapon like that through the streets."

"Yeah, it's not exactly subtle," Eavha agreed.

"I'm not leaving it." Dearmead's grip tightened on the staff as he narrowed his eyes.

They didn't understand what the spear meant to him. The way it had been carved specifically for him, to hone Dearmead's power when he used it. It had taken him weeks to craft it. Eaon had sat beside him in their secret hiding place—a cavern behind a waterfall near the guardian training barracks—sharpening the stones for

Dearmead when the carving dulled them. Compared to the wands made in Bernt the staff was rudimentary at best, but Dearmead had put his blood into the wood. He would not abandon it.

"Take the spear head off and let me use it as a walking stick," Eaon suggested, keeping his eyes on his boots. The strangeness of having his feet covered in conjunction with the lingering weakness from his surge made him unstable. Having something to lean on wouldn't hurt.

Eavha raised her brow, looking between Eaon and Dearmead as an awkward silence filled the den. It was the first time he had spoken to Dearmead since Wyldeden. But as the tension lingered, Dearmead began to unbind the spearhead from his staff. The stone went in one of the shopping bags before he passed the staff to Eaon.

He'd held Dearmead's staff before, but this time he felt an energy pulse up through his hand, turning the weapon into an extension of his arm. The wood hummed with power as he lowered the end of it to the ground, leaning on it to keep his balance.

Everybody was staring.

"Can you feel that?" he asked them.

"Yeah, we are not going to be able to walk down the street without drawing attention. You might as well have 'witch' tattooed on your forehead." Eavha dragged her hands down her face.

"Jealous?" Eaon poked his tongue out, purposefully ignoring the way Dearmead was still staring at him.

"Low blow, rogue." She gestured vulgarly, amusement pulling her mouth into a smile.

It only lasted a moment.

"We take the back streets," Kaelean said sternly. "Don't walk too fast and keep your mouths shut."

Picking up a shopping bag, she gave each of them a pointed look before leading them back into Pirevia.

Aside from the odd glance in their direction, the group went mostly unnoticed. Kaelean and Eaon faked idle chatter about the theaters being closed for the memorial and the inconvenience of losing all that gold she'd bet on the last hunt they'd had.

The farther they got from the palace the dirtier the streets were until even Kaelean pulled the hood of her cloak up. They kept to the shadows as inconspicuously as they could, but the people who lived in this area weren't used to seeing strangers.

Eavha tugged on Kaelean's sleeve and raised her chin in the direction of two women across the road who had stopped washing their clothes in the trough out the front of their house to watch the witches, deep frowns on their faces.

"Oh! My boot," Kaelean complained loudly, stopping to crouch.

Eaon took a canteen of water from one of the bags and made a show of taking a long drink.

Normal. They were normal city folk, just passing by. Even Cinn shook out his feet and sighed dramatically.

The women muttered to each other and went back to their work. Eaon returned the canteen, sweat dripping down his back. They were close. A few more minutes and they would reach the alley Kaelean said ran around the circumference of the city, heavily patrolled by guards.

Slipping between two compact buildings, they skulked in the

shadows until a patrol passed by, disappearing around the bend. All four witches abandoned their shoes as they silently darted across the alley to face the enormous stone wall. Cloaks went into the bags and Eavha tore the skirt of her dress at the knees. Eaon watched as she and Dearmead found cracks in the stone, hoisting themselves up and quickly scaling the wall.

The shame of being too tired to climb was an ugly feeling, and he pushed it far down inside himself as he retrieved the canister of soil Kaelean had stashed in one of the bags. She hastily drew spellmarks over her face, rolled her shoulder and began to shift. Eaon had never seen her do it, his eyes widening as her body turn to clay.

Lupanis. A common beast of the northern territory with an appetite for fresh meat. He'd encountered one when he'd stayed with the Northern Mountain Clan and had hoped to never see one again.

Cinn loaded up on bags before climbing onto the back of the lupanis, scrunching his face as he clenched his knees and tightly gripped the loose reptilian skin. Kaelean crouched back on her haunches and leaped in an impressive vertical arc, claws sinking into the stone like butter.

Shuddering, Eaon kept an eye on the road and waited for Kaelean to come back. Between him and Cinn, Eaon knew staying alone in the alley for a few minutes was the better choice, but it didn't stop his heart from trying to beat its way through his ribs.

A little farther down the cobblestone path, a woman appeared from the shadows. Eaon recognized her and swore as she pointed in his direction. Two guards emerged beside her.

His grip tightened on the staff, but he was unskilled. Dearmead had taken it upon himself to teach Eaon to defend himself, but it wouldn't be enough against those heavy steel blades.

Kaelean dropped to the ground beside him and growled viciously at the guards, who shouted for reinforcements. Eaon threw a cloak over Kaelean's back and was careful not to let his feet touch her skin as he climbed atop her. His hands felt clumsy in the gloves, but he tucked the staff under his arm and held on as Kaelean readied herself for another leap.

"Oh, shit," he gasped as Kaelean jumped. Seeing the speed and power of the lupanis was one thing, but feeling the muscles beneath the skin coil and harden, the air whip his face as they flew through it, was an entirely different matter. Digging his knees in tighter, he sent a silent prayer to the Lover—*Please, not yet.*

At the top of the wall, Eaon could see Eavha and Dearmead making their descent. Cinn crouched in the muddy bog below, knife drawn as he surveyed the vast space between them and the cliff.

"We need to move!" Eaon called out to them.

To their right, the city gates were being opened. Guards were spilling onto the bridge.

Kaelean dropped and Eaon nearly screamed at the sudden freefall. Mud splattered them as she landed, and Eaon quickly slid off. Despite the stress lining Cinn's eyes, his mouth was tight with suppressed laughter.

"Never again," Eaon gasped.

Eavha and Dearmead dropped to the ground and quickly redistributed the bags before running for the cliffs. Guards on horseback were racing across the bridge to cut them off while others were diving into the mud to chase them on foot.

Kaelean sprinted ahead and peeled off, snarling at the guards drawing bows and arrows.

They were not going to make it.

A flash of movement to his left.

Eaon whipped his head around and spotted a spindly figure running alongside him among the reeds. She had green skin, swamp-silk hair and a tiny glowing pixie on her shoulder. She caught his eye and grinned toothily, crooking a finger at him before darting suddenly to the side.

The air split as an arrow flew by his ear and sunk into the mud a few feet ahead.

Eaon whistled sharply, then turned to follow the nymph.

Without hesitation, the others followed him.

CHAPTER 34

EAON

The thick bog came to a crest and gave way to a shallow fen. Tiny faces peered out at them from behind shrubs and reeds, their large, shiny, black eyes tracking every movement. The guards and riders still chased them, slowed by the mud, but their aim true. Kaelean had a number of arrows sticking out of her hide, but they didn't seem to be slowing her down. In fact, Eaon thought she was putting herself in their line of fire on purpose.

Ahead, the nymph Eaon had followed leaped over a line of mossy rocks and large mushrooms, disappearing from sight.

No, not a line.

Slowing to a stop, Eaon realised the stones and fungus made an enormous circle. A faerie circle.

"Wait."

Eavha sprinted past him and skipped over the rocks, vanishing.

"Of course," Eaon groaned, chasing after her.

Dearmead and Cinn were right behind him, but Kaelean skidded to a stop and growled.

Inside the faerie circle was a haven of mangroves, the water deepening significantly. Crouched on the roots of the trees were dozens of nymphs, many with pixies the size of his thumb perched on their shoulders or hovering nearby. Standing in water up to her knees, glaring at them with cloudy white eyes, was a swamp hag. Even hunched over, she had to be seven feet tall with long, double-jointed limbs disproportionate to her body. Cloaked in pond scum, hair matted with reeds the same colour as her sagging skin, and baring needlelike fangs at them, she took a lurching step forward.

None of them so much as breathed as the nymph Eaon had followed scurried to the hag, chattering quietly.

Another arrow shot past them and buried itself in the water. Eaon looked back to see the guards cresting the hill.

Kaelean growled once more before stepping over the faerie ring, snarling and exposing her canines at the hag.

The guards came to a stop.

"Fuck. *Fuck*," one of them cussed, putting an arm out to hold back another before he could tumble across the line.

"They can't see us," Eavha whispered.

Eaon hissed silently at her and held a finger to his lips.

The third guard to arrive drew another arrow, aiming blindly into the swamp, but the first guard grabbed his arm and lowered it.

"You want to deal with whatever's on the other side?" he snapped, taking a wary step back.

All around them, the fae were gathering. Watching. Daring the humans to step over the line. The hag rose up to her full height, clutching a warped wooden staff in her hand.

"No harm," Eaon whispered, wracking his brain for what little Fae he knew how to speak.

His father had taught him a long time ago. He'd also told him to stay away from the Old Ones.

If you ever see a golem, a hag or a troll, any of those old kind of fae, just run. Run, and never return to that place. Iron and silver won't work and they have more magic than most witches will ever know. They never forget a scent. If they hunt you down, you'll be lucky if they just kill you.

More guards were arriving, one stepping out from the crowd with a scowl.

"Don't, Marcus. It's sacred."

Marcus sneered and, with a deliberate kick, broke the circle.

The magic veiling the swamp fell.

A symphony of hair-splitting screeches burst Eaon's eardrums as every faerie in the fen began screaming. The hag's howl of fury weakened the bladders of more than a few of the guards, who turned around and ran. The rest raised their weapons.

The hag aimed her staff at them. Mangrove roots snaked through the water, twisting around the ankles of the trespassers and dragged them beneath the surface. Nymphs pelted the men with rocks while the pixies swarmed, stealing arrows from quivers, untying shoelaces and poking men in the eyes with their tiny fists. Kaelean raced into the fray and tackled down the first horse cresting the hill.

Marcus grinned and raised his sword.

Dearmead lunged for Eaon, grabbing the staff still in his hand and raised it just in time to block the blade swinging for Eaon's head. The metal sunk into the wood, but it did not break. Eaon felt the injury to the staff in his very bones, stirring up the silky cold that lived inside him.

Dearmead hissed and dropped the staff, shaking his hand as his palm blackened.

Marcus swung again, and this time Eaon swung back. Deflecting the blow aimed for Dearmead, Eaon spun and slammed the wood into the guard's side.

Magic surged down his arm, tunneling through the staff and directly into the human. Marcus didn't have time to scream as his flesh melted off his bones, his essence bleeding into Eaon in a pearl of ecstasy. The life forces all around the fen blinked into his awareness, ripe for the taking.

Dearmead.

Eaon turned quickly, but the magic hadn't touched him. Cradling his hand, the decay hadn't spread beyond the line of contact. Eaon's mouth fell open, but Eavha's scream tore him from the shock.

One of the guards had snuck around the foray and cornered Eavha and Cinn by a decomposing log. Armed with only a knife, Cinn had thrown himself between the sword and Eavha, the blade sinking so deep into his chest it had to be sitting in his lung.

Without thinking, Eaon aimed the staff at the guard. His power whipped from him, lashing out at that one man who promptly began to wither. Another pearl burst inside him.

Giddy, Eaon pointed the staff at another guard.

Another.

Another.

Another.

The high soaked every fiber of his being in a pleasure unlike anything he'd ever experienced. His mouth salivated as he imagined what it would taste like to take the hag. The lupanis. The necromancer.

Eavha.

"No," he gasped, staggering back.

The refusal angered the magic and it writhed as he tried to rein it in, clawing at him to get out. It was too strong. It had fed —tasted—and now it wanted more.

More. More, more, more.

Eaon could taste his own blood as he sunk to his knees. Someone grabbed his wrist.

Flinching, Eaon raised his head as Cinn slid his hand up the sleeve of his shirt. Dropping the staff, Eaon tore off his gloves and grabbed Cinn, unleashing the evil inside him.

Cinn whimpered and sagged, face crumpling.

"I'm sorry. I'm so sorry." Eaon clenched his eyes shut and emptied out the stores of power that seethed at the kinner whose essence it couldn't take.

The fighting didn't last much longer; the clacking of the staff above his head assured him that at least he hadn't hurt Dearmead too badly, and the thinning out of screaming men meant the Pirevians were either dead or had fled.

As soon as the pain eased, Eaon let go of Cinn and lowered himself into the water, resting his spinning head on a thick root. Cinn collapsed beside him, an awful shade of gray, but his chest still rose and fell in hitching breaths.

The fen had gone silent except for the rasping breaths all around him.

"Don't." Kaelean's sharp word cracked the dusk air.

Eaon forced himself to open his eyes and turn in her direction. The witch had her hand over Eavha's mouth.

A few of the fae were repairing the circle, but most were still as stone, watching in anticipation. The hag tilted her head, baring her yellowed teeth, while the nymph stood beside her, smiling.

"Don't show them gratitude," Kaelean warned. "You'll just indebt yourself and believe me, you don't want that."

Kaelean was in bad shape. Arrows were still stuck in her back, blood soaking the tattered rags of her dress while she grew increasingly unsteady on her feet. Eavha slipped her hand over the torn flesh, but Kaelean shrugged her off.

"If we leave, they will attack us," Dearmead said quietly, eyes scanning the fen for a way out.

Eaon tried to get up but the world tilted and he heaved against the bile pushing up his throat.

Kaelean groaned and collapsed to her knees. When Eavha tried to help her, she shoved her away. The rogue hung her head and pressed her hands into the wet soil. A swell of magic oozed from her and every plant in the vicinity perked up, a sense of wakefulness that didn't belong outside of Anfar humming through the fen. Eavha took a few steps back, looking around as the fae began to chitter excitedly.

The rogue sat up and pulled her hands from the soil, cupping a water hawthorn bud. All around them, the fen started blooming with the white flower, a thick cloud of nectar sweetening the air. The nymphs were bouncing in glee, but the swamp hag waited until every new bud had fully bloomed. Then she turned and scuttled away.

Trembling, Kaelean dropped the hawthorn. Eavha knelt beside her, muttering under her breath before grabbing the shaft of an arrow in one hand and resting the other near the entry point.

Dearmead retrieved Eaon's gloves, filthy from the swamp water, and handed them back to him.

"So you were paying attention during our secret lessons," he smiled sadly as he crouched beside Eaon.

"Are your hands okay?" Eaon croaked, exhaustion weighing too heavily to pull the gloves back on yet.

"I'll live. Eavha can look at them later," he said, moving his hands where Eaon couldn't see them.

Kaelean howled as Eavha pulled the last arrow from her back. Beside Eaon, Cinn was groaning and trying to sit up, holding his shredded chest together as it stitched closed.

They were all hurt. Eaon had no right to be complaining. Body like jelly, he shoved his poisonous hands into the wet leather and grabbed Dearmead's staff, forcing himself to stand.

"Help him," Eaon said, raising his chin at Cinn, who looked ready to pass out.

Dearmead waited, lips parted as if he had something to say. Deciding against it, he went to help Cinn sit properly. Eaon found one of their bags up on the fen and drained a jar of tonic. It wasn't for magic depletion, but he would take what he could get to stave off the fatigue.

"We need to move. Before more guards come," Kaelean panted, staggering to her feet.

Nobody argued, the five of them holding each other up as they limped from the fen.

CHAPTER 35

AISLING

ALL SEVEN OF AISLING'S ADVISORS WERE SEATED IN THE council room, but her mind was elsewhere. All night she had worked on the letter she would send to her parents, inviting them to Hyrsch. Planning the assassination of her mother and choosing a patsy.

It wouldn't be enough to make her mother miscarry. None of her advisors or spies had confirmed her mother's condition, which made her wonder how Nevan knew. If this was some elaborate trap. Or if it was even true. If it *was* a test from her parents to see if she would strike, the Sparrow Coven would hang her for treason. Then Nevan would have a clear path to the throne. So was this a scheme of his, then? To weed her out without having to do the deed himself?

She couldn't lose the kinner, but she couldn't risk advertising her knowledge of her mother's condition either. But if the rebels in the city took an opportunity to assassinate their oppressors . . .

"Princess Aisling?" Farralt called.

"What?" she snapped.

"We asked if you would like us to start scouting the wastes for oil deposits, as the traveler recommended." The condescension in the old witch's tone was palpable.

"Obviously. Any more asinine questions? Do I need to command you when to shit and piss, too? Or can you figure that out for yourselves?"

She reveled in their chagrin. They were her advisors, but they'd been chosen for her by the king after she'd freed the demi-kin. She knew their quintessential purpose in Hyrsch was to keep her in line.

The door burst open and the guards in the room drew their swords. It was just Nora.

"Did you send it?" she panted, face flushed and holding a crumpled letter in her fist.

Aisling stood, ice sliding down her spine. "This morning."

"How dare you interrupt—"

"Shut it!" Aisling's nostrils flared as she glared at Farralt. "One more word from you and I'll use your skull as a croquet ball."

She held his stare until he averted his eyes, keeping his chin raised. The exchange had given Nora a moment to catch her breath.

"There's been a . . . surge, in Pirevia. Prince Nevan's court has been decimated. His prisons are empty."

For a moment, Aisling forgot herself. A wicked grin splashed across her face. "And my brother?"

"Not counted among the dead, but he hasn't made a public appearance yet. Rumors have him bedridden."

"A shame," she cooed.

"Should I send someone to intercept your invitation?"

Aisling could almost see the chessboard in front of her. The rook was down, but the endgame was approaching quickly. Whether she was ready or not, it was time to get her pieces into place.

"No. Thank you, Nora."

Her Second furrowed her brow but nodded, retreating from the room. Her advisors looked to Aisling expectantly, the suspicion and hostility in their eyes unable to touch her in her glee.

"Who have you invited to the city?" Farralt's tone was not as wary as she would have liked.

"The king and queen," she told them, deeply satisfied by the way many of them flinched back.

"It's always an honour to welcome your parents, but the demi-kin made it sound as if—"

Aisling raised her hand, slowly resuming her seat. Rolling her shoulders, she jutted out her chin as she surveyed the anxious faces around her.

"Prepare yourselves. We will be hosting Imsa this summer."

PART III

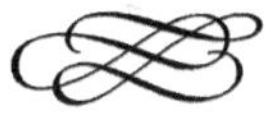

MIND, BODY, SPIRIT

CHAPTER 36

CINN

He didn't know how long he'd been in the dark. Long enough that he didn't remember what the sun felt like anymore. Didn't remember much of anything. The dripping in the corner of the cell was slightly off beat with his slow heartbeat; the incessant sound had driven him to screaming more than once. But the sound also meant water. Every so often, the pool of it grew large enough for him to wet his tongue. Lately, he'd had trouble moving enough to reach it. He was wasting away. Could feel it in the bite of stone against his bony frame. There was a blessing in that, too; there wasn't enough left of him to keep contemplating if it was possible to eat himself.

"Cinn."

Kaelean snapped her fingers in front of his face. He blinked away the dark and shoved her away from him.

He barely remembered the trek up the cliff and back through the heather field. As soon as they were beneath the trees again, Eaon had collapsed and Kaelean had called it a day.

Now she hissed at him. "Six . . . seven times I've saved your ass. You could be a little grateful."

Grateful.

Cinn snarled at her and climbed to his aching feet. If he had the energy, he might have grabbed the knife from his boot. It wasn't William's knife, but it was better than nothing.

"It had to be done," Kaelean argued, clenching her fists. "I didn't want to do it, but you wouldn't have come with me if I had explained."

It *had* to be done? Horseshit.

Cinn stepped up and spat in her face.

Kaelean's hand whipped up and grabbed him by the throat.

He lifted his foot and took out his knife.

"You put that thing near me and I will bury you alive."

Smirking, he slashed at the wrist holding his throat. Quicker than his eye could follow, she grabbed his wrist. Her foot hooked around the back of his knee, but he expected it and grabbed a fistful of her hair as she yanked him off balance, taking her down with him.

The ground cracked on impact.

Kaelean muttered under her breath and the soil softened beneath him, clinging to him as it dragged him down.

There was shouting, and then Kaelean was being pulled off him. Someone pried his fingers out of Kaelean's hair before lifting him from the sinkhole that was still trying to swallow him whole. He spat at her again and she snarled viciously.

Eaon whirled on Kaelean.

"What in the Lover's realm was that?!"

"I warned him!"

Cinn brushed off his clothes, glaring at the witch. He wished the others hadn't intervened. Let him drag her under with him and see how she fared.

Eavha stood between Kaelean and Eaon, lecturing them both. He didn't care what she was saying. All he could see was the dark.

He lunged for her again, wetness on his eyelashes.

Eaon grabbed him and hauled him back. "Cinn, stop. Stop."

"You're welcome." Kaelean curtseyed.

The darkness turned red. With nothing else to do, he screamed wordlessly at her until he tasted blood in his throat. Eaon held him tighter.

"Ignore her. You're fine. You're alright now."

Breath hitching, he struggled away from Eaon and stalked off into the bush. The witches started arguing again, but he didn't care. He just wanted to be alone.

They followed him.

He walked for hours until Dearmead caught up and pointed west. Huffing through his nose, Cinn turned his stomping in the new direction, sneering at the clovers crushed beneath his boots. It was stupid, but destroying them made him feel better. The trail of petty vengeance continued until someone whistled sharply. Reluctantly, he slowed down and turned back. The witches had gathered by a cluster of trees.

Dearmead started climbing one while the females sat down so Eavha could work on Kaelean's wounded back some more. Warily, Eaon came over to stand beside him.

"Kaelean said she stashed your things here. Dearmead also hid supplies nearby."

Cinn's chest ached and he glanced at the rogue witch, who pointedly ignored him.

"You have every right to be angry with her. We're all angry with her, but she won't leave until she's heard what Yomra had to say," Eaon explained. {I won't tell them your name if you don't want me to.}

His name.

Cinn clenched his eyes shut, pushing it away. He wasn't a lost little boy running from monsters anymore. He wasn't a slave or a brother or a cadet. When he went into that dark, he'd let himself become nobody. But that version of him wasn't compatible with who he was now, either. His name meant nothing.

{I want to go home.} Cinn sniffed, rubbing his jaw against his shoulder as he opened his eyes again.

"Look at me." Eaon grabbed Cinn's elbows and slouched so he could look the kinner in the eye. "I will personally make sure you get there. It might take a while, but I swear to you I will get you home and make sure no witch ever bothers you again."

The boulder sitting in Cinn's chest rolled away. He could breathe.

Dearmead dropped back out of the tree with a dirty sack made of an old blanket. Cinn ran for it.

Nobody spoke as he knelt on the ground and untied the knots, spreading his belongings around on the open blanket and retrieving William's silver knife. A piece of him slid back into place as the blade went back in its scabbard, secured around his waist. He took out the small wooden box and opened the lid. Everything was still there. His snail shell was a little chipped, but mostly intact.

"What is that?" Eaon asked, crouching beside him.

Cinn hovered over the box, guarding it as he looked around

the group of witches. Eavha and Kaelean were still busy, and Dearmead had left to forage for food. Chewing his lip, Cinn leaned back and showed Eaon the box.

"What are they?" He asked, tilting his head as he inspected Cinn's little collection.

{Mine.}

"Do they do something?"

{No. I just like them.}

Eaon smiled. "They're lovely."

Cinn nodded and closed the box.

He would go home. Close the chapter on this part of his life too. Tuck it away and never think about it again.

Eaon had promised.

CHAPTER 37

EAON

Eaon was so tired.

Tired of walking, tired from using his magic, tired of stress. The novelty of having controlled his magic had worn off and he was growing unsteady on his feet again. Only knowing that they weren't safe until they got to Anfar and Dearmead's promise that his supplies were close by kept him moving.

When they reached another tall tree and Dearmead began to climb, Eaon took the opportunity to sit down. Eavha, too, was looking a little pale. Kaelean got her some water and something to eat from their shopping bags.

"You're pushing yourself too hard. Your magic has only just come back," Kaelean told her.

"So I should have let you bleed to death? Let Dearmead's hands turn gangrenous?" Eavha jutted out her chin, even as she took a handful of dried apricot.

"You heal to perfection. Aim lower," Kaelean said, sitting down to massage her feet.

"You're both covered in scars. I hardly call that perfection. And besides, I'm a Nemuse. We have a reputation to uphold."

Despite his exhaustion, Eaon rolled his eyes. "Did you hit your head?"

"Excuse me?" She raised her eyebrows at him.

Eaon waved a hand at the bush around them. "You and I are all that's left, Eavha, and look where we are. I think it's safe to say our reputation is sufficiently tarnished. No need to give yourself an aneurism trying to impress the parrots and rats."

He didn't expect her to look so hurt.

Dearmead dropped from the tree with a large traveler's pack, stuffed to the brim.

Eaon's vision blurred, nostrils flaring as he took in the familiar patches and stains on the canvas. "That's my father's."

Dearmead's eyes widened in a flash of panic as he took in Eaon's incensed expression. "I didn't know what else to use. There was too much to take when I left."

"We had nothing and we managed."

Dearmead put the bag down, arms hanging limply by his sides as closed his eyes, taking deep, measured breaths. Eaon recognised the stance as Dearmead's trying-not-to-lose-his-shit pose. It wasn't usually directed at Eaon.

"Well." Kaelean stood, clearing her throat. "It's getting late. I'll build us a shelter."

She moved a distance away and began collecting long branches and sticks. Eavha went to sit by Cinn, who'd settled onto a soft patch of grass to look at his strange collection again.

"You want to talk about it?" Dearmead asked through clenched teeth, finally looking at Eaon.

"Yeah, let's talk about it," Eaon snapped, stuffing his hands beneath his arms.

"I regretted not following you every day," Dearmead started. "Every day, Eaon, I almost packed a bag and came after you."

"That almost warms my heart."

"I'm sorry."

The words were not a comfort.

"Well, don't be. It's not your job to take care of me. I never should have asked to you come. That was selfish."

Eaon could take care of himself, but he couldn't help that he had hoped he mattered enough to someone that they would want to try anyway.

"No, I should have come." Dearmead dropped his shoulders, stepping forward. Eaon turned away.

"You had your family, and all that stuff with the breach going on."

"I should have come."

"Plus, you know, everything was insane. I . . . I'm like this now, with this magic, and that's not what you signed up for."

"I should have come."

Eaon swallowed the ache in his throat and straightened his shoulders. "But you didn't."

"I'm here now," Dearmead pleaded.

"Why?"

Dearmead hesitated, running his hands through the hair that was falling out of his braid, framing his dark, weary face. Eaon clenched his fists beneath his armpits and looked away—he wouldn't be tucking those loose strands back again any time soon.

Glancing toward the others, Dearmead sighed. "Let's do this then. I'll explain everything."

He crouched over the traveler's pack and opened it up. First, he pulled out a few of Kailevi's shirts and handed them to Eaon.

The smell of them made him ache for Wyldeden like he never had before. Then Dearmead passed him a stack of papers and a small book that Eaon had left in his unk's room.

Eavha came over and Dearmead pulled out a box of vials and herbs, as well as her Blessing Charm.

"I found it like that near the Boab as I was leaving," he explained. The hair wound around the old daisy stem had snapped in the middle, the strands fraying. Eavha held it delicately, staring at it in shock.

"I thought I lost it," she breathed.

Kaelean had noticed that the conversation was changing and left her pile of branches to join them. Eaon spared her a glance, grateful for the attempt at privacy, before looking back to his papers. It was the timeline he'd been making to trace the blight plaguing their family. An itch at the base of his skull made him shiver.

"Everything went to shit after you left," Dearmead started as he pulled out more things: a pot they could use to boil water over a campfire, travelers' rations and waterskins, as well as a translating dictionary that Eaon had been working on since he was fifteen. "Elder Esther sacrificed herself in Eaon's place to restore the Balance and to atone for failing to teach Eavha 'proper respect' for the Spirits."

Eavha gasped, covering her mouth as her eyes welled. Eaon's insides twisted painfully. Another unnecessary death that was his fault.

"Then the high priestess banned traveling. Banned scouts or guardians from leaving the Boab. She put Keil and Peartar at the witchmark to arrest anyone who tried. Even for burials. The other elders argued, and then . . . twelve of them died in a week. Then . . . my family. My ma. Daete, Trumard—fifty, since you've been gone. And the high priestess doesn't seem to care about any of it. Some of the priestesses have been saying she won't even pray for answers as to what we've done wrong.

"Scouts still managed to get word from the dryads when you . . . you had your surge in the meadow. It was a relief to know you were still alive, but I also knew that if anybody could figure out what in the Lover's embrace was going on, it was you. And thanks to that surge, I knew where to start looking. I couldn't track you, obviously, but I could track what I thought was a demi-kin. That's how I found you.

"I know that as soon as I go back, as soon as I show my face, they'll excommunicate me for breaking the high priestess's commandment, but . . . I'm desperate. She'd forbidden the healers from investigating the disease—"

"It's not a disease," Eavha interrupted. "There was no disease in Eaon when he died. There was nothing wrong with him at all. I hate to say it, but I've been thinking about it a lot. It's probably a curse."

A curse. Even as his stomach twisted at the idea, Eaon nodded in agreement. He'd suspected Aadya was a liar, but . . .

"Wait." He froze, frowning at the thoughts speeding by too quickly to catch them. One of them was important; he could feel it in the urgent way his heart started galloping. Grabbing the back of his head, scrunching his hair in his fist, he tried to slow his brain down. "Who did you say was guarding the Boab?"

"Keil and Peartar. Why?"

Eaon rifled through the loose papers on his lap, sure he'd just seen those names. Pulling out a single sheet, he scanned the list quickly.

"They're on my list."

"What list?" Eavha asked.

"Witches who suddenly appeared on the census after the rogue coup fifty years ago. Who proceeded over the funerals for the elders and your family?"

"Aadya."

"All of them?"

"Yes."

Lorelei had plenty of priestesses on hand, so why was only Aadya overseeing the funerals of witches dying from the curse? Aadya, who was also on his list.

"What—" Kaelean started, but both Eavha and Dearmead shushed her, watching him think.

"How many high guardians are there?" he asked, counting the names left on his list.

"Twenty," Dearmead answered.

Twenty.

Everything was too loud, the air too crisp, the setting sun too bright. Every nerve in his body was coming alive until he could taste the night songs of birds in the trees nearby. His thoughts fell out of his head in glowing orbs, spinning around each other in an endless dance of connectivity. The paths between them shone with color as varied as the rainbow, ruby red sparks leading him towards the truth.

"I'd be willing to bet these are their names." He handed Dearmead the list, massaging his temples. "I'd be willing to bet they were all rogues before they got inside Wyldeden. Before the high priestess *let* them inside and then *employed* them. Why, even after all this time, she still insists on them wearing those masks. So we can't see who they are and realize they shouldn't be there."

Dearmead frowned, glancing between Eaon and the paper. If he guessed at how Eaon had put together the theory, he didn't mention it.

"She's obviously behind the curse, too," Kaelean added. "Sounds exactly like the kind of thing Lorelei would do."

Eaon stilled.

None of them had said the high priestess's name.

"How do you know Lorelei?" Eavha's wary tone matched the suspicion growing in Eaon's gut.

Kaelean raised her chin and gave them all one of her cocky smiles. "Because she was my heir back when I was the high priestess of Wyldeden."

CHAPTER 38

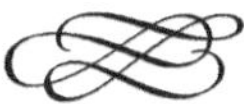

EAON

Cinn glanced at them all, but went back to playing with his feather.

"It may come as a surprise," Kaelean teased, "but the Anfar Forest Clan once resided in the Anfar forest. Nine hundred and forty years ago, give or take, we were at war with the Sparrow Coven. Your history books will call it the Third War."

"Anfar was losing, so the clan retreated to Wyldeden," Eaon said. He knew their history well.

"Our high priest was killed and the role fell to me. I was thirteen. Out of desperation to save our people, I tore a hole in Terra's realm and settled Wyldeden," Kaelean said, nodding. "I wasn't lying when I said I grew bored of clan life. Once the Treaty was made and the wards rose, I didn't know what to do with myself.

"Two hundred years, and I had nothing better to do with my days than experiment with my considerable blessing. So I did what I did. It wasn't forbidden at the time because nobody had ever thought to try it before. But the council disapproved and tried to overthrow me. I refused to step down.

"Soon, my guards started turning up dead in their homes, so when I replaced them I had them wear masks to keep their identities a secret. They stopped dying. And I was so busy keeping an eye on those who openly opposed me that I forgot to watch out for the witch I trusted most. Lorelei. She was powerful, but impatient and greedy, apparently. She ambushed me and helped the elders throw me from the home I had made for them."

"But . . . your brands . . ." Eavha shook her head, rubbing her own palms.

"They had to make a special iron just for me. The marks you have wouldn't have kept me out, but the ones I have would probably have killed you." Kaelean sighed, then smiled again. "Clearly they still aren't strong enough because I managed to tear another hole into the realm. Lorelei sensed the intrusion, since she was now the high priestess, and there are worse things they can do that excommunicate you, so I left. I only risked breaking that seal again to spy on you two."

"But . . . she's our high priestess. She never would have cursed us. It would offend the Mother *and* the Lover. Right?" Dearmead shook his head.

"Sorry, little witchling, but Lorelei's love of power was always greater than her love for the Spirits. I was trying to weed that out of her when she betrayed me," Kaelean spat.

"But, why?" Eavha asked, voice thick. Eaon grimaced. His sister had admired Lorelei; the idea that she had targeted their family for some reason would be hard to take.

"I can make a solid guess," Kaelean admitted, the shadows

growing longer over her freckled face. "After spending time with you, Eavha, I think she was threatened by you. So she decided to get rid of you in the most ridiculous, convoluted manner possible, just to be a pompous hag. And now she's cursing anyone who threatens her position."

Despite himself, Eaon snorted. "Tell us how you really feel about her, why don't you."

"Nobody in my family would dare threaten her," Dearmead said, ignoring Eaon.

"It doesn't make sense," Eavha added. "What does any of this have to do with the rogues? Why didn't she just have one of them kill me? Why my whole family?"

"We don't know for sure that there even are any rogues, either," Dearmead pointed out, avoiding looking at Eaon despite the faint colour on his cheeks. He knew the way Eaon's mind could turn paranoid when an episode was coming on, but that's not what was happening.

Kaelean shrugged. "I repeat: Pompous, theatrical hag."

"No," said Eaon.

All the pieces of the puzzle were screaming a symphony in his head. Shadows were dancing with tendrils of faelight, revealing the patterns of the universe as his mind continued to race and race and race and race . . .

"This started long before Eavha was born. Lorelei might be powerful, but she can't predict the future and she doesn't know enough about the Lover to have pulled off a curse like this. Besides, it didn't start with us. There were other clans who've been through this.

"So, what if Lorelei staged the invasion, let the rogues in because one of them was Morvish? Yomra wore a hood over her head to hide her tattoo. Hoods aren't a requirement to be a priestess, but guess who's always wearing one. Aadya.

"The other rogues are *her* entourage. And Lorelei wanted to know who would replace her, but Aadya only got a last name so she just cursed the whole family. Once we were gone, she asked again and got the name Bayfield. This is what she does. She is the real blight on the world."

Kaelean, Eavha and Dearmead stared at him with mixed expressions, but he couldn't focus on them. The lines of fate had woven a net over the bushland for miles in every direction. Everywhere he turned, he could see the threads. It was so beautiful. So impossibly beautiful.

"That's a lot of assumptions," Eavha said gently, giving him a pitying look. "I don't think we should jump to any conclusions without some kind of evidence."

Eaon frowned. The evidence was all around them.

"Regardless, we're going to have to confront Lorelei, aren't we?" Dearmead sighed, pinching the bridge of his nose.

"If we're going to stop your family from ending up like mine, then I think so," said Eavha. She got to her feet and began rifling through the bags.

"The curse didn't follow you two when you left Wyldeden. Perhaps it's time to close the pocket of spirit realm and leave the curse inside it," Kaelean muttered to herself, but Eaon and Dearmead heard her anyway.

"You can't," said Dearmead. "The people there . . . it's their home. Most of them have never been outside the Boab. They won't survive out here."

Eaon was about to argue that he and Eavha had managed just fine but, if he was being honest, it had been a close call.

"You underestimate our people." Kaelean narrowed her eyes.

"They are a different people than the ones you left behind," Dearmead said, holding up his hands in deference. "If we take them from Wyldeden, we condemn them."

"Here," Eavha returned and handed Eaon a small glass vial. "It'll slow things down a little."

He blinked at her, distracted by the wisps floating around her head.

"But I can see everything."

"I know." Eavha smiled sadly. "But you won't sleep otherwise and we have a long journey tomorrow."

Kaelean glanced between them and Dearmead, but nobody wanted to explain. Eaon didn't want the tonic, but he knew it would only get worse if he didn't nip it in the bud now.

"Thank you," he said, taking the vial and downing the content.

The four of them sat in silence as they tried to process everything that had been said.

No matter who was behind it, or what was going on, there was a curse in Wyldeden. Eaon owed the clan nothing, but he didn't have it in him to abandon them the way they had abandoned him.

Eaon sighed deeply, burying his face in his hands. He was going to have to go home.

Despite the heaviness in his body, Eaon was too wired to sleep, so he volunteered to keep watch while the others slept. Only his promise that the hallucinations had stopped made them trust him enough to do so.

Kaelean had built a fire and, in an unusual display of apathy,

Cinn had curled up in front of it with his back to the forest. He too didn't sleep.

"What are you thinking about?" Eaon whispered, chewing his fingernail as he sat down against a tree beside the kinner.

Cinn shook his head. {Trying not to.}

"Yeah," Eaon sighed, rubbing his palms over the sides of his head. He couldn't seem to stop thinking about Wyldeden. About the curse. Lorelei and Aadya. About Dearmead's ma. "I wish I could stop."

Cinn nodded and pulled out his feather again, brushing it over Eaon's face. Swatting him away, Eaon wrinkled his nose and leaned back.

"Careful. I don't want to accidently ruin it."

Cinn frowned and put the feather away. {I trust you.}

"Makes one of us." Eaon turned to the darkness so he didn't have to see Cinn's response. "I'm not even sure who I am anymore. Twenty-four years I spent being the most useless witch in my family, and now suddenly I'm this . . . monster."

Eaon took a deep breath and let it go, easing the tightness in his chest. He was moping, which was pointless.

After a moment, Cinn sat up. Holding his box of trinkets, he pulled out a button and passed it to Eaon. It only had one hole.

"Huh. Weird."

He made to hand it back to Cinn, but he shook his head and closed Eaon's fingers around it.

"Wait . . . you're giving this to me?" Eaon frowned. "No, I can't . . ."

Cinn nodded, holding on to his closed fist. Eaon couldn't quite explain why his heart was squeezing so painfully.

"Thank you."

Cinn smiled sadly, then let him go to lay back by the fire.

For a few minutes, Eaon sat and stared at the strange gift. Taking off one of his gloves, he ran a thumb over the surface, feeling its smooth, cold hardness. Cinn was definitely strange, but the button meant something to him and so it meant a lot to Eaon.

Placing it carefully in his pocket, he stretched out his legs by the fire, keeping his gaze on the forest.

"Do you want to know what happened today?" he asked.

Cinn nodded, so Eaon explained about Kaelean and Wyldeden, and even about the talk he'd had with Dearmead. He couldn't stop himself from looking over at the sleeping male as he did, eyes roaming over the familiar shape of him. He'd thought he would never see him again, and he didn't know if it was worse now that he had.

When he finished talking, Cinn put his feather away again and signed.

{You promised to make sure no witch bothers me again.}

"I did. And I will. But I think I have to take care of this first. People are dying," Eaon explained, an apology on the tip of his tongue.

{I want to help your home, too.}

"What?" Eaon blinked.

{I want to protect your home too,} Cinn repeated, lowering his weary gaze. {You help me. I help you. Friends.}

Eaon's chest hurt again.

"You don't have to, Cinn. It's not your fight. You'll still be my friend."

{I want to. I want to help someone instead of hurt them.}

Eaon closed his eyes, just for a moment. He felt that sentiment in his very soul.

"Alright then. I won't lie and say it wouldn't be nice to have a kinner on the team."

{I will even promise not to try to kill Kaelean again.}

Eaon snorted. "Now that's a fight I'd give a tooth to see finished."

Cinn tilted his head and frowned at Eaon. {A tooth?}

"You know, because of the fae story about giving a tooth . . ." At Cinn's increasingly perplexed expression, Eaon smiled. "I'm guessing you don't have that tale in Hyrsch."

{No.} Cinn chuckled. {Will you tell me?}

"Sure." Eaon rolled and cracked his neck, fondling the button in his pocket. "Though I've never told it in Nirnish, so bear with me."

{Of course.}

And so Eaon spent the night telling faerie tales to Cinn until peace settled over both their heavy hearts.

CHAPTER 39

AISLING

T HE SPRING MORNING WAS RATHER LOVELY, SO AISLING TOOK her chess set onto the balcony to ponder over her next moves over a cup of tea and a plate of pastries. She had once again found herself in a predicament on the board. The power pieces had always been her favorite, but her opponent had used her pawns well and cornered Aisling once again.

Sighing deeply, she thought about the demi-kin pawns she had waiting at the bridge for further instructions. In particular, she was thinking about Owen Turlough.

Aisling knew exactly who lived on the farm just outside of Belden where Owen had found the kinner. She made a point of keeping tabs on those who brought the demi-kin into her city, making sure they saw as little resistance as possible from the Oford lords. But after some digging, she'd discovered Owen's history with the farmers and she now had doubts about his report on what had happened. Had the kinner escaped, or had Owen let him go?

Having him lead the squadron into Anfar might have been a poor decision, but she wasn't entirely out of options. A new game was being played now and she couldn't afford to make the same mistakes. To make her brother's mistakes, either.

Sipping her tea, Aisling reached over and moved her last pawn one place.

"Farralt," Aisling called after her least favorite advisor as the seven of them rose to leave the council room. "Wait here a moment."

The witches all paused, glancing between one another until finally abandoning their comrade to whatever whim the princess had. Farralt returned to his seat, waiting for Edwina to finish collecting the paperwork scattered over the table. The servant left and, with only Clayton with them, Aisling lounged back in her seat and waved a hand toward the drinks cart in the corner.

Farralt sat patiently until Aisling turned her penetrating gaze on him.

"You want *me* to fetch . . ."

"Well, I'm not going to get it myself," Aisling cooed dangerously.

Swallowing his rage, Farralt went to fetch her decanter and a couple of glasses. Aisling kept her face neutral, trying not to show how much she enjoyed tormenting him.

"Do you have any pressing matters to contend with at the moment?" she asked once he had poured her a glass of wine.

"A few, Your Highness," Farralt admitted guardedly.

Aisling sat and waited, staring at her glass. It took Farralt far too long to realize what she wanted. His face burned when he realized.

Good. Be enraged.

Farralt tested the wine and Aisling waited to see to see if he would react to a poison before taking a sip herself. Of course, she had servants at her beck and call to do these things for her, but they were not the pawns she needed right now.

"Delegate them," she said. "I want you and a small number of your guards to meet my deployment at the border of Anfar."

Farralt stilled, hand at the base of his own glass.

"At the border? Perhaps Ler would be better suited."

"No. You." Aisling sipped again and gazed out the colored-glass window. "You were Terranian before you became a Sparrow, correct?"

She sensed him flinch at the taboo. Their alliances from before the Passing were meant to be left behind.

"I was," Farralt said through gritted teeth.

"Then you should feel right at home amongst the trees. And as my most trusted advisor, I need you to be my emissary."

"Emissary?" Farralt practically choked on the word. On the insults and praise she had delivered.

"There is a Terranian necromancer and a Returned residing somewhere in the forest, cast out as rogues by the Anfar Clan. I want them here, but it needs to be a peaceful encounter. We don't want to end up like Pirevia, Lover have mercy." Aisling put a hand over her heart in a blatantly mocking gesture. "The soldiers I have at the border are fine, but they don't have the silver tongue that you do."

Farralt had gathered himself enough to sneer. "These soldiers are some of your slave-converts, I assume?"

"They are, and you will be respectful."

Farralt had complained the loudest about her decision to free the demi-kin and had often requested to be sent to Nevan's court instead. She had refused him out of spite.

"As you wish, Your Highness."

"You will depart immediately. Make your preparations and I will have Edwina bring you yours and Owen's orders before you go." She drained the rest of her glass and ran a finger over the rim. "And Farralt?"

"Yes?" He was already half standing.

"Fail me, and I'll drop you into the Womb myself. Understood?"

Farralt blanched and nodded earnestly before leaving.

Aisling poured herself another drink and sighed heavily, loosening the tight laces at the front of her bodice. All the wine had given her a soft belly—as if her courtly dresses weren't restrictive enough already.

The door opened again and Nora came in, striding to the seat beside Aisling, glancing at the wine glass. "Is everything alright? I thought we weren't due to meet until later?"

Aisling turned to Clayton, who nodded and left the room.

"Sit." Aisling waved a hand at the chair Nora stood behind and waited for her Second to settle. "The farmers at Belden."

Nora was silent.

"You know them."

"I know of them."

"I think they need to disappear."

Nora didn't answer her, and when Aisling finally looked over she wasn't surprised to see how pale her Second had become.

"Do you think I am wrong?"

"I . . ." Nora considered her words carefully. "I do wish to know exactly what their offense is."

Aisling chose her words just as wisely. "There is reason to believe they played a more influential part in the attack on Ralph and the others. People who attack members of my court do not go unpunished."

"You think Owen is lying about what happened?" Nora's voice became hostile and Aisling raised her eyebrows.

"Did I say that?"

"You didn't need to."

Aisling drank, clicking her tongue as she gazed back out the window, surveying her city below.

"Do *you* think he is lying?" she asked softly. "If you tell me he isn't, I will believe you."

Nora took a long time to answer.

"I do not think he is lying. If the Copelands had a hand in the attack and they let him live because of their connection with him, he would have told me. And I would have told you."

The words were surprisingly earnest. Aisling finished her wine and closed her eyes.

"Swear it," she asked, throat thick. "Swear to me the Copelands are innocent."

"I swear it on my life." No hesitation.

"On your husband's life?"

"Yes."

"On your future child's life?"

Nora flinched. Then, "Yes."

It was enough.

"Alright. But Nora?" Aisling opened her eyes and leveled a cold stare at her Second. "I am growing tired of not being able to punish the people who have wronged me. I want that damned laundress."

"I will make it a priority," Nora said as she stood, bowing deeply before heading for the door.

CHAPTER 40

EAVHA

EAVHA SAW THE STORM COMING.

They all took the opportunity to wash the bog off before waiting out the rest of the downpour beneath the flimsy shelter Kaelean had built. Eaon had backed himself as far from the rest of them as possible, sipping at another dose of tonic. He hadn't stopped talking all morning, and she doubted he would be quiet any time soon.

"Alright." Kaelean cradled a cup of steaming turmeric tea they'd managed to make. "I've given you sloths enough time. Tell me what Yomra said."

Eavha blinked, having almost forgotten the Morvish witch entirely. Of all the Spirits, Morvia was the least understood. The spirit of stars, of prophecy and dreams, did not deign to meet witches during communion. Not even the grandest temple could lure her from her realm, and for that, she was scarcely worshiped. She did not bestow blessings, did not involve herself in their affairs.

Except in Qiri.

The only Morvish witches south of the mountains were those who left the recluse territory, but they were few and far between.

"You might not like it," Eaon warned her.

"It's vague, no doubt. Morvish witches take classes on how to be as stupidly unhelpful as possible." Kaelean rolled her eyes, but there a soft, affectionate smile on her lips. She had lost a friend, Eavha reminded herself. An old one.

"She told me I would have all the pieces of the puzzle soon. And that I am who I need to be, so stop fighting it. Which, I suppose, came to pass."

"What about me?" Eavha asked.

"Um, she said you had forgotten where your strength truly came from and to start again. And that you should be careful, and trust yourself, because power corrupts."

"The wording can be important, Eaon," Kaelean warned him.

"That's what she said."

"My strength." Eavha bit her lip and pulled the broken Blessing Charm from her pocket. "Start again."

She'd felt it, hadn't she? When she'd brought Eaon back, she had felt her essence fraying. What if she wasn't really as powerful as she thought? What if her blessing had only been as strong as it was because of a charm? Perhaps that was why she had been having so much trouble with her healing since then. It was more than just a depletion of magic. Its source had been broken.

She was a fraud.

"Cinn was told to go to a place called Ahrenhale. Which I guess is in Qiri, because I've never heard of it. He should find someone named Moyra Thorne and that she would have the answers."

"What?" Eavha dropped her hands, glaring from Eaon to Cinn. "How come we get vague nonsense and he gets literal instructions?"

Eaon shrugged. Kaelean scratched her neck.

"It's strange for Yomra to be so direct. As much as I'd love to go home and throw Lorelei off my throne, perhaps I should take the kinner to Ahrenhale instead."

"No," Eaon snapped. "No more decisions on his behalf from you. Cinn wants to come to Wyldeden, and then I'm taking him home."

The rain pounding on their shelter was the only sound as Kaelean and Eaon glared at each other. Eavha shared a wary glance with Dearmead, who'd grown tense.

"Yomra did not give her life just so—"

"That was her choice. Let Cinn make his own for once."

The air crackled and the ground trembled beneath them, magic fracturing from Kaelean like the epicenter of a world-shattering earthquake. Eaon pulled off his gloves.

"You really want to do this?"

"Both of you need to stop it!" Eavha slammed her hands down on the ground, making Kaelean recoil. Sweat broke across her skin as she realized she'd just scolded one of the most powerful witches in Nir.

Mother shield her.

"If you're not going to do that when it's helpful, don't do it when you're not getting what you want," she continued.

"As I said after Cinn stormed off and had a tantrum, it's an all or nothing manifestation, and I am *tired* of repressing my every emotion to control it. Unlike some other people here, I'm not willing to crumble a city but, believe me, if you keep pestering me I will happily bury the lot of you."

Eavha didn't believe her. She'd taken a volley of arrows in the back for them and had been worrying after Eavha since they'd left Pirevia.

"You're nine-hundred and fifty years old," Eaon scoffed. "I'm twenty-five and I've managed to refine something monstrous within two seasons. So what's your next excuse."

"Is that what you're calling it? Refinement?" Kaelean sneered.

"Alright, just stop it!" Dearmead snapped. "People are dying and this isn't helping them. Use your blessing or don't, I do not care right now. I've buried enough of my family. If the kinner wants to help then let him help, and you can all deal with after . . . after."

Eaon's face reddened as he averted his eyes and nodded. Kaelean huffed, but nodded as well.

"Well, the rain is easing. Let's pack up and move on. I'd like to have a plan before we set foot in Anfar. Lover spare us if the dryads get wind of what we're doing."

Nobody argued with her as they shuffled out of the shelter. Eavha wound her hair into a knot and picked up one of the supply bags, watching her brother trudge along, pulling his gloves back on.

She could tell he was making an effort not to cave into whatever impulses were driving him. Growing up, these more frantic moods had never been as much of a concern as his fatigues until, one day when he was nineteen, he'd followed one of his hallucinations to the top of the tallest waterfall in Wyldeden. Dearmead had been with him and tried to talk him down, but Eaon had jumped right off the cliff. He'd broken his arm and nearly drowned, but had laughed the entire way to the healer's clinic.

Kaelean and Dearmead were discussing the logistics of

getting back inside Wyldeden, which wasn't a conversation she could contribute to. And as much as she liked Cinn, she could hardly talk with him, so she hurried to walk beside Eaon instead.

Taking one of his gloved hands, she squeezed.

"Do you want to talk? You know it helps sometimes," she offered.

"Thank you, but no. It's wearing off, I think. I'm getting tired."

"Do you think you're heading for another low mood?"

"Of course I am. I killed hundreds of people the other day and nearly lost my mind doing it." Eaon pulled his hand away. "No offense, Eavha, but I don't think talking to a healer is going to help me with that."

"Why? Because you don't think I can understand?" Her eyes began to burn. "I just found out all of this, all those people in Wyldeden, our family, is probably because of me. Because Lorelei is jealous of me. And all those people who died in Pirevia? It only happened because I took you back from the Lover . . ."

"Eavha, you can't take that all on yourself." Eaon shook his head.

"Why not? You seem intent on doing it and you didn't even get a choice in the matter."

Eaon frowned. They walked in silence for a while until Eavha realized he wasn't going to respond to her.

"You haven't been able to shut up all morning, and now that I actually *want* to listen to you, you don't want to talk?" Eavha teased. It didn't earn a smile. Barely even a reaction.

"I think I preferred it when I was useless."

Eavha's throat was suddenly very tight.

She'd called him that. She knew what the word meant to him,

and she had used it against him anyway. The bitter taste of it still lingered on her tongue.

"You were never useless, Eaon," she said softly.

He didn't seem to register her words, so she took his hand again and squeezed hard.

"I wasn't fair to you. I'm sorry."

"You're hardly the first person to say it."

Eavha would never forget the day Eaon had come home from elementary school and been forced to explain to their entire family that his teacher had declared him too meagerly blessed to be useful to the clan. The first Nemuse ever born who would have to be a laborer.

It had not gone well.

That was the night Eavha had begun to make the Blessing Charm, terrified she would end up like her brother and desperate to do anything to encourage her magic to bloom sooner.

It had worked, but the way their family had celebrated Eavha's success had broken Eaon. She'd seen it, and done nothing. Brewed his tonics and healed his bruises, but had distanced herself from him and had never offered to listen to the way he suffered.

Eaon was suffering again now. Because of her choices.

Setting her shoulders, she took a deep breath. "I might not have been the first, but I will be the last."

The next person to speak ill of her brother would regret it.

As the sun lowered, they once again stopped for the night by a large pond. Eavha went to collect some water for boiling, taking her Blessing Charm with her. Crouched by the still water, she stared at the broken charm and shook her head.

Born from fear, and broken in it.

"I've met a few necromancers in my life."

Eavha flinched, not having sensed Kaelean coming up behind her. Carefully, she unbound the coronet on her head and shook out her reddish curls.

"Not many dare what you did," she continued. "Even less are successful; their Returned come back with broken souls and half a mind, bodies continuing to rot until they have to be killed again just to put them out of their misery. These were powerful witches who had practiced their craft."

Eavha twirled her broken daisy stem. "Thirteen years of charm work probably would have helped."

"You think that using a charm makes you any less impressive?" Kaelean tilted her head. "A charm is only as strong as the witch who makes it. You ought to know that. Same as the potions and tonics you brew."

Eavha bit her lip. She did know, but it didn't stop the shame that had been chewing on her all day.

"Did you even have the slightest clue what you were doing when you went into that abyss?"

"You know I didn't. I told you that."

"You did, and I asked you again to remind you that what you did was extraordinary. Whether your true power lies in healing or in charm work, you are still a very powerful witch. We will likely need that power again one day. So start again." Kaelean put her hand over Eavha's to conceal the broken charm.

She let herself shed a single tear as Kaelean helped her lower her hands into the pond and release the broken flower. They watched silently as it floated away, slowly sinking to the muddy bed below.

"When we are home again and getting our people back in shape, I would have you appointed as my heir, Eavha."

Eavha whipped her head around, eyes widening as she stared at Kaelean. The wicked grin spreading across her face was terrifying.

"Did you ever doubt you would ascend?"

"No." Eavha's voice shook. "And . . . yes, of course, I will be your heir."

Kaelean grinned wider as she turned her face up to the setting sun, catching the last of its warmth. "Then start a new charm and let's go kick that Lover-abusing donkey out of my house."

CHAPTER 41

EAON

A FEW HOURS BEFORE THEY REACHED ANFAR, THEY DECIDED to stop and eat. As Eaon shoveled in a large bowl of raisin muesli from the traveler's rations, he watched Cinn and Dearmead train together. If the kinner was coming to Wyldeden, he needed to be prepared to fight a witch if he needed to. His scuffles with Kaelean had demonstrated how unprepared the kinner was to fight someone so much faster than him.

Dearmead kept knocking Cinn down, but the kinner always got back up, undeterred and ready to try again. If Eaon didn't know better, Dearmead almost looked like he was enjoying battering him.

Cinn made a T with his hands, panting hard on the ground once more.

"I'll get you some water," Dearmead said, not waiting for Eaon to translate before stalking off.

Cinn glanced back, looking between Eaon and Dearmead.

He knew the history. Eaon had explained everything during his initial meltdown.

{Want me to punch him in the face by accident?}

Eaon smirked. {You can't even stop him from punching *you* in the face.}

{What about . . .} Cinn looked down to his crotch and jerked his knee up.

An awful snorting laugh tore from Eaon's throat, earning a curious look from everyone else.

"I don't like you two having a secret language," Kaelean muttered.

Eaon made a gesture and Cinn chuckled.

Carrying a waterskin, Dearmead returned with a sour expression on his face, tossing the drink at Cinn with more force than was strictly necessary. Still, Cinn caught it and tried to contain his laughter.

There was another conversation that needed to be had that Eaon had been avoiding. It would be better to get it over and done with before they reached Anfar, so Eaon finished his muesli and stood up. "Dearmead."

The guardian looked to Eaon, then nodded when Eaon signaled they should take a walk.

"Five minutes!" Kaelean called after them.

They didn't go far, sitting down on a fallen tree a good five feet apart.

"I wanted to say I'm sorry about your ma," started Eaon.

Dearmead shrugged. "She was a nasty old crone anyway."

"She was still your ma. And I'm sorry. About all of them."

Dearmead closed his eyes, taking a moment to gather his thoughts. Eaon was more than happy to wait.

"I don't know how you did it," he finally said. "I'm scared,

Eaon. Scared enough to come out here and face you. Scared enough to have been prepared to beg you for help."

The words were spears straight to his heart. Shuffling closer, Eaon carefully placed a gloved hand on Dearmead's shoulder.

"You're my best friend, Dearmead. I'd do anything for you." No matter how bitter and angry he was sometimes, it was still true.

Dearmead put his head in his hands, bracing himself on his knees. He was right. They had to move faster. Who knew how many more witches would succumb to the curse before they could get there because they were too busy arguing, or because Eaon was tired.

"Is Kaelean a better high priestess than Lorelei?" Dearmead asked, straightening but avoiding looking at Eaon.

Lowering his hand, Eaon stood up and brushed off his pants. Clearly Dearmead was done being vulnerable.

"Let's go ask her."

Eaon walked right up to where Kaelean was getting ready to move again and crossed his arms. She looked up at him, narrowing her eyes at the hard expression on his face.

"Before we go any farther, I want to know that we're not going to Wyldeden just to replace one selfish high priestess with another."

"Excuse me?" Kaelean raised her eyebrows.

"Why should we let you be high priestess again?"

Dearmead had taken a seat beside Eavha, looking faintly amused as Eaon stared down Kaelean.

"How about the fact that I don't go around killing people to advance my own agenda?"

"It's a start."

"Eaon!" Eavha scolded. "You're being rude."

Cinn was watching, so Eaon started signing as he spoke. "It's a fair question. The clan threw you out. What are we going to tell them when we bring you back?"

Kaelean sat back and gave Eaon a once over. Her beady eyes were not as hostile as he expected them to be.

"Dearmead said the people are different now. I can't tell you how I would be different to Lorelei because I don't know what she has done."

That was also fair. Eaon took a step back and stopped himself from looking back to Eavha and Dearmead as he asked, "How do you deal with travelers and laborers?"

Kaelean looked between the three witches, frowning.

"What do you mean 'how do I deal with them'? What is there to deal with? Travelers have one of the most dangerous roles in the entire clan. I would never ask someone to do it, but I was always grateful to those who did. And laborers? Laborers are the backbone of our society. We rely on them to keep things running so we can use our blessings to tend to what we need to tend to. That's why we celebrate the twenty-first day of each month. For the twenty-first elder. The elder laborer."

Eaon stared at her, waiting for her to explain the joke. She stared back, confused by his confusion.

"Things are very different now," Eavha said softly. "There is no elder laborer. We don't celebrate the twenty-first. And traveling is one of the only options for witches who don't have enough magic to . . . do other things."

To be useful. It was drummed into them from the moment they were born. Be useful to your family, to your clan; serve a purpose, or you are not welcome.

"She sends witches *without magic* into Nir?!" Kaelean screeched. "Is she insane? And what did she do with the elder laborer? Who organizes the laborers? How does anything get done?"

"Laborers aren't really organized. They're kind of just . . . traded," Dearmead explained, cringing. "They're not thought of very highly. More like possessions. A lot of families don't take care of their laborers."

"You mean slaves," Kaelean said coldly. "That bitch has enslaved my people."

The silence was suffocating. Slowly, Kaelean turned to look at Eaon again. He had not made it a secret he had little magic before his encounter with the Lover. The roles they were talking about were the roles he had been made to fulfill. Traveling with Kailevi had been a reprieve from laboring for the family, and he'd stepped foot in Nir much younger than most other travelers. His ma had practically tossed him out herself, desperate to get him away from her relatives.

"I said it before, but I will say it again," Kaelean said, her voice low and hard. "I tore myself apart when I was thirteen years old to protect my people. All of my people. In the seven hundred years I have been gone, I have never once forgotten them. I have never once gone to sleep at night and not prayed for them. My very blood powers the portal that keeps them safe inside that Boab, and I still feel the beat of its life in my veins. When I return home, I will do what I have always done. I will serve. I will protect."

"Even Lorelei?" Dearmead asked.

Fire burned behind her black eyes as Kaelean's lip curled up in a sneer. "The moment she stopped caring for every single witch in that clan as if they were her own blood, she stopped being an Anfar witch."

Eaon's heart was beating too hard, too fast. He walked away for a moment to collect Dearmead's staff, just in case he had another surge. Cinn came to stand beside him.

"I heard Eaon tell Cinn how Lorelei had you beaten." Kaelean reached for Eavha's hand as she flinched. "I am gravely sorry that happened to you. She is a liar. Necromancy is not a crime. It's a carefully regulated magic with many laws and few masters, but it is not a crime. Lorelei was always fanatical about the Lover, more so that then others Spirits, so I assume she did it out of jealousy that your power might outshine her own."

Eaon's knees weakened and he grabbed a hold of Cinn to keep himself standing. Not a crime. He'd known it was taboo in other clans, and most necromancers joined the Sparrow Coven anyway where such magic was practically worshipped. But . . . not a crime? In Anfar?

Eavha could go home. It was dawning on him what displacing Lorelei really meant for them. The curse wasn't the only poisonous thing in Wyldeden.

"So, to answer your initial question," Kaelean continued, getting to her feet to survey them all properly. "I am not innocent, and I will not lead Wyldeden if my people do not want me. But I will help you get rid of Lorelei regardless, because my people deserve better."

Eaon couldn't stop staring, but the shock of it was wearing off. He held his own weight, gripping the staff tightly as he took a step forward. Kaelean met his gaze and held it.

"If you are lying, I will kill you."

Eavha gasped and hissed at him, but he ignored her.

Kaelean didn't look away. Instead, the true high priestess of Wyldeden grinned.

"I'll hold you to that."

CHAPTER 42

CINN

ONCE AGAIN, CINN WALKED AMONG THE ANCIENT, SENTIENT trees of Anfar. Their towering trunks and sprawling canopy dwarfed him as he followed the witches deep into the wild.

For weeks.

Every morning and evening, he trained with Dearmead. Eavha had joined them a few times and Cinn had shown her more thoroughly how to wield a dagger. Of all of them, she was the most vulnerable and Cinn didn't like the idea of her being unable to defend herself. She held the blade like it was a poisonous snake but smiled and nodded and let him train her.

As they walked each day, Eaon continued to teach him to sign. Eavha joined them for those lessons too.

They were still a few days away from Wyldeden the first time Cinn landed a blow on Dearmead, knocking the witch to the ground. Raising his fists into the air, he threw his head back. Victory!

Eaon laughed hysterically as Dearmead got to his feet, rolling his eyes.

"Shh," Kaelean hissed, becoming still. The rest of them quieted, listening.

A breeze whistled through the old trees; the creak of heavy, moss-covered boughs above. Cinn scanned the green-and-yellow foliage for signs of rogues. They hadn't encountered one the entire time they had traveled with Kaelean, and he wasn't eager to find out who was dangerous enough to try.

Kaelean crouched, sniffing the air with her tongue poked out between her lips. She looked just like the lupanis, poised like that. The beast was as much a part of her as her magic, as if she was never really just one thing anymore.

"Demi-kin," she hissed.

"In Anfar?" Eaon frowned deeply, translating for the others.

Kaelean sniffed again. "Lover-blessed witches with them. Royal escorts."

Every muscle in Cinn's body went taught.

Eavha took his arm. She pointed to a nearby tree, then pointed up.

Maybe it made him a complete and utter coward, but he couldn't face it again. He let Eavha take him to the tree and let Eaon give him a boost so he could jump for the lowest hanging branch and haul himself up. Eavha followed, climbing high enough that the approaching threat would have to crane their necks to see him, assuming the witches didn't scent him first.

The two of them perched on a branch overlooking the small clearing below. Hands shaking, Cinn handed Eavha one of his blades. She nodded, face hard, taking it without hesitation.

Below, Eaon removed his gloves. He kept the spear though.

Dearmead leaned against a tree beside him and crossed his arms, flexing the hard muscle beneath his dark skin.

Kaelean had disappeared.

For a few minutes, nothing happened. Nobody moved. Cinn wasn't even sure he was breathing, but Eavha's soft hand on his back kept him steady.

A twig snapped. Leaves crunched under boots. A dozen demi-kin soldiers came crashing through the shrubbery, panting heavily. Among them were three witches. The silent, predatory way they walked was enough to set them apart, but the dark gold of their uniforms compared to the burgundy the Hyrschan soldiers' cemented the division.

Two of the witches were covered in weapons: swords, hatchets, knives—so many that Cinn wondered how they could even walk with so much extra weight. The third was leaner than the others and sported a thick gray beard.

"Do either of you speak Nirnish?" the third witch asked as he stepped forward.

"Maybe." Eaon tilted his head as he appraised the trespassers. "I hope you have a good reason for being in Anfar."

"I do. Her Highness, Princess Aisling Aurnia of Hyrsch, Daughter to the King and Queen of Nir, Liberator of the Demi-kin, cordially invites you to Imsa."

Cinn had no idea what that meant.

"Me?" Eaon put a hand to his chest. "You mean to say our crossing is not a coincidence?"

"Pardon me for not explaining."

"Or introducing yourself."

The bearded witch blinked, the muscles in his jaw twitching.

"Yes. My name is Farralt of the Sparrow Coven and I'm here as an emissary of the princess. I asked the dryads to lead us to you, and they were happy to oblige. Take their willingness as a sign of goodwill on our behalf."

The soldiers shifted their weight as they glanced around at the trees. None of them were standing close enough to the witches to properly protect them if Eaon and Dearmead decided to attack.

One of them was familiar. His curly black hair and tired sandstone eyes were hard to forget. Cinn tensed, tempted to leap from the tree and let the questions spew from his mouth.

Are the Copelands okay? Did you protect them? Is it safe to go home?

Eavha grabbed his bicep as Cinn's breaths came quicker.

"And why does this princess want to see me?" Eaon asked, bewildered. "Does she often lower herself to the company of rogues?"

The larger of the two other witches sneered and glanced across at the demi-kin. Some of them glared back, tightening their grips on the hilts of their swords.

"The princess is not averse to unusual company," said Farralt, struggling not to chuckle. The other witch failed to demonstrate such control and a number of the demi-kin soldiers snarled in response.

"Well, Farralt." Eaon narrowed his eyes, having noticed the hostile exchange. "You can tell your master that I will not see her, and not to send any more of her dogs, lest I put a leash on you."

The witches lost their amused expressions.

A wave of relief washed through the demi-kin and they immediately began to turn away. Farralt had gone red in the face, raising his fist and digging in his heels.

"Halt!"

The demi-kin paused. One soldier with a brutal scar across

his left eye stepped forward with his hand still securely on the hilt of his sword. "Our orders were to make the offer. The witch has declined."

Owen, the soldier Cinn recognized, stepped forward as well. "It's time to go home."

"Do not forget your place," Farralt snarled.

Every thought emptied out of Cinn's head.

There was a metal collar around his neck again. His brother was being whipped. *Do not forget your place again, or the next time I'll skin you alive.*

"This conversation is over when I say it is over," Farralt continued. "Where is the necromancer? I demand you all meet Her Highness for Imsa."

Cinn was going to throw up. Eavha held him tighter, but he shrugged her off and leaped from the tree.

"Cinn!" Eavha called after him.

He landed poorly, rolling a few times before scrambling to his feet. Everyone was staring at him. Owen's face drained of color.

A feral snarl loosened the bladders of a few demi-kin, and as Kaelean stalked out from behind a shrub in her lupanis form, their bowels followed.

"Leave," Eaon said tightly. "While you still can, heretic."

"What did you call me?" Farralt hissed.

A dark aura shadowed the gathering, crackling against Cinn's skin. For once, the cold wasn't coming from Eaon. Both he and Dearmead had fallen into a fighting stance, but that wouldn't help them if the emissary had a power like Eaon's.

Cinn pulled out his silver knife and flung it with the skill of a half-trained cadet. It sunk into Farralt's neck with a wet thud and the magic dispelled. Snarling, faces reddening, the other two witches drew their weapons. So did the scar-faced demi-kin and Owen.

"We're not dying for your arrogance," Owen warned.

"Then you will hang for your treason."

The Sparrow witch lunged for Owen, who roared in defiance and met the witch's blade with his own. The other demi-kin followed.

Eaon, Dearmead, Kaelean and Cinn stood there and watched in shock as, in the space of a couple of breaths, the twelve demi-kin soldiers slaughtered the two Sparrows.

Only heavy panting and the whistling wind disturbed the stunned silence in the clearing. Cinn walked slowly to Farralt, braced his foot on the witch's face and yanked his dagger out of his neck. He turned to Owen.

"We mean no harm," the scar-faced demi-kin said, returning his sword to his waist and raising his bloodied hands. "The Sparrows don't speak for us. We came to make the invitation, and now we're happy to leave."

Kaelean made a low sound in her throat, stalking around them, but Dearmead said something that gave her pause. She quickly shifted back into her natural form.

"If you were anything but demi-kin," she hissed, "I would gut you where you stand for trespassing. I will ask the dryads to lead you out, but you tell that Sparrow bitch that if she breaks the treaty again, even for Imsa, I will not be so generous."

"Yes, ma'am."

"And," Eaon stepped forward, letting the aura of his magic swell just a little. "You tell her that if she doesn't leave the kinner alone, I will make what happened in Pirevia look like a scratch compared to the lashing I will unleash upon her city."

An array of bobbing heads and hushed prayers were his

answer. Kaelean approached a tree and began hissing at it until a spindly figure made entirely of bark emerged.

Cinn kept his eyes on Owen. The soldier didn't look away.

"They're safe."

Cinn narrowed his eyes.

"Go home."

Home. Two places warred for the title.

Cinn looked back down at the corpse beneath his foot. Aisling's emissary. As grateful as he was to Eaon for trying to protect him, Cinn had a message of his own to send to the princess.

He drew the Sparrow witch's heavy sword, bracing himself awkwardly. Hefting the steel over his shoulder, he took aim and brought it swinging back down. The first hack didn't do the job, so he lifted the sword again and swung it down with more force. A third time cleaved the head right off.

Grabbing it by the beard, he picked it up and flung it at Owen. The demi-kin caught it, cringing only slightly.

"Message received."

CHAPTER 43

NORA

THE DAWN WAS CLOSE AS NORA TRUDGED HOME, A SPLITTING
headache making it hard to bear even the firelight burning in the
glass streetlamps. She'd bled all her resources dry trying to
identify the missing laundress with absolutely nothing to show
for it. If the woman had any brains she'd be long gone from the
city anyway. The chances of Nora finding her were abysmal.

As she turned into her street, she spotted a familiar
silhouette leaving the house. Nora was about to call out to her
when a man darted out from the shadows across the
cobblestones. Siobhan waved and waited for him, looping her
arm in his before strolling off.

Another dead end in the hunt for the rebel, but Siobhan
meeting men in the dark hours of the morning was still a cause
for concern. Her contract stated she was not to have relations
with other males as long as she was trying to conceive for the
Turloughs.

For half a moment, Nora considered following her. The sharp

stabbing pain in her left temple convinced her not to. She would confront Siobhan when she returned.

Inside, the house was silent. It was too early for even Paulette to be awake. Nora went to the kitchen first and made herself a cup of willow bark tea, taking it to the bedroom with her. She needed proper sleep. It had always been hard to relax when Owen was away, but Aisling's questioning of the Copelands had reminded her that Owen had omitted information about the kinner's escape.

Placing the tea by her bedside, she looked around for where she had left her nightgown. It wasn't in the wardrobe or the bathroom, or anywhere in the room. Grumbling, she went down to the laundry assuming one of the servants must have taken it. She'd rather sleep in a dirty nightgown than naked.

Except it wasn't there, either.

"I swear, Siobhan, if you're taking my things we're going to have real problems," Nora muttered to herself as she stalked back up to the main floor and down the hall to Siobhan's private room.

The surrogate was rather tidy, her generous double bed made up and all the belonging's she'd brought with her from her village packed away nicely. If she had half a mind, Nora would have felt guilty for going through her things but she couldn't think past the pounding in her head. She just wanted her nightgown.

Nora opened a trunk inside the wardrobe and stilled.

"No," she whispered, reaching down to pull out a clump of curly brown hair. A wig. There was a second one, blond, underneath it. A guard's uniform. A servant's uniform.

A laundress's uniform.

Nora slammed the trunk closed and left the room.

Back in her own bedroom, she sat down and sipped at her

tea, staring at the wall. There had been a mistake. Her head was pounding, she was sleep deprived . . . she was hallucinating. Obviously that was what was happening. She would check again later. Ask Siobhan.

There would be an explanation.

~

"Miss?" Paulette's gentle voice roused her from a deep sleep. "I'm sorry to disturb you, but there's a messenger."

Nora sighed, running her hands over her scalp. "Are they in the parlor?"

"Yes, miss."

"Thank you, Paulette."

"I'll whip you up something to eat. It's good to see you, miss."

Nora made herself sit up in time to smile at the woman, then got out of bed and quickly changed out of her crumpled uniform into a comfortable pair of pants and a long cotton tunic. With slippers on her feet and rubbing the crust from her eyes, she shuffled to the parlor.

"Good afternoon, ma'am," the young boy bowed and handed her a note.

"Afternoon? Damn it," she sighed. Noticing the brown mark on the back of the boy's neck, Nora went to a compartment in a tea cart by the window and pulled out a few coppers. "Thank you. Be well."

"Be well to you too, ma'am." The boy beamed, hurrying from the house.

Nora sat down and peeled open the sealed letter.

"Oh," Nora stood up quickly. "Oh. Oh. Paulette! I don't have time!"

"What's the matter?" Paulette came rushing back out form the kitchen. "Is it Mr. Turlough?"

"He's back in the city. I'm being summoned. I have to go." Nora hurried back to her room, pulling out another set of uniform.

Paulette still managed to convince her to shovel down a few bites of warm oats as she ran out the door, but she didn't care about food. Or sleep. Or what she may or may not have seen in Siobhan's room.

Owen was home.

Aisling was already sitting on her throne when Nora arrived, a cold and impassive expression on her face. Along the walls stood over twenty guards while, behind her, six of her advisors were sharing nervous glances. Nora stepped up on the dais and stood to Aisling's right. She was about to question why the princess was so tense when the doors opened. The soldiers shuffled in, still filthy and exhausted from their travels.

Owen wouldn't look at her.

The soldiers knelt, General Tomson at the head of the formation. The male was getting older, but Nora thought the lines on his scarred face were particularly poignant today. His hands trembled as he removed a satchel from over his shoulder and placed it on the floor.

"Your Highness."

"What happened?" Aisling snapped.

Frowning, Nora glanced sideways at the princess. She didn't

have the glaze over her eyes that she sometimes had when she'd drunk too much the day before, so her poor temper was unusual.

"Farralt, Hollik and Tollen are dead."

The advisors stiffened, quiet muttering breaking out.

"What. Happened."

Her tone silenced the room again.

"The rogue witches declined your invitation. Farralt refused to accept their response." Tomson spoke very carefully.

One of the advisors, Orla, a witch so old her physical appearance had even started to age, stepped forward from the line, eyes black with rage. "Yet every single demi-kin returned unscathed. Did any of you even try to defend your superiors?"

"The royal infantry is a joke," another spoke up.

Aisling raised a hand and, once again, silence descended upon the throne room. "Bring me the satchel."

Shoulder's aching from the tension rife in the room, Nora stepped down and retrieved the bag at Tomson's feet. From the weight and smell of it, she had a pretty good idea of what was inside.

"I don't think—"

"I know what it is. Give it to me." Aisling demanded, holding out a hand.

Nora carried the bag to Aisling, stepping back and covering her nose as the princess pulled Farralt's decapitated head out and held it up for all to see. There were gasps and sobs from the line of advisors. Someone vomited.

Whoever had cut the head off had done a bad job of it, but the torn flesh at his neck was the least awful part. The cloudy eyes and bleached lips turned Nora's stomach.

Aisling had no apparent visceral reaction as she turned the head from side to side, inspecting it. Clasping it with both hands, she sniffed deeply at the decomposing flesh. When it didn't give her the answers she wanted, she stared into the sightless white eyes and began to mutter in a language Nora didn't understand. The air crackled with energy, making the hairs on her arms stand up straight.

A minute passed. Two. Aisling's eyes had grown unfocused as she continued to chant almost silently.

Finally, the air fell flat again. Aisling sagged slightly in her seat and let the head drop unceremoniously on the marble floor, a loud splat echoing through the chamber.

"General Tomson tells the truth. Farralt was killed and decapitated by royal blades wielded by one of the rogue's companions. A shame you didn't bring me a body part from the others so I might have seen how they died as well."

There was the slightest ruffle of unease among the soldiers.

"We . . . couldn't carry their bodies, and would never defile their remains the way the rogues defiled Farralt."

"Your commitment to respect endears you." Aisling sat back and wove her fingers together, creating a shelf for her chin as she surveyed the soldiers. "Owen. Come forward."

Nora's breath caught, turning to stare at the princess. Aisling didn't even glance in her direction, her hard gaze locked on Owen as he stepped forward and knelt beside Tomson.

"Your Highness."

"Did you know that most Sparrow witches can see a corpse's moment of death?" she asked, venom coating every word.

"No, Your Highness." Owen managed to keep his voice steady, also avoiding eye contact with Nora.

"Well, it's a very useful little trick when dealing with matters of justice. I bring it up because, while you were away, body parts washed up in the eastern port village of Oford. They belonged to the three soldiers who accompanied you on your errands in Belden. I hoped to glean more information about the incident at the Copeland farm, so I had them delivered to me just this morning."

As the color began to leech from Owen's face, Nora forgot how to breathe. She looked from her husband to the princess, back and forth, begging one of them to tell her what was going on. Why hadn't Aisling brought this information to her first?

"Can you guess what I discovered about their deaths, Owen?"

"I can explain, Your Highness."

"You will. But right now, I'm going to give you the chance to tell me the truth about Hollik and Tollen. Because if I get a hold of their bodies and find out you were equally responsible for their deaths as you are for your brethren in Belden . . ."

Nora didn't hear the rest of the threat through the ringing in her ears. Her vision was blurring, her head too heavy and too light at the same time.

Owen had lied. She knew he had lied, but she'd never thought . . .

The sudden movement of a few of the guards made her suck in a deep breath that cleared her head. Some of the soldiers had made a run for the doors, but the guards lining the wall stopped them.

"It was just the two of us," General Tomson declared, rising to his feet. "Owen and I did it. The others had no hand in it."

"They were complicit," Aisling hissed. "Archirion, see that all these soldiers find their way to the dungeons. I will be down later to discern the truth."

"No," Nora gasped, gripping the throne to keep herself steady.

"Quiet," Aisling snapped at her.

"What kind of circus are you running here, Aisling?" Orla asked, stepping forward as Archirion and the guards wrangled the soldiers toward the door that would take them to the dungeons.

Nora watched Owen go, keeping his shoulders set and his chin up. Still, he didn't look at her.

Bastard.

"Enough!" Aisling shouted at the remaining advisors. "Meet me in the council room. I will explain everything shortly."

Despite their suspicious looks and quiet muttering, the advisors made their way out of the throne room. Aisling sat quietly, waiting for the guards and soldiers to finish clearing out.

Once it was only Nora, Clayton and Aisling left in the room, the princess finally turned to face her Second.

"I didn't tell you about the bodies because I didn't want you distracted, and there wasn't time to discuss this new information with you earlier."

Nora was either going to vomit or pass out. Her whole body was shaking.

"I don't know what would be worse," Aisling continued. "That you knew, and lied to me, or that you were completely ignorant to the fact that your husband is a rebel. Either way, I'm one wrong word away from denouncing you as my Second."

Nora didn't care. "Please. Show him mercy."

"You know I cannot do that. It would look like preferential treatment and send entirely the wrong message. You'll be lucky if I can convince the council not to let you hang beside him."

She could see it. Owen swinging lifelessly by the neck. The noose tightening around her own throat.

"What message are you worried it would send?" Nora

choked. "That you're not cruel, like Nevan is? Not calloused like the king and queen?"

"I cannot—"

"Do you really think continuing to kill them, to torture them down in your dungeons, is going to work?" Nora interrupted, blood pulsing in her temples as an insatiable urgency took over her. "It hasn't worked for you yet, and it never will. Not with the rebels, not with the kinner."

"Enough," Aisling hissed.

"No," Nora stepped back, hands balled into fists. "I should have said this a long time ago, and if you're going to hang me like a traitor then I might as well get it off my chest. What you did to that boy was wrong, and it got you nothing. What you are doing to the rebels will get you nowhere. How many times will you say you're not like the rest of the Sparrow Coven in Dusarn, and yet walk their path anyway? Walk it, because you're too much of a coward to forge your own."

She stood there, shaking, breath hitching while Aisling stared at her murderously. When the burning in her eyes became too much, she didn't bother to wipe away the tears that slid down her scarred cheeks. She had sworn to be by Aisling's side for any and all of her endeavors, but that was when Aisling had been the spearhead of peace. This business with the kinner had poisoned her, and Nora would not ignore the rot any longer.

"What would you do if you were me?" Aisling finally asked, her tone softening.

There was no denying what Owen had done. There was no way around the confessions that had happened in this room today. Aisling needed a reason to be lenient where she had always been unyielding.

Nora's breath trembled and she closed her eyes.

"I have a strong lead on the missing laundress from the kinner's escape. I was waiting for proof before bringing her in, but . . . tell the council you offered Owen leniency in exchange for information, and that he provided her name."

"He killed three royal soldiers and likely two Sparrow witches. The name of some random rebel will not be enough to excuse him. To explain her worth, I would have to tell them about the kinner. They will report it to the Coven."

Aisling would be in trouble for keeping him a secret, but Nora held her stare. She didn't care if it looked like begging.

Setting her jaw, Aisling lowered her voice.

"Who is she?"

Nora swallowed and turned her face up to the ceiling. "Siobhan LaTour."

"Your surrogate."

"Yes."

Aisling's nostrils flared as she stood from the throne and Nora flinched. She wouldn't put it past the princess to slit her throat herself.

"You disappoint me, Nora. Bring the woman in."

"You'll spare Owen?"

Aisling stopped as she stepped down from the dais, looking back with something close to pity in her cold eyes.

"I will try."

CHAPTER 44

NORA

THERE WAS A THICK WALL BETWEEN THE WORLD AND NORA AS she entered her house, the laughter of children and Paulette's stern warnings for them to get out of the kitchen barely penetrating. Like a ghost, she wandered down the hall and found Siobhan sitting on the kitchen counter again, smiling and swinging her legs as she watched the demi-kin children play.

"Beg your pardon, miss. There must have been something in the water this morning that has sent the young ones mad. I said *outside with the lot of you,* before I cook you in a stew!" Paulette chased them out the back door.

Siobhan lost the smile on her face, getting down off the counter.

"Paulette said there was news about Owen. Is everything alright? You look terrible." The human woman brought her a glass of water, but Nora just put it down on the wide kitchen island.

"Come with me a moment," she said, voice thick as she turned back around and left the kitchen.

Siobhan followed her to the guest bedroom where Nora let herself through to where she'd found the trunk earlier. She opened it, revealing the pile of disguises that had not miraculously disappeared during the day.

"What is this?" she asked. The calmness of her voice felt wrong, but there was nothing inside her. No rage, no fear. As if someone had picked up all her emotions and put them in a box, stashing them in the attic.

Siobhan had gone very still, her posture tensing. "Why were you in my room?"

"Who were you with this morning? What is all this?"

"I really wish you hadn't found that."

As if she too had no feeling, Siobhan walked calmly toward the nightstand.

"You are under arrest." Nora's voice trembled and she clenched her fists, trying to keep it together enough to do this.

Siobhan picked up a slip of parchment and passed it to Nora.

"What is that?"

"Read."

With one hand on the handcuffs looped in her belt, Nora took the paper. She recognized the handwriting on it immediately; she had seen a note like this nearly every month since hiring Siobhan, but this time the words were different. Nora's mouth went dry as the walls began to close in on her.

"You're pregnant."

She didn't make it to the bed—Nora sat down right there on the floor and stared at the doctor's note. Pregnant. They were going to have a baby.

"I will not go to the palace willingly," said Siobhan. The cheerful farm girl that Nora had gotten to know had disappeared, and in her place stood a pinch-faced woman of spine. From within the nightstand, she pulled a dagger.

"You need to leave," Nora gasped, head spinning. The air was too thin and the ground too magnetic. For a few seconds, she closed her eyes and focused on wriggling her fingers on the carpeted floor.

"Sorry, what?"

"Pack a bag and go."

When Siobhan didn't speak again, Nora took a steadier breath and opened her eyes. The dagger was hanging limply in her hand, a deep frown on the human woman's face.

"Aisling knows it was you."

The air left Siobhan in a hushed whoosh as her face whitened. Moving quickly, grabbing a large satchel, she began to pack things from the trunk: wigs, false teeth, envelopes that Nora could only guess held false identity papers.

The last five years, everything Nora had done had been to build an easy life for herself. To build a family. Now her husband was a traitor, their surrogate a rebel. It was all slipping away.

"There are horses out the back. Take one to Belden." Her voice sounded flat and dead, even to her.

"The farm town? Why? I have contacts at South Wharf."

"There is a couple there who know Owen. They will keep you safer than anyone else is able to. As soon as I can get him free, Owen and I will join you and disappear."

"Get him free?" Siobhan paused. "Nora, what's going on?"

"I'm not even sure I know. But please, trust me. Find the Copelands and wait for us."

Siobhan looked Nora over, still sitting on the floor. The human crouched down beside her and took her hand, placing it over her stomach.

"We will wait for you."

Nora closed her eyes again and nodded.

CHAPTER 45

CINN

THE SUN WAS ON ITS DESCENT WHEN THEY STOPPED AT A fallen maple log a few dozen paces away from the looming shadow of the Great Boab.

Cinn watched Kaelean shrink into a tiny field mouse, then picked her up and held her in his palm. Those beady little eyes stared at him, as if daring him to crush her. He could, if he wanted to. A part of him did. A part of him wanted to squeeze and watch her squirm, just so she knew what it felt like.

He put her in the pocket Eavha had sewn to the inside of his shirt and took a calming breath. Eaon caught his eye and gave him a knowing look.

"Remember, you don't have to have an answer for everything they ask. You don't have to lie perfectly. You're just distracting them until we can take care of the curse," Eaon reminded him.

Cinn nodded and fondled the parchment in his pocket with the note Eavha had scratched out.

{Will you be alright if your magic surges?}

Eaon smiled tensely, gripping the staff still in his gloved hand. "I will be fine."

Eavha came and gave Cinn a careful hug. He stopped her from pulling away entirely and untied the belt that held the silver knife from around his waist. Carefully, he tied it around her instead, adjusting it for her dominant left hand. The folds of her skirt hid the scabbard from view, and the belt wasn't so obnoxious that it would draw attention. Eavha bit her bottom lip as she stared at it, giving him a small smile.

Cinn nodded before leaving the three of them at the spot where they would rip open the barrier between Anfar and Wyldeden.

As he neared the Boab, there was a strange tingling of magic in the air that made him want to turn around and run. He was not welcome. He was not of Anfar. Not a witch. Craning his neck, he tried to see the canopy high above them, but it disappeared above the tangled branches of surrounding trees. The bark seethed with an almost tangible power that weakened his knees.

Swallowing the lump in his throat, Cinn wandered around the trunk looking for the crease that was the entrance to Wyldeden. Normally there would have been scouts in the forest to report on his presence, guardians that would have stopped him from even getting this close, but they were all locked inside now. Nothing but Kaelean's spell was left to defend it, the witches inside vulnerable to another attack and enduring the murdering whim of their high priestess.

Cinn found the witchmark and laid his hand on top of it. The mouse in his pocket squirmed.

The magic is tied to me, Kaelean had explained. *I'll feel it when you touch it, but so will Lorelei. She will not be able to ignore it.*

Sure enough, minutes later, the magic in the air intensified and the smell of pollen and nectar permeated the air. Backing away, Cinn watched the crease in the tree widen. Through the portal, he could see a meadow and a crystalline lake, but the view was quickly obscured by ten masked guardians filing through the crease and into the forest.

Trailing them was a witch Cinn assumed was Lorelei; rich earthy skin and large curls, wearing a dress of moss and a diadem of branches and acorns. Eyes that seemed to turn like the earth, the colors ever shifting in tones of green and brown, appraised him. The opening in the Boab closed. The witches were speaking to him, but he couldn't understand them.

Cinn stood still and looked the witch over with a cocky smile that he'd practiced over and over these last few days. Reaching into his pocket, he focused on not letting his hand shake as he offered the note.

One of the guardians took his note and read it before passing it to Lorelei.

"You understand Nirnish," Lorelei said, folding the note. "But you do not speak and require a translator for the Southern Mountain Clan's sign language."

Cinn nodded, confirming he understood her.

Lorelei's eyes were gleaming as she gave him another once over. "You reek of magic."

Slowly, trying not to appear wary, he turned his back to them and lowered the collar of his shirt to expose the mark on his neck. They'd been prepared for Lorelei to be able to sense Kaelean, even in mouse form, and they were relying on her not ever having met a kinner before.

"Kinner," Lorelei was physically shaking, licking her lips. "I thought your kind had abandoned Nir."

Cinn held out his arms and bowed with a flourish.

Lorelei spoke to one of her guardians who promptly opened the portal again and disappeared inside.

"I've asked him to fetch one of my elders who may understand you. I would very much like to know why a creature such as yourself has come to my humble home. They won't be long."

Within minutes, the portal was opening once again and the guardian returned with an older male witch covered in peppery brown hair, a few laugh lines around his eyes. Cinn doubted the male had done much laughing of late, however, as his face was drawn and wary, a profound sadness pulling at the corners of his mouth.

A mouth that popped open as he stared at Cinn. Lorelei and the elder shared a few rushed words before the male stepped forward and held out his hands. Eaon had trained him in the customs of the clan, so he let the elder take one of his hands in both of his.

"The high priestess tells me you understand Nirnish?"

Cinn nodded.

"And can use the Southern Mountain Clan's winter language? I'm afraid I am not as fluent as one of my . . . a witch I used to know, but I'm sure we will manage. It's an honor to meet you. My name is Bodhi."

The smile Cinn gave the witch was kinder.

"What is your business in Anfar?" Lorelei asked, narrowing her eyes at Bodhi.

{I was cursed some years ago and my voice was locked. I was told there was a powerful priestess here that could help.}

He had practiced the sentences with Eaon until he knew them by heart. Utter nonsense, of course, but the lie would get him through the door to Wyldeden.

Bodhi translated in the human language so Cinn could confirm the words were close enough to what he'd meant to say.

Lorelei grinned wolfishly and spread her hands.

"I would be glad to assist you, though I would ask how you heard of me, and how you found us," Lorelei asked as she tilted her head.

{Travelers from your clan spoke of your power when they visited the Mountain Clan I stayed with.} Cinn told the lie they had perfected on their journey south. {The location I interrogated from rogues.}

"Ah." Lorelei put a hand to her heart. "It warms me to hear that my people speak so highly of me."

Bodhi pursed his lips, keeping his eyes on the kinner's hands.

"Before I allow you inside of Wyldeden, you will need to take a vow of forfeit. You must forgive me for putting the safety of my people first," Lorelei explained, putting her hands together as if begging.

{Of course. I expected as much.}

"Normally I would request a forfeit of life should you bear any ill-intent to the clan, but considering the Lover is unlikely to take you, will you vow to forfeit, perhaps, your freedom instead?" Lorelei asked.

She won't be able to resist the chance to study you, Kaelean had told him. Cinn could see it in the shine in her eyes, the way she couldn't stop rolling and chewing her lips, that he could very well refuse to take the vow and she would still let him in. Just not as a guest.

{I have no ill-intent, so I am happy to make the vow,} Cinn signed.

He repeated the words of the high priestess as best he could with his hands, aware that the elder watched him closely. The vow was not a lie. He really didn't plan to harm the clan. Just her. Still, he started sweating as the possibility of being trapped again became very real.

Lorelei was practically bursting as they finished. There was a tight squeeze in his chest as the bond snapped into place.

Once again, the portal opened.

The mouse in his pocket stayed utterly still as they crossed the threshold into Wyldeden.

CHAPTER 46

EAON

EAON HAD THOUGHT EAVHA WOULD WANT TO BE THE ONE TO make the witchmark Kaelean had taught them, but her cheeks pinked as she asked him to try instead. She didn't trust herself and he couldn't convince her to try.

Kaelean had assured Eaon that he had the strength to do it if Eavha couldn't; what he lacked was control, so that was what he had focused on these weeks they had journeyed south.

Unlike the spellmarks Eavha used to amplify her power, Kaelean had taught Eaon a few tricks on how to dampen his. Witches learned faster than humans, but trying to cram years of magic training into a handful of weeks was still a challenge. Forcing himself to practice until he vomited, or passed out, had been unpleasant but worth it; he didn't feel like a storm in a jar anymore, waiting for the glass to shatter from the pressure within.

Regardless, Eavha and Dearmead cast a protection spell over

themselves as Eaon prepared to cast the mark. Kaelean had needed to teach them those spells as well.

"This is ridiculous; do they teach you nothing?" she had complained. "What do you all do all day in there? Skip around making flowers bloom?"

Eavha's cheeks had burned hotly because, yes, that was exactly what she had spent her elementary years learning to do.

"Why train warriors when there is no war?" Dearmead had countered.

"Yes, why be prepared for the worst when you could all just die, instead?" Kaelean had narrowed her eyes. "At least with all your useless flowers your mourning pyres would have smelt nice."

The three of them had stared at her in confusion, having to have another long conversation about the way grieving had changed since Lorelei had ascended.

Kaelean's ability to cuss colorfully had impressed even Eaon.

"You mean the Lover isn't offended by our grief?" Eavha's eyes had been brimming with tears.

"Not grieving is like saying they weren't worth anything to you." Kaelean grabbed fistfuls of her hair as she paced. "You're saying that the person the Lover decided was *perfect* isn't even worth you missing. That's the true insult. Lorelei's radicalism was a welcomed challenge, but Lover spare me, you can't tell someone not to grieve!"

A rock hit Eaon in the back and he spun around to glare at his sister, who raised her eyebrows as she tossed a second stone in her palm.

"Um, *ouch*."

"You were spacing out." Eavha shrugged

Dearmead was frowning at him. "What's wrong?"

"Nothing. Except now my back hurts," Eaon grumbled as he stalked toward the broken, moss-covered log that Kaelean had used to bear the mark once before.

"Oh, spare me." Eavha rolled her eyes, tossing the stone away.

Dearmead followed Eaon, still fussing. "You've got that look on your face like you're having another existential crisis."

"And?"

"Focus. Both of you," Eavha scolded.

The three of them waited in silence until they sensed the surging in the forest as the portal to Wyldeden was opened. Spellmarks for concentration and control were drawn in mud on Eaon's face, but it didn't stop his hands from shaking as he sliced open his arm. Eavha and Dearmead stood behind him, the thrum of their protection spells almost distracting.

Eaon's power stirred as he pictured the witchmark he had to draw and dipped his fingers into his bleeding wound.

No killing right now, he told it.

It churned inside him, dragging its claws through his lungs.

Eaon drew the first line with Dearmead's spear across his lap, ready to take the brunt of his surge if his magic decided to lash out. He drew the second line, his head pounding, sweat rolling down his back. The air thinned, carrying scornful whispers. Dearmead and Eavha glanced around, hearing them too. The very fabric of the world trembled, reality blurring as Eaon dipped his fingers into his arm again and spread the blood in an arc between the two lines. The shadows darkened as the whispers grew louder, frantic, the weight of them pressing down on him. Wordless urgency rattled his veins, skin tingling as a slimy fear oozed through his gut.

"Hurry up," Eavha hissed.

There was no way Cinn was enough of a distraction for Lorelei to not notice this. Then again, nobody had noticed when Kaelean had done it.

Blood dripped from Eaon's nose as he drew the final curve, red spots flashing behind his eyelids. The mark pulsed as the spell sealed, the oppressive presence dissipating as quickly as it had come on.

Eaon staggered to his feet.

"You did it." Eavha covered her grin, face pale. "You really did it."

"Yeah, and I'm never doing it again."

"Thank you," Dearmead said, shivering as he passed Eaon a canteen of water and the last of the tonic they had brewed for him. The magic would have been unpleasant for them at such proximity, too.

Downing the lot, Eaon shoved the bottles into his pack before stepping through the tear in the world he'd made and into the golden-lit forest of Wyldeden.

It was exactly how he remembered it and yet it was so different. It still didn't feel like home—there was no sense of relief as he put his feet in the velvet soil—but it no longer felt like a cage, either.

Quickly, the three witches dashed through the forest, knowing it didn't matter which way they went, they would eventually end up on the outskirts of town. On the border of their very own estate, in fact.

Eavha moaned at the sight of their house. The garden had

not been tended to in a long time, and there was no food growing on the vines.

"It's unoccupied," Dearmead assured them. "Nobody wanted to move into the house of an extinct bloodline."

"Not extinct. Not yet." Eavha gritted her teeth before darting across the open land.

Moving quickly, keeping low, Eaon and Dearmead followed her to the door to the Nemuse estate. The wards Eavha had painted on every window had faded, but Eaon's hands started prickling where his brands had scarred. Eavha hissed and rubbed her hands on her skirt as they crossed the threshold, crouching low beneath the window.

"Well, the wards work," Eaon groused.

"We won't be here long," Dearmead assured them. "Just until night falls and we can sneak into the city. You're sure the book you need is here?"

Eaon raised a single eyebrow at Dearmead.

"It's just a question."

"A stupid one."

"Stop it," Eavha hissed at them. "Just go get it."

Eaon took the spear with him as he stalked through the dusty halls toward his unk's office. Everything had been moved since he'd left, so it took him a moment to find the leather-bound tome that he'd dismissed so quickly during his studying. *Willful Illness* had sounded promising, but it had been about black magic, not malignant diseases. Aadya had been their presiding priestess and had ruled out a curse—like the naïve fool he was, Eaon had questioned it too late.

Returning to the kitchen, Eaon passed the heavy tome to Eavha who immediately opened it and started scanning the contents page.

Dearmead had already started changing back into his guardian leathers so that, if they were spotted, he wouldn't stand out quite so much. Eaon couldn't help but stare at the new scars on his friend's body; the ones he'd gotten trying to rescue him and Eavha from Pirevia. Dearmead had once cringed at the idea of venturing outside the Boab, yet, for his family, Dearmead had escaped Wyldeden and braved Anfar alone. Had tracked Eavha and him to an alien city and planned a prison break with nothing but a little Terra magic and his spear.

Eaon clenched his fists and wiped his still-bleeding nose on his shoulder again.

"Here," Eavha said, putting the book down. "Detection of curses."

"Anything on how to break one?" Eaon asked, pulling the book a little closer.

"No, but the methods are likely to be as varied as the curses themselves. Once we find the altar it was cast at we will have more of an idea of what the actual curse is, and then we can figure out how to break it."

"Assuming the kinner can buy us enough time to do all that," Dearmead sighed, pinching the bridge of his nose.

"Cinn," Eaon said flatly.

"What?"

"His name is Cinn. Stop calling him 'the kinner.'" Eaon gave the book back to Eavha. She would have more luck figuring out what to do; she was better trained.

Dearmead's face reddened.

Eaon focused on getting his nose to stop bleeding.

Once it had, he pulled clean pants and one of his father's shirts out of the pack to change into. Dearmead knelt up to look out the window as he did.

CHAPTER 47

CINN

Wyldeden made the heather meadow Cinn had been so awed by look like a patch of weeds, but he tried not to look too impressed by it as the high priestess led him to a circle of houses. Each was made of polished stone, had a crystal gate and a perfect little garden bursting with a bewildering variety of flowers and berries.

Bodhi, Lorelei and two guards came with him as they entered one of the houses. The lounging space was furnished in intricately carved mahogany and upholstered in soft silk, but it was the ceiling, covered in wisteria and glowing buds that cast a soft, glittery light into the room that had Cinn's jaw slackening. To the left was a kitchen, the counters filled with of exotic fruits and golden pastries. Across the room lay two open doors; one seemed to be a bedroom, the post of a canopy bed woven out of oak branches just barely visible, while the other appeared to be a bathing room.

"This is my guest house," Lorelei explained, gesturing to the five witches kneeling by the wall. "And these are some of my laborers. They're trained to be pre-emptive, so you won't need to ask for anything. Though if you have any trouble with communication, please let me know."

Cinn's stomach turned as he looked to the witches, who remained still and silent. The sadness that weighed on Bodhi wasn't mirrored in their faces. Just an emptiness, a blankness that he was far too familiar with.

"Between you and I," Lorelei spoke quietly, stepping closer to him. "I have tried them all, but the fourth one is the most skilled at *service*, or the third if you're that way inclined."

It was an effort to remain impassive as Lorelei winked at him.

"I will leave my Wolf and Fox with you, if you don't mind. But take some time to refresh yourself, then join the elders and I for our evening meal. We shall discuss your curse in the morning."

Cinn could barely nod.

The two guardians stood by the door after Bodhi and Lorelei left, so Cinn didn't dare relax his mask of superiority. He took his time as he wandered the house, orienting himself with its layout before selecting some fresh clothes and taking them to the washroom.

He went to close the door behind him but two laborers had followed him, slipping inside. One began to pump water into the large wooden tub while the other reached forward to begin undressing him.

Stopping her, Cinn shook his head, then turned to the male filling the tub and shook his head again. He knew how to run his own bath, and he certainly didn't need anyone messing with his clothes. The two witches gave each other a glance, but quickly left the room.

Once the door was closed, Cinn put the change of clothes down on the floor and took the mouse out of his pocket. Kaelean immediately started to shift, and Cinn began pumping the bathtub to cover the sound of it. The water was perfectly tepid and had the same shimmery quality as the lake.

Kaelean sat by the door with her ear pressed against the wood, a finger to her lips.

Ignoring her, he got in the tub and took the time to clean himself properly. His mere presence had bought the witches at least until morning to do what they needed to do and the dinner tonight would give him the opportunity to figure out exactly which elders might give them trouble when it came time to deal with the priestess.

Dearmead had explained who the remaining elders had been before he left, so Cinn had a rough idea who he needed to get a feel for. Herbe, the elder guardian, was particularly loyal to Lorelei considering his job was to keep her safe. He was more likely to kill Kaelean on sight than pause to hear what she had to say. There was Milnova, the keeper of law, and Bodhi the elder teacher, who Dearmead and Eaon both thought would be their best chance at finding allies. They would want to know the truth and may already be suspicious. The two elders of trade and agriculture were not big politicians, but the elder scout would be paying attention. Which only left the elder messenger, because the others were all dead.

The witches hadn't told him to do anything but waste time, but if there was anything he could do to make things easier, he would try. If not for Eaon, if not for Eavha and Dearmead or Kaelean, then for the slaves waiting to serve him in the living room.

～

A few hours later, Kaelean was back in his pocket as he followed the masked guardians out of the house. Even as the sun faded, the air stayed warm and the shadows cast themselves only softly over the valleys and crests of the city around him.

The guardians led him to a large arching pavilion made of glittering quartz, the posts covered in climbing ivy and sweet jasmine flowers. Regular guardians watched over the structure as laborers milled around, tending to the circular table laden with fruits, cheeses and wine. Cinn recognized Bodhi, deep in a serious discussion with one of the other elders. On the other side of the table, two other males howled with raucous laughter as they drank heavily, snapping their fingers at laborers to bring more wine. Clearly the clan's predicament was lost on those two.

There were more than the eight elders he was expecting to see, and Lorelei had not yet arrived. The heirs apparent also sat at the table, along with a female whose heavy robe made her stand out like a bloodstain on a white shirt. While the others were all dressed in what passed as finery in Wyldeden, the female sat quietly with her gray hood raised so that her eyes were hidden in shadow. Cinn knew enough about Aadya, Lorelei's favored priestess, to recognize her. That she was here meant the others had a clear passage to her quarters tonight.

"Ah, the kinner has arrived." Bodhi noticed him and stood, pulling out a seat beside him. "I'm sorry, I haven't managed to catch your proper name in all this time."

Cinn smiled and walked around the table, ignoring the sets of eyes on him.

{Do you all speak Nirnish?} he asked Bodhi.

"No, unfortunately. Shayella here is in charge of the scouts, so she knows most languages. Von is our traveler apparent, so he is fluent in many languages as well. Maybe even yours, actually," Bodhi said. "Von, do you know much of the Southern Mountain Clan's winter language?"

"Their winter language?" Von raised his heavy brow. "Not much, I'm afraid. I visited during the early autumn but I acquired some books on the subject for our libraries anyway."

All conversation died abruptly. The guardians straightened and the laborers dropped to their knees, bowing their heads.

Lorelei was making her appearance.

All the elders and heirs stood as the high priestess meandered her way through an archway and took the empty seat beside Aadya. Only once she was settled did everybody else return to their positions. Lorelei started praying in Terranian and the elders muttered along softly.

Kaelean shuffled in his pocket.

Cinn glanced around to make sure he wasn't being watched before reaching into his shirt and slowly taking her out. He set her on his lap and tried to sit still as she scurried down his leg.

With a final declaration, Lorelei ended the prayer. Conversations resumed, but many had directed their attention to the high priestess.

Dinner was a jolly affair and Cinn gorged himself on the fine food and drink. The wine was far too potent, so he switched to juice after one sip. He waited until most of the elders were tipsy before getting Bodhi's attention.

{What were the prayers about?}

"Oh, just the usual things." Bohdi waved a hand as if swatting a fly, spilling a little of his wine as he did. "Gratitude for this and that. Do you pray?"

{Not normally. I've always been interested in your spirits though.}

"We have some of the most beautiful temples east of the Spine here. I would be happy to take you on a tour in the morning. If you're not busy with Lorelei of course."

{I would enjoy that.}

Any excuse to delay that meeting.

Kaelean hadn't returned by the time dinner was finished.

Cinn let the guardians lead him back to Lorelei's guest house, trying not to be too obvious as he looked around for a field mouse.

Inside, the five laborers were still on their knees by the wall. Cinn didn't miss the way a couple of them tensed upon his arrival. One female couldn't help but glance warily at the guardians before lowering her head.

The two masked males stood silently by the door, apparently planning on guarding him the entire night. His stomach churned, and without thinking too much about it went and tapped all five laborers on the shoulder and crooked a finger telling them to follow him as he went to his room.

Once inside, Cinn closed the door. The laborers immediately started undressing.

Cinn shook his head, waving at them to stop. He didn't know how to explain, so he took one of the females by the arm and led her to the bed, put her in and tucked her under the sheets. He pointed until a couple of the others followed suit, then led another to the chaise lounge beneath the window and found some more blankets for them.

Then he took his position by the door and watched the handle for movement.

After a moment, a soft voice called out behind him. "Sorry, but what do you want us to do?"

He turned and raised his eyebrows, not having expected any of them to speak Nirnish. The first female he had led to bed was sitting up again, tucking a stray piece of hair behind her ear. Cinn put his hands together and lay his head down on them.

"Sleep? You want us to . . . sleep?"

Cinn nodded. Then pointed at his eyes, then to the door. He would keep them safe.

There were quiet whispers throughout the room, but finally the female gave him a grateful smile and lay back down in bed, closing her eyes.

CHAPTER 48

EAVHA

They waited until the night was deep, then made their way to the Sanctuary. Getting inside was easy. There were hardly any guardians about and none that were properly awake; such was the sanctity of the priestesses. Nobody in Wyldeden would even consider troubling them.

Eaon, Dearmead and Eavha stood outside the Holy Library. Deep underground, the library was the keeping place for the oldest and most delicate books. No guard was needed because the warding spells on the door were so intricate that only a handful of priestesses even knew them. Less were able to cast them.

Of course, Kaelean knew the wards well. She had created them.

Dearmead leaned against the wall with his hands over his uptilted face.

"I can't watch this. I can't believe we're doing this."

Eaon rolled his eyes. "I used to sneak into libraries all the time."

"I know, but I liked to pretend I didn't so I never had to report you," Dearmead groaned. "My Head of House would kill me if he knew I was here."

"Mother of all, get the stick out of your ass, Dea," Eavha sighed as she finished tracing the complicated series of spellmarks over the door. The butterflies in her stomach from having actually used strong magic again made her smile and the click as the latch unlocked was deeply satisfying.

They were alone in the dim library, but some of the ancient books had such a potent aura it was like its own presence. Like the trees in the forest, Eavha got the distinct impression the books were watching them.

She walked silently along the cold granite floor, peering at the titles. Many weren't in Terranian so, as they searched for more information on curses, she and Dearmead hissed for Eaon to come and translate.

"What about this one?" Dearmead asked, stepping back as Eaon went to inspect it.

"I . . . I actually have no idea what language that is," Eaon grimaced. "It looks Fae, but not the Fae that I know. But wait, look at this one. Might have a spell for your . . . you know. *Problem*."

"Eaon!" Dearmead hissed. "This is serious."

Eavha didn't want to know.

"This one's called *Death's Blessing*. Volume two," she called out.

Eaon came around, still smirking at himself. He dropped the expression when he saw the book Eavha was pointing at.

"Do you feel that?" he asked breathlessly.

Eavha shook her head, looking between her brother and the book.

Eaon raised his hand, gloved fingers hovering millimeters from the cracked leather spine. Eavha could have sworn the room grew colder.

"Where's volume one?" he whispered.

Eavha searched the shelves nearby while Eaon carefully removed the book. The pages were yellowed inside.

"Not here."

"Maybe we should check Lorelei and Aadya's offices," Dearmead whispered.

Eavha smirked. "Now you're talking."

"Not now," Eaon shook his head. "Dinner will be over soon."

From the doorway, a fourth voice spoke up. "I'll get Cinn to distract them tomorrow."

Eavha jumped and covered her mouth to muffle her scream as Kaelean poked her head into the aisle, sniffing at the book in Eaon's hand.

"Shouldn't you be with him?" Eaon snapped.

"He's fine." Kaelean rolled her eyes. "I wanted to see how you were going for evidence?"

"Did the timing work? She didn't sense us?" Eavha asked.

"As far as I can tell."

"And did she want to wait until morning to check his curse?"

"Just like we predicted. Cinn will buy us as much time as possible, but I will need to be with him when Lorelei goes looking for a curse that isn't there."

Eaon nodded, holding the thick book he'd chosen close to his chest. "I'm going to read this tonight, and we'll get into their offices tomorrow once they're working with Cinn."

"Well, try not to take too long. Cinn looked like he was going to lose his shit when he saw the laborers. If he goes on a murder spree, I might just join him. But, you were right. Bodhi and Milnova will side with us, and many of the heirs will as well. None of them like the way things are going, and Lorelei's not even trying to hide her abuses from them anymore."

"Their offices are connected to their suites, so, unless you know a spell to make us invisible, tomorrow is the soonest we can risk going in. We put up with this shit our whole lives, I'm sure the two of you can keep it together for one day," Eaon snapped, then turned towards the ajar door. "We need to go before we get caught."

Ignoring the stunned look on Kaelean's face, Eaon stormed off.

"Be safe," Eavha said softly, quickening her pace as she and Dearmead went after him.

Back at their house, Eaon sat on one of the wicker armchairs in their living room with a large candle and poured over the repugnant book they had stolen. Eavha prepared them some food in the kitchen while Dearmead scrubbed off the remains of the wards on the windowsills.

"We grew up with this," Eavha muttered, glancing through the door to Eaon. He was so engrossed in the pages he didn't hear her talking to Dearmead. "He said *we*, but . . . I mean, I knew it wasn't great to labor but I didn't really understand. He never talks about it and I never asked him."

Dearmead's shoulders tensed as he wiped away the last of the stains on the kitchen window and moved to the doorway. "Don't."

"What?"

"Ask him. Don't ever ask him."

Eavha blinked, stirring the soup she was making, the excitement for a hot meal replaced with confusion at Dearmead's tone. "It's healthy to talk about—"

"If he wants to talk to you about it, he will," Dearmead's tone sharpened even further. "But don't ask him. He worked too hard to get past it."

Eavha frowned and turned back to her soup, testing the temperature on the tip of her tongue. It was ready enough. Preparing three bowls, she waited for Dearmead to finish cleaning the doorway.

"I'm glad he had you," she said as he rinsed his hands in the sink before taking his dinner. "I'm glad at least one of us was there for him."

Dearmead turned his face up to the ceiling and sighed. "I promised him I always would be, and then when it mattered most . . . I was a coward. He's never going to forgive me for that, is he?"

Eavha took the other two bowls and bit her lip. She wished she could answer that.

"Give him time, Dea."

CHAPTER 49

CINN

T HE NEXT MORNING, E LDER B ODHI TOOK C INN ON A TOUR OF the lakeside, explaining what the different meadows were for, the temples, the healing clinic, the guardian training center, the scout's intelligence center, the keeper's libraries, the trade market, the pastry kitchens, the mills and workshops . . . It was incredible. A city at peace with the land, a people that worked as a unit.

{It's beautiful.}

"Thank you. We are proud of what our clan has accomplished here," Bodhi said, but there was tightness in his eyes.

{Sorry if it is rude to ask, but there are twenty masked guardians and twenty elder houses, but only eight elders?}

"Ah, not rude to ask what is plain," Bodhi nodded. "We have had a bout of sickness recently and many of our elders have passed to the Lover. The heirs are still preparing for ascension."

{A sickness your healers couldn't help?}

"Our best healers were some of the first taken, unfortunately. We rely on the Spirits to purge our lands now."

{Then why did we not pray for it at dinner last night?}

Bodhi sighed deeply. "It's complicated. And you don't need to concern yourself, the blight will not affect you."

{I just worry that perhaps if your priestess cannot help her own people, maybe she cannot help me. If I am being honest, she is not the high priestess I was expecting to find here.}

He was taking a risk, but he had a good feeling about Bodhi.

The elder tilted his head and frowned, turning to Cinn.

"Sorry, I'm not sure I caught all that. Not the high priestess you were expecting?"

{The Mountain Clan spoke of a black-eyed mother-blessed witch. Has she passed?}

Bodhi stopped walking, his mouth popping open again.

"You . . ." he lowered his voice to near silence. "You speak of Kaelean Caesarea. Only Lorelei is old enough to remember her but, no, she has not passed as far as I know. She was excommunicated many years ago. How long ago were you at the Mountain Clan if that was who you were expecting?"

{Would she not be able to help with the curse in Wyldeden?} Cinn pushed, ignoring Bodhi's question.

"Curse?" Bodhi frowned, looking around for eavesdroppers. "Did I misinterpret?"

Cinn stared pointedly, waiting. The elder wiped his sweaty palms on his pants and quickly began walking again. He led Cinn to the Mother's temple but did not go inside; behind the towering structure, they were hidden from view beneath a cluster of pristine trees.

"What do you know?" Bodhi asked.

{Why can't we talk openly?}

"We are forbidden from talking about the disease. From trying to cure it. Lorelei says it is the Lover's will, and to leave it be, but . . . some of the others and I have done the calculations. At this rate, we will have no healers, no guardians by the end of the year. There will be no clan at all within a decade if the increased speed of the spread continues. We cannot do nothing; Lover's will or not."

Cinn could barely contain his smile.

{In Anfar, I met Eaon Nemuse.}

Bodhi stiffened, eyes widening. "Is he alright?"

Cinn nodded. {He told me this clan is cursed. Not plagued. I did not come here to break a curse on me. I came to break the curse on your people. And I did not come alone.}

Bodhi turned a sickly shade of green.

"Eaon . . . A bright witch. A very bright witch. Had he been more gifted he would have made a fine high teacher. He said it's a curse? He is here? How?"

{It's complicated,} Cinn told him. {But if you trust him, then trust me. This curse did not come from nowhere. Who does it serve?}

Bodhi did not answer, but Cinn could see the wheels turning in his head.

Priestesses and their acolytes were out in droves looking for Cinn, so Elder Bodhi led him down hidden paths throughout the city's narrow streets until they reached a rare-fruits store. The owner nodded at them as Bodhi and Cinn walked through the service door, down a hall and into a closed-off room. Waiting inside were two elders and four heirs. Each had received a whispering leaf from Bodhi calling for an emergency meeting.

Cinn recognized Milnova, of course, but was surprised to see Herbe as well. The witches were equally surprised to see the kinner.

"What is going on, Bodhi?" Milnova asked.

"Cinn here has confirmed what we have suspected for some time. The excessive deaths are not natural. He has come to help us."

The witches broke out into chatter that Cinn couldn't understand, but he watched Herbe carefully. Tugging at Bodhi's sleeve, he signed, {We are suspicious of the high guardians. How much does the elder know?}

Bodhi nodded slightly and turned to Herbe, having another conversation Cinn could not be a part of. They argued for a moment before Herbe cussed, clenched his fists and kicked out at a chair by the wall.

"He did not choose the high guardians," Bodhi explained. "Lorelei has always taken his authority over them away from him, but he still tried to deny the involvement of any guardians in what is happening. But we must be careful, regardless. He is unhappy."

Cinn nodded.

Waiting patiently, he let the witches discuss the information Cinn had brought them. He didn't mind being bored as he waited; the longer he could put off seeing Lorelei the more time he was giving the others.

Finally, the conversations died down and a few witches began to leave. Cinn looked to Bodhi again.

"They will support us," Bodhi said with a sad smile. "When

Kaelean presents herself, they will make sure she has a chance to speak."

Cinn smiled and nodded his thanks to each witch as they left. He'd helped rally his very own little rebellion. His brother would've been proud of him.

Finally, Cinn had run out of excuses to delay meeting with Lorelei. An acolyte found him and Bodhi by a market stall and guided them back through the city to the Sanctuary. The sun shining off the crystal surface off the building was blinding, but the gemstone finish on the exterior didn't follow them inside. Rich wooden floors and soft green walls gave the sanctuary a soothing vibe as he followed the acolyte to the reception room.

A boar masked guardian and Lorelei stood waiting, and the four of them made their way up a spiraling staircase to the top floors of the Sanctuary. Tapestries of deities decorated the walls between doorways, behind which Cinn could hear voices chanting and singing in chorus.

By the time they got to the top, Cinn's legs were burning from the climb. Compared to the guest house, Lorelei's suite was basic and minimalistic. She had four large desks with different potions brewing on each, a large cabinet full of jars with things inside them so bizarre Cinn wasn't sure he even wanted to know what they were.

"Please, take a seat." Lorelei pulled out a chair for him.

Scraping for seconds now, he wandered slowly through the room examining the tables and checking the view from the apex of the Sanctuary. From here, Wyldeden looked like it belonged in one of the picture books he'd once seen the human children reading in Hyrsch.

The guardian watched him through tiny slits in the mask, icy blue eyes hard and unwavering. Cinn's delaying would not be tolerated much longer, so, warily, he took a seat on the chair Lorelei had provided and braced himself. The high priestess rubbed her hands together before splaying them on either side of his face.

The magic probed at him like a feather brushing beneath his skin, tickling his bones. Within moments, there was a frown on Lorelei's face. Glancing quickly to Bodhi, Cinn gave a quick double blink. The elder nodded imperceptibly, then looked down at his feet. There was a tiny mouse sitting on Bodhi's bare foot, waving at him.

"Who did you say put this curse on you? I cannot sense it." Lorelei's magic twisted inside him, digging deeper. Being torn apart by it was going to be excruciating.

{Nobody did. There is no curse.}

Bodhi was sweating as he translated.

Both the magic and her hands dropped away. Lorelei's ancient gaze turned on him, every shred of graciousness and civility gone.

"You took a vow," she warned him.

{That I have no ill will to this clan.} Cinn nodded.

"If that is still true, then why did you lie to me?"

From the corner of his eye, Cinn could see Kaelean starting to grow.

{Because I believe that *you* have ill will toward this clan.}

The air hummed painfully against his skin. The wood of the chair softened, two branches from the woven back snaking over his arms and wrapping themselves around his wrists. More restrained his ankles, his waist and neck. Bucking reflexively against the restraints, Cinn grit his teeth to stop from snarling.

Lorelei and the guardian had noticed the lump of clay growing in the corner. The guardian moved to crush it beneath his foot, but Bodhi pushed him.

"I would hear what the kinner has to say."

Kaelean was growing faster.

The color drained from Lorelei's face as, finally, Kaelean took form, crouching and baring her teeth at the guardian aiming his spear at her.

For a moment, the tension in the room was dense enough to suffocate him. As he drew a steadying breath, twisting his wrists against the branches, Lorelei dropped to her knees and began sobbing.

"Thank the Mother you're here. I've been waiting for you for decades."

Kaelean and Cinn both stilled, frowning.

"Aadya. You have to stop her."

The high guardian turned and spun his spear, aiming a blow for Lorelei's head.

Lorelei raised a hand. As the staff came down and the wood touched her skin, it splintered. Harmless woodchips fell to the ground.

In one fluid motion, Kaelean leaped onto the guardian's back, wrapped an arm around his neck, flipped over and brought him crashing down onto the ground. Yanking off his helmet, revealing a shock of hair so white it was nearly translucent, she stomped the back of his head so hard he passed out.

"What's going on?" Kaelean turned and hissed at Lorelei.

"You're here. Mother has blessed us all; you're here," Lorelei was shaking, fingers pressed to her lips as she stared at the guardian. "I've been a fool, Kaelean. I've made such terrible mistakes and I can't fix it."

"Release the kinner. Now," Kaelean demanded.

The wood around his body retracted. Wrinkling his nose, Cinn added another scratch to the tally of how many times Kaelean had saved him.

"I'm sorry." Lorelei was still on her knees, looking up between the elder and Kaelean. "I . . . I . . ."

Kaelean stepped forward and slapped the witch across the face. "Snap out of it. My coven is here looking for the curse you put on my people. Explain. Now."

"Not me! Aadya!" Lorelei held her burning cheek. "I was so stupid. Fifty-five years ago a Morvish traveler came and I thought . . . I wanted to know who would dethrone me. I wanted to take measures. So I let her in, and she told me . . . she told me it would be you."

Lorelei dropped her hand, face crumpling.

"I sent out scouts to track you down, but . . . then the rogue invasion happened. Aadya wasn't a traveler at all, but a deserter. And she had a coven. We fought but some of them got inside." She looked down to the unconscious high guardian. "They took over. I've been her puppet for *decades*."

Cinn stared at her, shocked. Despite the hallucinations, Eaon had been right.

Bodhi crossed his arms, pursing his lips. "You never tried to—"

"I couldn't risk it. If she wanted to, she could kill us all. If I tried to tell someone, she would have. She . . . she communed with Morvia to find out who would be a threat to her master and only got the last name Nemuse. I thought . . . it was just one family. A sacrifice to protect everybody else. But then . . . then the Nemuses were gone and she targeted the healers. The elders, then the Bayfields. I can't stop her, but I knew you were coming. She'd already told me you would come. Please, you have to find her now. Stop her before—"

"The curse," Kaelean demanded. Cinn was still reeling from just how accurate Eaon's paranoid theory had been. He'd known he was clever, but he didn't think the others really appreciated just how clever Eaon really was. Even with whatever mental battles he had to fight.

"I don't know where she cast it exactly, but she keeps guardians outside her personal rooms at all times. Kept *me* under the surveillance of her guardians at all times." Lorelei wiped the tears streaking her cheeks. "I'll come with you."

"No. Bodhi, get the others."

Bodhi nodded and rushed from the room, quickly returning with Herbe and Milnova who promptly hauled Lorelei to her feet.

"Take her to the prison." Kaelean's black eyes razedLorelei, who didn't fight the elders. "I'll deal with you and your stupidity later."

Then to Cinn: "You with me?"

Cinn raised his chin and headed for the door.

CHAPTER 50

EAVHA

They had barely gotten out of Lorelei's office before hearing the high priestess's voice floating up the stairwell. Dearmead had shoved open a manually locked door to a supply closet in the hall for them to hide in as Lorelei, Bodhi, Cinn and a masked guardian made their way to Lorelei's office.

They were running out of time.

Outside Aadya's suite, Dearmead and Eaon stood guard while Eavha picked the lock. It wasn't as complex as the library's one, but it took a lot of concentration. As the bolt dropped, she pushed open the door and waited for the males to follow her inside.

The sun shining through the slits in the wall sent the pale stone walls glittering like diamond. The furniture was scarce but the arrangement of desks and shelves were stacked with jars and tools, scrolls and drawings.

Eaon froze, eyes widening as he fixated on a thick black book on one of the desks. The volume Eaon had speed read during the night had been filled with spells and hexes that used the Lover's blessing. Nothing on curses, but Eaon had felt confident that the first volume would have what they needed.

And there it was.

"Quick," Eavha said, rushing to the central desk, nearly tripping on the corner of a rug that had been turned up.

Dearmead paused to inspect the rug on the floor, kicking it back farther. "There's a cellar door here."

As he crouched down to investigate, Eavha reached for the book. The binding was burning cold. She hissed and pulled back her fingers. "Eaon, you'd better do it."

A wet thud echoed in response, and both she and Dearmead spun around.

Eaon stood there, eyes wide in shock as he looked down to the spear protruding from his chest.

The blood rushed from Eavha's face as quick as it was spreading down Eaon's shirt.

"No," Dearmead rasped.

Behind Eaon stood the wildcat masked guardian, holding the spear inside Eaon's chest. Beside him, Aadya tilted her head and gave an annoyed pout.

"When you spot a rat, it's best to set a trap."

The taunt was a distant echo. The only sound in the world was the wet rasp and gurgle of blood as it welled up in her brother's mouth and slipped past his lips. Eaon dropped Dearmead's staff, reaching up to hold the spear in his chest as if he couldn't quite believe it was there.

Dearmead came to stand beside Eavha, taking her hand. Eaon would not survive that wound, and she didn't have the power to bring him back this time.

The guardian yanked the spear out of Eaon's back, chunks of

flesh clinging to the stone. A wet whine cracked Eaon's throat as he crumpled. Eavha almost dove for him, but Dearmead pulled her behind him. Not only was there nothing she could do, but stepping forward would put her within the guardian's reach. Standing so close to him, she could feel the way Dearmead's body was shaking.

"I love you," he said.

Eaon choked on the blood in his mouth before collapsing in a heap on the floor.

She should feel something, but there was just emptiness.

"Now, just one left." Aadya pulled back the hood on her robe to reveal the constellation tattooed on her forehead.

The masked guardian readied his spear.

"Eavha," Dearmead said through gritted teeth, letting her go as he crouched into a fighting stance. "Break the fucking curse."

The words had barely left him before the guardian struck. Dearmead rolled and snatched up his staff, raising it to deflect a blow carving the air toward his head. The two of them moved like vipers and the crack of the staffs as they collided startled Eavha out of her daze.

She forced herself to peel her eyes away from Eaon's body and grabbed the horrible book off the desk. Racing for the cellar Dearmead had discovered was a mistake; the door was too heavy to open with one hand.

"Where do you think you're going, you mewling little grass-chewer?" Aadya's eyes flashed as she came around the desk.

Dropping the book that was blistering her fingers, Eavha backed away. As Aadya approached her, she shook the robe off entirely.

She wore no clothes underneath, but she didn't need to.

Running down the sides of her face, over her chest, arms and legs, were glistening green scales. Thick black claws clacked against the wooden floor as she kicked off the shoes she'd had hidden under the robe, scratching tiny marks in the floorboards with every step.

"Like it?" Aadya grinned, flicking her golden curls over her shoulder. A constellation tattoo of opalescent silver shone on her pale forehead. "A gift from my master."

One minute.

Eavha needed just one minute to get the cellar door open, grab the book and start down the stairs. Dearmead could not help her. The high guardian had backed him against the wall and it was taking all of Dearmead's training not to let the spear touch him.

"Your master must be cruel," Eavha's voice shook as she circled around towards the window. "You look hideous."

Aadya grinned, crouching low. "Oh, you have no idea."

Eavha squeaked as Aadya pounced, dashing for the window. She didn't make it before Aadya slammed her into the wall, reaching for a scalpel on the desk nearby.

"He is cruel. He is chaos incarnate, and he will bring an end to the Balance. His disciples have cleared the way now and the powerful will rule once more when—"

Eavha slammed her elbow into Aadya's diaphragm, crying out as the scales scraped the skin from her arm. Sharp, but pliable, her stupid healer brain noted as Aadya gasped emptily, pressing a hand to the soft spot beneath her ribs. It gave her room to turn; to grab Aadya's hair and yank her head down into the knee she brought up with adrenaline-fueled ferocity.

Bone crunched and hot blood splattered her skirt. Without

hesitating, Eavha shoved Aadya down to the ground and raced for the cellar door.

"Terra, give me strength," she muttered as she grabbed the handle and pulled. The wooden door felt lighter than before as Eavha threw it back, grabbed the book and flung herself into the dark.

Gritting her teeth through the iciness scalding her hands, half falling as she ran down the rickety spiralling staircase, she barely had time to take in the details of the room around her. It was dark, lined with lit braziers, and in the middle of the room . . .

An altar.

She only had time to notice that it was made of obsidian, had a white cloth spread on the top. Thick black candles sat in an arrangement surrounding a silver bowl filled with salt, blood and the still-beating heart of a sparrow. Pieces of parchment, many half burnt, were scattered on the floor.

Nemuse. Nemuse. Nemuse.
Bayfield. Bayfield. Bayfiled.

Slamming the book on top, Eavha quickly thumbed through the pages. But the words were a blur and she couldn't read as fast as Eaon . . .

Eaon.

Eaon, Eaon, Eaon.

Sobbing, she grabbed the book and swept it across the top of the altar, scattering the candles and salts, the delicate bones and bowls of blood. The clatter of them on the stone floor echoed through the chamber, along with an airy chuckle from directly behind her.

Eavha spun around.

Too slow.

Strong hands shoved her down onto her back atop the altar. Aadya climbed above her, scales catching the fabric of her skirt. Blood staining her face, one of Aadya's teeth were missing as she grinned down at Eavha, pinning her right arm and her throat against the cold stone.

"You think destroying my altar means anything? It doesn't. After you're both gone, I'm finished in Wyldeden anyway."

"Dearmead!" Eavha screamed as she bucked and thrashed under the Morvish hybrid.

Aadya scoffed, hovering inches over Eavha's face as she tightened her grip on her windpipe. "Stop fighting me, Eavha. Don't you know we're the same? I do not worship Death, especially not disguised as a Lover. My master will free this land of Death's embrace once and for all. Can't you see that this is bigger than you and me? Bigger than all of this? Please, Eavha. Be a good girl and die for me, okay?"

Vision spotting, Eavha choked on another cry for help. With her free hand, she scratched at Aadya's face, but the beast-witch just laughed.

Weak. She was too weak.

Unable to keep fighting, her arm dropped back to the stone. Her twitching fingers brushed something leather against her side.

Cinn's knife.

Fumbling, Eavha gripped the hilt of the blade.

'You are not weak,' Eaon had told her. Her eyes burned as she drew the knife from its scabbard, trying to blink the shadows from her eyes. She was not weak, but she was not a fighter. She had no great power to unleash. She wasn't a killer.

She was a healer.

"Go . . . rogue," she choked out. Lifting her heavy arm, Eavha aimed carefully before shoving the knife deep into Aadya's abdomen. The silver shredded through the scales easily.

Aadya gasped, her grip slackening.

Eavha coughed as she sucked in a painful breath, keeping her grip as steady as possible as she held the knife inside Aadya.

"Hold still, and you might not die," she warned her, cold fury curdling in her veins.

The sound of a single drip of water from the ceiling above echoed through the prayer room as Aadya shivered, arms trembling as she tried to keep herself upright. The Lover would not be kind to her if she died right now.

Another drip, followed by a feral snarl.

A lupanis stalked down the stairs.

"If she moves, she dies," Eavha said through gritted teeth, tears finally spilling over. Despite the way her arm was cramping from holding the knife so still, she didn't dare move as Kaelean shifted. Didn't dare look away from the agonized eyes of the witch above her.

"Let go," Kaelean said, her hand closing over Eavha's.

Carefully, Eavha uncurled her fingers from the hilt. Kaelean slipped a hand under Aadya's body to support her weight as Eavha slid off the altar.

Once she was clear, Kaelean twisted the knife.

Aadya's scream rattled the walls.

"That was for Eaon," she hissed in her ear.

Eaon.

Dizziness hit her hard. She forced herself to take a steadying breath before racing back up the stairs.

Dearmead, bloodied and in need of stitches, was sitting on

the floor against Aadya's desk, sobbing. Cinn was frozen in the doorway, eyes fixed on Eaon's body.

There was nothing she could do, but she went to kneel by her brother anyway. She didn't think before reaching for his face. Not until her skin touched his, and nothing happened.

CHAPTER 51

EAON

EAON STOOD IN DARKNESS.

The cold was infinite.

He did not want to be there.

Again.

Alone.

Nothing changed, but everything changed as someone, *something*, stepped out of nothing. Everywhere and nowhere, its body was a black hole, eyes like diamonds. The coldness swallowed him and he dropped to his knees.

You again, it said in a voice he couldn't hear.

Eaon's head emptied.

"I'm sorry."

He didn't know what else to say.

It came closer.

No, it didn't move. Space moved around it, drawing them closer.

Your sister begs for your life again.

"She needs me." Eaon could barely muster the words.

The aura around the Lover was breaking him apart. Lingering in the in-between would fracture him beyond measure. The gravity of the Lover's body was pulling him in. It was his only salvation.

Mother also begs for you.

Eaon froze.

The Lover came closer again, until the force of it was unbearable.

Nothing made sense. Leaning in, he could feel the warmth on the other side of that black hole. He wanted to know what was beyond.

You will stay with me one day, Eaon. But until this is over, until Chaos is at bay, you are forbidden here.

Eaon stared, the cold consuming him as the Lover folded back into the darkness.

CHAPTER 52

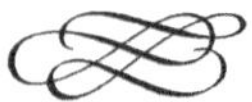

NORA

THERE WASN'T TIME FOR NORA TO LAMENT IN THE WASTELAND inside her. She stood by the window in Aisling's tower and watched the princess tuck a few loose strands of her hair away. Edwina had helped tease her slate-gray hair into a nest, adorning it with an ornate crown. No red today; Aisling's eyes and lips were painted in kohl to match the heavy gown dragging across the floor.

"This is your last chance to change your mind," Aisling warned Nora. "You don't have to do this."

"I know. But it's the only thing that makes sense."

"You are angry with me . . ."

"No." Nora stepped forward. The princess was so young still, despite the hardened look in her eyes. Placing her hands on the witch's shoulders, Nora leaned in to hug her. "It has to be done, and I trust you."

Aisling stood frozen. Nora smiled as she stepped back. She

just hoped that whoever replaced her could keep Aisling on the right path.

In the throne room, Aisling sat rigidly on her velvet pillow, chin high as the guards brought in the two prisoners. Owen and Tomson were still in their undershirts and slacks, faces darkened with grime and skin already sallow from the lack of light.

The lords and ladies of Hyrsch, Aisling's remaining advisors, and all the prominent members of the court were present and silent as the two traitors knelt before the throne, wrists in shackles, swords pointed at their backs. Nora stood to Aisling's right, eyes fixed on the chandelier above instead of her husband. She couldn't afford any more emotion today.

"Tomson Wiles and Owen Turlough, you have both been found guilty of treason, of murder, and of sabotage. I have consulted with my advisors and with the Spirits to determine what is to be done with you."

Nora's palms became clammy as Aisling rose from her seat, jutting her chin out as she appraised the crowd.

"We are all fallible."

The silence thickened. The advisors narrowed their eyes, looking between each other. The words were not what the princess had promised them.

"When I took my rule in Hyrsch, I vowed to liberate its people from tyranny. However, my responses to the rebellion thus far have been hypocritical, and thus I hereby declare the death sentence abolished within these walls."

Muttering broke out, but quickly stopped as Aisling continued.

"I will also hereby declare that the imprisonment of rebels is unlawful."

"Heresy!" One of her advisors shouted at her, spittle dripping from his chin.

Clayton drew his sword. "Order!"

The throne room fell silent once more.

"May word reach the rebels on both sides of this dispute that if they provide representatives, I will happily meet with them to discuss their concerns. Let peace reign."

Aisling paused to give her audience a moment to adjust, but Nora knew she wasn't finished.

"However," Aisling's tone darkened. The crowd visibly cringed. "I cannot allow the murder of royal subjects to pass, and I will not tolerate sabotage. And so, Owen, Tomson, and to all dissenters who choose not to bring your concerns to me civilly, your sentence is simple. If you do not respect my court, and you do not respect the laws of this city, then you shall leave. In the morning, a ship will leave for Pirevia and you will both be on it, along with the rest of the demi-kin prisoners. If you don't appreciate your freedom, you will be stripped of it."

Gasps rang throughout the room. Many of Aisling's advisors shocked faces began to twist into vicious glee.

Owen sank to the ground, head on the marble floor, shoulders shaking.

"Nora Turlough."

Aisling's clear voice brought hush to the room once more. She turned to her Second, and Nora bowed her head.

"You failed to report your suspicions about your husband's deceit, failed to identify the treason happening right under your nose, and you failed to capture Siobhan LaTour."

Nora stepped down from the dais to kneel beside her husband.

"No," he raised his head, bloodshot eyes bulging. "She is innocent. I—"

"Quiet, you damned idiot," Nora hissed at him. Then, to Aisling. "I accept these charges. I acted in accordance with the demi-kin rebels' wishes, and accept the punishment of exile."

"No! No, she didn't. She has nothing to do with the rebels." Owen was frantic, shoving at Nora to stand. The guards surrounding them ordered him to be still, raising their swords.

"I denounce you as my Second in Command. You will go to Pirevia." Aisling stated coldly, but Nora noticed the way the princess's chin wobbled.

Nora lowered her scarred head and nodded.

Owen sobbed as he pulled Nora to him, hugging her fiercely. The cell door clanged shut behind her. One of the normal cells in Aisling's dungeon, not the horrific torture chamber she had kept the kinner in.

"Get off me," Nora hissed.

Owen stepped back but kept a hold of her shoulders.

"Why would you do this? Why—"

"For the love of the gods, would you shut up." Nora shoved Owen's hands off her and stalked to the corner.

Owen followed her, eyes hardening.

"I'm sorry, my love—"

Nora shoved him back again, clenching her fists. "Don't you ever call me that again. Do you know what a tell is, Owen? A little tick a person has when they *lie*. This is all your fault, and you have the nerve to stand there and lie to me about being sorry—"

"I tried to tell you she was corrupt. I tried—"

"Aisling does more for this nation than anyone will ever know!"

"She's sending you to Pirevia and you're defending her!" Owen blanched.

This time Nora stepped in close, grabbing a fistful of his tunic and pulling him down to her level.

"Listen to me," she whispered, aware that they were not alone. "Tell who you trust and nobody else. Aisling's sending the demi-kin to Pirevia to usurp her brother. There's a plan, but we will not be there to see it through."

Owen's eyes widened as he pulled back.

"What?"

"Come here," Nora grabbed him again. "She has always planned to take Pirevia. She has always planned to unite the east against the Sparrow Coven."

For a long moment, they only stared at each other. After clearing his throat and glancing behind him, Owen asked: "So why are we not going to Pirevia, then?"

She could see it now—the part of him that had sided with the rebels. He was quick to adapt, to listen, to scheme.

"Siobhan is pregnant," Nora choked. "I figured it would be easier to escape a boat than this city. Once we're on the sea, we'll get overboard and make our way to Belden. She's waiting for us with the Copelands."

"Oh gods. Now? It's happening *now*?" Owen ran his hands over his head, then over Nora's. "Is it safe there? Does Aisling know she's the laundress?"

Nora bristled. "You knew?"

Biting his lip, Owen turned away. "I'm sorry."

Later. She would deal with that later. "Yes, she knows. And she knows about the Copeland's involvement with the kinner. But she's on a different path. They're safe. Siobhan will be safe."

Owen closed his eyes and took a deep breath. "We're having a baby. There's going to be a war, and we're having a baby."

There was no joy in his face.

Sagging, Nora took his hand. "You're a bastard, but I love you. We'll figure this out. But no more lies, okay? You need to trust me, and I need to trust you."

Owen nodded. Then looked over Nora's shoulder to the General.

"Tomson," he called. "Come here for a second."

The three of them huddled in the corner of the cell and planned.

CHAPTER 53

AISLING

"Go home, Edwina. I want to be alone."

Aisling didn't wait for her servant's reply before shutting the door in her face. Stripping out of her black dress, she guzzled three glasses of red wine before bothering to look for her robe.

The noon light spilled into her suite from the open windows, the fresh spring air blowing scents of the city below through the open balcony doors. Her chess set sat on the table outside. Wandering over, Aisling inspected the board.

With a sigh, she knocked over her king.

"Again, Davina? I really could have used a win today."

The female sitting across from her smiled sadly. In life, color had saturated Davina from her tarnished-gold hair to her polished nails. Her skin had been the richest earthy tone, eyes as green as ripe limes. Her dresses had drawn the attention of every male and female in Dusarn, but it had been her glistening smile that had drawn Aisling in.

Now, Davina was so faded that Aisling could see the railing of the balcony through her collarbones.

"I don't know, I thought today went well." Davina began to rearrange the pieces on the board to start a new game.

"Were we in the same room?"

"You're playing the pieces the best you can."

"What does it matter. You and I both know how this ends."

"I saw what happens. Not how it ends."

Aisling turned her face up to the clouds and groaned loudly. "Your Morvish ambiguity will be the death of me."

"It's no fun if we just *tell* you," Davina smiled wickedly. "You start this time."

Aisling sat and pushed forward one of her pawns. Davina quickly moved her own. If the palace burned down tomorrow, this chessboard would be the only thing Aisling cared to save. It had cost her half her fortune to have a witch from Bernt make it for her, but not even death could stop their game.

"You'll be with me, won't you? When it comes time?"

"Every step of the way, little bird. Until the very end."

CHAPTER 54

EAON

Breathing was the hardest thing Eaon had ever done. His body was impossibly heavy, his eyelids full of sand as he peeled them apart. A warm hand tightened in his own and a sun-kissed face appeared over him, mottled blue-green eyes wide. Eavha appeared, dark circles under bloodshot eyes that watered as she stared down at him.

"I have no idea how you are alive right now, but I swear on every single Spirit, Eaon, I will kill you for dying on me again." Her voice cracked as her breath hitched.

He blinked at her, throat scratching as he forced himself to speak.

"You look like shit."

"You should see *you*," she hissed, then pinched his ear lobe with her gloved fingers.

He didn't have the energy to laugh, or swat her away, or cry at the sheer impossibility that he was there to listen to her taunting. In fact, the longer he was awake, the worse the pain was getting.

"Here," she said, holding a cup to his lips. Cinn held his head so he could drink. "Poppy milk. Should put you out again in a minute."

"How long?" he wheezed, closing his eyes.

"A week. You're a couple more away from getting out of this bed. Rest, Eaon. Everything's okay now."

A few weeks later, Eaon was well enough to attend the sentencing of Lorelei and Aadya.

In all directions as far as anyone could see, witches crowded together, standing on the balls of their feet to try to see the podium. Even the laborers had been allowed to attend, the closest ones unable to stop themselves from looking at where Eaon stood with Cinn, just to the right of the platform. The braziers on each corner were lit, and standing in the very center was Kaelean and Eavha.

Kaelean had abandoned her furs, donning a more traditional Anfar gown, while Eavha wore the modest sheath of a priestess-in-training.

"Before we commence, I wish to take this moment to address the witches of Wyldeden," Kaelean said, her voice carrying across the rolling hills as if the very wind wished her words to be heard. "You do not know me, but you have heard of me. I will not shy away from the errors of my youth, but I return to you now with a clear purpose. The council has voted to reinstate me as your high priestess, but I will not take this stand unless it is also what the people want. So, after today, I will make my plans known and you may all have a say on whether you find me suitable to lead you."

Eaon raised his eyebrows. Other clans had democratic systems but he'd never taken the time to understand them properly.

Kaelean gave the crowd a moment to process what she had said before raising her arms, and it was a mark of how many of them already respected her that they all went silent.

From behind the platform, Dearmead and one of his brothers brought forward Lorelei and left her to drop to her knees. Eavha had found something in the far distance to stare at. For a long moment, Eaon thought Kaelean might rip Lorelei's head right off her shoulders and toss it into the lake.

"Rise."

Lorelei stood but kept her head down.

"Lorelei Messasure, you stand accused and found guilty of clan endangerment, willingly allowing a rogue inside the Great Boab. You also stand accused and have been found guilty of failing to correct this error, resulting in the near extinction of Anfar's most Sanni-blessed bloodline."

Lorelei had branded Kaelean seven hundred years ago. She had branded Eavha and Eaon after standing idly while their family died. The power in Eaon's blood ached to reach for her, but he clenched Dearmead's staff in one hand and fondled the one-holed button in his pocket with the other, turning it over and over.

"For these crimes, we the council have decided that you are forbidden from performing magic, and your blessings will be bound until you have proven capable of making wiser decisions with it."

Eaon stilled.

Lorelei began weeping.

"And, while not a crime by law, you are also guilty of heinous misconduct against the laborers and travelers of this clan."

Muttering broke out among the crowd again, and Kaelean gave them another moment before raising her hand. Those beady black eyes were inscrutable as she stared at Lorelei.

"Look at me."

Trembling with the effort of her crying, eyes flickering to the branding irons waiting in the braziers, Lorelei raised her head and met Kaelean's gaze.

"You will spend the rest of your life making up for what you have done, right here. You will be my laborer, and I will have you making reparations to the people you've hurt."

Eaon's stomach dropped as cold spread across his skin. Cinn took his hand out of his pocket, ripped off his glove and squeezed hard.

Lorelei was not being excommunicated. She would be allowed to stay in Wyldeden. She would not have to suffer the way he had been made to suffer.

Lorelei broke into loud sobs, collapsing back to her knees. Kaelean put her hands on either side of the witch's head, closed her eyes and let her magic swell. Everybody took a step back, especially when Kaelean started the incantation that would bind the witch's blessings. Lorelei wailed, and Eaon had to clench his jaw to stop himself from snapping at her. Not having access to magic was not the worst thing that could happen to her.

From the podium, Eavha looked down at him and he saw his own anger reflected in her eyes. She took a steadying breath, and Eaon made himself copy her. Over and over as they watched Kaelean's display of magic.

When the binding was complete, Lorelei collapsed,

hysterically clawing at her chest. Dearmead and his brother stepped forward to take her from the stage.

Once it was quiet again, Kaelean stepped forward to look over her people.

"The matter of Lorelei Messasure is now closed. As for the Morvish deserter and her coven, I have decided to call Imsa and consult with the leaders of the other clans she has inflicted herself upon before deciding what is to be done with her. But rest assured, she will never again pose a risk to any Anfar witch under my care."

As the crowd dispersed, Eaon kept his hand in Cinn's as he made his way up to Kaelean, ignoring the wary looks of the elders and heirs. Kaelean saw him coming and dismissed Milnova, raising her chin.

"Bind my blessing," he demanded.

Kaelean blinked at him, then sagged.

"If I could, I would, Eaon."

"You bound—"

"I used my Terra-blessing to bind another Terra-blessing. You would need a skilled Lover-blessed priestess to bind yours, and you and I both know that the Sparrow Coven are more likely to recruit you than help you."

Eaon glanced over his shoulder at Cinn, who shifted his weight and looked across the lake. Later. He would think about the possibilities later.

Kaelean watched Cinn's discomfort too, twirling a stray curl around her finger. "Take him north, Eaon. Get him to Ahrenhale."

"High Priestess!" one of the elders called to her, so she left Eaon and strode off the platform.

Cinn wanted to be free of his mark, and Eaon wanted to be free of his blessing. The answers were with a witch somewhere in the only other free territory in all of Nir; the Aurnias had formed the treaty with Anfar, but not even they were bold enough to move on Qiri.

"Eaon." Eavha nodded to a quiet corner near an old oak, so he followed her back down the platform until they had some privacy. "Are you alright?"

"Did you know what Kaelean had decided to do?" he asked.

"Only a few moments before the sentencing was announced. I don't know how I feel about it."

"It's different." Eaon sighed. "You'll have to let me know how it goes. I promised to get Cinn home."

"Can he wait a few hours?" Eavha looked to Cinn and smiled. "I want to show you something before you go."

Eaon asked him, and Cinn nodded.

"Great give me a moment to finish up here and we'll go." Eavha grinned, bouncing on the balls of her feet before rushing off to follow Kaelean.

Eaon sighed.

"Lover help this clan with the two of them in charge."

Outside their family's estate, a small group of witches had gathered, standing around a table full of pastries and fruit platters. Each one of them held a bag or a package of some kind, talking quietly among themselves as they sipped at goblets of bubbling white wine.

Dearmead was there. Selina, Teagan, and a couple of other teachers from the elementary school. A handful of laborers he knew from the years he'd worked as one were trying to mingle with a few of Dearmead's siblings toward the back.

"Happy belated quarter-century birthday, Eaon." Eavha smiled at him.

Eaon blinked. Twice.

"My birthday was months ago."

"Oh, was it?" She rolled her eyes at him and nodded to Cinn, who pushed him forward. Selina spotted them and stepped forward with a smile so large her eyes were watering.

"It's so good to see you again."

"This . . . this really isn't necessary," Eaon muttered, shaking his head, face burning.

From the bag hanging over her shoulder, Selina pulled out a parcel wrapped in parchment. Eaon knew it was books before he even took them from her.

"*History of the Swallow* and *Elementary Magic*." He smiled as he read the titles. "Thank you, Selina. I'm going to need these."

"No matter where you go or what you do, I hope you know I'll always be here. Always be your friend," she said, clasping her hands together.

Eaon gaped. He hadn't realized she thought that highly of him.

He was saved from having to reply as Elder Bodhi and Kaelean came up behind them, carrying their own parcels. The celebration might have been simple compared to the birthdays he'd celebrated for others before, which he was completely and utterly grateful for, but he was almost certain no other Nemuse witch had ever had the high priestess of Wyldeden attend.

"Eaon," Elder Bodhi smiled warmly. "Congratulations."

"Elder Bodhi." Eaon didn't know what to do with his hands as he bowed.

When Bodhi reached for his shoulder with gloved hands, squeezing tightly, Eaon nearly passed out.

"Do not ever bow to anybody in this clan ever again," the elder muttered, locking eyes with him as he raised his head. Then he held out the gift in his other hand. A simple patch depicting an owl, sewn with gold thread. "When you come back, you may train as a real teacher if you wish."

Throat too thick to thank Bodhi properly, Eaon could only bow his head again as he accepted the offer.

"Ma and Da would be proud of you," Eavha whispered in his ear, slipping something into his pocket. He could tell from the weight it was some kind of carved amulet.

"Shut up before you make me embarrass myself in front of all these people you ambushed me with," he hissed at her, but couldn't muster any real bite.

Kaelean stepped forward, eyes glittering as she held out a small, wrapped gift.

"It's not another Vertlyn tangerine, is it?" he narrowed his eyes.

She grinned wider, but her arms drooped slightly. "I'm not sure I ever actually apologized for that."

"No, you didn't."

"Perhaps one day I can make it up to you."

"Perhaps I'll just poison you for your millennium celebration and we'll call it even."

Kaelean cackled, tossing the gift at him. He didn't have a spare hand, so Eavha caught it for him before swapping out the books and patch so he could accept Kaelean's gift.

Unwrapping it, his heart skipped a beat. Of course this is

what she gave him. He lifted the bloodied spearhead in his hands.

"Is this . . ."

"It is."

"That's twisted, even for you."

Kaelean curled a strand of hair around her finger and gave him a wily smile. "Objects hold power, Eaon. Not many people get to hold the object of their demise in their hands. Use it wisely."

He was tempted to stick it in her ear. "Thank you, I think."

"I am never inviting you to a party ever again," Eavha sighed at her, then nodded toward the table. The others were waiting their turn.

Dearmead handed him a shoulder-height staff that had been carved with complex spellmarks, trading it for his old damaged spear.

"It's nothing like something you could get from Bernt, but it will work better than a guardian's staff," he explained, shifting his weight as Eaon took the gift.

Not just a staff, but a proper wand. Even through the glove, he could feel the magic imbued within the oak.

"Did you carve this?" Eaon asked, astonished. The way the spellmarks interlocked with each other looked like layers of twisting branches, delicate leaves filling the blank spaces between the gouges. "It's beautiful."

"Kept me busy while you were recovering."

Eaon found himself smiling his first genuine smile at Dearmead since before he was branded.

"Thank you."

It didn't take long for him to accept the rest of the guests' gifts, deeply grateful for the assortment of clothes and foreign coins that he could take with him while traveling. Then he endured the singing before begging everybody to eat before the heat in his face burned off his skin. Once everybody had begun to feast and gossip, he quickly looked at the amulet Eavha had slipped into his pocket. A willow tree, with a loop in the top and a long piece of twine threaded through it so he could wear it around his neck.

Looking up, he searched for Eavha among his friends. When he caught her eye, she winked and signed: {Thank you.}

Eaon frowned, mouthing, "What for?"

{You save my life.} She pointed at his hands, and Eaon looked down to the amulet again. Not just a willow tree. *Their* willow tree.

There was a tap on his shoulder, and he quickly turned away before he started crying. Cinn had kept back during the gift giving and Eaon imagined he felt a little left out. Pocketing the necklace beside his odd button, he smiled at Cinn.

"We won't stay much longer," Eaon promised.

Cinn rolled his eyes and slapped Eaon's arm, shaking his head. Then he looked back to Dearmead. {You can stay if you want to. I can find my own way home.}

"I promised to ward the farmhouse for you."

{I can live without them.}

Eaon snorted. "Immortality jokes? Really?"

Cinn wrinkled his nose.

"I'm sure you'd be fine, but I promised. You defended my home, I will defend yours," Eaon insisted. "Besides. I could use some time to figure out what I want. I have options now, you know. Maybe I'll teach, maybe I'll travel. Maybe I'll labor for my sister. I'm still Head of House, and she'll be here alone . . ."

Eavha's laugh rang through the dandelion field, her hand

braced on one of Dearmead's brother's arms. The male looked ready to faint at the attention.

{She's not alone.}

"Still. I need some time."

Time to decide what to do with his life. Time to decide what to do about Dearmead. Realistically, they wouldn't have much of a future even if they could get past what had happened. Eaon couldn't have much of a future with anyone as long as his skin held this so-called blessing from the Lover.

The more he thought about it, the more he wanted to leave. Immediately.

Cinn put his finger under Eaon's chin and raised his head. Then he hugged him. Hard.

It might have been the best gift he'd had all day.

CHAPTER 55

EAON

Nobody noticed as Eaon snuck inside to pack two travelers' bags. One for him, one for Cinn. Most of his new gifts went in, as well as a couple of waterskins and some rations. Though, if he hadn't already been proficient at gathering from the wild when he'd been a traveler, he was now.

The door behind him opened and Eaon turned to see Dearmead staring at the two bags on the table. Wandering closer, Dearmead's rough fingers caught on the canvas as he ran them over the pack.

"Where are you going?" he asked, stopping so close that Eaon could practically taste the heat of him.

"I need to get Cinn home. I promised," Eaon explained, tucking his hands under his arms.

"Right now?" Dearmead frowned, glancing back to the party.

"Soon."

"Alright. I'll come with you," Dearmead offered.

An offer that stole the breath right out of his lungs. Once upon a time, that had been all Eaon wanted.

"Stay." Eaon's voice cracked on the word.

Dearmead flinched.

"Things are so . . . tense. I need someone here that I trust to keep an eye out for Eavha. Who can get her out if the clan turns on her again," he explained.

After a moment, Dearmead nodded, straightened his stance and dropped his hand from the pack. "Of course. Maybe when you get back though, you could take me to see the snow?"

"Yeah, maybe," Eaon smiled sadly. He thought he might have had enough of the cold.

"You are coming back, right?" Dearmead frowned.

"Yeah." Maybe.

Eaon reached over to give Dearmead a squeeze on the shoulder before leaving him to say goodbye to Eavha. Carrying two packs with him, it wasn't a mystery to his sister what he was doing as he approached. Quietly, she led him aside, keeping her voice low.

"I'll try not to take too long," Eaon started.

"Let's be honest, Eaon." Eavha shook her head, smiling lopsidedly. "I've seen you out there, and you come alive. Even when it's awful, you thrive in it. You never belonged here, and I understand that now. So go. Be free. But come and visit some time, okay?"

Eaon raised his eyebrows. Then smiled.

"I love you."

"I love you too, you damned rogue."

"Watch it." He pointed at her, a teasing gleam in his eye. Then his shoulders dropped. "I asked Dearmead to stay here. If it looks like things are going wrong, he'll get you out."

Eavha gave him a knowing look and took his hand. "We did the right thing, didn't we?"

"I think so." Eaon grimaced. "I hope so."

Cinn interrupted them, and Eavha beamed as she hugged him fiercely.

{Thank you,} she signed smoothly. {Be welcome me all time.}

Cinn smiled and nodded, giving Eaon an amused glance. Then he took her hands in his and raised them to his lips, bowing his head. Eavha blushed.

Kaelean had noticed them and came over, looking between the two males.

"You're not going north, are you?" she asked in Nirnish, a deep frown of disapproval on her brow.

"Lover be damned, Kaelean, let him go home for a minute before he has to think about what Yomra said," Eaon snapped.

But Cinn held up a hand to Eaon and stepped forward until he was eye to eye with Kaelean. The look on his face could only be interpreted as a warning. If the new high priestess had any sense in her head, she would not push Cinn on this.

After a long, brutal minute, Kaelean just smirked.

"Say hello to the humans for me." She tilted her head. "And don't get lost, my little cinnamon biscuit."

Cinn's face turned beetroot red.

As realization broke, Eaon burst with laughter.

CHAPTER 56

CINN

Nine Days Later

"No, no." Eaon stopped Cinn. "If you're talking about excrement as an action, it's like that, but if you're calling someone a piece of shit then it has the thumb knuckle out. See?"

The lessons and harrowing journey back through the Dividing River had kept him thoroughly distracted as they'd crossed the border into Oford, but every step in the direction of the farmhouse sent his heart skittering.

Cinn stopped paying attention as a barbed wire fence appeared in the distance. They were at the north-western boundary line, closest to where the orchards were laden with bright, sweet-smelling fruit. As if in a trance, Cinn approached the fence, eyes glued to the top of the posts. On the one closest

396

to him sat a black river pebble with a streak of striking turquoise across the top. It was beautiful, and completely out of place. On the next post to his left, a large insect wing had been nailed to the wood. The colors in it shifted in a mesmerizing metallic pattern.

They were for him. The Copelands had left them out for him.

Pocketing the pebble, he made a mental note to walk the boundary line later to see what else they had found for him.

"You're no better than a magpie," Eaon teased.

As they climbed carefully over the fence, as the shade from the fruit trees cooled his damp skin, he almost couldn't believe that this was real. That he was truly home.

Someone gasped. Cinn whipped his head around to see William halfway down a ladder, carrying a basket of apples.

"Cinn?" the farmer's voice broke.

Cinn's eyes watered as he smiled.

William dropped the basket as he jumped off the ladder, rushing at the kinner and pulling him into a fierce hug.

"Gods, oh gods, it's you. You're home."

Cinn held on to the farmer, relishing the solidity of him.

"Sarah!" William shouted over his shoulder. "Come quick!"

Within a moment, the sound of a long skirt brushing the grass preceded Sarah as she hurried toward them.

"Cinn!" she screamed, running faster. "Cinn! Oh!"

Her body crushed into him as she hugged him too. Joyful sobs broke through the remains of his composure, and he didn't care if Eaon heard him.

The three of them stood there holding each other for a very long time, crying quietly. Sarah let go first, but kept a hand on his arm as if to make sure he stayed right there. William kept an arm over his shoulder as they both turned to take in Eaon, who had stayed a good distance back.

"That is not the witch you left with," William noted.

Cinn shook his head and smiled at Eaon, wiping his cheeks.

"Hello," said Eaon. Both the farmers jerked. "My name is Eaon. It's nice to finally meet you, Mr. and Mrs. Copeland."

Sarah and William stood there staring at Eaon, slack-jawed. Cinn chuckled silently, raising his hands.

{Why are you being so formal and weird?}

Sarah gasped as she watched him sign.

"It's a witch language," Eaon explained to the farmers. "I learned it while traveling, and taught it to Cinn so we could talk."

"Would you . . . I mean, if you're not in a hurry, would you teach us? Tell us what happened?" Sarah asked, a hand at her throat.

Eaon smiled and bowed his head. "I have nowhere I need to be."

With that, the four of them walked toward the farmhouse, which hadn't changed in the months Cinn had been gone. The cat was still lazing in the sun, ignoring the chickens who pecked at the long grass around the raised vegetable gardens overflowing with produce.

"I'll make you some biscuits." Sarah beamed, holding his face in her hands and shaking her head, eyes brimming with unshed tears. "And then we'll do something about the state of you. Of both of you. Eaon, that hair! What do you boys do out in the forest to have it end up like that?"

Eaon's eyes widened, a hand reaching up to grab the strands tickling his shoulders. Cinn just grinned. Yes, everything was exactly the way he remembered it.

William saw the smile and hugged him again. "I can't believe it. I can't. I'm so glad you came home."

In the kitchen, a young woman with long black hair stopped cutting potatoes. Cinn froze, and only Sarah's hand squeezing his shoulder kept him from backing out of the house.

"Well, you look better than the last time I saw you," the woman said, putting the knife down.

That voice. He would never forget that voice.

Cinn dropped to his knees and covered his mouth as he looked up at the woman who had freed him. Smiling, she got down on her knees in front of him and took his hands away from his face.

"We have so much to talk about."

North, Yomra had told him.

North, Kaelean had insisted.

North was where the answers were. Moyra Thorne was waiting for him.

Right then, he didn't care.

He was home.

ACKNOWLEDGMENTS

Having to write an acknowledgements section was a dream I didn't know I had until I sat down to do it. This book is the culmination of decades pretending that I could do anything else with my life than tell stories. It never could have happened without the support of my family—Mum, Dad, thank you. From the bottom of my heart, thank you.

To my dear friends Sam, Logan and AJ, without whose enthusiasm I never could have grown the spine to share my work with the world, I'm so very grateful for everything that led us to know each other. Also, my editor, Kat. You don't know what it meant to me to have the first stranger I shared my work with be you, someone so patient and encouraging. I couldn't have done this without you.

Finally, to James, who taught me about death in a way I never wanted to know; and to Sammy, who taught me about life like I'd never imagined I'd experience it. Thank you both.

ABOUT THE AUTHOR

Alex Clifford is an emerging author from the coffee capital: Melbourne, Australia. She has spent the past decade studying creative writing, interior design, sociology, psychology, and secondary education. As a neurodiverse, queer, widowed, single-mother, Alex is excited to bring her unique perspective to the fantasy genre for many years to come. For more on Alex Clifford's upcoming work, visit: www.alexclifford.com.au

You can find her on social media at:
    Facebook: facebook.com/AfsCliffordBooks
    Twitter: @AfsClifford
    Instagram: @almost_alex
    TikTok: @alexcliffordwrites

KEEP READING FOR A SNEAK PEAK
OF BOOK 2 IN THE WITCHES OF
WYLDEDEN CHRONICLES . . .

KAELEAN DIDN'T HEAR A SINGLE PROTEST THE ELDER'S HURLED at her. As soon as the messenger had barged into the temple, Eaon's name on his lips, Kaelean had already been moving towards the Boab. For Eaon to be calling for help, it was serious.

Striding across the bridge, she kept stumbling over the length of her stupid—

"—fucking dress!" she hissed.

Shedding her gown, she bit her fingertip until it bled and drew hasty spellmarks on her face. The lupanis was faster than she was, and though she'd sworn to never absorb another form, she wished she had taken something that was even faster. If she ran at full speed without stopping, it would still take her almost two days to reach the human farm.

Ignoring the stares of witches offended to see their high priestess naked, Kaelean shifted and charged through the portal to Anfar.

~

She sensed the magic wards surrounding the human farm long before she came within visual distance of it. It wasn't Eaon's fault that he'd practically put out a beacon to his location—there was a fine line between casting a powerful enough spell and casting something too pungent, and he'd never learned to walk that line.

Exhaustion had slowed her down the past few hours, but as she scented the Sparrow witches surrounding the farm, she found the strength to push on.

Her muscled limbs burned from having not rested, but she would demand more from them this day. She'd rip herself and the whole Mother-made world to shreds if Eaon or Cinn were hurt. It went against all her instincts, but she couldn't help that she loved their stupid faces. After the last time, she'd vowed to never form another coven, but here she was. Whether they liked it or not, they were hers now.

The sparrows were chipping away at the fence posts surrounding the farm. Some were sleeping on the ground while others cooked over a small fire. Eaon's spell work might have been excessive, but it had worked. Those sparrow-scum heretics weren't getting through any time soon.

Or at all.

Slowing, she counted the enemies: ten, eleven, twelve. Four necromancers and eight Returned.

Her stalking slowed to a stop as she took a moment to catch her breath. This would not be an easy fight. Despite her thick scaled skin, the claws and teeth she knew could crush bone, could rip apart stone, she trembled like the thirteen-year-old witchling she'd been the last time she'd faced off against

Sparrows. Nevan didn't count. He barely counted as a witch at all.

Quietly, she backed away. This was not a fight for the lupanis.

Shifting back into a witch, Kaelean knelt in the dirt and bowed her head, threading her fingers under the earth. It warmed beneath her palms, leaning up to brush her lips as she muttered a spell. The Terra blessing in her soul rumbled, shuddering its way down her arms, her hands, and into the ground. The rumbling grew louder, the ground shaking and cracking under her silent command.

Spirit of the earth, from thee I am descendent and to thee I give my all. Terra, keeper of our foundation, bless me once more. Take my enemies

She raised her head just high enough to watch the Sparrows rising from the ground, panicking as the soil softened beneath their feet. Softened, until no matter how they scrambled, it swallowed them to their knees. Their thighs.

"Witch!" One of them shouted, pointing in her direction.

Kaelean hissed and rolled to the side as an arrow loosed, splitting the hair by her ear. The ground solidified as she broke her hold, leaving the Sparrows trapped.

Ducking behind a tree, breathing hard, she drove her hands back into the earth.

Take my enemies.

The ground cracked, the sound of a mountain being cleaved in two, as the soil didn't just soften, but began to part. Screams filled her ears, arrows thudding into the tree she hid behind, unable to find their target. Spears of magic shot for her, hitting the trunk. The tree groaned, rivalling the earth in its complaints as it crumpled to one side.

Swearing, Kaelean raced for the next thick-trunked conifer,

but another dark, cold spear of power had it crumpling before she could reach it.

Gritting her teeth, she fled through the forest around the border of the farm until the encampment was too far for their magic to reach her.

Too far for hers to reach them.

"Fucking sparrows," she spat, then leapt into the branches of the pine beside her and stalked along silently, making her way back from above.

A number of the Sparrow-scum were training their arrows at the surrounding bushes. Others were digging furiously at their legs.

She had a minute, maybe, until they began to free themselves.

Glancing through the branches, her sharp vision spotted a prone figure lying outside the farmer's house, arrows sticking out of their body.

White hot rage shredded any sense of self-preservation she had left.